St. Martin's Paperbacks Titles
by Jeff Rovin

Fatalis

Vespers

TEMPEST DOWN

Jeff Rovin

St. Martin's Paperbacks

TEMPEST DOWN

Copyright © 2004 by Jeff Rovin.
Excerpt from *Rogue Angel* copyright © 2005 by Jeff Rovin.

Library of Congress Catalog Card Number: 2003016865

ISBN: 0-312-93480-7
EAN: 9780312-93480-4

Printed in the United States of America

St. Martin's Griffin trade paperback edition / March 2004
St. Martin's Paperbacks edition / May 2005

St. Martin's Paperbacks are published by St. Martin's Press, 175 Fifth Avenue, New York, NY 10010.

10 9 8 7 6 5 4 3 2 1

PROLOGUE

RED

ONE

Brackettville, Texas

In 1938, when Major Tom Bryan was minus thirty-one years old including womb time—his fate was determined by some farsighted member of the 75th Congress. This gentleman, whose name Major Bryan did not know, but who was probably from Texas, put together a committee that put together a report that decided the United States did not have sufficient pilot-training facilities to meet a military crisis should a crisis occur. The gentleman further recommended that such a facility be constructed in Texas, in Corpus Christi, a swath of bay-front where it was sunny an average of 255 days a year and not so hot that your ears hurt just from moving when you breathed.

The rest of Congress took a look at the U.S. military, took a look at the world situation with Germany and Japan acting more and more like pit bulls at a rib roast, and said okay. In March 1941, the new naval air station opened for business. Nine months later the Axis gave birth to World War II.

By war's end, thirty-five thousand aviators had learned their skills at NAS Corpus Christi. It was on its way to becoming the world's largest pilot-training facility. Today, Training Air Wing Four lets loose an average of four hundred highly qualified fliers every year. Of course, most of them did not fly the way Major Bryan did. They usually landed back at Corpus Christi and not on a plain some six hundred miles away. Also, their airplanes had engines.

The short, muscular Bryan was alone in the twenty-two-meter-long sailplane, a pearl-white, straight-winged, high-performance glider with a nearly clear, slightly bulbous cockpit. The aircraft looked like a banana on a stick with a high T-tail and long, skinny wings dropped behind the pilot. The beauty of the plane was that if it showed up on radar at all, it looked like a big bird. With oxygen and a pressure suit the pilot could come in from fifteen to twenty thousand feet. He could launch from Florida and land in Cuba, from Saudi Arabia and land deep in Iraq, or from Pennsylvania and land in Virginia if the states ever went to war and he was called to fight for the home turf. Depending on the thermal currents, he could ride for just about as many hours as he could stand to soar, loop, dive, and rise again.

After being towed aloft by a Cessna, two miles out into the Gulf of Mexico, Bryan swung the gleaming bird around and pushed her toward the northwest. His destination was Brackettville, twenty miles southeast of Laughlin Air Force Base. His mission was twofold. First, he had to try to get into Laughlin's airspace without being asked to ID himself. Second, he had to land in a field and find a parcel that had been left there by a fellow member of his L.A.S.E.R. unit, Capt. Paul Gabriel. Of course, there was a time limit. If he did not find the package by 6:00 P.M., the results—he had been told—would not be pleasant. His commanding officer, Gen. Benjamin Scott, was inclined toward understatement.

The setup was fine with the major. He enjoyed high-risk scenarios. Otherwise, there would be no reason to hold the position of field commander for the U.S. military's new Land Air Sea Emergency Rescue unit. Since L.A.S.E.R.'s formation nine months before, the goal of the multiservice team had been to be able to get anywhere, at any time, to rescue trapped or stranded military personnel. That included extracting undercover intelligence operatives and rearming or retrieving troops under fire, cut off by an act of God, lost in bad weather, or simply broken down where traditional search-and-rescue operations could not reach them. It was not a job for underachievers.

This run, for example.

Bryan was not a pilot. L.A.S.E.R. was stationed at the Corpus Christi NAS for logistical reasons. It was a good staging area for air activity. He left the flying to others who had spent years in a cockpit. But sailplanes were different. There were a stick, two pedal controls for the rudder, and elevator controls. That much he could handle. It was similar to being in a rowboat. The pilot could feel the currents; the air was damn near solid. The one difference—and it was a big one—was that without a rowboat a man could still tread water. But Bryan didn't let that bother him either. Keeping the plane aloft, and intact, was part of the challenge. He had done test runs in two-seaters with an experienced pilot in the backseat. Except for the hard, ass-bone-numbing landings, he had done all right. And even the best pilots had those, Bryan was told.

"The lift at ten feet vertical is not very significant," his instructor—also a man of understatement—had told him. "Setting down at all is pretty impressive."

Bryan figured gravity would take care of that. All he had to do was make sure he was upright.

The major was running silent. If this were a real mission, there would be no communication between himself and his point of origin. The only concession to safety was a transponder that sent a high signal once every twenty minutes. The beep lasted less than a half second. Someone had to be listening for the sound to hear it. Bryan once had to parachute into a Tarlac jungle to evacuate a rescuer. The newbie, a Delta Force lieutenant, John Johns, had broken his leg on a jump to rescue a spy, a Philippine army scout ranger, who had been captured by the Abu Sayyaf terrorist group. Those things happened from time to time, but it was one of the most embarrassing turns extraction personnel could endure. It was far worse than the humid, hundred-plus heat and mouse-sized mosquitoes that called Tarlac's tropical jungle home. Bryan had been to some lousy places—Iraq in the summer, the north pole in the winter—but the four days sloshing through rivers that were hotter than coffee were his least favorite. He managed to save the ranger, then went back for the Delta Force lieutenant, who had found a

grove of mahogany trees and stayed buried under a pile of
leaves for three days. He'd stayed hydrated and fed by sucking
roots and worms. He was proud to have fought and defeated a
kingfisher for the rights to the territory.

The trip to Brackettville wasn't fast, but Major Bryan had
enjoyed a mostly smooth ride since the towplane had cut him
loose just over six hours before. He was following landmarks
on a mini-laptop strapped to his right thigh. Linked to a military
global positioning satellite, the image scrolled in all directions
as the glider moved in those directions. Bryan also had a dome
compass on his left wrist, just in case the laptop died or the sun
was so bright it killed the display with glare.

For the past half hour the major had been at six thousand feet
and holding. When a red star indicating Brackettville scrolled
onto the four-by-six-inch LED monitor, Bryan used a combination of pedals and stick to begin his slow descent. The thermal
currents were not as active at this hour as they were in the
morning. There was relatively little lift though the air was busy.
It bumped and rolled under the wings, tilting him several degrees with each knock. He compensated with the pedals and
stick as he continued to drop. The digital altimeter clicked past
three thousand feet. Clouds were spotty and he avoided them as
he watched the ground. Once he dropped below one thousand
feet, the heated air would not be ascending with sufficient force
to keep him airborne. There would be nothing for him to rise
on. He would have to set down. When he did, he needed to be in
the target area.

Holding the stick in his left hand, the thirty-four-year-old officer touched a button on the computer with his right. His blue
eyes squinted. His leg had to stay where it was to keep his foot
on the pedal, but the sunlight coming through the window threw
a glare on the monitor. Bad planning. He undid the Velcro
straps to get a closer look at the monitor. He touched a button to
overlay a grid.

"Okay, champ," he muttered. "The Nueces River is nine
point two miles behind me due east, which means that I need to
set down in what is just coming into grid-mark D4, which is
three miles to the northwest." Bryan looked out the right win-

dow and smiled. "And there are the two knolls in D4. We are on target."

The major tucked the laptop into the small section of seat between his legs. He could still see the monitor there if he needed it. Toggling the elevators and ailerons, he nosed the sleek aircraft down and felt his stomach go up. He pulled back slightly to level off. He would have to circle the target wide to cut his height and still come in relatively level. The lumpy air continued to rock him. He had to hold the laptop tighter with the bottoms of his thighs.

"Those muscles are gonna hurt in the morning."

So would his tarsi, from dancing on the pedals all these hours. The interesting thing about being what was called a versatile mission specialist was that you were continually discovering parts of the body that most people never paid attention to. On the north pole training mission, which involved recovering a dummy missile that had been fired from a military satellite—strictly speaking, not a violation of United Nations resolution 55/122 on the peaceful uses of outer space, since the projectile was unarmed—Bryan had done something he had done countless times. He was using a pocketknife to pry the three-foot-long missile from an icy ledge and matter-of-factly put the thing in his mouth. The knife began to freeze to his upper lip and he had to yank it free. That hurt like red burning hell. What hurt more was that he couldn't kiss his fiancée for a month when he got back. That probably didn't have a lot to do with her breaking off the engagement. The long separations and that he was now working closely with Lt. Woodstock Black were mostly to blame. It didn't help that there was nothing between Bryan and Black except close proximity on role call. But Patty couldn't handle that. She ended up marrying some rich yacht guy who lived on his boat. Bryan hoped they both drowned.

The major punched through a small cloud—it was the most direct route and he was busy keeping the sailplane level—as he dropped below twelve hundred feet. There was no time left to circle. He had to commit.

His heart kicked in its adrenaline-rush contribution as his gloved hands clutched the increasingly free-moving stick. It had been cold aloft; now it was warmer, plus he was perspiring from the wrists down. Without air to resist, the stick was disturbingly easy to move. Conversely, it produced little change in his course. He was slicing through the air with increasing speed, or what seemed like increasing speed, as the ground rose to greet him. He did what he could to remain as level as he could. His instructor had told him to keep the nose above the horizon, about ten degrees, to compensate for the loss of lift during the descent. He did that. He was moving forward with a ground speed of about sixty-five miles an hour. He was at five hundred feet and change. A few moments later he was at four hundred feet. He stopped using the altimeter and eyeballed his descent. He picked out a flat stretch of plain. He knew the scrub and gullies would seem a whole lot larger when he was tearing through it, but he would have to deal with that. Or rather, the plane would.

A plane on the plain.

It seemed funny, for the second that Bryan thought about it before the ground closed in and the wheels made rough contact, first starboard, then port, then starboard, then port, then both, each time with an ugly bounce before the nose finally settled in. He felt each jolt in his butt and up his back to his skull, as though he'd thought a chair were somewhere but wasn't and he'd sat down hard on a concrete stoop. The contours of the landscape added to the discomfort as the plane hopped and kicked like a mule. Or at least, what he thought a mule would do. He didn't meet a lot of them growing up in suburban Philadelphia.

Still, it was good to be down. He was still speeding ahead, but Bryan didn't feel as if he'd nose over. It was simply a matter of riding this out.

Bryan kissed the pedals with his boot, as he'd been taught. The wingflaps raised and the sailplane slowed. The major was impressed that the aircraft continued to move dead ahead despite all the knocks it took. The weight of the wings, on the ground, had something to do with that, he decided. They probably served as counterweights. Such a simple machine, but so damn marvelous.

After what was probably about a minute—the seconds counted out by the "knocks and rocks" as they called tear-assing across open terrain in a jeep—the plane just died. It was as though the aircraft had never even been active. There was no hum of a motor, no venting of vapors, no anything. Just stillness. Except in and on Major Bryan. His flesh was still electrified, sweat had filled every part of his pressure suit and was still leaking here and there, and his hair was soaked and cool under his helmet. The oxygen mask he had been wearing at the higher altitudes was hanging from the right side of the helmet. A moment ago it had been jiggling like turkey wattles. Now it was still.

"The turkey has landed," he said with mock-importance.

The forced-air ventilation had stopped when the plane did. It was getting hot and stuffy fast. Bryan reached to the left, raised the two latches, and popped the dome. The outside air provided no relief. But then, this was Texas.

Bryan strapped the laptop onto his leg and rose. He was used to riding in cramped seats of trucks and cargo planes and military helicopters for extended periods, hitching rides wherever he could get them. But he wasn't typically applying pressure with both feet for that entire period. His legs were so weak they tingled when he tried to stand. He had to grip the sides of the cockpit to keep from dropping back into the seat. After a few minutes he managed to get them under him and climbed from the plane. He gave it an appreciative pat on the side as his feet touched down with a crunch. Dust clouds flew from both feet. He removed his helmet and set it in the cockpit. He drew sunglasses from a vest pocket and slipped them on.

"On laptop," he said as he punched the buttons. "Or are you a thigh-top? Got to be PC with my PC."

He selected LOCAL VIEW from the menu and brought up a map of the region. The computer was too large for his arm but it was awkward looking at the monitor on his thigh. He was standing there with his leg twisted at the ankle as if he were checking a run in his stockings. He would have to tell the R&D guys to come up with something better. A heads-up display for the helmet visor, for example.

He looked at the map, figured out where he was and where he had to go, and started toward it. The local map had a countdown clock on top. He still had forty-two minutes and change to locate whatever it was that General Scott had sent him for. Plenty of time.

The prize was located at square G21. Unlike the laptop's larger view, which plugged into both the global positioning satellite and the sailplane's compass, and kept the picture scrolling, Bryan had to use the mouse pad to move around the local map. Another ungainly action. He could just picture one of General Scott's field units coming out here to plant whatever it was. If it was something important or dangerous, they would probably have been out here today. Possibly before dawn, before it got this hot. They might even be watching. Looking down at the straw-colored dirt and dirt-colored weeds, Bryan flipped a nondirectional bird, just in case they were. The only thing he hated more than screwing up was being caught by surprise. The only thing he hated more than that was someone *thinking* they had pulled a "gotcha"—

G21 was just a few yards away. He stopped. He looked around. He made a sour face. No one had been here. There were no tracks anywhere. Farther in the southwest, where Patton's army had drilled before heading to Europe, tank treads were still visible in the earth. But there was nothing here. No tire treads or strut marks from helicopters. Nothing.

And then he realized what he was looking for. What was supposed to happen.

Bryan looked over at the real-world counterpart to G21. He wanted to know exactly where it was. About ten feet ahead, in a flat stretch of nothing. He knelt where he was and removed the thigh-top. He took his lip-searing Swiss Army knife from another pocket. He turned the computer over and used the tiny screwdriver to take off the battery panel.

Two tiny packages were stuffed inside, along with a tiny cadmium battery. Obviously, whatever larger battery the unit had been designed to accept had been replaced by something that would give Bryan just enough juice to get here.

He set the computer on the ground and studied the packets.

One of them was filled with silver particles. It had a tiny computer chip and what looked like a small detonator cap attached to it. The other packet was filled with a red powder.

"That devious prick."

Bryan used a knife blade to pry loose the package with the silver particles. There were no wires attaching it to the other package. And why should there be? The device wouldn't need them. Bryan left the computer where it was and strolled toward G21. His legs felt fine now. He was juiced. Avoiding what he had hopefully just avoided was like using steroids.

The major stopped within a yard of G21. Holding the packet like a beanbag, he tossed it ahead. It hit the ground with a spangly sound and a little burst of dirt-cloud. A few seconds later the packet flashed big and white. The global positioning satellite had sent a signal to the computer chip, which had turned it into an electrical impulse. That had triggered the detonator cap, which had ignited the packet of magnesium particles. Had Bryan walked over here with the thigh-top, the same thing would have happened. With one major difference. The flare would have split the second packet, which contained red dye. The tint would have stuck to his suit, hands, and probably his face. It would have stayed there for days.

The popped cherry. A spray of red to signify that someone was no longer a virgin. It was usually planted in pillows, lockers, bath towels, or shaving kits. It left a big, fat, visible sign that kept someone from getting cocky. It reminded them that they were in the game but still new at it. The ribbing they took helped to reinforce that sense of humility. If Bryan had gone back wearing it, the jokes would have gone on long after the dye had faded.

Bryan smiled. He watched as the magnesium flare died to a whitish fog, then sputtered and vanished. He had to admit it was a smart mission. Scott didn't like his people taking anything for granted. Especially senior officers who were often putting other lives in jeopardy. That was worse than virginity. It was irresponsibility.

Bryan kicked dirt on the packet to make sure the fire was out. Then he returned to the glider. A small 3324SE secure phone was tucked behind the seat. It was the same phone Bryan and the other L.A.S.E.R. team members took on missions. It fit neatly in a briefcase and also contained a DSP-9000 tactical radio ciphering system for remote units. He yanked it from the cockpit and walked back along the fuselage. After checking the ground for scorpions, he plopped cross-legged in the shade of the wing. He rang the general's office. Scott's aide put him right through.

"Target achieved, sir," he said.

"Glad to hear that, Major. Did you have a good flight in?"

"Uneventful. It's a nice machine. Oh, and, sir? I did not—repeat—did *not* acquire a sunburn."

Scott laughed. "So the team from Laughlin reported. They're watching from the hills. They caught your little signal to them. Had you seen the unit up there?"

"No, sir," Bryan replied. "That was a 'just in case.' "

"In case what?"

"In case I was being watched."

"Should I call that to the attention of the med officer, Major?" the general asked. "Are you becoming paranoid?"

"I'd call it a preemptive strike, sir."

"Okay, Major. I'll buy that. What made you suspect the computer?"

"The fire-retardant layer in my suit would have protected me from the flare," Bryan said. "The computer was the only thing outside of it."

"Very good."

"Thank you, sir. Did the AFB pick me up on radar?"

"You were observed but not footnoted," Scott said. "The signature was apparently similar to a circling buzzard. A very clean passage."

Major Bryan felt, then heard, the beat of helicopter rotors. It sounded as though it was coming from the hills. It was difficult to tell because of the echo. Probably the spy boys coming to get him.

"Your ride out will be there in a few minutes," Scott said. "Unless you want to wait for the tow and fly your buzzard to Laughlin."

"No, thank you," Bryan said. "I want something with an engine and a little legroom."

Scott congratulated him again as a black spot of a helicopter appeared in the distance, smudged by the ripples of ground heat. Bryan uncrossed his legs and stretched them full, even the toes. That felt good. The whole thing felt good.

For the moment. And in his business, that was the best he could ask for.

Major Bryan got a lift back to NASCC from Lieutenant Perry, a pilot with the Forty-seventh Aerospace Dental Squadron. They flew a T-37B Tweet, a twin-engine training jet in which the trainee and pilot sit side by side. Perry told Bryan that when his hitch was up, he hoped to run for Congress from his home district in Louisiana. Bryan wasn't sure that service in the ADS was going to be a major asset running for public office, though the lieutenant did have a killer smile. That was just as important.

Bryan had never thought of military service as a means to an end. That seemed crass. To him, it was about serving the nation and its citizens. In that respect, he couldn't have done better than landing with L.A.S.E.R.

The L.A.S.E.R. team was an outgrowth of the Disaster Preparedness Center at the Corpus Christi Naval Air Station. Early in its evolution the base was directed to monitor hurricanes, cyclones, and tropical storms that were moving through the Gulf of Mexico. As defined by charter, the Command Mission was to provide within areas of responsibility as assigned by the Commander, Naval Meteorology and Oceanography Command, operational meteorology and oceanography services to the Armed Forces of the Department of Defense. In 1963 that mission was expanded to include rescue operations at sea and in regions of intense flooding, which the NAS was well equipped to do. Their teams were trained expressly for those activities.

When Gen. Benjamin Scott was transferred to NASCC from the Pentagon, he made it a priority to expand the activities of the DPC. He did that partly because it was necessary and partly because he was angry "at being backwatered to the NAS." Apparently, some conflict in Washington had threatened to become a court-martial if General Scott did not request the relocation. At first, Bryan heard, General Scott had resisted. He was a fighter. He liked the work he was doing at the Pentagon, running the National Emergency Airborne Command post. The NEAC was a rapid-response team that responded to domestic crises and worked to prevent them. Those included acts of God, acts of terror, military accidents or security breakdowns, and domestic disasters. Eventually, however, he yielded to direct pressure from the chairman of the Joint Chiefs of Staff. The president was running for reelection and he didn't want Scott's problems to make it seem as if the military were above censure.

It was never proven whether the issue that forced him to request the transfer, that he had slugged a fellow officer, a French officer, was bona fide or not. Major Bryan did not know the circumstances; the complaint and transcript of the hearings of the board of inquiry were sealed. But Major Bryan had a theory about the event. When Bryan was a kid, his favorite novel was *The Count of Monte Cristo*, in which Edmond Dantes was wrongly persecuted and imprisoned. He fought back with incredible fury, not resting until everyone who had helped to frame him had been destroyed. A man didn't do that if he was guilty. An officer did not start life over again, set himself a formidable goal on an impossible timetable, and succeed unless he had something to prove. He would only do that if he was innocent.

At least, that was Major Bryan's view.

So the sixty-three-year-old General Scott had moved himself and his wife, Wendy—a retired air force captain—to Texas, where he worked the friends he had in Washington, especially those who felt he'd been screwed. Over the next two fiscal years they put more and more money into the DPC so that Scott could refashion and expand it. He collected a team composed of hazardous-duty volunteers from the different services. He selected the best of these and took everything that was wrong with NEAC—including the noncentral location, the shared personnel, and especially the bureaucracy—and created L.A.S.E.R. Within two years, NEAC had been so severely downgraded that virtually all of its activities were being run from the NASCC. By General Scott.

Scott had already gone home by the time Bryan arrived. The general obviously considered the phone debriefing to have been sufficient. Bryan went to his quarters on the base, took a shower, then went to the mess hall for dinner. Though he had been here for nine months, Bryan did not know many of the officers outside L.A.S.E.R. It was a curious thing. In times of peace, the rivalry between services was intense. In times of war it was even more intense. Everyone wanted to be the first ones in, wherever "in" was—a beach, a bunker, a city. Support for whichever unit took point position was absolute, but the competition was still there.

L.A.S.E.R. was multiservice. Among members, the rivalry came second to the needs of the unit. Outsiders had a somewhat different view. Rather than pick and choose the L.A.S.E.R. members they would associate with, the sailors at NASCC avoided them altogether, save for the obligatory salute or the occasional "good morning" among equals. There was nothing impolite about it; that's just the way the services were run—"We're number one and you're not." It didn't make for easy socializing.

Bryan grabbed two cold sandwiches that were left in the racks—pinkish, pig-looking meat of some kind, on whole wheat for the grainy needs of the now health-conscious navy. He sat on a plastic chair, wincing as he settled on a seat that was still sore from the sailplane landing.

Fewer than a dozen people were spread among thirty-odd tables. One of them was a member of L.A.S.E.R., army lieutenant Woodstock Black. Woody hadn't noticed Bryan enter because she had her back to the door and was reading. The twenty-nine-year-old explosives specialist did not know the meaning of the word "downtime." If she wasn't reading scientific papers and journals—chemistry had been her college major—she was studying engineering or geology textbooks to teach herself about stress points and where structures, metals, and natural formations were most vulnerable. She'd once freed soldiers from a cave in Afghanistan because she'd recognized the feldspar wall as plagioclase and knew how to punch through it using just detonator caps. Woody once said that she was the worst nightmare of her former-hippie, UC Berkeley, philosophy-teaching unmarried parents: a politically conservative soldier who blew things up for the Establishment. Maybe her parents had had a different plan for the young woman, but Bryan liked having Woody at his back. Any details he missed in training, during planning, or on a mission he knew his sharp-minded subordinate would sweep up.

Halfway through his second sandwich, Bryan saw Paul Gabriel stride in. Gabriel was a marine captain and house-in-motion, thick and solid with arms like oak trees. His head was the dormer, no neck with these big window-eyes. He was L.A.S.E.R.'s strategic offense officer. Scott had taught his people to look at rescue operations like combat: the enemy was a situation, not a group of individuals, but it was still powerful and unpredictable, it still had to be contained, and lives had to be preserved. Like Bryan, Gabriel was a veteran of the first Gulf War. Unlike Bryan, Gabriel was sorry to leave. Like General Patton, who had wanted to fight the Russians after World War II while he already had troops in Europe, Gabriel had wanted to go into Kuwait and seize the oil fields, then double back and finish Iraq after they figured they were safe. It would have saved the United States a second trip.

"It made tactical sense," the six-foot-five Gabriel had explained to Major Bryan and General Scott when he was first interviewed for L.A.S.E.R. "If we had that extra oil, we wouldn't have to care what the rest of the oil-producing countries did, didn't do, thought, or wanted."

Gabriel's outspokenness concerned Bryan a little, but Scott had responded to it. The general's happy embrace of Gabriel's USA-centric idea was the one and only time Bryan had wondered whether Scott really had punched that French officer.

The captain tapped Woody on the back as he passed. She turned, saw him, smiled warmly, and saw Bryan at the same time. The smile broadened. While Gabriel got a can of Dr Pepper from the dispenser, Woody closed her magazine and walked over. She pushed short blond hair from her eyes as she sat down.

"You made it," she said. Her eyes held his. They were looking for the answer to a question she hadn't asked.

"Yep," he replied.

"No excitement?"

He rolled a shoulder. "Nothing. Certainly not a red-letter day, if that's what you're asking."

"Yes!" she said. "I knew you'd dodge the bullet."

"So. Did everyone know about the dye but me?"

"Not everyone," the lieutenant replied.

"Who's 'not everyone'?"

"Gabriel, the general, and me. We knew." Woodstock added apologetically, "Someone had to rig the packet to blow."

"Traitor."

"Patriot. Orders."

"I see."

"But I did it under protest," she said, "and I'm glad you weren't tagged. Especially with the Laughlin boys watching."

"Tell me, did the general have anything else planned if I took a paint ball? He's big on follow-through."

Gabriel arrived. He threw his log of a leg over a chair back and saluted as he sat down. "Major—it would have been bad for us all."

"How so?"

"Public humiliation." Gabriel popped his Dr Pepper. "Pure Benjamin Scott. A gentle kick in the pants. I'm not sure what, but one we wouldn't forget. The bad thing is, not many people will know that you succeeded."

"Why is that a bad thing?" Bryan asked.

"People should know you're the best," Gabriel said. "They'll respect you."

"If people think you're the best, they'll watch even closer to see you stumble," Woodstock said. She picked up her copy of *Product Engineering* and leafed through it. "Or they'll call you out to prove themselves. I'd rather just do my job and feel like I earned sack time."

"I'm not convinced," Gabriel said.

"Let me ask you something," Woodstock said.

"Okay."

"You're lying on your deathbed—"

"Nice—"

"Hear me out," she said. "You're lying on your deathbed and your final thought is about your life's work. Would you rather be thinking, 'Paul Gabriel, you did your best' or 'Paul Gabriel, you got your name in lights'?"

"Both," he replied.

"No. One or the other."

"One *leads* to the other," he insisted.

"Not necessarily," the lieutenant said.

"Then I can't answer that," Gabriel said. "Life isn't so clear-cut."

Bryan grinned. "Sometimes it is. You get painted red or you don't. We succeed on a mission or we don't."

"Exactly," Woodstock said.

Gabriel shook his head. "There are textures to everything."

Bryan drained the plastic container of orange juice and rose. "This is too heavy for me right now. I'm turning in. Do we know what time we're getting dunked tomorrow?"

The first Monday of every other month was big-scale disaster rehearsal for the full L.A.S.E.R. team. Typically, Scott organized the destruction of specially built structures or mothballed planes, trucks, buses, choppers, tanks, or other vessels. Tomorrow was an old destroyer.

"Eight A.M. call," Woodstock said. "I've got to get there early to punch a hole to let the bay in, so you get an extra two hours' sleep."

"Excellent," Bryan said.

"I'm still waiting to get that midair transfer the general's been talking about," Gabriel said. "I've got a twenty-dollar bet with Captain Puckett that says there's no way he's going out at the end of a canvas tether, getting banged around the atmosphere as he's lowered into another plane, and not blow chunks."

"And you base this opinion on what research?" Woodstock asked. "The man *is* a pilot. I've seen him do tight barrel rolls, one after another after another."

"I know. It's just a psych. I want to see if it works."

"You pull him down a notch in the L.A.S.E.R. big sausage-hang ranking, and you rise, is that it?"

"He'd do the same to me."

"You're both insane," Woody said. "But speaking of bets, pay up."

"Shoot, I don't have any—"

"I saw the wad when you put a buck in the pop machine. Pay."

"Okay, okay." Gabriel wore an unusually contrite look as he shoved a large hand in his small pocket. He used two fingers to fish out a thin wad of bills and peeled off a ten.

"What's that for?" Bryan asked.

"Nothing," Gabriel said.

"He bet you'd come back looking like a lobster," Woody said.

Gabriel frowned at her. "Thanks."

"What, I can't play sausage hang with the big boys?" she asked.

"Excuse me, but you bet against me?" Bryan complained.

"It was just a 'bet,'" Gabriel said.

"Against me."

"Not really. It's not like it was a wish or what I thought would happen. It was just a wager."

"Against. Me."

Woodstock smiled at Gabriel to soften the blow as she rolled her magazine, said good-night, and left the mess hall.

Gabriel watched her go. "That was good."

"She kicked you in each nut, ping and pong, and then left to hit the hay." Bryan clapped the larger man's shoulder. Then he grabbed his juice container, tossed it in the trash can, and walked off.

"Sir?" Gabriel called after him.

Bryan turned.

"I just want to say, Major, that my balls notwithstanding, I'm glad."

"About what?"

"That I lost."

Bryan grinned. "Now *that's* the measure of a big man, Captain. Good night."

"Good night, sir."

Major Bryan left the mess hall feeling not so bad about his bruised tailbone. Come morning, that would be healed.

PART ONE

TEMPEST

ONE

Kings Bay, Georgia

Dr. Charlotte Davies watched as the sleek black submarine slammed through the air.

It was late, and she should have been at home watching TV, but her tired eyes never left the computer-simulated run on the twenty-one-inch monitor. The TOP—transit observation point—was a spot three meters above the sweeping tail. That position allowed for optimum visibility of the ramjet envelope. Rear Adm. Kenneth "Stone" Silver once described this perspective as "the butt end of a bullet." That pretty much pegged it except there was no impact. Charlotte and her team hoped to keep it that way.

The thirty-three-year-old Ph.D. watched as glittering shock waves fluttered past the hull. They were like a curtain of tightly packed silver streamers, kept clear of the submarine by an invisible ovoid that stretched from the nose of the ship to its stern. The Egg, as it was nicknamed, was the heart of what Charlotte and her team had been working on for nearly seven years.

Despite the sense of motion, Charlotte herself was not moving. Just the opposite. She seemed bolted to the swivel chair in her cubicle. Attentive, but also slope-shouldered from exhaustion, too tired to move. A marine engineer specializing in fluid dynamics, she was studying the COMSIMP—computer-simulated prototype—as it literally flew along inside a self-generated envelope of gas. The Tempest class submarines used a process called supercavitation to create the submerged bubble. The bubble eliminated liquid drag by pushing water from the submarine. It allowed the object to race ahead using twin aft propellers that also moved the submarine through the water. The steam turbines that ran the screws were themselves powered by a nuclear engine that delivered a ramjet-force 2,900 shaft horsepower.

Right now, the simulated *Tempest A* was traveling at ninety knots, nearly five times the speed of a conventional submarine. It didn't so much resemble a traditional submarine as a finless barracuda, down to the slightly elongated lower jaw and majestic, unswept tail for stability. The forward-facing jaw extension housed the sensors that cued the submarine's rear-mounted ramjet fans.

Ironically, the only noise in the cubicle was coming from the computer fan. The whirring sound complemented the on-screen image. It was Sunday and no one else was around; Stone Silver had given the team the day off and insisted they take it. As project director, and a civilian, Charlotte was entitled to decline. The silence helped her concentrate.

A grid superimposed over the computer-generated image provided the scientist with specific reference points to evaluate the craft's performance. The submarine was moving within the maximum tolerable deviation of .05 degrees laterally and less than .01 degree along the vertical plumb. This "shuddering," as Charlotte called it, was due to constant changes in water temperature. The cooler the water outside the bubble, the cooler the oxygen-carbon dioxide-nitrogen mix inside. If the air cooled too much, the bubble would shrink. If that happened, sensors inside the submarine alerted the hull, which warmed to heat the air. This was accomplished with one of two sets of capillary systems inside the hull. When the vessel was in the water, one set of capillaries filled with finely filtered, highly compressed seawater. These were heated as necessary by the steam turbine. The other set of capillaries used hydrogen drawn from the water as ballast.

"I like what you're showing me, Socs," Charlotte said. She gave the monitor a pat on its "forehead."

Early in the project, Charlotte would have thought it was a sign of cabin fever to be talking to her computer, let alone have a name for it. Or to think of it as a friend, which she did. Not now. Bearded with curled, yellow Post-it notes from her colleagues, the computer reminded her of an etching of Socrates she had once seen. And it was indeed a wise, silent sage who revealed things to her. Sometimes they were happy things, sometimes they were unpleasant things. But the computer was never dishonest, unreliable, or unavailable. If there were another requirement for friendship, Charlotte didn't know it. Despite the Defense Automation Resources Management Act, which mandated that military computers, monitors, and other hardware be replaced and donated to schools every two years, she had resolutely refused to surrender Socrates. Especially when he gave Charlotte good news, which happened more and more of late.

According to Socs, the COMSIMP was working just fine. She had made modifications to the program based on input from sea trials with scaled-down prototypes. In theory, then, the full-sized *Tempest D* should also function according to plan. But as Charlotte's plasma physics professor Dr. Norwood used to remind the class, a theory is at best an artful, educated, hopeful guess. It is not a fact. Since graduating from MIT seven years before and coming to work here, Charlotte had learned that reality repeatedly. Her talent for troubleshooting, as well as her ability to listen to and synthesize all opinions, had gotten her the Tempest directorship the year before. The job hadn't reduced her hours at the computer console, though. It had just added to the hours she worked each week. At least half the man-hours she had spent here were used to fix things that did not work as planned.

How many hours would that be? she wondered. Seven years, maybe 320 days a year, twelve to sixteen hours a day.

It was a lot.

The workstations alone gave some indication of the time the scientist had spent here. Her cubicle smelled of coffee, an odor that had been soaked up over time by the four canvas-faced walls and everything pushpinned to them—the printouts, the photographs, the laminated charts with grease-pencil markings. Even her Bounce-scented jeans and button-down, white blouse could not cover that smell. Or the smell in any of the other twenty-four cubicles at the Naval Submarine Base at Kings Bay, Georgia. Each cubicle had its own "olfactory personality," as she preferred to think of it, from sweat to pepperoni pizza to her favorite, metallic pencil sharpener.

Not that Charlotte minded. The facility, nicknamed the Ant Hill, was a giant sandbox with all the pails, shovels, and top-of-the-class scientists you could want. A sandbox that had been built just for them.

"It's the kind of place where, historically, ten billion dollars buys you a prototype, some part of which always spits and crackles like a July Fourth sparkler before crapping out," Rear Admiral Silver had told her when she'd first come to interview here. "I've worked at a lot of those. I want to lose that reputation."

Charlotte liked his approach, which was one reason she'd agreed to work here. That, plus the personal challenge. She was a civilian, female scientist in a world made up mostly of horny sailors and highly opinionated, socially awkward, bordering-on-helpless male scientists. Her group alone had one deputy chief scientist, Dr. Mike Carr, eleven theoretical scientists, twenty-three engineers, four computer-simulation programmers, and five navy liaisons. All of them had been working sixty-, seventy-, often eighty-hour weeks. What was more astonishing than the time spent was that they had worked those hours with unflagging passion. For security reasons she could not even access the Internet from her computer. Being at the Ant Hill was all about "the work." The Tempest Project hadn't left the project director any time for a social life. But then, none of her dating and married friends got to play with toys like the *Tempest*.

While part of her tired mind watched the screen, another brain part went cherry-picking through the years. She remembered all the failures, the victories, the deadlines, the frustrations, the theories, and—damn you, Dr. Norwood—the newer theories, the old-new revised theories, the arguments, the cold coffee, and the even colder burgers and fries. There were births and resignations, and the quick looks at photos from confirmations and bar mitzvahs, class plays, and even weddings. She reflected briefly on what was probably the biggest void of all: unanswered e-mails back at her house. From the start Charlotte had prioritized those. At the top of the answer list were e-mails from the Pentagon and fellow scientists, followed by family (mostly answered), friends (some answered), classmates (few answered), alumni fund-raisers (deleted unread), and a sad handful of former boyfriends (deleted, then blocked). She had hoped to get through some of that over the next few weeks, while the *Tempest D* was en route. But she wouldn't. Lives and billions of dollars were going into the water. She wanted to review as much of the work as possible to make sure they hadn't missed the kinds of bugaboos that harmed NASA, such as a leaking O-ring, the use of "yards" when it should have been "meters," or potential ejecta that could strike vital components.

Even if everything checked out, the project was still a work-in-progress. Supercavitation had worked in computer simulations. It had worked in the ten-foot-long model they had built and tried in an indoor pool down the hall. And it had worked in the twenty-five-foot-long model they had built for secret trials in St. Andrews Sound, to the north of the base. In two days the field unit would set out for Antarctica to undertake the sea trial phase of the project. They would board and sail the 120.2-foot-long *Tempest D*. Only then would they know for certain whether everything would work. Only then would theory become fact.

The hazel-eyed scientist finished studying the computer simulation. She was confident she had not missed any variables. That done, she popped in the DVD recording of the St. Andrews trials. The video was shot from the model's tail camera, a fiber-optic thread run to the antenna. She went to the menu and accessed the most recent recording. Charlotte wanted to compare, once more, the real-life deviations from the computer simulations. She also wanted to study data from the sensors that monitored the capillary flow. The hull of *Tempest B* had leaked on occasion. It had taken them a while to determine that the leaks did not come from without. They came from the ramjet vibrations impacting the seams. The larger *Tempest C* nearly sank them, due to a near-catastrophic explosion when hydrogen in the capillaries became too hot due to the steam turbines. Stone had to resell the team to the brass at the Department of Defense, using his promise of success as collateral to buy the scientists time and money. After that, the redesigned diesel-fueled *Tempest C* had held fast through three different sea trials.

The model went through maneuvers she had watched at least one hundred times. She tried to watch it fresh. She had to. Sharing the responsibility with dozens of other scientists and consultants did not ease the burden. She tried to imagine how the full-sized model would work. The untested *Tempest D* was nearly five times the size of the largest model the team had built. The supercavitation fans displaced twenty-five times as much water. Though that didn't increase the pressure per square inch, it did increase the surface area on which that pressure was exerted. Though they were bonded together with water-resistant cyanoacrylate—"cal," a form of "superglue"—there were more seams that could break, more and larger components that might react differently inside the underwater air pocket. Had they used enough cal? They could heat or cool the air pocket, but had they missed a way the south-polar climate could affect the capillaries themselves? They had installed high-frequency generators to repel whales, but what if they encountered one that was deaf? It could happen.

Charlotte sat back. Her eyes blurred for a moment. She blinked them back into focus. She studied the small, white numbers that flashed on the grid. The water temperature had warmed, the bubble had expanded, and the submarine had yawed to the northeast by .03 degrees. It righted itself quickly. If everything worked the way it should, the *Tempest D* would be fine.

She took a sip of lukewarm coffee from her USS *Louisiana* mug. The Trident class vessel was based at Kings Bay. The short, black-haired woman finished viewing the trial. Her brain could not process any more data. She shut the DVD function and sat back. Everything seemed "right and ready," as they said in the navy. She had not noticed any new potential trouble spots. The numbers worked. The theory worked. The only question now was whether the submarine itself would work.

It would, Charlotte told herself. The Ant Hill crew had already endured their "July Fourth sparkler" with the *Tempest C*. They had paid their dues, gotten their accidents out of the way.

The scientist drained her mug. The caffeine hadn't helped. She was beat. She pushed the chair back from the desk and got up. As she walked around her small cubicle, she unrolled the sleeves of her button-down shirt. Moving about usually got her energy level back up. Not just because of the walking but because she fancied the security guard watching her. It was the only excitement she had these days. Everything in this underground section of the ultra-high-security facility was done in the open. Security cameras monitored everyone's moves. Cell phones were not permitted down here. Bags were searched upon leaving. Even the drains were checked for capsules that might be washed down to a waiting accomplice in the sewer.

Charlotte thought about the drain duty as she took her mug to the kitchenette near her cubicle. The military was responsible for emptying the filtered traps that had been installed at the other end. She wondered if any of those kids thought they'd been rooked by the "see the world" and "learn a trade" ad campaigns.

At least she felt as though she had got what she came for. Even when things got rough, it wasn't "too much work," it was "experience." Making peace between the scientists and the military wasn't "aggravating," it was "goal-oriented." Even the name of this place got Charlottized in her mind. She told herself the name Ant Hill was inspired by Antarctica, in whose waters they would be field-testing *Tempest D*, and not because all the engineers and military personnel moved around underground like bugs.

Charlotte placed her mug in the drainage rack. Stretching, she walked slowly back to her cubicle. All she could think about now was how good bed would feel. Deep pillow, cool sheets, open window. White bedding, cool breeze—her own private south pole. She wished she were going to the real one.

The submarine would be traveling south, to the isolated Weddell Sea, on board the *Abby,* a refitted tanker. Because an international treaty prohibited the use of the region for military purposes, it would be sailing under the banner of the Chesapeake Bay Oceanic Foundation, a facility run by the Smithsonian Institution but funded by the Department of Defense. It was one of the dirty little secrets of the scientific community that several oceanographic facilities along both coasts were financed by the Pentagon. This arrangement enabled the DOD to outfit deep-sea vessels for surveillance as well as to conduct secret sea trials like the *Tempest D* operation.

Charlotte's cubicle had no door. Only one thing could be done in private down here, and even that was subject to spot checks by security personnel. She took her Boston Red Sox windbreaker from a hook beside her desk. She put it on and took a key ring from her pocket. Removing the DVD from the computer, she put it in her desk and locked the drawer. Physical theft was difficult to pull off down here, and the only computer systems that accessed the Internet were monitored by base security. If you were on-line, so was a member of NES—naval electronics surveillance. If you were on the phone, your calls were digitally stored. At first it made Charlotte uncomfortable that she had no privacy. Charlottizing it, she looked at the surveillance as having given her a leg up on real-world life in the twenty-first century.

Grabbing her New England Patriots cap and fraying MIT backpack from beside the desk, she hefted it over her shoulder and headed toward the stainless steel elevator. She entered a six-number sequence on a keypad. The door opened and she rode three floors to ground level. Stepping from the elevator, she headed toward the exit. There, she ran her ID card through the door lock. The young security guard acknowledged her with a wave from his high-tech outpost between the inner and exterior doors. The booth was made of bullet- and bomb-proof glass and housed a chair, a desk, and a series of cameras. Displays were built right into the glass. She could not see them but the sentry could. Everyone who entered and left was metal-detected and videographed in visible, infrared, and ultraviolet light. If a person tried to leave with something more than he or she had brought, a scanner would tell the guard. The doors would lock, other guards would arrive, and the culprit would be detained.

Charlotte stepped into the unseasonably warm night. She walked along the curving asphalt path to the adjoining parking lot. High chain-link fences surrounded by barbed wire girded both areas. She did not like looking at them. They made the facility feel like a prison. She looked up, as she always did. A crescent moon had risen above the line of oaks. Jupiter was hanging bright and clear not far from the moon's cusp. The cool, white stillness of the moon and the planet made her smile. Relaxing like that made her realize how tense she had been. Charlotte knew herself well enough to know that she would review the test data dozens of times before the *Tempest D* was finally lowered into the sea. Just as when she used to play Intellivision video games with her little brother back home in Norwalk, Connecticut, you never knew when something on the TV screen would strike you in a different way, send you in a new direction to new discoveries.

A strong, balmy wind moved across the compound from the east. She could not see the ocean but she could smell it. Instead of breathing machine-circulated air she yawned down an invigorating sea breeze. Instead of seeing pixels she continued to look up. As her tired eyes adjusted to the darkening skies, she saw early-evening stars. She had spent her entire life at the shore. She knew the constellations and she knew the planets. She seemed to be at home everywhere but on land.

She reached her red Camry, beeped it to life, and climbed in. After starting the car she rolled down the window and took another long, slow breath of air. She closed her eyes. It was sweet. She wondered how the air tasted in Antarctica. If they didn't need her here, she swore she would stow away. What a bummer. She sighed and pulled away from her spot.

The scientist lived in a small, thirty-year-old ranch house on a quiet cul-de-sac in Kingsland, eight miles east on Georgia Highway 40. It wasn't her dream house and she had always intended to find another. She had never had the time.

Now it was home. Charlotte used her ID card to pass through the electronic gate. She got a wave and a smile from the night sentry, Sergeant Zavala, and headed through the still evening. The crickets were inactive this early in the night, this late in the year. There were few other cars. Yet as silent as it was, Charlotte tried to imagine how unutterably quiet it had to be at night in Antarctica. She imagined standing on the deck of the converted tanker, layered in cold-weather gear, maybe hearing the wind, maybe the engine, but filtering those out and hearing nothing else.

Did the ice make noise constantly? she wondered. Would she hear it creaking and splitting off bus-sized chunks along the coast of Graham Land, day and night? Not that there were more than a few hours of night there at this time of year.

Charlotte smiled as she thought of Antarctica. She contemplated the vastness of the Weddell Sea, a body of water whose sounds and smells and winds were probably as different from those of the Atlantic and the Pacific as she could imagine. And as Charlotte tried to picture it, her eyes shut and the wheel turned free. The car ran off the road, hopped over an embankment, and rammed headlong into the trunk of a two-hundred-year-old oak.

TWO

New York, New York

"Dad, I'm not sure Sally should be eating that."

Twenty-seven-year-old food writer Elizabeth Silver-Jackson was sitting on a vinyl-covered stool to the left of her father. Elizabeth's daughter, Sally, was straddling the knee of her grandfather, Rear Adm. Kenneth "Stone" Silver, who was feeding the three-year-old girl with chopsticks. The three were eating at Chew-Chew, a popular new sushi restaurant on Twenty-eighth Street and Third Avenue.

Silver was dressed in khaki trousers, a beige shirt, and an olive green blazer with an American flag pinned to the lapel. It wasn't a uniform but he wore it as if it were; the pants and shirt were crisply pressed. He sat straight, as if he were on the bridge of a battleship. But at least he was here. When Elizabeth was growing up, that was a rarity.

Beyond a dark hardwood bar, a conveyor belt carried plates of sushi past diners. Patrons removed the dishes they wanted and the plate count was later tallied by a waiter. Three dishes were in front of Elizabeth and six in front of her father. Another four plates sat edge to edge, spread in a semicircle in front of Sally. The brown-haired girl was wearing a Winnie-the-Pooh jumper and scattered spots of soy sauce were on a napkin tucked in her neckline. She was patiently fussing with her own wooden chopsticks, trying to hold them the way her grandfather did. Occasionally he would help her, his big, sun-bronzed hands dwarfing her pale fingers. But the girl's determination was equal to his own and she continued to struggle with the chopsticks as she chewed.

"What's wrong with what Pooh girl is eating?" he asked his daughter.

"It's *raw* fish," Elizabeth said.

"Yes, it is. That's what they serve at sushi restaurants."

"It's *one* of the things they serve," Elizabeth said. "I thought we agreed that Sally would only have cukes and avocados. Raw fish is susceptible to ciguatoxins, scombroid poisoning, parasites."

The rear admiral mugged a look that said, *I'm impressed.* "Did you write an article on that?"

"For *New York* magazine." It came out a bit more defensively than Elizabeth had intended. "Contaminants are a real problem with sushi."

"Hushed up by the big sushi conspiracy, no doubt." Silver smiled.

Elizabeth made a face.

"We used to catch six-foot eels off the deck of our patrol boat in Vietnam, gut them in the dinghy, and eat them right there," Silver said. "None of us ever got sick. Shot at, sleep-deprived, trip-wired, and one of us blown all to heck, yes. But not a single case of scombroid poisoning, or whatever it is."

"You were lucky," Elizabeth said.

"Very." He touched her face.

"Awwwww," Sally said.

Elizabeth blushed and ate a piece of her own squash roll. "Anyway, that was the Mekong Delta. This is Manhattan."

The rear admiral took a bite of tuna sashimi. "I'm sure it's fine. But we'll stick to the veggies if it makes you happier."

"Thanks," Elizabeth said.

He smiled at her, then at Sally, who was wrestling a California roll with her chopsticks. He helped her snare it and move it to her mouth. "Bull's-eye!" he told his granddaughter.

Elizabeth looked down at her plate. She hated being short with her father. The ladies spent most of their time in New

York, where Sally went to private preschool. Elizabeth's husband, Congressman Sander Jackson, came up on weekends when Congress was in session. Her father lived in Kings Bay, Georgia, where he was working on one of his top-secret projects. It was the story of her youth all over again: she did not see her father a lot. She missed him. She wanted him to miss her and respect her instead of just coming onto the bridge and running the ship.

"This shooshi is chewy," Sally said.

"I'll bet that's one reason they call this restaurant Chew-Chew," the officer said.

"Really?"

"Really."

"What's the other reason, Grandpa?" the young girl asked around a thick mouthful of rice.

"My guess is it's the conveyor belt," the rear admiral said. "You see how it runs around the restaurant just like a train?"

Sally nodded.

"Well, what sound does a train make?"

"Choo choo!" she said.

"You figured it out! Only instead of delivering passengers, that food train delivers dinner."

"That's funny." The girl laughed into her hand.

"I think the conveyor belt gets people to *chew-chew* a whole lot more," Elizabeth added. "You see something pass and you say, 'Hey, that looks nice,' just like we did with those roe wrapped in seaweed. It doesn't take long for those plates to add up."

"You're probably right," her father said. He leaned closer to Sally. "You want to know a secret?"

"What?" she whispered conspiratorially.

"That's how the navy gets money from your daddy."

"How?"

"We show him and the other members of Congress pictures of things and then they buy them."

"What kind of things?"

"Big shiny jets and missiles and boats and satellites," Silver replied.

"What's a saddlite?" Sally asked as she tentatively raised a second piece of California roll from the plate.

"A satellite is a robot that flies through space and protects you," her grandfather told her. He didn't help this time, but cupped his hand under the California roll in case it fell.

"Is it like an angel?" Sally asked.

"Just like one," he replied.

"Is Grandma a saddlite?"

Stone Silver didn't answer immediately. Sally managed to get the California roll partly into her mouth with the chopsticks. She finished the job with a finger. Elizabeth used a napkin to wipe a grain of rice from her daughter's cheek.

"No," Elizabeth said softly. "She's a special angel." The young woman looked at her father. "That's nice. You're feeding her raw fish *and* propaganda."

"Is that what you think?"

"Spy satellites as *angels*, Dad?" Elizabeth replied. "What does that make the National Reconnaissance Office? God?"

"Pretty much," he said. "Otherwise you and your fellow southpaws wouldn't be so scared of them."

Elizabeth shook her head. "Not all New York journalists are leftists. We understand privacy issues. We're humanists. Unlike the military, we don't have a coordinated agenda."

"Would you sleep better if the military were uncoordinated?"

"I'd sleep better if there were a civilian oversight board, as Sander has suggested."

The officer smiled at Sally but was looking at his daughter. "Pooh girl, your mom thinks that I propagandize. Can you say that word?"

Sally smiled and made a noble attempt. It came out "popagundice."

"*Very* good," he told her. "Can you guess what it means?"

"Feed sushi?"

"In a way." He laughed. "It means that you try to convince someone your ideas are better than theirs. Which you shouldn't have to do when those ideas have been tested by time and events." He used his chopsticks to offer the girl a piece of her mother's roe sashimi. Sally took the entire piece in her mouth.

Elizabeth turned back to the counter. She picked at her side salad. Strike two. The woman did not like getting into political debates with her father. She felt dishonest when she said nothing, disrespectful when she did. And angry because it was another way they wasted time when they were together.

She snuck a glance at his long, familiar face. It was bronzed by years spent under foreign suns and held the softest blue eyes she had ever seen. Seeing them turned her into a little girl again. A little girl who was sitting beside her daddy as they drove onto a base, men saluting him and he turning to wink down at her so she wouldn't feel left out. He had always been kind and patient with her, just as he was with Sally. But Elizabeth disagreed with his right-wing politics and he with her liberalism. The breach had been exacerbated when she'd married a liberal New York congressman five years earlier. She wished one of them could get past that. Maybe if they spent more time together, they could.

"What time is your plane?" Elizabeth asked, trying to put a little sparkle back in her voice. And bracing for strike three.

"Eleven," the rear admiral said. "Why?"

"If you can hold off another day, maybe leave late tomorrow morning, I'll drive out to Mom's grave with you. I've been thinking that Sally is old enough to go."

The rear admiral's expression flattened. He selected a plate of octopus sashimi from the conveyor belt. He picked up a piece and pressed it onto the well-worn mound of wasabi he had in a small dish.

"I have to get back."

"Are you sure, Dad? You're already here—"

"Next time," he insisted.

Elizabeth returned to her salad.

It had been nearly a year since Nancy Silver had died of pancreatic cancer. She had been fifty-three. Elizabeth's father had been up from Georgia three times since then but he had not been to Queens to visit the family plot since the funeral. Elizabeth had gone twice, once with her husband and once by herself. She sensed that her father was avoiding the reality of what had happened. He had been away so much he could pretend Nancy was "at home" and he just wasn't seeing her.

"Are you going home today, Grandpa?" Sally asked.

"Yes, tonight."

"Why?"

"I have to, Pooh girl," he replied.

"Why?"

"I have a meeting very early tomorrow morning."

"To sell new things to Daddy?" Sally asked.

A little of the rear admiral's smile returned. "No. I'm meeting with some very special people about a very important machine."

"What machine?"

He leaned toward her. "I can't tell you. It's a big secret."

"Can I go with you?"

"I wish you could. But after the meeting I have to go away for a while."

"Oh?" That was the first Elizabeth had heard of a trip. Her father had been hidden in Georgia for so long she had forgotten that he used to go for extended periods to places around the world. "How long is 'a while'?"

"A month or so."

"Some place interesting, I hope," she said.

"A place I've never been. I'm looking forward to it."

"Great," Elizabeth said. "I hope you'll be able to tell us something about it when you get back."

"Maybe a little."

Elizabeth smiled. "I'll take what I can get."

Her father put his big hand on hers and gave it a little squeeze. Suddenly, there weren't any politics. Whatever opposite poles they found themselves on politically—or even on the question of scombroid poisoning—they always ended up back here. Dad and daughter. Elizabeth was grateful for that.

They went for a walk after finishing their meal. The Jacksons lived on Gramercy Park, on the tenth floor of an eighty-year-old brownstone. They walked to the gated square at the center of the neighborhood and went in. It was a pleasant night, with a late-autumn sun and a bright, early-autumn moon. Sally played count-the-stars while Elizabeth and her father walked slowly behind her.

It was strange. Elizabeth had her husband and their daughter. They were the focus of her life. She felt whole. She could not imagine what it was like for her father. He had no other children. His only "family" were his colleagues in Georgia and his buddies from the River Patrol Force in Vietnam. They had spent two tours of duty traveling the waterways in the Mekong Delta, battling Vietcong guerrillas and clearing the way for the joint navy-army operations of the Mobile Riverine Force. Elizabeth's bedtime stories were about those missions. Her dad told them in secret, so her mother wouldn't hear—just as he did with Sally. She grew up hearing about "Gumby" Meyers, who was always squeezing shapes in clay to stay calm. About "Blade" O'Hare, who, her dad insisted, could cut a fly in half whenever one buzzed by. About "Compass" Carlyle, who never got lost. Elizabeth wondered if they called each other those names or if her dad had made them up to keep the stories kid-friendly. Only later did she learn about how the men had put Vietcong prisoners in piranha-infested waters to persuade them to give up information. Or how the patrol boat was once strafed by friendly fire. Or how Gumby had died when he'd stepped on a land mine. Her dad was the only one who had stayed in the navy. He was probably the only one who found the adversity invigorating. Her dad was like that.

As they walked, the rear admiral's cell phone beeped. He excused himself and turned away. He did not keep it on his belt but inside his jacket, in a buttoned pocket. There were numbers programmed into its memory that he did not want lost if he lost the phone or was pickpocketed.

Elizabeth watched as his ramrod posture grew even stiffer. She knew that stance. He had received bad news. Her first thought, involuntary and instinctive, was that something had happened to her husband. She looked over at Sally for comfort. But then reason took hold and Elizabeth realized that she would have gotten that call, not her father.

After a moment her father turned back. His expression was grave.

"I've got to go."

"What's wrong?" Elizabeth asked.

"One of my people . . ." His voice choked as it faded. He walked quickly toward the park gate.

"Sally!" Elizabeth yelled. "We're leaving!"

"Where are we going?" the young girl asked as she ran toward her mother. "Is Grandpa coming?"

Elizabeth told Sally that Grandpa had to get back to the airport because of work. Sally accepted that without comment. She was a savvy little New Yorker. At times her mother had to postpone outings and playdates because of deadlines. The young girl intuitively understood about responsibility. She was without question the rear admiral's granddaughter; maybe that was one of the reasons Elizabeth fought him on things that probably weren't significant. Sometimes, like now, she didn't see enough of herself in her little girl.

None of which mattered at this moment. Taking her daughter's small hand, Elizabeth followed her father as he jogged toward Twenty-first Street and into the apartment building. Fifteen minutes later the two women were hugging the rear admiral before he climbed into a cab.

THREE

Kings Bay, Georgia

Rear Admiral Silver flew to Atlanta, then hopped the Delta shuttle to Jacksonville International Airport in Florida. He drove north to Kings Bay. There was little traffic and the forty-mile drive took just over a half hour. Silver remembered little of the flight from New York or the drive.

Upon arriving at the base, Silver learned that the sentry at the northwest gate had heard the car crash and had sent an Emergency Response Unit to investigate. The car had taken the hit on the driver's side and had been flattened. The ERU dispatcher who had called him had said that only the airbag had prevented Dr. Davies from being crushed into the backseat. Unfortunately, that hadn't prevented the engine from being slammed into her lap. It took the ERU twenty-five minutes to extricate her from the wreckage. She was taken to the Naval Ambulatory Care Center at the base. Silver went there, to the office of the chief of surgery, Capt. John Smolley. Silver learned that Dr. Davies had been conscious but completely disoriented when she'd arrived. Smolley had given her a FAST scan—Focused Assessment with Sonography in Trauma. External bleeding was limited to the left shoulder and arm. However, her spleen had ruptured, there were severe renal lacerations and pelvic exsanguination, and her liver had been crushed. Dr. Davies spent two hours in surgery before, as the chief surgeon put it, "We just couldn't shunt, suture, and trans-fuse anymore. Everything failed at once."

"Do we know what happened, what caused the crash?" Silver asked.

"The head of rescue said there were no skid marks, no at-tempt to decelerate," Smolley told him. "The road was dry and the brakes appear to be intact. We're doing the toxological drill, but frankly, sir, it looks as if the young lady simply shut her eyes and drifted."

Silver didn't want it to be that simple, that preventable. It cheapened life. You fell asleep and missed a ball game. You didn't fall asleep and die.

He thanked the surgeon for his efforts, then sat alone in the quiet room. Boxes of sample drugs, file folders, and journals were piled high around him. The medical knowledge and hopes of humankind surrounded him. The reality of what medicine could not do sat inside him making it difficult to think, to breathe.

Silver put in a call to the Camden County sheriff. Sheriff Robson investigated all accidents on public roads. The deputy-in-charge did not know anything more about the accident than the ERU. She said the car had been impounded pending word from the base. The sheriff's department was not sufficiently well-equipped to look for sabotage. Silver said that someone would be there to collect the car right away. Hanging up, Silver called the naval base's Emergency Management Office. The EMO was not affiliated with the Emergency Response Unit, which was a division of the Medical Office. The EMO sup-ported the activities of Submarine Group 10 and helped local authorities when the area was hit by storms, fires, or nonnatural disasters. The EMO had a truck en route to the sheriff's office within ten minutes. Silver also called Jacques Dryer, Kings Bay press liaison. The regional dailies would not lock up their early editions until 2:00 A.M. Silver wanted the PL to put out a death notice saying that Dr. Davies was working on upgrades to Tri-dent submarine guidance systems. That would forestall questions the local obituary writers would have about what she was doing at the base.

She was running the show, Silver thought grimly. It was the first time he had thought about the Tempest Project. Now that he did, he wondered what the *hell* they were going to do without Charlotte Davies.

That was for tomorrow. Right now, he had to call Charlotte's parents. The ones who had invested countless hopes and even more years. Rising slowly from the armchair beside the desk, the rear admiral sat in the captain's chair and logged on using his password, so he could access Charlotte's dossier to get the phone number of her parents. He looked at her pictures. Color mug shots, front and side. He realized how much he was going to miss the way she waved her hands excitedly when she thought of something everyone else had overlooked. And her humility, her evenhandedness. He'd miss her.

Silver scrolled down to her contact information. Karen and Dick Davies lived in Norwalk, Connecticut. Silver had been to Norwalk several times. There was a restaurant in town, the Yankee Doodle Inn, he used to visit on his way to the submarine base at Groton on the Long Island Sound. Norwalk was a busy, mid-sized city about an hour from New York. A lot of families, a strong sense of community. A lot of people probably knew Charlotte. The hurt was going to be widespread. In a way, that might be good for the Davieses. They would not have to suffer alone.

It was late. He was going to catch them watching the news or sleeping. Something ordinary that would never seem ordinary again.

If Charlotte had been a servicewoman, the news of her death would have been delivered in person by an officer and a chaplain. Because she was a civilian, Department of Defense policy was to give her next of kin the "fatality notification" ASAP. Because Silver had spent so many years in laboratory-based research and development, this was a first.

He punched the number into the chief of surgery's phone. This was going to be bad. Charlotte's parents didn't even have "deer ear," as the base psychologist called it, to cushion them. The families of servicemen and -women always reacted to a rap on the front door with a start. The anticipation was low intensity but it was never turned off.

The phone rang three times, but it felt like many more.

A man answered, "Hello?"

"Mr. Davies?"

"Speaking." A touch of sleep was in the man's voice.

"Sir, this is Rear Admiral Kenneth Silver. Your daughter works for me here at the Kings Bay Naval Base." He said "works" by accident. He didn't correct himself.

Dick Davies said nothing. The late-night call and Silver's solemn voice was probably the equivalent of a knock on the door.

"Mr. Davies. I regret to inform you that Charlotte was involved in an automobile accident earlier this evening. Base medics reached her quickly but were unable to pull her through."

There was a short pause. "Who are you? Why are you doing this?"

"I'm Rear Admiral Kenneth Silver. And I'm sorry to say, sir, this is not a crank call." It was important that he remain patient and calm.

"I'm going to call Charlotte right now—"

"Sir, your daughter was brought to the base hospital suffering severe trauma. We lost her in surgery. I'm very, very sorry. Charlotte was a wonderful and intelligent woman, a beloved co-worker."

"But we spoke with her last night. This isn't possible."

"I'm very sorry."

In a "condolence class" required for senior officers, Silver had been told that repeating condolences in a somber voice reinforced the reality of the event. Acceptance would only come over time.

Mrs. Davies was talking in the background. She wanted to know what was going on. Her husband repeated what Stone Silver had told him. He could picture her expression—frozen and disbelieving. He could taste the sickness rising in her chest. Silver had had a little time to adjust to the loss of his wife. The feeling of unreality was no less intense when it finally happened, but at least there had been a diagnosis, treatments, possibilities. There had been time to say good-bye.

"Jesus. Jesus. What are we supposed to do?" Dick Davies asked.

"That's up to you, sir." Silver heard Mrs. Davies crying in the background.

"Up to us? My wife is hysterical—we can't even think. I can't believe this."

"I understand. If you want to come here we can arrange for your flight. Or we can have Charlotte taken home. Why don't you talk about it and let me—"

"We'll come down," Davies interrupted. "I don't want Charlotte to be alone."

"Of course," the rear admiral said. "Let us take care of this."

"Yes. All right."

"Mr. Davies, I want to tell you again how very sorry we are for your loss."

"I still can't believe it," Davies said. "Charlotte was such a sweet girl, *woman*. She worked so hard. How could this happen?"

Silver said nothing. What could he say? He didn't know why it had happened.

No one spoke for quite some time.

Finally, Mr. Davies spoke. "Just tell me one thing. Tell me that what our daughter was working on really mattered. Tell me we didn't lose our Charlotte for something unimportant."

"One day I will tell you what she was in charge of," Silver replied. "You will be extremely proud."

"We've always been proud of her," Davies said. "But thank you. It may help to remember that."

Silver gave him his cell phone number, told him to call if they needed anything. After the rear admiral hung up, he sat and thought about Charlotte. Or rather, about himself and Charlotte. He had pushed her to stay on schedule and within budget, and she seemed to take the pressure well. But you never knew about these things. Soldiers who seemed to be in lockstep with a drill program or battle plan sometimes cracked. They took the responsibility so seriously that they didn't get enough sleep or worked out potential scenarios until they were confused and distracted. He could imagine that happening to Charlotte. He could imagine it now that it was too late to help her. He wondered what hairline fractures they may have missed in her, or in the skulls of the other project members.

He logged off and rose slowly. Without Charlotte Davies monitoring the tests at Kings Bay, they would have to rely on Dr. Carr, the chief scientist. He was thirty years old, a wunderkind, but he tended to rely too much on data and not enough on intuition. Missions like this often required some seat-of-the-pants command. Silver did not know if he trusted Carr with the project, and he did not think Captain Colon would be comfortable trusting Carr and the lives of the *Tempest D* crew.

But this was not the time or place to make that determination. He would go to his office, where he could gather his thoughts, then use the secure phone to call Ernesto Colon and the other team leaders to tell them the news. Protocol for top-security projects did not permit calls about key personnel to be made over open lines. He would meet with the entire team in the morning as scheduled, which was where many of them would first hear the news.

FOUR

Kings Bay, Georgia

"Slaying with artillery is easy. Slaying with comedy—that's tough."

If Capt. Ernesto Colon ever got up the guts to do an act—and he wasn't sure he ever would—that was going to be his opening line. The thirty-nine-year-old, prematurely silver-haired officer had been at the Muddy Tracks coffee bar Sunday night, as he was most Sunday nights. Muddy Tracks was a converted railroad warehouse built in the days when trains mattered. Along with the regular mix of military and civilian patrons, he had been listening with pain and awe as locals and the occasional "big name" did stand-up comedy. The captain understood what it took to face an enemy. But to face a crowd of people from different backgrounds, values, and politics, all of whom were daring you to make them laugh—that was a mystery. Comedy was something he'd like to do when he retired from the military. A big audience of soldiers was out there and no one since Bob Hope had tried to reach it. Plus, Colon had a lot to say.

Colon had listened to comics until closing at 1:00 A.M. Then he spent a little time showing one young lady and her equally enticing cousin from New Jersey the bay by starlight. They also shared the north-Georgia merlot they kept in the trunk. He did not have a lot to drink, but he had enough. Colon didn't get back to his quarters until three, but he had needed the R&R. Hell, Rear Admiral Silver had ordered it. He was about to sail to cold hell and back. He would catch up on his sleep aboard the *Abby*—unless things went well with her commander, Dr. Angela Albertson, in which case, who needed sleep? Besides, he did not need to be super-alert in the morning for Rear Admiral Silver's "meet-and-greets" with the combined military and tech staff. He had worked his handpicked crew for months and he had worked with the technical support groups for years, giving them a seaman's perspective of their plans and prototypes. Even if Colon was not completely alert, that was okay, which was one reason he loved the military: the rules for interaction were laid out.

That hadn't always been the case for him. He grew up improvising his way.

Born in San Juan but raised in Fort Lauderdale, Florida, Colon was not just the shortest kid on the block—and now, at five feet eight, one of the shortest men in the navy, which made him ideal for submarine service—he was also the only one who spoke little Spanish. His parents had insisted that since they were in Florida, they should speak Floridian. As it happened, the young Ernesto spent more time with his parents than he did with other kids. The other Latinos considered him *un pequeño traidor*, "a little traitor," for being one of *los muchachos blancos*, "the white boys." Growing up, the young boy went from fisticuffs before or after and sometimes during school to laughs at home. His father drove a public bus and his mother worked at a laundry. His parents' English, though heartfelt, was severely fractured. Ernesto would correct them over dinner or when they watched television, and they would often belly laugh over the things they said, whether it was about scrubbing his face with "soup" or helping his mother "grocer chopping." He actually kept a notebook with little drawings of himself washing his cheeks with clam chowder or killing the supermarket clerk with an ax. If he'd had any artistic talent, he might have become a cartoonist. A semester at Broward Community College taught him two things. One: He did not have the talent. Two: The answers to the kinds of questions Colon asked were not in books, they were in doing. School wasn't for him. Instead, one day—he vowed, when he found the courage—he would become a comedian.

The older he got the more absurd that old ambition became. He often wondered if he had grown backward, or dematured. The kid who had wanted to do something cerebral became the adult who was an adventurer.

Captain Colon went to sleep. He did not check his voice mail until the alarm buzzed at six-thirty. When he did, there was only one message: to call the rear admiral on the Micro-TAC. It wasn't an unusual request. They only discussed Ant Hill business on an encrypted line, the Motorola MicroTAC technology with its compact Elite XC handset. Since so many participants in the Tempest Project were civilians, Silver wanted them carrying cell phones that were virtually indistinguishable from nonsecure phones. Spies were everywhere around bases and in Washington. Hooked to a belt, a unit like the Elite XC was less likely to draw attention than standard, slightly bulkier military-issue secure phones.

Colon called.

The cafeteria meet-and-greet no longer seemed like a formality. He wouldn't be weaving in and out of pockets of well-wishers. Worse, he had no idea what they would do when it was over.

The captain dressed quickly and rushed to the Ant Hill.

FIVE

Kings Bay, Georgia

The only people Rear Admiral Silver had called the night before were those individuals who had to know at once about the death of Charlotte Davies. The ones who had to be thinking about what came next. The only ones he had spoken with at length were his superiors at NORDSS, the Pentagon's Naval Office of Research and Development, Submarine Systems. The admirals, led by Van Grantham, were noncommittal about proceeding with or postponing the test run. They did not have all the information about Dr. Davies's replacement, Dr. Mike Carr. It wasn't just a question of his scientific knowledge and his familiarity with all aspects of the project. How he got along with Captain Colon and the other members of the science team were also important. So were his leadership skills.

Rear Admiral Silver forwarded copies of Carr's quarterly psychological profile. Conducted by a Pentagon psychiatrist, these tests not only looked for signs of mental fatigue and intrasystem tension but also checked on stress at home. Professional disappointments accounted for 33 percent of the insiders who became foreign agents. Personal problems with parents, spouses, or fiancées accounted for the other 67 percent.

When asked, Silver told the board that Charlotte Davies's psych profile had said she was fine, save for a tendency to "overdemand both personal results and consensus." In other words, she took on too much. Obviously, Grantham pointed out, that was a warning Silver had missed.

Silver recognized that as Grantham's opening shot of CYA—cover your ass. If the project suffered any setbacks, Grantham had just told the rear admiral where the Congressional Oversight Committee would plant their flag.

Silver had been awake most of the night reviewing Carr's personnel files. The Hawaiian-born Carr was not a people person the way Charlotte had been, and that mattered. Working as liaison between a military crew and a tech team required communications skills and tact. But his professional credentials were strong. Before the navy had grabbed him, the thirty-year-old Caltech quantum engineer had worked as a graduate student for the institute's affiliated Jet Propulsion Laboratory. His specialty was supplementary spacecraft drive systems for NASA's ion-propelled solar sails. He was accustomed to thinking about materials in a below-freezing environment, something Charlotte had had to learn. But he was definitely checklist-oriented. Caution first. In theory, that was good. In practice, it minimized Joe Guinea Pig, as the military called their test pilots and maiden-sail seamen. A professional crew could usually push or finesse their way over a technological speed bump. Silver's attitude was that they should be given the final word. Not just because they were on-site, but because they had the most to lose.

By very early morning Silver had not reached any conclusions about Carr. He'd grabbed three hours' sleep, then dressed to go to the meeting. Before leaving, he spoke briefly with the EMO's chief investigator, Paul Roman. Roman and his team had spent the night dismantling the car and studying the brakes, steering, tires, and other key components. Silver was not surprised by the findings, though they did make him sad. Nothing was wrong with the car. In a strange way he wished it were otherwise.

It was a half-mile walk from Silver's quarters to the Ant Hill. Though he was entitled to a driver, he preferred to walk. The extra man could be better used elsewhere. More importantly, those ten minutes of solitude allowed the rear admiral to reflect on whatever issues he was facing. Usually, the open air was enough to clear his mind and give him a fresh perspective. Not today.

Silver had told everyone to meet him in the commissary. Though not the largest room at the facility, it was the warmest. When the old shipyards were replaced by the Ant Hill, Silver had commissioned murals showing the history of submarines. Not the vessels but the people. The Englishman William Bourne, who, in 1580, first theorized that a submarine was a possibility. Cornelius Drebbel, a Dutchman who built the first working model of a submarine in 1623. Marin Mersenne, a French priest, who ascertained in 1634 that a cylindrical shape was best for submarines. David Bushnell, a Yale man, who built a submarine called the *Turtle* in 1776 and used it to attack a British ship in New York harbor. There were many others, including the centerpiece, a portrait of cotton broker Horace L. Hunley, who, during the Civil War, used his fortune and influence to advance and standardize the science of submarines. Silver wanted the team, especially the civilian members, to understand that they were part of a long and distinguished history of human achievement.

By the time he arrived at the meeting, roughly a third of the personnel were already there. They were seated quietly at the cafeteria-style tables. Some were drinking coffee, a few were chatting, most were just sitting quietly. They were all wearing "moon pies," as his Polish-born grandmother used to describe pale, sad expressions. Obviously, everyone had heard the news. Some had worked closely with Dr. Davies; some—like Lt. Brance Michaelson, Colon's number two—barely saw her during the course of a week. But all of them knew her work and her dedication. They also knew the scientist's importance to the project.

He poured himself coffee and then sat on the short edge of a table to confirm the rumors. Silver told them that the funeral would probably be held in Connecticut but that there would be a memorial service here. New arrivals clustered around the rear admiral, listening without comment. Dr. Carr was among them. Most looked at the scientist with long, questioning glances, but he was impassive. Silver said that nothing had been decided about the status of the Tempest Project. No one seemed surprised.

The rear admiral finished his impromptu briefing by saying that the address of the Davies family would be posted, but that cards and flowers should be ordered on-line and sent without return addresses. Foreign operatives sometimes infiltrated local post offices to snag information about civilian employees of government installations. Kings Bay was certainly a potential target. When the U.S. navy began designing the nuclear-powered *Nautilus* in the early 1950s, the high incidence of atomic engineers working in and around the Electric Boat Company in Groton, Connecticut, was noted by Soviet "observers"—nationals who were not trained or authorized to infiltrate facilities, only to watch. Believing that a new generation of submarine was being built, they would go to diners the scientists frequented after work and collect paper place-mats, napkins, and newspapers they found in the trash. Numbers that had been sketched and circled on a discarded matchbook suggested that the top speed for the ship would be at least nineteen knots, much higher than that of conventional submarines. That scrap of information made it imperative for the Soviets to accelerate their own nuclear submarine program. The arms race accelerated in earnest. That the Soviets were able to steal nuclear weapons secrets at this time and build their own bomb made security an even more pressing issue.

And just as now, paranoia had gone from medium boil to high, Silver recalled.

Captain Colon had entered the commissary moments before the rear admiral began speaking. Colon stood just inside the doorway, his arms crossed. He was outfitted with his usual sense of purpose: eyes ahead, shoulders squared. There was no "moon pie" here, Silver noted. When the short talk was over, the scientists and crew dispersed into smaller groups and Colon made his way over. He snapped off a salute, then apologized to the rear admiral for not having contacted him sooner. He said he had not collected his messages until this morning.

"You were off duty," the rear admiral said.

"So were you, sir," Colon replied.

"I'm not the moving target you are," Silver said with a forgiving smile.

"Poor lady," Colon said. The men continued to speak as they walked toward a corner of the room. "Her folks are where— New York?"

"Connecticut."

"That's right. She rooted for the Pats. We ought to find out if they have a kids' charity, make a donation."

"Nice idea," Silver said.

The men were quiet for a moment. The minimum respectful silence. Then Colon said, "I assume, sir, you spoke with NORDSS."

"I did. They're reviewing the timetable and options. We'll be talking again at ten o'clock."

"Did you get a sense of things one way or the other?"

"No."

"You'll forgive my asking at this time, sir, but the *Abby* is due in today and my crew is hyped and primed. I'd like to let them know what the game plan is ASAP."

"I understand. What's your feeling, Captain?"

"My call would be 'go.' You, sir?"

"If NORDSS bucked it down to me, my inclination would be the same," Silver said.

"You don't sound one hundred percent."

"I'm not." The rear admiral looked for Mike Carr. He was not surprised to see that the scientist had left. The men stopped and Silver faced Colon. "You know the problem as well as I do. Dr. Carr is untested in the key-man spot. If it turns out he can't handle this, there's no one else who can do the job."

"With respect, we don't need one man," Colon said. "We can assemble a backup tech team to act as liaison with the *Abby* and the *D.*"

"A committee can't run this end of the operation," Silver said.

"No, sir, but we could inform Dr. Carr that there's been a change, that either you or I would be making the final decisions regardless of who is monitoring the data flow," Colon said.

Silver didn't feel like debating the matter just now. "Let's wait until the admiral weighs in. Until then, this is just talk."

"Yes, sir," Colon said. "Sir, there is one more thing."

Silver looked at him. He knew what Colon was going to ask. The question no one else would.

"Do we know if the crash was an accident?"

"The EMO's preliminary report says it was," Silver quietly informed him.

"I only asked because of that whole no-return-address thing."

"I understand," Silver said.

Colon said nothing more. Silver had grown up in the era of Cold War fear where a Communist was under every bed, but the younger officer had been raised in an era of conspiracy paranoia and terrorist plots. The government was out to get you. Foreign governments were out to get you. UFOs were out to get you. Admiral Grantham was a student of the Roswell flying saucer scare; he maintained that the era of paranoia began there, fostered by the federal government, as a means of deflecting public attention from real problems, real terrors. Which wasn't to say the idea of sabotage was out of the question. It was just less likely than the captain might be inclined to believe. If the car had been tampered with, the Defense Intelligence Agency would be all over Kings Bay and everyone in it. The Ant Hill would be "decontaminated," the workers grilled, and the entire system flushed of personnel regardless of what was found.

Silver looked around. There was no paranoia here. Not at the moment, anyway. There was only sadness. What had originally been planned as a rally of sorts, a chest-thumping send-off for the crew of the *Tempest D*, was instead a wake.

The question was whether it was just for Dr. Davies or for themselves as well.

After leaving the briefing, the rear admiral went to his office, poured himself coffee, then began to read the preliminary report from the coroner. He had barely gotten through the overview—stating that there was no evidence of drugs in Dr. Davies's system—when Grantham called. There was still an hour before a decision was due; Silver guessed that NORDSS wanted to be rid of the responsibility for this as quickly as possible.

He was correct.

"We continue to stand behind Tempest and believe its implementation is in the best interests of national defense," Grantham told him, as though he were reading from a prepared statement. Perhaps he was. "But we are removed from the daily operations and cannot fairly judge the readiness of the team to undertake the scheduled trial. We leave that decision to you."

"I understand," Silver replied. That had been the formal proclamation. The arm-around-the-shoulder part would come next.

"What can we do to help you with this, Stone?"

"Nothing I can think of." Silver didn't bother to ask what they thought of Dr. Carr's dossier; he already knew. They found nothing to object to and nothing outstanding to support. If Tempest went ahead and worked, NORDSS could claim they had approved Carr by not disapproving. If the project went south, they could tell the Congressional Oversight Committee it was Silver's decision.

"Have you got a ballpark for me?" Grantham asked.

"By ten," Silver replied.

"That's less than an hour from now."

"Yes, sir. I've had a long night to think about it."

"That's true," Grantham said.

The admiral asked for copies of the reports from the coroner and the EMO and Silver promised to send them. The conversation ended quickly after that.

Silver leaned forward and stared at the steam rising from his coffee. The phone call had been like the Japanese Bunraku puppet theater Silver had taken Elizabeth to see when she was seven or eight. The players went through predictable, stylized motions. The entertainment was in the comforting familiarity, not in any surprises. It seemed silly for two men to be going through this charade, but they had. It was a rehearsal. If the test went ahead and failed, there would be a hearing. Then they would do the performance again for an audience. An audience of congressmen and top brass.

Silver refused to let that influence him. In the end, there was one compelling reason to launch on schedule. It had to do with who they were. CYA notwithstanding, the U.S. military did not wait for something to be certain or easy. If they did, he'd be paying taxes to the queen.

Silver finished his coffee and asked his orderly to have Captain Colon and Dr. Carr come see him.

SIX

Louisa Reef, The Spratly Islands

"Adversity is healthy," Wu Lin Kit's father, Yan, once said to the eleven-year-old. "Do you see?"

"I do, Father."

The younger Wu did not see, but he believed. He believed because his father said it, spoke it in his deep, confident father's voice that seemed to start somewhere around the knees and gain resonance as it ascended. A voice trained for theater in the Beijing Opera School and roughened by the fat, hand-rolled cigarettes he was never without.

"Misfortune requires you to focus, or there is no escape. Hardship forces you to react in new and resourceful ways, ways that are usually correct. Onstage, the unexpected gets the attention of your fellow performers and thus the attention of the audience. Receiving a surprising look or line-reading from another actor causes you to stay alert. That helps you grow. Do you see? From dirt and rain comes flowers. Bad things can be good."

The elder Wu had made those remarks nearly twenty years ago, over bowls of sticky white rice and steamed vegetable dumplings at a wooden table in the marketplace. It was a week before the opening of the Yan Theater in Shanghai. Though the thickly bearded actor had been talking about his trade, Wu would soon realize that what he said also applied to life.

As now, for example. Wu was drawing his strong index and middle fingers from the nose of *Shao Xiao* Chen Lo Pei. From his reaction, it was clear that Chen had been surprised.

Wu's long fingers had been inserted backward into Chen's nostrils, their sharp-nailed tips hooked outward and tugging hard in that direction. The pressure, plus the forceful digging of the fingernails against the soft inner flesh, caused the taller man to yelp and dip forward, his big arms pinwheeling. When the thirty-one-year-old finally removed his two fingers, the *shao xiao*—a naval lieutenant commander—stepped away from him.

The bald-headed Chen vigorously rubbed the bottom of his nose with his right hand as he glared at his opponent. After a moment Chen stopped rubbing his nose. The forty-one-year-old turned and kicked the cinder-block wall of the small warehouse. His rubber-soled slipper made a dull scratching noise.

"That isn't good for your knee," Wu told him. "The wall has no give."

"At least I know what to expect from it!" Chen said bitterly. "Is this what they teach you in the Tenth Bureau?"

"I don't understand."

"How to cheat? You're all about deception, aren't you?"

"If you mean the scorpion's tail, it's a legitimate maneuver." Wu stood down, lowering his arms from chamber—the strike-ready position with elbows bent and extended back, the arms hugging the top of the rib cage. It was also a position from which to defend a rear attack, with an elbow strike.

"Legitimate among streetfighters, perhaps," Chen complained. "Not here."

"Lieutenant commander, we are always in the street."

"Are we?" With a snarl, Chen snapped a quick, low right-leg kick at the groin of his attacker. It was an angry, poorly conceived maneuver. For one thing, Chen had announced his intent with his expression. For another, being in the street did not mean acting impulsively. Wu blocked the kick by raising his left leg slightly, bending it at the knee, and lightly brushing the kick aside. When Wu put his left foot back down, he did so a long step closer to Chen. Wu could have come down hard on Chen's instep. He did not. But he was crouched low, left arm in chamber, ready to strike, the right arm in front of him, ready to block or strike. Wu was ready to hit his opponent in his belly, up into his chin, or at an angle into his groin. Even though the men were close together, striking power did not come from a long, arcing blow. It came from twisting the waist. Wu could break his opponent's rib even if they were only an inch apart.

Obviously, Chen had not expected his adversary to block the kick or to approach. He had not expected defense to become attack. But that was Wu's way. Chen waited a moment, then put his right fist in his open left hand and bowed his head slightly. In Chinese martial arts, that signified peace. Wu returned the gesture. Then Chen jabbed a finger at his own head.

"Here," Chen said, his voice echoing off the corrugated tin. "That is where your 'street' is. You create enemies where there are none. They are out there, not here." He pointed in the direction of the sea.

"You wanted to spar, to practice what the navy taught you," Wu said quietly. "We did that."

"What I wanted to do was train! You *fought*. There's a difference."

"I was taught that when a man steps in the arena, he must expect anything. That includes the results, which he must accept without excuse."

Still looking at Wu, Chen shook his head as he left the foam-filled vinyl mat. He continued to grumble as he crossed the concrete floor. He maneuvered with sharp, angry turns through the rows of supplies in sacks and boxes. Behind him, on the other side of the small exercise area, was ordnance in fat crates. The wooden boxes were covered with gray tarpaulins to protect them from the humid summers in the South China Sea.

Wu put on his slippers and followed a moment later. His baggy pants blew in the breeze, air racing up his legs. As he walked, Wu undid the traditional knot in the thick black belt of his kung fu attire. He slung the cotton belt around his damp neck. This was the way darker belts came to signify advanced standings in martial arts: They picked up perspiration and dirt over the years, indicating greater experience.

The lieutenant commander was not wrong. Wu was a street-fighter. Proudly so, and always looking for bigger streets to challenge him.

Wu Lin Kit worked for the Guoanbu—the Guojia Anquan Bu, the Chinese Ministry of State Security. He was the junior director of Remote Field Operations for the Tenth Bureau, the Scientific and Technological Information division of the MSS. The Tenth Bureau had been established in 1989 to support the other nine bureaus, which were not equipped to collect data on the high-tech innovations and capabilities of foreign powers. Two years later the MSS had also established the Eleventh Bureau, which concentrated on computer and Internet surveillance and counterintelligence. Those people were the kind of men and women Chen would enjoy, reasonable and predictable. Whatever aggressions they had were worked out mentally as they found ways to break through firewalls created by other electronics geniuses.

The work of the Tenth Bureau was more active. The agent's job was to move, to gather intelligence by signal interception, by placing or becoming a mole, through break-ins and theft, computer hacking, and observation at test sites and laboratories. Many of these operations were conducted jointly or with the support of the other MSS bureaus and military divisions, in particular the team of Mui Yu-tang, director of Second Bureau, which was responsible for foreign intelligence. That was the prestige group. That was the one Wu hoped to join, and one day to run.

At the moment, Wu was working with Lieutenant Commander Chen at this small, temporary base in the South China Sea. It was not a dream position, but was a good one. Though the facilities were not geographically remote, the facilities were primitive. They were located on the northern end of tiny, unoccupied Louisa Reef in the Spratly Islands. Portions of the more than one hundred coral reefs, islets, and sea mounts in this island group were claimed by China, Taiwan, Vietnam, Malaysia, and the Philippines. The archaeological record put China here as early as A.D. 110, when the expansionist Han dynasty had sent out naval expeditions. China had established this particular outpost three months ago when Brunei had begun fishing off the shores of the reef. Beijing did not want the sultanate to attempt to establish its own claims in the region.

Wu had been here for two days and would be here for less than a week. He had come to review procedures for reconnaissance of the other islands. This would include "dinghy runs" around the islands, communications surveillance, and bugging the piers of the larger harbors. His senior director in Beijing had also asked him to monitor the security for a research team that was coming from the mainland. The primary natural resources in the Spratly Islands were fish and bat guano, which was harvested by the few native islanders. However, scientists believed that the area was also rich in gas and oil reserves. Three senior geologists from Hunk Luk Fuel were going to be diving off Half Moon Shoal to the southeast of Louisa Reef. They were going to search for evidence to corroborate what was suggested by satellite observation. The Guoanbu also wanted to make sure that their operation was not being watched by anyone else.

Wu stepped into the warmth and white-wine light of midmorning. Shanghai had always been hazy, perpetual smog blocking the sun. When he was in places like this, Wu thrived. It was as if his skin were passing vitamins to his organs, his blood, his soul. The gentle morning sea breeze also felt refreshing. Despite the way it had turned out for Chen, Wu had gotten a good workout, mostly from throwing Chen and maneuvering him into armlocks and neck holds. The military really let men like Chen down. They taught them to use muscle instead of technique. Finesse. Misdirection. Deceit. Those were the surest, least costly ways to win battles. Done in the name of country or family, in the preserving of "face," these were honorable activities.

Wu let the jacket of his *gi* hang open. The light wind caused the fabric to billow slightly around him. He smiled. It felt as though he were being lifted slightly from the scrub. Feeling like the Flying Swordsman of legend, Wu looked across the dusty shore to the cove where the type 520T Houjian-class large missile boat was at anchor. The vessel was used primarily to ferry supplies to the little settlement, though its six missiles could

reach any of the islands within the two-hundred-mile-wide
stretch. A two-man watch was on deck. The rest of the twenty
crew members were ashore, most of them working out on the
small beach or writing e-mails on a shared laptop computer. Wu
had spent some time with one of them, Pan Shiying, one of two
radio operators. Pan was the son of a lumber boatman who
sailed the Hong Kong–India trade route. Pan loved the sea and
he knew these waters and their history. He was using a metal
detector to search for treasure. According to him, this was one
of the islands where the notorious Scottish pirate Captain
William Kidd had hidden some of his treasure. Wu wished the
young man well. Alone among the crew, Pan was showing initiative. Wu was also moved by something the young man had
said:

"If I ever find treasure, I'm going to give it to my father so
he can retire. He wants to garden, not sail on a lumber ship. He
wants to give something back to the soil."

Wu understood that desire to help his family. He remembered the night the gangsters had come to his father's theater.
They'd entered the backstage area unannounced. They'd maneuvered Yan into a corner and told him what it would cost to
remain in business. His father refused to pay.

Unfortunately, it did not work out well for Yan. He was not
given a chance to reconsider. The four men broke the actor's
right knee with a tire iron. Yan spent six weeks in bed and was
never again able to walk comfortably. He acted, but only as an
old man with a cane. He was still doing that, bragging about
how, at fifty-six, he still required makeup to play those parts.

That was why Wu believed what he had said to Chen. For
Wu, for the people of the Tenth Bureau, the field of conflict was
the world, and the world was a street, full of shadowed alleys,
dead ends, and dangerous individuals. Even in misty sunlight.
But Wu didn't expect a soldier to understand that. Theirs was a
profession built upon rules of engagement. In Wu's world, victory came through the unexpected, just as his father had said—
and also through stealth. Wu had learned that part of the lesson
when he'd tried something he had seen at the local cinema.
He'd stuffed a scarf from one of the theater's costumes into the

gas tank of the local gangster's automobile. He set it on fire and ducked behind a building as the car exploded. To protect his son, the elder Wu sent him to a local Shaolin master to learn martial arts, so that he could defend himself if the gangsters came looking for him. They did not. They were too busy fighting among themselves to replace their boss.

Wu's father never did pay the extortion money. And Wu, who had once hoped to become a movie stunt actor, went in a different direction. While he was still at the Shaolin school, Wu's fighting skills had caught the attention of the director of Central Security Regiment. Wu was recruited, an invitation a good citizen did not turn down. He served in the regular army for two years, and then in military intelligence for three years before shifting to the CSR, the division of the army responsible for the security of China's political leaders. The CSR was the successor to the 8341 Unit, the division of the People's Liberation Army that had overseen the security of Chairman Mao Tse-tung. The 8341 Unit had officially been decommissioned in 1976, because it had too high a public profile. All of its operations, though, were simply moved underground. Wu had not yet decided whether certain people chose Guoanbu or whether the profession chose people. Not that it mattered. This was the way it was. This was the way *he* was.

The intelligence officer took a long breath. The incident with the gangsters was twenty years ago, yet the rage he felt was so immediate. Maybe that was the real difference between men like Chen and men like himself. The anger, the hate, the humiliation, the frustration. Those feelings were always right there, behind his eyes, in his throat, in every joint of every finger. Maybe that long-ago explosion had burned the street into him. Not that the cause mattered. There was no changing the result. Wu knew exactly what it took to survive.

With a final glance toward the pastel blue water, Wu turned and walked toward the tents that served as the seamen's barracks. His private tent was on the north end, fifty meters from the end of the reef. The scientists had set out before dawn in a twenty-two-foot motor launch. They would be arriving at Half Moon Shoal around ten-thirty. Wu would talk to them via a two-foot portable satellite dish overlooking the sea to the south-east. The uplink would also allow him to monitor the communications of anyone else using radios or cellular phones in the region. A radar download would enable him to watch for approaching ships or aircraft. If Wu was away from the tent or asleep, a pager would alert him to any activity.

This operation would take three days. When the scientific team was finished, they would return to the reef and an aquaplane from the mainland would come and get them. Then Wu's superior, Director of Remote Field Operations Liang, would send him somewhere else on the globe. Perhaps that was another reason Wu held so tightly to his internal compass. The external one was constantly changing. That internal compass had been a part of his makeup since childhood. Early in his martial arts training Wu Lin Kit had learned how to find his center, to focus his *chi*, his energy, to strike hard and fast. He remembered one day in particular, the day of his twelfth birthday, because of a gift he had received from his sensei, his teacher. Master Hun had come up from behind, unannounced, and kicked upward between Wu's legs. If the young boy had failed to feel the master's foot and shin ascending, if he had failed to tense his gluteal muscles in time, the result would have been extremely painful. Wu defended himself correctly and completely and was presented his yellow belt in recognition of the accomplishment, removing him from the realm of the white belt novice.

That was how Wu liked things to be: promotion under fire. Growth.

The unexpected.

Wu returned to his small tent and sank into a canvas-back chair. He felt centered now, too, with the instruments of his craft around him. He studied an e-mailed weekend intelligence summary sent by Chin, the director of remote field operations, to all his agents. Like Director Chin, the summary was terse and impersonal. Substance only. When Wu was finished, he pressed one end of a headset to his ear. A radio receiver in a small briefcase sat on the card table along with his laptop. A fresh breeze carried salt air through the open flap causing it to flutter like a great seabird.

Wu spoke with each of the three Hunk Luk Fuel geologists. He was pleased to hear that it had been a productive first day. It was strange to hear Dr. Peng, the reserved paleobiologist, sounding so excited.

The Spratly Islands sit on the Pacific plate. During his mission briefing, Wu had learned that this massive geologic formation is passing slowly under the Australian plate, movement that thrusts long-buried sediments to the surface. If silt from the seafloor contained a significant amount of animal and plant remains—the major component of petroleum—there was a four-in-ten chance the site also contained oil. Beijing felt it would be worth establishing a presence here if it kept Brunei or other nations away from attempting to exploit these stores.

After listening to the report and writing his daily update for the Guoanbu, Wu received an alert from his laptop. The Eleventh Bureau routinely monitored communications to, from, and on American military bases. Jumps of any kind were rarely irrelevant. When Wu had first joined the Tenth Bureau, he was surprised to learn that the Chinese also used their Washington, D.C., embassy to monitor calls placed from the Pentagon to nearby pizza parlors. Before any major action, officers typically worked late and ordered in. The previous night, comm monitors at the embassy had picked up a spike in secure cell phone communications from a base in the nearby state of Georgia.

All cellular and radio activity was monitored by a fleet of ships that sailed international waters along the coast of the United States. There were six ships in all, from yachts to fishing boats to oceanic research vessels. Their scanners swept every signal going to and from bases from the Air Warning System in Maine to United States Central Command in Florida, inland to the nation's midsection. Ships in the Gulf of Mexico and the Pacific Ocean completed the coverage. Unsecure messages could be listened to. The contents were usually unimportant, but they enabled the Chinese to pinpoint the location of key personnel. If a high number of admirals and five-star generals were absent, chances were good they were at the Pentagon planning something significant. Otherwise, the number of calls and signal type—secure or unsecure—were all that the ships could determine. That was often enough. Usually, Sunday was heavy with open calls as sailors called their families. This was different. Though the Eleventh Bureau telecommunications specialists could not ascertain the content of the calls, a spike in secure communications usually meant that maneuvers or military action was imminent.

The Eleventh Bureau had contacted the Tenth Bureau, which had notified Wu, because of something else that had happened at the base. Because of the communications spike, the Tenth Bureau had gone back to digitally stored satellite surveillance of this region. They were looking for increased transit of warships or aircraft. Images showed just one thing out of the ordinary: a small, re-outfitted oil tanker arriving seven days before at the Kings Bay Naval Base. However, computer enhancement of the images revealed that the waterline was extremely low on the hull. That suggested the vessel was empty. Wu accessed the Guoanbu database on oil activity. He had spent days reviewing those files before coming here and knew his way around them. The U.S. navy did not store oil at the Kings Bay facility. They kept it in bases located in the states of Florida and New Jersey. Clearly, the navy would not have been filling the tanker at Kings Bay and sending it out. Not with oil, anyway. Indeed, according to subsequent images, the tanker had not left the base. It was probably moored inside the large shed at the northern end of the bay. That was the only structure big enough to accommodate it. A check of old Russian images, stolen from the surprisingly accessible satellites, was stored in the database. They showed nothing but open harbor at that site. The shed had been constructed within the last six years.

Wu went on-line and checked the weather in that area. The climate was temperate, with considerable annual cloud cover. There would be no reason to erect a structure to protect vessels from the elements. It had been built to keep observers from seeing whatever was going on inside.

Wu added these findings to his daily report. He also requested that someone in the Tenth Bureau's photo analysis department attempt to identify the ship and get its history from the Ministry of Foreign Trade. The ministry's Maritime Bureau would be able to trace the ship's registry.

Wu felt a rush of pride at the effectiveness of the Guoanbu. They did not have the technological advantages of other nations, but they had one quality the intelligence services of other nations could not touch. Their parts did not work at cross-purposes. There was only the job to be done, the goal.

They had *chi*.

SEVEN

The South Pacific

South of New Zealand and north of the Balleny Islands, a man was alone. Below the sea, the sense of isolation was even stronger. Even with his sixty-eight-man crew, Sr. Capt. Chien Gan felt alone. He felt privileged to be commanding the first all-Chinese submarine of the twenty-first century, the Song-class *Destiny*. There were no Soviet parts, no Russian naval advisers, nothing that had not been contributed by Chinese naval engineers and built by the personnel at the Wuhan shipyard. Still, as he recorded in his log, the four stars on his shoulders and twenty-six years aboard submarines had not prepared him for this.

The intercom above his small desk buzzed. The silver-haired officer saw the light flashing above the small plate that read TORPEDO ROOM. Chien put his pen down and touched the green button. It glowed red.

"Go ahead."

The officer on the other end was Lt. (j.g.) Hao Hark. This was the first time the senior captain had sailed with him. Hao was a meticulous officer and the senior captain had been impressed by his vigilance.

"Captain, torpedo tube three has gone dark. It could be a filament problem. We're going in to make sure."

"Thank you, Lieutenant. I'll have Captain Biao slow to ten knots."

"Thank you, sir."

The senior captain tapped off the torpedo room intercom and tapped on the bridge. Captain Biao answered. The cruising speed of *Destiny* was fifteen knots. Biao had been running her at twenty-two knots to see what did and did not come apart at the submarine's top speed. Though Biao had the bridge, any actions involving the torpedo tubes, even passive activity such as an engineering check, required the approval of the senior captain. Chien notified the bridge and Biao gave the order to slow. Then the senior captain went back to his log.

Chien didn't like the book they had given him. It had been bound with glue, not thread. When it opened, it cracked. Chien would include that in his final report. Sloppy workmanship was something the senior captain did not tolerate.

A loose binding or a loose filament, he thought. It all mattered, some of it more than the sophisticated equipment the *Destiny* had on board. The helm had computers attached to sensors to monitor hull integrity, seam stability, and other aspects of the vessel's construction. But for Chien, the filaments in lightbulbs had always been the best indicator of excessive vibration that, over time, could compromise welds. The computer readings were pure; it told them how much "shake" there was. Filaments were interactive; it told them how vibrations that were tolerable on paper could be detrimental at sea. Before computers the captains also relied on water in a cup, kept on flat surfaces around the ship. If the water sloshed, that was all right. That was normal submarine movement. If the water rippled, it meant dangerous structural flexibility. Unfortunately, that technique could no longer be used. Back in the late 1970s, if one of those cups had spilled, an ensign had grabbed a rag and swabbed the water. Now, with the ship's reliance on electronics, a spill could be catastrophic.

The captain completed his entry and rose. The stateroom was small, just two by three meters. Just like one of the caves from his childhood. Chien stood five foot three, so there was sufficient headroom. That was one reason he had been selected for submarine service. The other reason was that he had been raised in a small village high in the mountains. That was where the navy recruited submarine crews. They were accustomed to breathing thin air. That background was an asset, given the way ventilation systems regularly broke down on the old Ming-class vessels, variants of the Soviet Romeo-class ships that were obsolete when the Chinese built them. Chien had always suspected that the Chinese spies were allowed to steal those plans so the Russians could drown enemy sailors.

At first the young man had resented being taken from the heights and thrown into the depths. But it introduced a new world to him, a world that knew no boundaries. At sea, one could go anywhere. It was both fitting and gratifying for the fifty-seven-year-old senior captain to be commanding this new generation of vessel.

They were just two weeks into the mission, which was scheduled to last one month. The previous six months had seen them operating primarily in tropical waters—the Philippines, near Guam and Midway, then all the way to Hawaii. Those trips had produced only minor technical problems. But those waters were also extremely moderate. Here, on the fringes of south polar currents, they would be cruising at greater depths, executing sharper maneuvers due to the canyons, and experiencing cooler water temperatures which could cause the ship's alloys to react in different ways.

The unknown didn't bother Chien. Growing up, he had always been eager to find out who or what was behind this crag or in that cavern. Perhaps he sought the mountains out because they frightened him. He looked for the familiar, the small, in any new place; some indication that people had been there. Smells, for example. At seven thousand feet the air was not thick enough to scatter the particles widely. Sometimes the smells were of cooking from a village miles away. Sometimes the odors were diesel fuel from a military patrol moving to or from neighboring Tibet. At times he could even smell the tobacco of men watching goat herds on distant peaks.

The senior captain rose and unbuttoned his olive green shirt. He hung it and then his trousers on wooden hangers behind the door. Hangers were a good indication of stability as well. If the clothing didn't sway, the vessel was under control. Then he lay down on the aluminum cot perpendicular to the desk. A small shower, with a head inside the unit, was across from him. A closet was beside that. Chien clicked off the desk lamp. The room vanished. The cabin's doors had two-layer rubber edging. In the event of a hull breach, that would help keep water out and air in. There was no light, save for the glowing white numbers of the digital clock on his desk and the green buttons on the intercom. No sound came from outside the door; the crew were silent whenever the captain or senior captain were in quarters. In the dark, lying on his back, Chien listened to the sound of his ship as it filtered through the walls, ceiling, and floor. He heard the gears engaging—high and low, some close by and some not. There were occasional clinks and clangs, and like a distant waterfall, the constant sound of the sea moving past. Chien was familiar with all the sounds, though their order, volume, and frequency depended upon the course, speed, depth, and trim of the *Destiny*. Like the mountains and their smells, the vessel felt alive.

Tonight they were also reassuring. In the light he was alone. In the dark he was part of the ship, part of the sea, feeling currents that washed around him like the mountain air of his ancestral home. . . .

EIGHT

Kings Bay, Georgia

It wasn't fair to Stone Silver, to Colon's crew, or to the rest of the Ant Hill team. But Ernesto Colon couldn't help it: He did not like Mike Carr. It was a downer just being in the same room with him, as they were now, sitting in the rear admiral's office, side by side in aggressive silence.

Mike Carr was not a team player, unless the team was his. He didn't understand negotiation or compromise. Three years before, the two men had had their first brawl when Carr had refused to change the position of a rear stabilizer. It cut 1.3% of the view from the commander's periscope. Colon did not want to hear that sonar could compensate: He wanted an unobstructed 360-degree sweep. Eventually, Charlotte told the team to move the stabilizer. That required a redesign of the aft section and, thus, the location of two top, rear-mounted propulsion fans. Carr avoided Colon for a month. On another occasion Carr had asked that plasma monitors be installed in the computer stations instead of traditional electron tube screens. His reasoning was sound: They would have far greater resolution of downloaded satellite images, among other imaging considerations. But the inert gas that was used to transmit the light in plasma systems became unstable in sharp turns on the simulations. Carr wanted to install the units and solve the problem at sea. Colon could live with the lesser resolution and one less headache. Again, Charlotte had sided with Colon. The battles even got down to square-foot details. Just a few weeks ago, a panel in the com-section could not be removed easily for repairs because of the location of a ventilator. One or the other had to be moved. Colon felt that ease of repair should take priority. If they couldn't fix the hydrogen-removal system that gave them ballast, nothing else would matter. Carr suggested training the sailors to lie on their back and pop the four screws where they were, rather than having to reroute the air shaft. Carr had won that battle. Colon was still pissed.

Each week it was two or more "something elses" where science and function clashed. So the two men sat resolutely quiet in Rear Admiral Silver's office. They were waiting for Silver to finish with his aide in the closet-sized room out front. It was almost comical to see poor, six-foot-five CPO Ron Farmer tucked into that small outer office. The Oklahoma native was a good-natured kid who didn't seem to mind. The rear admiral's office wasn't big, but it was larger by half than the other offices and cubicles. It didn't have a window but the fluorescent lights were white and thorough.

Silver was giving Farmer instructions for a very, very low-keyed naval participation in Charlotte Davies's funeral. The rear admiral wanted a large, red-white-and-blue floral arrangement from "her friends at the office" but no other indication of where or for whom she worked. He also wanted someone watching the funeral home. Silver wanted to know if anyone came and asked questions about what Charlotte had been doing in Georgia.

She was running a smooth ship, Colon thought. Not like this other bonehead would do, given the chance. Hopefully, Silver wouldn't give him the chance. He'd give him Charlotte's job, but with restrictions.

What was most frustrating about Carr was not that he disagreed with Colon. If Colon were engaged in combat against a Russian or Chinese officer, he could respect the enemy's abilities. Not here. The *Tempest* wasn't supposed to be a pure-science wet dream. It had to be a functioning, habitable, first-and-foremost user-friendly vessel. One of the first things a good commander learned is that you shouldn't try to change the instincts of a new recruit. One of the first things Colon had learned at the naval air station in Pensacola was that reactions were hardwired, like a man automatically protecting his groin in a fight or picking up something to read before hitting the head. To override those instincts took moments that would be better applied against a threat. Colon knew what a sailor's instincts would tell him to do. Carr did not. He reminded Colon of the surfers Colon had encountered in Puerto Rico, at Tres Palmas. They'd laze at their tables, around plates of *mofongo* or *chicharrónes de mero*, plantain balls or fresh fish nuggets, and pray for the storms, cold fronts, and low-pressure pockets that brought on big waves. Never mind what that did to the livelihoods of fishermen, farmers, and those dependent on tourism. Forget about the floods and battering rains. These lanky, vacant-expression congers wanted their fucking waves.

Silver returned. He tossed his notes in the bin marked SHRED as he returned to his desk.

"Gentlemen, NORDSS has left the go, no-go decision to me," the rear admiral said as he sat. "I've considered our assets and I've thought about the risks. I've decided I want *Tempest* to launch, as scheduled."

Neither Carr nor Colon moved. But Colon cheered inside.

Silver fixed the scientist with his sharp eyes. "Mike, how do you feel about taking Charlotte's place?"

Carr thought for a moment, then replied, "Very uneasy."

The two naval officers stared at him. Colon had been sure Carr would jump on the offer like a pit bull at a rib roast.

"Why?" Silver asked.

"To begin with, this is not the kind of job one steps into without preparation. There is too much at risk."

"Steps into?" Colon said. "You've had six years to prepare!" Colon hated "no-can-do." He loathed it more than he disliked candy-ass surfer boys.

"I've had six years of working with the team and buttoning up the technology," Carr said. "But I don't know all the science the way Charlotte did. She lived it. Last week I came to work at seven in the morning and found her sleeping upright in her chair, one of the *Tempest B* sims playing. I'm willing to bet that's what she was doing last night. She fine-tuned the programs, looked for cracks and leaks, left no rivet or current or thermal variation unexamined. She earned the project director's chair."

"I appreciate your honesty," Silver told him. "Most people would have thumped their chests and said, 'Bring it on.'"

Colon took a quick hit from Silver's eyes. He didn't know whether the rear admiral was telling him *Like you* or *Don't open your mouth*.

"But I'll tell you something," Silver went on. "I've spent my life assessing people's abilities, whether they're fit to command or even date my daughter. I wouldn't have pulled the trigger if I didn't think you could do this. And it's not as if you'll be alone. You'll have top support here and from the team at sea."

Carr was silent.

"If we stand down now, we have to ratchet the process back to zero," Silver went on. "You know the drill. We'd have to re-assess the weather conditions, the currents. We'd have to wait for another clear zone in scheduled Russian and Chinese patrols, in the number of research vessels crossing the region. We run the risk of losing our own edge."

"Hell, we even have a window in seal migration so we don't screw them up and piss off Greenpeace," Colon said. "We need someone in that seat and you're it." Colon couldn't believe he was arguing *for* this guy to take the job. But the rear admiral was right. Carr would have top support here and at sea.

"Mike, I guess I'm not really clear on what needs to be done," Silver said. "We've got computer sims for virtually every conceivable situation. You can bring them up in seconds with the troubleshooting protocols right there."

"I know that, Rear Admiral. I contributed to a number of those programs."

"Then what's the problem?"

"I'd like to ask the captain something," Carr said.

"Please," Colon said. One tight word with an affected chime at the end. That was his attempt at being affable. This was going to be good.

"You're at sea. Suppose I detect a loose hydraulic valve that was not vital to the ship's operation but could affect a future Sonar Warning and Control Antenna placement. What do you do?"

"I get on with the primary mission and look into it when we get back," Colon said.

"I'd stop and fix it," Carr said.

"Even if it threw off the timing of everything else?"

Carr nodded. "That's the way a good scientist does things. Working here, I've discovered that the military holds things together with chewing gum until you reach port. I can't do that."

"You don't have to," Colon said. "You'll be here, safe. We'll be the ones who have to worry about it."

"Captain, please," Silver said. "Mike, it's true that we sometimes—not always, but sometimes—do what you described out of necessity. If a destroyer is clipped by a torpedo or a mine or a terrorist charge, or an aircraft carrier takes an injured bird and suffers damage, you may not have much choice."

"It's called CIA, command-in-action," Colon said. "That's when you take whatever measures are necessary to get you through whatever the problem is."

"And who decides what's necessary?" Carr asked.

"The on-site commander," Silver replied. "You know that."

"Yes. The problem I'm having is that we're not in a combat situation," Carr said. "This isn't even a shakedown cruise. It's a test run of a new vessel. It's an engineering mission."

"With sailors risking their lives," Colon said. "That makes it a military operation. That also means there's a chain of command. *That* means even if we don't always like the way the military does things, we do them anyway because we're professionals."

"In my business, the chain of command is ascendant, not descendent," Carr said. "A professional builds on what he knows for certain."

"Mike, you just lost me," Silver said.

"Rear Admiral, this is a mission to study a vessel we all designed and built," Carr said. "A scientist doesn't get a better laboratory than the real world. Charlotte was able to live with a military mission that was science-driven. For me, it's the other way around."

"Nice work if you can get it," Colon told him. "Unfortunately, things *aren't* that way."

Carr raised his hands in surrender. "Which is why I can't take the project director's chair."

Colon shook his head angrily. "I don't believe this. You'll hold up this mission because of a loose screw in a nonessential section of the ship?"

"I won't do something in a way I know isn't the right way to do it."

"Your way," Colon said.

"If you like."

"I *don't* 'like,' Doctor," Colon replied. "The military has paid your bills for six years."

"To do my job, which I've done. Now you're asking me to take Charlotte's job. I'm honored, I'm flattered, but I can't do it. Not the way the job description is written. You can't let desire or instinct or bravado run over scientific procedure. At least, I can't. That's how you end up with the *Titanic*."

"It's also how you sail a tub like the *Santa Maria* from Spain to America," Colon replied.

"Gentlemen, that will be all," Silver said. He sat back and put his fists together, knuckles to knuckles. He looked at Carr. "Mike, I can't force you to run this operation. We can put together a team to work as mission directors, but they wouldn't be as effective as one good man. I don't want to go that route. You're the deputy director. *You're* the one good man."

"I'm sorry, sir, but—"

"Hear me out," Silver said. "I believe your reservations are sincere. And I can't order you to continue with the project. But I want to make very sure I understand something. I get the feeling you could live with the lack of sim-time. What you're saying is that if we ran this as a scientific mission, you would take Charlotte's place."

Colon's neck turned to ice.

"I believe I would, yes," Carr said.

"No 'I believes' or 'ifs,' " Silver replied. "Can you do the job backed by the other team leaders?"

"Yes."

"No," Colon said, shaking his head. "Sir, with respect, this is a bad idea—"

"I'll talk to you about that in a minute," Silver said.

"Sir, you can't let a civilian run a sub! That's how you ram fishing vessels—"

Silver ignored him. "Mike, if you'll wait outside, I'd like to discuss this with Captain Colon."

"Of course."

Carr left, shutting the door behind him. The chill on Colon's neck had spread through his arms and rolled down his spine. It was as cold as what he saw in the rear admiral's eyes: the CIA apparatus about to iron-heel Colon into submission.

"You were out of line," Silver said.

"Sir, I'm sorry, but he just snookered us. He set us up so he could run the operation."

"I don't believe that. I think he's sincere."

"About taking over, yes—"

"About his concerns. The question is, what do we do?"

Colon couldn't believe this was happening. He couldn't believe the rear admiral was considering the man's back-door coup. "Fortunately, sir, I don't have to make that decision. Sir, I still think—"

"If you did have to make the decision?" Silver asked.

"I'd run it with a team before I put Carr in charge," Colon said. "Sir, he's saying he can't get over some personal anal shit for the good of the project."

"Can you?" Silver asked.

"Yes."

Damn him, that was good, Colon thought. *Nice trap, perfectly sprung.* "I'm a naval officer. I'll do as I'm told, even if my superior officer allows a civilian to command a military mission."

"The president does all right," Silver said.

Shit. Another point for Silver. Colon should have anticipated that one, too. But he was tired and he was angry and he was a little hungover. He was most angry at Carr. He'd worked hard to command this operation and he didn't want to lose it because of loose SWACA screws. He'd recover because he had to, but this rankled him. He was even angry at Charlotte Davies for having watched over the sub and its crew but not herself. He wanted to go to her cubicle and yell at her—

And that was the first time it really hit him. Charlotte Davies was dead.

"Ernie?"

Colon looked over. "Sir?"

"Are you with me?" Silver asked.

"Yes."

"It looked like you went somewhere."

"No, sir." Colon squared his shoulders. He was thinking about what Charlotte would think of this dustup over issues that would probably never come up, or not matter much if they did. She would probably give this one to Carr. And she was a fair woman. "Truth is, I think I just came back."

"Glad to hear that." Silver smiled. "Look, Ernie. As far as I'm concerned, this is effectively the same mission we've planned all along. I think Mike is a little intimidated by what he has to do. He's looking for some kind of comfort zone. When he takes the chair, I don't think he'll be unreasonable. We'll have the team leaders stay a little closer to him than they were used to with Charlotte and have them run the sims with him when he's not watching dataflow. It's going to be all right."

Colon rose. "You're probably right, sir."

"I like the sound of that. Never mind what we call Mike Carr, or what his specific duties are. When the mission is over, he'll be the guy who sat at a computer in Georgia while you made history at the south pole. Your picture will be the one they paint on the cafeteria wall."

"It'll be the *Tempest*'s portrait that goes on the wall. You haven't spent much time at sea. Do you know what I'll get?"

"What?" Silver asked.

"Tomorrow morning the crew will check the mission roster and see Dr. Mike's name on top, not as project director but as mission commander. I'll go to my station one morning and find a little G.I. Joe doll in a lab coat sitting in my chair, probably with a tiny slide-rule and stubby pencil."

"I see."

"It won't be pretty."

"Well, if that happens, there'll be an upside," Silver said.

"What's that?"

"Maybe he'll introduce you to Barbie."

That was a truly bad joke. Colon tried to smile but it probably came out as a wince. Still, he appreciated the rear admiral's efforts to lighten things.

Silver thanked the captain and reminded him about the 6 P.M. science team meeting. He would like Colon to attend. The captain said he'd be there and left the office. As he did, he passed Mike Carr. The scientist was standing with his back to the rear admiral's office, looking out at the hall. Colon decided he would try again, just once more, to suck some life from this lemon.

"Look, Mike. I'm sorry if it got a little rough in there. I don't react well when someone asks me to do a one-eighty without the proper turn radius."

"I didn't ask that," Carr said. "I told the rear admiral what my issues were—"

"Okay, I know that." *Jeez, the guy didn't know when to stop fussing. He fuckin' won! He could show some grace.* "What I want *you* to know is I'm on board. I'm with you. I want this to work. We *need* this to work."

"I agree."

"Great. We've got a final briefing scheduled for six. I'll see you in the conference room?"

Carr nodded. He didn't smile but at least he kept his mouth shut. Colon headed into the corridor.

Chief Petty Officer Farmer called after him in his low, slow Midwestern drawl, "Captain Colon, sir?"

Colon stopped and turned. "Yes, Farmer?"

"I hope you don't mind, Captain sir, because I didn't mean to be listening in. But it sounds to me like you're fielding new ideas. If you are, then I have a suggestion for you."

"Do you?"

"Yes, sir. I was thinking that maybe we should rechristen the *D* in Dr. Davies's honor. You know, we've got the *Abby*— maybe call her the *Charlotte* or the *CD* or even the *Doctor of the Bay*, which happens to be my personal preference. Anyway, I think we should do something like that."

Colon smiled. "*Doc of the Bay.* I like that, Chief Petty Officer. And we can still call her the *D.*"

"Yes, sir."

"That's the best idea I've heard today," Colon said. "I'll tell Cleveland to stencil that on the con."

"Thank you, sir," Farmer said.

The rear admiral called Carr back into the office and the scientist turned to go. He still seemed to be wincing slightly. Or maybe that was a smile. With Mike Carr and most of the other scientists, it was difficult to tell what they were thinking or feeling. Those men and women seemed to have two expressions: scrunched-in-thought or neutral-with-defeat.

But Colon did not want to think about them right now. He wanted to go upstairs to surface level and walk along the covered promenade to the Shed. He wanted to tell Major Cleveland about the unofficial name change and then have a good long look at the *D.* Major Gregory Cleveland was the officer in charge of dry-dock operations. He lived and worked in the Shed, where the *D* and her refitted tanker-transport were being kept.

Colon decided not to take the elevator but went to the stairwell. He ran up the four flights of concrete stairs. It felt good to get his heart chugging, to experience the burn in his legs, to hear "Anchors Away" playing in his head, sounding just as it had the first time he'd worn his dress blues in a parade in Pensacola, with his parents in the grandstand and the vice president of the United States on the viewing platform.

Don't lose that feeling, the captain reminded himself. *That's really what this is about.*

It wasn't about a little setback but his years of labor and decades of preparing for this command and the success he had achieved by actually reaching this point. It was not about the titles of the players but the ship herself. It was not about the turf war they had just fought but the country they all served. And all of that was pretty damn special, he had to admit. Plus one more thing.

He was alive. And right now, that, too, suddenly seemed precious.

Major Cleveland once described entering the Shed as like walking into a big sock. He was right.

Outside, the Shed was a cinder-block structure with a corrugated-tin roof and rain-rust on the exterior walls. It sat on the bay and was designed to look like an old ship's repair shop. If spies noticed the structure, they probably wouldn't think it housed anything of importance. Inside, the Shed was not so simple or innocent. The "neck" of the sock was stretched through an eight-foot-wide entranceway on the shorter side of the rectangular building, an air lock that covered the outer door and led to the main area of the Shed. Captain Colon closed the door behind him and walked ten feet to the inside door of the air lock. A guard was seated at a small desk. The sergeant at arms stood and saluted the captain, then she parted the slit canvas. She used a key to open a second door. Colon stepped inside the rest of the sock, the main room of the Shed. It stood forty-five feet high, seventy-five feet across, and two hundred and twenty feet long. Thick black canvas was draped everywhere, double layers stretched loosely across the ceiling and walls. The canvas was used to mute sound, block the brutishly bright work-lights, and seal the interior from anyone who might want to have a peek from the outside. On the opposite side of the Shed were the wide doors that led to the harbor and the open sea. They, too, were covered with canvas.

A concrete walkway followed the inside walls of the Shed. It was wide enough to accommodate the compact three-cylinder tractors that were used to move parts of the *D* to and from the submarine.

Twenty-odd workers were in the Shed. Most were inside the converted tanker that filled the structure. Run by the Smithsonian's Chesapeake Bay Oceanic Foundation, the *Abigail Adams* used to be the *Hornet*. It ran oil to drums in bays, inlets, and harbors that were not large enough to accommodate mid- to large-sized tankers. The DOD had selected it because the hold was large enough to carry the kinds of maneuverable, manned, and unmanned minisubs they were developing for future off-shore reconnaissance. For most of its five years under Smith-sonian Institution control, the *Abby*, as she was nicknamed, had been used to transport research vessels used to conduct geo-logic surveys, study marine-animal migration, and chart cli-matic changes. The vessel had been to both poles, something the Pentagon had insisted on so they would know whether the *Abby* could function reliably in polar weather. They also needed to establish her presence around the world so she would not at-tract attention wherever she showed up. She had just returned from the Weddell Sea, a trial run for the Tempest mission.

The science missions of the *Abby* were under the command of Dr. Angela Albertson. Unlike Mike Carr, the tall, athletic African-American did not have a military off-switch in her brain. The thirty-one-year-old was happy not to go to commit-tees and boards to beg for grants. She had all the money she needed to conduct research, as long as she was ready to drop it to do Pentagon business. And she was. She was particularly ea-ger to be involved in this mission. She had been given a general briefing about the supercavitation drive, a form of propulsion that would make submarines of the U.S. military exponentially faster and more strike-ready than any other underwater force on earth. She was supposed to study its impact on the marine envi-ronment in the wake of the drive. The Pentagon wanted to make sure it did not send marine animals so far off normal migratory paths that other nations might notice and try to observe or block a Tempest. The nature of the drive had to be kept secret.

Major Cleveland was at his desk beside the *Abby* when Colon arrived. He rose and saluted. His expression lacked its usual sparkle and a question was in it.

"Morning, sir."

"Morning," the captain said, saluting. "The *D* get loaded without any trouble?"

"Yes, sir. We've got the hooks in, just checking the release circuits now."

"Good. Major, I need a favor."

"Of course."

"I want you to have 'Doc of the Bay' painted in small letters on the front of the *D*. That's 'doc' with no 'k.'"

Major Cleveland stared at him.

"'Doc.' 'Doctor.' For Charlotte."

The major's beefy features grew a little smile. "Yes, sir. That's sweet. Whose idea was that?"

"CPO Farmer."

"Good kid. Sir? What about the mission?"

"You'll be getting an official notification from the rear admiral," Colon said. "But just between us sea jockeys, we're still a 'go' for tomorrow."

The major's smile blossomed. "Now *that's* the kind of tribute Dr. Davies would really appreciate. Thank you, sir."

Colon went around the desk and walked up the aluminum ramp. He could hear soft clanging and softer voices as well as an occasional sizzle and pop coming from within the *Abby*'s hull. The helmsman, former naval office Dr. Howard Ogden, was reviewing a checklist.

"How do we look?" Colon asked.

"She's hooking up without complaint," the thickly bearded oceanographer told him. "Mostly."

"Mostly?"

"The towline retractor doesn't like having the weight, like a wild horse with a bridle. It's been catching somewhere. We've got a team on it. Should have it fixed by tonight."

"In enough time to run all the tests?"

"More than enough time," Ogden said. "Major Cleveland said he'll drown me if we're late."

"That's what you get for being a civilian," Colon said.

"Sorry?"

"Can't submit a formal complaint for abuse."

"Ah. If I thought he were serious, I'd be worried."

"I am serious!" Cleveland said as he walked up the plank with Ensign Rosedale and a can of white paint.

Ogden frowned.

Colon glanced at Ogden's printout. "I wouldn't worry too

much about the towline. Using it is like being a hooked fish. Good for the fisherman, bad for the fish."

"Understood, sir. We'll have it working just in case."

Colon nodded and continued along the deck of the *Abby*. He made his way toward the stern. The deck was dry; he was used to ships being slippery with sea mist, even vessels in harbor. The forward section held the V-shaped bridge, while the mid-section was the science center, which consisted of a slender observation shack with sonar, communications, and other electronics below. Just aft of it were the crew's quarters and mess. The stairwell at the ship's stern led to the hold.

Dr. Albertson was on the bridge. She saw Colon walk by on the lower deck, then ran out to join him. She was dressed in short shorts and a San Diego Sea Planet T-shirt. Colon hadn't been thinking much about women today.

He did now. She was a great-looking woman, though when she came closer, he could see that her eyes were bloodshot.

"How are you?" he asked.

"Okay. Sorry I didn't get to the briefing. I wanted to be here when the *D* was pulled in."

"Understood."

"With Dr. Davies—was it an accident?"

Colon nodded. "Fell asleep at the wheel."

Angela shook her head slowly. "Poor soul. Charlotte Davies was one of the good people."

"Amen."

"What about the mission?" Angela asked. "We've been working this morning as if it's going ahead—"

"It is," Colon told her. "Dr. Carr will be running the science team."

"I don't know him very well."

"You're lucky."

"Ouch."

"Well, we don't get along—"

"I gathered."

"But he'll be fine."

"He seemed pretty absorbed in the few meetings I had with him. Not absorbent, if that makes any sense."

"It does and that's a good description. Meanwhile, Doctor, speaking of falling asleep—you'll forgive me, but you look a little tired."

"I am. We came through the Caribbean, got knocked around a little."

"You were down there in Kim?"

She nodded. "We held up in Antigua till she got down-graded to a tropical storm. Then we bulled through to get here in time."

"Well, you do your checks and then get rest. We need you at one hundred percent tomorrow."

"You'll have it," she promised.

"No, I mean it."

"I'll rest. I promise. When we sail from the bay, I'll be all over the ship with binoculars, cameras, and computers. Make it look and sound like we're on a real science mission."

"Thanks."

"Now I'd better get back to it, make sure all the hammocks and food are properly stowed," Angela said.

Angela left and Colon watched her go. She didn't hear him clop down the stairs so she probably knew he was looking, which was fine. They had flirted a little the times they'd been together, never anything serious. Now Angela had been in a storm-swept ship with a couple of nerds for a couple of days. She would be around *him* in a confined space for a couple of weeks. He wanted her to know he was interested. They'd suffered a loss, he'd had to eat some shit, but life went on.

The canvas made the Shed extremely dark and still. It kept the air thick with sea-smell. Visiting the hold was like being born. The glow reached out to you, and when you stepped inside, it was like entering a new world.

The *D* sat in its steel cradle like an artisan's handcrafted model. It was that, of course, but it had been built by dozens of brilliant and dedicated individuals, and it wasn't a display piece. The blue-black submarine was cloaked in four stark white beams from spotlights fore and aft, starboard and port. Most of the activity was centered near Colon, at the nose. The towline was located there. One end was attached to a rotating

cuff in the nose; the other was on a three-foot-diameter spool
attached to the roof of the hold. Four naval engineers dressed in
powder blue jumpsuits were making sure the three-hundred-
foot copper-cadmium line had no rough spots that might catch
the spool or another part of the strand. Two other engineers
were on ladders making certain the spool itself was not what
had caused the line to catch. They were checking the side-
mounted axle and carefully applying a subzero-formula VCI—
volatile corrosion inhibitor. What they used to just call grease
when Colon first started sailing. That would keep the joints
from rusting or freezing. The towline would not be significant
once the engines were fired up. It would be popped from the *D*
the way a sailplane cuts loose from the motored aircraft that
pulls it upward. The line was there in case the engines did not
light the way they were supposed to and the *D* had to be reeled
back into the *Abby*.

Ensign Rosedale was there as well, painting the new nickname on the forward hull of the submarine.

The engineers on the outside saluted when they could. Men
were inside the *D* as well. Colon could hear them working. He
did not go in. He did not want to bother them. He had simply
come to gaze at his girl.

Now this *was a sexy woman,* he thought. Smooth and
shapely and requiring special handling, which was fine with
Colon. He liked that challenge.

He stood with his hands clasped in the small of his back, just
looking. There was a tart smell of shaved steel, a worked-metal
smell that permeated dry docks everywhere. It was like visiting
McDonald's in a strange city. Wherever you were, it was a
smell from home.

"One more day," he said. His voice was lost in the grinding
of the tow-spool. Not that it mattered. He was sure she had
heard him.

Colon continued to stare for several more minutes. Then he
turned and left the hold. He thought he caught a whiff of the
deodorant Charlotte used to slather on in her cubicle because
she didn't always get to go home to shower. Maybe it was just
his imagination. Maybe it was left over from her last visit.

Or maybe it was Charlotte checking things out. He'd like to believe that.

As he neared the air lock he thought back to the beginning. To the blueprints and computer constructs, the simulations and models. He thought back to two days ago when he and Charlotte had come to the Shed to run tests on the antenna after the casing had been installed. Charlotte had been focused on the work, as always. But as they'd left—were right here, in fact— Colon had caught her glancing over her shoulder. He saw her look back and for the first time her expression seemed to be relaxed. Content. It seemed a small thing then; now it seemed large.

He was glad he had shared the moment with her.

The science team meeting was held every Monday afternoon at 6:00 P.M. and usually ran an hour. This one took longer. Silver—and now Dr. Carr—wanted to make sure the leaders of the science and engineering crew knew the timetable and had the most recent pages in their playbooks. Once the *Abby* left the base, they would be monitoring every minute of the voyage from a small command center. The emphasis would be on the condition of the *Tempest D*. It would be watched like an astronaut in orbit, with sensors attached to key elements from hull to fans, from sonar to capillaries. The team at Kings Bay would make sure the submarine was unaffected by temperature, sea conditions, and any gremlin that might happen by. If problems were detected, engineers on board could deal with them.

The team leaders presented qualified "all-clear" assessments. With the exception of the towline and a few other minor components, everything on board was functioning as expected.

When the roundtable ended, Silver shooed everyone out to phone Admiral Grantham with an update. Colon was sure the top brass would be pleased. After all, Grantham and the others had nothing to lose. It was the crew's life and Silver's reputation that were at risk.

There was a saying among officers that a good general should be prepared to become a soldier, if necessary. The rear admiral was like that, which was probably why they got along relatively well. The rest—

The rest won't know the thrill of what we're about to under-take, Colon thought. Neither the risks nor the rewards nor the heightened living of life.

Maybe that's why the word "brass" fit them so well . . .

NINE

Louisa Reef, The Spratly Islands

Wu was lying on his back, on his folding cot, the top of which was outside the tent. The canvas flaps were hooked open and Wu was looking at the stars. In Beijing, because of light pollution, he could only see a few lights in the night sky. An unimaginable number of them were visible here, including the cloudy band of the Milky Way. What patience the ancient sailors must have had to make sense of them. What a frightening adventure each journey would have been.

Wu was startled when his phone beeped. He slipped on the headset. Chin Liang, director of Remote Field Operations for the Tenth Bureau, was calling Wu personally. The junior director was impressed. It was the same time in Beijing as it was here, and Chin was an early riser.

"We've identified the vessel and checked its registry," Chin said. "Your instincts were correct. It does not appear to belong where it is."

Neither do I, Wu thought. The trick was not to be noticed.

"We have permission to turn the S3 from Washington to the naval base," Chin went on. "It will give us an oblique view of the area from the southeast. That will be a perfect vantage point to watch your shed."

The S3 was the Sentry Surveillance Satellite. It was one of the first sophisticated spy satellites China had put into orbit, capable of taking high-resolution, black-and-white images with details up to a half meter. It was positioned in a geostationary orbit over the American capital. The satellite was operated by the People's Liberation Army Air Force, Sixth Research Institute, which was responsible for signal-intelligence collection from around the world.

"For how long will we have it?" Wu asked.

"The grant is open-ended."

"That's quite a coup. It would suggest there is more going on at the base than just the phone calls and that mini-tanker?"

"One very significant thing," Chin told him. "There was a fatal automobile accident very close to the base. It occurred shortly before those telephone calls were placed. The *Florida Times-Union* newspaper, which covers the area, reports on-line that the driver was a physicist named Charlotte Davies. She held an unspecified position at the naval base for several years. No other vehicles were involved. Apparently, Dr. Davies fell asleep while driving home."

"Overwork," Wu speculated.

"Very possibly. But on what? Kings Bay is a support base for America's Trident ballistic missile program. The primary missile refit facility is located there. They don't conduct research."

"As far as we know."

"Exactly," Chin said.

"Do the photographic analysts think this building is a part of that process? It's constructed quite far from the other facilities."

"True, but it's also built over relatively shallow water," Chin said. "We checked the National Geographic charts of the bay. The harbor at that point is not sufficiently deep to hold the submarines of base Squadrons Sixteen or Twenty."

"Could it be for the construction of a new generation of missile? The United States navy would want to locate such a facility far from the submarines in the event of an accident."

"That's one possibility," Chin said. "We went on-line to look into Dr. Davies's publications. She is a plasma physicist from MIT. I queried the chief scientist in our own naval sciences laboratory. He described plasma physics as working with extremely hot gases that have some of the properties of liquids.

He said they could be used for everything from propulsion systems to stabilizers to current conductivity."

"In other words, anything," Wu said. "New missiles, new engines, maybe mini-subs."

"Yes. But I feel this is something we need to watch and the PLAAF agrees. If the vessel that you discovered leaves, and the waterline is significantly higher, that could mean it is carrying parts elsewhere, perhaps taking something away from the area for testing. If so, we will want you to go and see it."

Wu felt a flash of excitement. "Me, sir?" he said modestly.

"It was your discovery," Chin said.

"I'm honored by your trust."

"Hopefully, Dr. Peng will be sufficiently well along that he won't need you any longer."

"Dr. Peng will be fine," Wu assured Chin. "He was showing uncharacteristic bravado when we communicated earlier. I think this kind of work appeals to him and the team."

A shooting star flicked sharp and white through the darkness. His village had traditions about such objects. Wu wasn't sure if he believed them, but they were fun to consider. If the object moved from east to west the observer was going to find wealth. If it went west to east, he was going to enjoy happiness. If it shot from south to north, he would have good health. And if it flew north to south, he would be taking a journey. The trail of this one was due south. There was another part of that tradition. If the course led south into land, the trip would be brief. If the course led to water, the move would be permanent.

Director Chin once again congratulated Wu for his good work, then told him to get some rest. Wu said he would. He placed the secure phone in its cradle and lay back. He continued to stare at the skies.

It was strange, Wu thought. Here they were discussing hot gases and attack missiles while he was looking at the stars. *They* were made of hot gases but they provided planets with light and warmth, not death. They could be reached by missiles but only if those rockets were used for constructive purposes, not death.

The *chi* of humankind was on a strange and unhappy course.

The only way to divert that was through the equality of nations, of men. Wu felt fortunate that his job, his life, was about achieving that goal. Comforted by that thought, Wu closed the flaps of his tent and went to sleep.

Wu was awakened shortly after 6:00 A.M. when the local phone beeped. It was Dr. Peng. The scientist reported seeing what looked like a fishing vessel a half kilometer northwest of his position. Wu was up at once, dressing as he hurried to the missile boat. Commandeering a sailor on the dawn patrol, Wu took a motorized dinghy to investigate. Rounding a small projection of rocks, the Guoanbu operative saw a weather-beaten forty-foot ship that smelled of fish. Tuna, he saw, as the nets were pulled aboard. With the rising sun to his back, Wu approached the ship. Two men came to the side, shielding their eyes from the blazing horizon. They looked Vietnamese. Wu spoke to them in Vietnamese. They responded. He suggested that they go away unless they wanted to get caught in the weapons test his colleagues were planning.

The men looked from Wu to the shore to Wu again. They motioned frantically for Wu to hold the test and shouted that they were leaving. The vessel coughed up speed and set out.

Wu smiled. He savored the exchange, the power of words backed by appearances, the fear it generated. As his sensei used to tell him, "A warrior doesn't need strength. Just the proper technique."

Wu watched the boat sail away. The actions of the crew convinced him they were fishermen. First, they seemed genuinely panicked. Second, if they were spies, they would have challenged his claim or at least asked questions about the weapons. All they did was flee.

Wu went to shore and waited with the scientists until it appeared the vessel was not returning. Then he went back to his reef, utterly satisfied. Those fishermen would not return. They would tell others not to fish here. With just a few words, Wu had in a small way altered the *chi* of civilization.

He couldn't wait for the chance to play on a larger field.

TEN

Kings Bay, Georgia

For Dr. Angela Albertson, leaving port—any port—was always the most exciting part of a voyage. At that point, anticipation ended and doubts had to be put aside. The test of one's resources began. As her father, successful independent filmmaker Temple Albertson, used to say about any new enterprise, "That's when the learning meter starts to run."

Growing up on the fringes of Beverly Hills, Angela was always close to the water. She could swim in their pool before she could crawl, and the sea was her playground long before it became her avocation.

Now Angela Albertson was a marine paleobiologist, a scholar of extinct sea creatures. After obtaining her Ph.D. from the University of California, Santa Barbara, she had spent two years working for the Field Museum in Chicago, but became frustrated trying to raise money—ironically—for fieldwork. She didn't want to buy whatever fossils the museum put on display. She didn't want to show fiberglass casts made from fossils in other museums. Angela wanted a real protosphyraena like the one that had been donated to her beloved Los Angeles County Museum of Natural History. She wanted to display fossilized remains of ichthyosaurs and elasmosaurs that *she* had found. In her two years with the Field she was able to put together a single five-day excursion to Kansas to search for mosasaur remains. She found some nice but fragmented specimens in what used to be the Western Inland Sea. She wanted to return for further digging but it didn't happen. Like modern Kansas, the museum was dry. So were the other institutions she approached for funding.

Now, thanks to the U.S. government, working through the Smithsonian Institution, there was money for research and access to sites worldwide. Most of the time she was her own boss. The rest of the time she was working with interesting people like Captain Colon and Rear Admiral Silver. She hadn't gotten to know either man well, but she would. It was more than a weeklong sail to the Falkland Islands, where they would make a final weather and sea-traffic check at the British Royal Navy Meteorological Station in Stanley before covering the remaining nine hundred miles to the test area. They would be in the region for three days, then return home. In seventeen days—longer, if they ran into a storm or rough seas or anything else—on a ship the size of the *Abby*, with the extra hands they were carrying to run the *Tempest D*, they would all get to know each other well.

Right now, though, standing on the bridge beside Dr. Ogden, Angela did not want to think about the people. Only the moment. And the incredible device in the hold. It was exciting to be part of something new, to contemplate the spin-offs. Freeze-dried coffee was invented to keep soldiers caffeinated and alert during World War II. The personal computer and home video cameras were offshoots of miniaturization done for the Apollo moon program. Supercavitation was a new area of science. There was no way of knowing how it might benefit private industry in the years to come. Perhaps it would lead to new kinds of aircraft or automobile engines to replace internal combustion. It might create the next generation of hovercraft, allowing boats to compete with aircraft for shipping or passenger travel. It was all very exciting.

All that in addition to the thrill that never grew old, the thrill every captain who ever sailed must have felt. The thrill of leaving. The slow start as the ship maneuvered from shore. The changing feel of the swells as you left the wharf and made for the open sea. The waters were no longer tentative or tame. You were no longer a keeper but a passenger. That transition was extraordinary. It was the moment when Angela felt the magnitude of the seas. Setting out, even to sail the few miles from the condominium she owned in Santa Barbara out to Santa Rosa Island, she always felt insignificant and vast at the same time, vulnerable to the massive force below yet able to go anywhere on the planet. Able to feed yourself by catching what was below, gather water from the rains, become as free as a person could be.

The trip through the bay took under a half hour. Dr. Ogden had studied the navigation charts carefully. He always did. He knew the traffic lanes in the bay as well as the depths and currents. He also knew the Atlantic from his own naval days. Ogden had been Angela's lab partner her last year at UCSB. They became lovers, then friends, which worked out much better. Through Ogden, a former navy meteorologist, the DOD had hooked up with Angela.

The sea was somewhat choppy at this hour. The spikes of charcoal-gray water threw up hard, oily spray along with the occasional plastic bottle and rotting piece of driftwood. Creaks and metallic snarls were coming from below, in the hold. Seated on a high swivel seat, Angela used the color video monitor in the console to watch the *D*. The submarine was secure in her suspended berth. The sounds appeared to be coming from the towline spool. The two *D* crewmen on morning watch did not appear concerned. Captain Colon was down there as well, strolling slowly back and forth the length of the submarine. The rolling of the deck did not interrupt his pace. That was the mark of a true sailor: However long he had been away from the sea, his sea legs never left him.

When they reached the Atlantic Ocean, the waters were even bolder. The waves weren't as choppy but they were larger. The crests were higher, the dips deeper, the swells fuller. Colon continued to walk without breaking stride. The captain was ready, Angela was ready, and the *Abby* was also ready. The recent test run had brought them to the outskirts of the Ross Sea. The vessel had been able to take the cold, though Ogden had asked for extra drums of propylene glycol for both the *Abby* and the *D* in case they were needed. The *Abby* was going to be close to the ice shelf but not near any of the research stations. As a result, there were no landing strips, no staging areas. Because of the top-secret nature of the cargo they would not be permitted to call for civilian rescue ships if they got into trouble. And it would be difficult for military rescue to get to them quickly.

But they had taken precautions, including stowing a portable med lab in the hold. The third scientist permanently attached to the *Abby*, ichthyologist Dr. Aguina Grande, was qualified to operate the unit. Roughly the size of a phone booth, the PML contained essential life-preservation equipment ranging from a defibrillator to a "pressure equalizer pocket," a water-filled suit used to treat someone who was suffering from decompression sickness.

They had planned for what Rear Admiral Silver described as "the known and the conceivable," down to a towline umbilical cord for their newborn. As a scientist, though, Angela was concerned and excited by what was known as the Coelacanth Factor. The coelacanth was a five-foot-long prehistoric fish believed to be extinct for two hundred million years, until December of 1938, when one was captured by a fisherman off the coast of South Africa. Its discovery forced ichthyologists to open their minds to the kinds of creatures that might inhabit the world's oceans. Every science, virtually every experiment, had its Coelacanth Factor, something that added to human knowledge and also forced the brain to think in new directions.

As the sleek, untimid *Abby* made her way through open seas southeast at twenty-five knots, toward the West Indies, Angela wondered what their Coelacanth Factor would be.

ELEVEN

Louisa Reef, The Spratly Islands

Wu Lin Kit's mind was on the other mission, the one he was already imagining, as he wrote up the incident about the Vietnamese fishing boat. The large target was out there, the bigger street, the one he had always been drawn to. He could feel it and he wanted it.

When he was finished with the report, he climbed to a bluff and went through his late-afternoon workout. He did his *forms*, a series of slow, ritualistic, dancelike moves that simulated martial arts combat. Done at regular speed, these motion studies were lethal. When he finished, he returned to camp and did his daily language studies; Wu spoke seven languages but wanted to know more and was currently studying Russian. Then he had dinner with several of the seamen, after which he hiked out past a slippery breakwater on an isolated section of white-sand beach. The sun was down, visible only in the faintest hot-pink edges of clouds in the western sky. The stars were not yet out, and the low moon was a faint glow behind a layer of nearer clouds.

The sound of the waves, low but forceful, made him feel as if he were alone on the reef, in the islands, on the planet. He knew, though, that he was not. He kept the secure phone with him, sitting on a rock like a black crustacean that had been washed from the sea.

Wu walked into the warm water. He was standing there, trying to keep his balance on the crawling sand, when the phone beeped. Chin Liang was on the line.

"There is movement at the American naval base!" Chin said excitedly. "I've just seen the satellite images. The tanker is emerging and it is riding lower than in the images you discovered."

Wu's world was suddenly in perfect balance. He did some quick computations. "It's very early over there."

"Just past dawn," Chin replied. "But we don't think the timing was an attempt to be secretive. The tide is high in the bay—"

"They needed the depth and buoyancy."

"Exactly!"

"Is there anything unusual about it, apart from what we can't see? Crew size, gear?"

"Not that we can tell, though the night-vision capability of the S3 is not very good," Chin said. "We should have full sunup in about fifteen minutes. We will have another round of photographs then. In the meantime, the first pictures have been sent to your computer. I'll forward the others as soon as they arrive."

"Thank you."

"Is everything still quiet at your site?"

"Extremely," Wu told him.

The men agreed to talk again after Wu had had a chance to study all the images. The operative hung up and returned to his tent. He opened a canvas chair under the blossoming stars, booted his laptop, and sat facing the sea. The first two pictures loaded quickly. They were dark, as Chin had said. Wu could tell that the hull was much lower, but he could not see much else. The second set of images was already coming in. It was lighter now, still not full daylight. But there was enough light to make out some surface details of the vessel.

Drums and crates were being stored on deck, under canvas tarpaulins. Obviously, the hold was full, which was not a surprise. What caught Wu's attention, though, was a hint of metal underneath the windblown fabric. That could be significant. He waited impatiently for the next picture. It would have been taken about three minutes later, when the vessel was farther out in the bay. Where the wind was probably a little stronger. When the canvas flap was indeed a little higher. The image began to download. Wu magnified that section of the S3 photograph. He clicked on it and asked his basic but efficient photo-enhancement program to sharpen the image and compensate for distortion caused by ripples in the warming atmosphere.

He got a sharper, purer picture showing magnesium-white drums. Eagerly, Wu logged on to the Guoanbu database. He went to the files of U.S. military chemicals. He had heard—perhaps it was propaganda—that American soldiers were such illiterate creatures their chemical containers had to be color-coded rather than labeled. Because of television, they found it easier to remember colors than words.

Whether it was true didn't matter. Wu found what he was looking for. The drums appeared to contain propylene glycol.

It was like watching a drama on television. A good one. Each new scene was a revelation, another clue in the mystery. The only difference was that this was real. The outcome mattered.

The canvas chair was cool and damp with sweat from his thighs. The lights of the campsite were turned off as the men retired. The patrol boat was also dark. The only sounds were the soft slosh of the retreating tide, the hum of the fan in his laptop, and what sounded like *mooing* from somewhere at sea. The foghorn wail could be a humpback whale. From August to October, the leviathans left Antarctica for the South Pacific to spawn. Wu had a great deal of respect for the animals; it was a formidable journey.

Wu heard them all without really listening. His attention was on the computer. It was rare to have disparate pieces come together in this fashion, in a way an opponent never foresaw. If Wu interpreted the data correctly, this could be quite an intelligence coup. The Chinese had an international reputation for "dirty hands" intelligence, consisting primarily of moles on-site or bribing and blackmailing people for information. Nearly 80 percent of their intelligence did come from dirty hands operatives. Wu wanted to change that. He wanted parity with nations like the United States, Russia, and Israel. He wanted to bolster the Chinese capacity to collect what the British called armchair intelligence. Even if that chair was made of canvas and aluminum.

The intelligence officer watched patiently as each new picture appeared. Once begun, the downloads took thirty seconds. Each picture first appeared as a blurry mass of gray tones, one that became sharper with every two-second-long scan. Wu was waiting for a second piece of information, one that would let him interpret with confidence what he was seeing.

The drums on the ship's deck had been the first key to figuring this out. They appeared to contain propylene glycol. A deicer. Unlike the more commonly used ethylene glycol, propylene glycol was not a danger to marine life. It was the only deicer that was not subject to international hazardous-materials regulations.

But that alone was not enough to determine absolutely where this ship was headed. It helped his suspicions to note that the vessel did not follow the coast of the United States. The ship had made a dramatic turn to the southeast, headed out to sea. That suggested a southward voyage that had been charted to steer along the east coast of South America.

But that was still not enough. Not yet.

Wu watched the downloads as 10:00 P.M. approached. That was approximately the time when the American ship would pass out of range of the S3. For the first time in a long time Wu felt tense. He didn't want this one to slip away. Not when he was so close. Finally, at ten minutes to the hour, he watched as three successive images showed the vessel turning its satellite dish. With eager taps on the keyboard Wu stored these images separate from the others. He needed three to triangulate the position of the dish relative to the position of the S3. Like the legs of a tripod, they could be traced to a single point.

Wu shifted the saved images to the Guoanbu satellite database. This site had been framed in the mid-1990s using information found on the public Fourmilab Switzerland Web site. Internet users could visit the site and view the earth from a selection of several hundred satellites. Since satellites had to remain at a collision-free distance from one another, Guoanbu astronomers used the Fourmilab data about height, longitude, and latitude to chart the space lanes that were open to military satellites. Working with dirty-hands records of secret shuttle-mission military launches—the size and thrust of the boosters used, their trajectories, the length of the burn—as well as detailed telescope studies of the skies, Chinese scientists had been able to create a detailed map of earth-orbiting military craft. This was added to the web of weather, communications, and scientific satellites.

The satellite database told him that the vessel's satellite dish was pointed to a spot 997 kilometers above the earth at 61°8'S, 101°21'E. With rising excitement, Wu looked up the coordinates. They were the location of a nonmilitary satellite, the Polar Bear, located in a stationary orbit over the south pole, where it reported on weather patterns.

Wu sent the data to Beijing and immediately called Chin on the secure line.

The American ship was going to Antarctica.

TWELVE

The South Pacific

Sr. Capt. Chien Gan had long ago learned that two aspects of submarine life required lifestyle adjustment. The first was discipline. Not just military discipline, but chronometric discipline, the need to keep "surface hours." In a world that was often without sunlight, where time zones were crossed and recrossed with some frequency, it was necessary to keep a schedule that resembled "a day." Gan kept his shipboard clocks on Beijing time and conducted the ship's day as if they were at home. If the senior captain allowed those boundaries to change and lapse, the crew would become disoriented. It would be subtle, but subtleties mattered in a submarine. No man was dispensable and no man could afford to become unfocused.

The other quality submariners required was patience. It took time to move from place to place. Surface ships could travel relatively quickly. They navigated on what was essentially a two-dimensional surface. Submarines moved in three dimensions, with haphazardly shaped cliffs and valleys as well as multidirectional currents and clouds of detritus that made travel hazardous. Slow travel was difficult; high speed was brutal. Wherein came the pressure of command, and of this command in particular. As the flagship of a new generation of submarines, the *Destiny* had to prove she could handle the dangers as well as respond efficiently and effectively to crises and emergencies whenever and wherever they arose.

Such as now.

Captain Biao had received a message from the deputy director of military intelligence in Shanghai, home of the naval intelligence division. He was to divert from his current course for a rendezvous in the Spratly Islands. The senior captain was standing at the ballast control panel in the *Destiny*'s control room when the coded e-mail arrived. Chien had been watching the crew prepare for a fire-fighting exercise, one of two they conducted weekly. The control room, which also included the attack center—where Biao was seated—was located directly below the conning tower. Biao informed the navigator of the new coordinates before passing the printout to Senior Captain Chien. The pass-along was a courtesy; orders from headquarters were always implemented at once, and incontrovertible.

The rendezvous was to collect a passenger, a Ministry of State Security operative named Wu Lin Kit. The message contained no information about the man, which was not unusual. The MSS, the Guoanbu, was among the most secretive and influential organizations in the nation. The communique did not even tell the captain their destination. That would be provided by the operative.

Situations like this were always awkward. When an individual like Wu came aboard, he became the de facto commander, what they called an overcaptain. Like the senior captain, Yuen Biao was happy and honored to serve. But the presence of an overcaptain created conflict. A commander tried not to give an order that might be countermanded. And the crew waited a moment longer than usual to see if an order would be reversed. Both situations were counterproductive. If the overcaptain had his own personal agenda, he might also seek to humble the captain, assert his own command style immediately. Those situations did not happen between a captain and a senior captain because there were clear rules of conduct. With a Guoanbu operative the dynamics were sure to be very different.

Naturally, all of that would be managed. What would be of

greatest concern and interest to Chien was the nature of the request. An order like this could be as simple as shuttling an individual from one country to another. But Chien didn't believe that was the case. The senior captain had read the weekly intelligence briefing for the region. Reconnoitering operations were ongoing in the Spratly Islands. The operative in question was probably part of those. If he had been moved there as part of a phased shift to another location, the MSS would not have waited until now to turn the *Destiny* around. Something must have come up that demanded his attention. Also, the individual was not being moved the quickest way, which was by air. Whatever this was, either the operative had to be inserted somewhere clandestinely, or else he was being moved to study an activity at sea.

They would know soon enough. Right now the crew had a drill to conduct; it was a bad idea to lose sight of routine because something extraordinary had occurred.

The ballast officer indicated that the crew was ready to undertake the fire-fighting drill. Chien asked the team leader, one of the sonar operators, if he was ready. The young sailor made sure his infrared thermal imager was operational. That would allow the team to "see" hot spots and extinguish them. The other participating members of the drill had their masks, hoses, and fire extinguishers ready.

Captain Biao went on the intercom and made sure the rest of the ship's crew were at their fire stations. In some cases that simply meant getting into the nearest doorways and bunks. In the event of a real fire, it would put them in places where the thermal imager operator would not mistake body heat for fire. Rescue units would also know where to find them.

The captain hooked back his sleeve and glanced at his watch. The team's objective was to reach a fire aft—signified by an "X" made of red duct tape—at the electrical switches just forward of the turbine generator. They had to get there and put it out in two minutes. He pressed a red button to sound the fire alarm. The deep bell echoed everywhere, as if someone were banging the hull itself. The team of six raced through the hatch to the reactor compartment, the squad leader in the rear shouting to keep the others running. They ran in tight, hunched positions, hugging their gear in front, shifting this way and that so they could clear the narrow corridors as cleanly as possible. Alone among nature's creatures, only humans could achieve this: chaos with a sense of purpose.

Senior Captain Chien remembered when he'd first participated in a shipboard fire drill, toward the end of his third week at sea. He had just gotten over the nausea that most new recruits suffered, not from the ship's motion but from the recirculated air that often included petrol fumes, cigarette smoke, and rank seawater that spilled into the bridge hatch whenever they surfaced. Chien was in charge of two weapons-loading hatches when the captain, a four-foot-eleven martinet, ordered him to take a place in the squad. Chien was twenty-one. He had seen others run drills; he was confident he could do it. The submarine was a Han-class, nuclear-powered attack boat, 120 meters long. Chien had always had the sense that it was a fairly small vessel until he had to run from one end to the other, holding thirty pounds of oxygen tank and hose and hopping the lower lips of the hatchways with someone shouting "Fire! Fire! Fire!" in his ears, on an offbeat with the alarm. It was, in fact, a very, very large ship. Chien noticed door handles, pipes, ledges, and projections he had never seen before. He also felt them against his shins, hips, arms, and skull. It took several drills before the young seaman knew to avoid these things in the dark—which he had to do on his fourth drill.

Perspective changed, depending on circumstance. But a commander could never go wrong by depending upon a well-drilled team.

Which was why Chien hoped their diversion was simply an escort mission and nothing more. The agents of the Guoanbu were accustomed to working on their own, cutting their own paths.

Independence and submarines were not just a poor mix, they were a potentially deadly one.

PART TWO

L.A.S.E.R.

ONE

Corpus Christi, Texas

Morning always held a special charm for Benjamin Scott. It was a curtain beyond which there was always a surprise. When he was growing up in Wabash, Indiana, it could mean he'd have to work his butt off in his dad's general store. It could mean he'd learn new things or fall asleep at the dinner table because he was dead tired. It could mean a ball game in the park or chores around the house.

If it was a Sunday morning, it was usually a stew of good and bad. Every Sabbath began with church, but that usually led to a matinee at the local movie house, the Bijou. It was an old vaudeville theater that had become a movie theater full-time during World War II. As a small boy, Benjamin would go with his granddad and sit on his knee and watch westerns and war movies and even jungle adventures and cheer with the men and women. Benjamin grew up wanting to be like Randolph Scott and Clark Gable and, of course, John Wayne. As a teenager in the 1950s he didn't like the way Hollywood went negative on war, hand-wringing its way through combat in films like *Paths of Glory* and *Pork Chop Hill*. They showed the blood but not the glory.

As it turned out, both versions were right.

War was a heroic mess. He had experienced that in Vietnam, serving with the Thirty-first Infantry Regiment. They fought at

Quang Ngai, Chu Lai, and up and down the Que Son Valley, keeping Vietcong guerrillas and the North Vietnamese regulars from occupying the coastal lowlands. The village of Hiep Duc was an especially wicked place, earning members of the allied Fourth Battalion two Medals of Honor for virtually the same battle a year apart. It was a nonstop, day-and-night, physical and emotional hell. It cost the lives of men, but so did most other endeavors. Driving cars, exploring space or the sea, taming lions, and studying volcanoes. Going to bars and even falling in love. The difference was that war built men and men built worlds. Scott believed that when he was a young lieutenant fighting in the jungles, carrying the idealism of those Sunday matinees in his heart and helping to make those heroic visions a reality. But the bloody reality was never far from his mind or any of his senses. Especially smell, which was something the movies missed. War reeked of gunpowder, mud, and rot. It was filthy with the stench of bodies and blood that had come from them, often days before you found them.

Then there was the morning he would never forget. The day he woke and met Gen. Augustine Dupre, head of the Fifty-fourth Air Intelligence Wing, *Commandement de la Force Aérienne de Combat.*

Scott had met a lot of top-of-the-line French soldiers, especially the men of *Les Anges Vengeurs*, the Avenging Angels, mercenaries who came to finish the job French withdrawal had left undone. But Dupre, the son of a Vichy collaborator—Dupre *père* had believed it was better to save lives by cooperating with the Nazis—was convinced that the job of intelligence was to prevent or subvert wars, not to wage them. Not a day passed without General Scott damning that coward and everyone who believed in appeasement.

And blackmail.

Scott tried not to think of that as he walked to the mission command center. It was morning and he hoped it would take him to a good day.

Scott had been getting his grandfather's pocket watch cleaned at L.A.S.E.R.'s repair shop when he got the word that the unit was airborne. Granddad Scott's watch had been with

Scott through two wars. He believed, in some supernatural corner of his brain, that if the watch ever stopped, he would die.

The MSC was a roomy outhouse located next to the eyewash station at Hangar 24. It was large enough to house Scott and his communications officer, Corp. Evan Vandenburgh. A satellite dish was on the peak of the slate roof. Even though the drill would be taking place just two miles out to sea, well within normal radio and video range, protocol dictated that all communications had to come through a secure uplink. Scott had no problem with that. The digital images and sound gave the computer far more detail and flexibility during a mission. It also gave the computer more material to work with when Scott and L.A.S.E.R. did their postgame wrap-up.

Vandenburgh half-rose and saluted the general when he arrived. Rising fully would have necessitated removing the headset that allowed the corporal to listen to the team. That was not permitted. Once any member of L.A.S.E.R. had set out, the comm officer had to be in unbroken contact with the team leader. For the first two hours, that team had consisted only of Lt. Woodstock Black and Ensign Galvez. Now it consisted of eight members, including Woodstock, under the command of Major Bryan.

Eight of L.A.S.E.R.'s twenty-five members were being shuttled to sea by a Blackhawk helicopter, which was kept at their disposal for training and surgical rescues. For longer-range missions they would use a C-130K Hercules transport, which was large enough to carry the Blackhawk to wherever it was needed. It was large enough to host the World Series, Scott had once remarked to the team. That idea appealed to Dr. Moses Houston, their medic, who came from San Diego and felt his beloved Padres could use some hands-on SWAT-style rescuing.

General Scott shut the door and stood behind Vandenburgh. The general preferred to stand during drills and missions. If he sat, he just bopped his knees up and down and made people anxious, which affected their performance. Standing only intimidated them, which affected their performance, too, but in a positive way.

The general watched the twenty-one-inch monitor. The color

video, showing the inside of the helicopter, was being shot with Major Bryan's helmet-mounted microlens camera. The optics weighed 1.75 ounces and were run from a small pack on his back. A four-inch antenna provided the uplink. Every team member had a camera, and Vandenburgh could jump between them as necessary. The corporal could also do frame-grabs from the video, which enabled team members at the command post to analyze situations in detail. If members stood side by side, the corporal could even generate three-dimensional images of whatever they were seeing. That helped the computer to pick out routes through fires, building collapses, and other situations where the dust was too thick for human eyes to see. Vandenburgh could usually remove dust from images by boosting obscured light sources and color.

The red lights were lit over the buttons on his control panel, which meant Vandenburgh had already run the tests and all the cameras were functioning. General Scott reached for a headset as well as a cardioid mini-microphone hooked to the radio unit. He slipped on the earloops so he could listen and clipped the microphone to his lapel. During a mission, he was the only outsider in contact with L.A.S.E.R. Unlike the omnidirectional units used by the crew—which gathered surrounding conversation and sounds and sent them home for recording and analysis—the general's microphone was set to pick up only his voice. The unit also dampened sounds beyond a radius of one hundred millimeters. That prevented comments made by the comm officer or anyone else in the room from bleeding into the broadcast. The general's voice was piped directly into the helmets of each team member. The transmission program was such that the general's remarks came through the left ear while local conversation came through the right. In loud situations, the microphones were often the only way team members could hear each other. Unless Scott saw a danger the field unit was missing, he was careful not to distract the team members when they were in a hot zone.

The general greeted Bryan and wished him well. He said nothing else. There was no kidding before a mission. Some field commanders like to keep their teams relaxed. Not Major

Bryan. Once the plane, chopper, or truck left the base, it was a humor-free zone. Maps and blueprints were reviewed, gear was checked and triple-checked, video was studied, and outside activities such as reading or listening to music, or even staring out the window, were prohibited.

The Blackhawk reached the target, an old destroyer. The 1939 vessel was going to be sunk for retrieval practice. The air force had developed new automated reflotation devices that could be worked remotely. They wanted to test them in a relatively level area of the sea where the robots could be retrieved if they malfunctioned. General Scott got permission from the project commander in Washington to let him sink the destroyer.

Lieutenant Black had gone out in a patrol boat just after dawn. She and another scuba diver from L.A.S.E.R.—her protégé, Ensign Davis Galvez—had planted explosives in the anchored destroyer. Woody set the charges to blow remotely from a keypunch unit she carried with her. Major Bryan wanted his team to go aboard while the ship was sinking so they could experience the shifting decks, the changing pitch, and the rising water. Their goal was to rescue four dummies that were trapped in the engine room.

General Scott's heart began to jog. It always did before his team went into action. L.A.S.E.R. was his child, dearer to him than anything except his wife and reputation. And at times, in the small hours of the night, he stared at the ceiling and realized—unhappily, but undeniably—that L.A.S.E.R. mattered more in certain ways. It was a true extension of how he saw himself, dedicated and unafraid. Except while he had been tested, L.A.S.E.R. had not. Drills were careful simulations. They were not reality.

A countdown clock was on the shelf in front of Scott. The digital clock was sandwiched between a backup computer and a secure phone that would ring the office of Comdr. Noah Adams, the NASCC executive officer. The phone was there in case they had an emergency and needed air or naval support. It had never happened in the nine months L.A.S.E.R. had been in existence, but Adams had a summary of every training mission on his computer, whenever the team went out. If a crisis did occur, he would be able to order the appropriate response.

With his pulse throbbing even faster, Scott watched as the chopper reached the target. He could see the open door through Bryan's camera. He experienced the same rush he used to feel before leaving a utility chopper in Vietnam. Up until he would actually exit the UH-1 Huey, his body would feel like bagged lightning. As soon as he hit the grass or beach or mud, the internal charge was transformed into function.

Here, it was different. He was a soldier who wasn't going on a mission. He was a father throwing his baby into surging seawater.

He was an armchair general who couldn't even sit down.

TWO

Corpus Christi, Texas

It didn't look or sound dangerous. In fact, it seemed kind of comical to Major Bryan. There was a muffled pop and then a big bubble rose from the side of the faded gray destroyer. It was the USS *Bundy* and it had a long if unusual history. In the fall of 1940, the year-old vessel had been sent to Great Britain as part of the Destroyers for Bases agreement, which allowed the United States to help arm England for the fight against Hitler. It was recommissioned the HMS *Meadowood* and it served in the North Atlantic for four years before being transferred to Russia as the *Cherkassov*. In 1946 it was converted to an anti–submarine-warfare vessel and remained a part of the Russian fleet until the man who had redesigned her defected to the West in 1956. The U.S. navy—which had assumed the vessel was sunk—asked for its return. The destroyer was given back, largely because the ASW components didn't work well and the Soviets wanted the United States to think that was the best they had. Renamed the USS *Bundy*, it sat in a shed at Camp Pendleton in Southern California until the end of the Cold War. It was turned over to the NASCC, where it was going to become part of a museum display until funding was cut. Now it was going to be destroyed.

Well, it's a fitting end for a warship, Bryan thought as one of the chopper crewmen kicked an aluminum ladder overboard.

Like a Viking desiring to enter Valhalla, it needed to die with a sword in its hand.

The lead-weighted ladder hung straight and steady in the prop wash and high ocean winds. The chopper was twenty feet above the deck of the ship. Woody was the first one out. She wanted to enter the engine room in advance of the others to make sure that all the C-4 had exploded. Triggered by a detonator cap, the puttylike substance, composed primarily of RDX—cyclotrimethylenenetrinitramine, a relatively stable white crystalline—can be shaped to dictate the shape and direction of a blast. Sometimes, however, impurities in the oil and waxes used as an inert medium prevent some of the RDX from detonating. On rare occasions particles are blown away, unexploded. Sometimes they strike something else so hard they detonate; sometimes they do not. But even a pinhead-sized particle, blasted from the body of the C-4, could destroy a person's foot if stepped on against a concussive surface. For that reason, Woody coated the exterior of her plastique with a red dye. She wore a colored gel over her visor that caused even the smallest stray pieces to stand out.

As Woody had planned, when the team reached the deck, it was tilted to the starboard between five and eight degrees. They would have the exact readings later, when digital video being shot from the Blackhawk was analyzed. The initial tilt was due to the influx of water on that side, just below the waterline. The destroyer would level out nearly flat again as the water started spilling toward the port side. That would take about five minutes. By that time, according to plan, the team would have reached the rear access stairwell. Within minutes, the aft-heavy vessel would then sink in that direction, where the engines were. Major Bryan wanted to be in the engine room by then.

Each of the eight soldiers on this mission was dressed in a yellow wet-suit with vulcanized-rubber slippers for traction. They wore helmets similar to the ones worn by bicycle riders in case anyone slipped or something fell. They had a single 240-liter oxygen tank buckled to their back with a plastic mouthpiece. If the destroyer shifted unexpectedly and they found themselves trapped underwater, they would have a half hour of air. Capt. Paul Gabriel carried a liquid-fuel cutting torch to slice through any metal that might get in their way. He was toting a heavier but safer liquid-fuel tank instead of compressed gas. It was less likely to explode under pressure or suffer fuel-line backflash, the accidental igniting of ambient fumes around the torch.

He looked anxious to use it, Bryan thought as they left the chopper. Ever since the chopper had been airborne and the major had informed the team their target was four dummies dressed as marines.

With Bryan at the head, and Woody at his left elbow, the rest of the team moved single file across the relatively dry deck. They had to pick their feet up fully rather than walk normally since the rubber "booties" tended to grab whatever they touched. The wind was a modest ten knots but seemed louder as it whistled through Bryan's helmet, but not as loud as the groaning of the ship as it took on water. Bryan put a gloved hand on the poop rail as they made their way forward; he could feel it shivering with each small shift and tilt. It amazed the major how solidly these vintage boats were built. Despite the added weight from roughly two thousand gallons of seawater, none of the old rivets popped, nor did the old hull plates buckle or snap. They would have felt the jerk. The designers back then didn't have computers to help design blueprints, but there was a lot to be said for the muscular construction of these old warships.

The group reached the hatch. Major Bryan stood aside while Sgt. Bernie Kowalski came forward. Kowalski was their structural man, seconded from the Coast Guard. He was like a doctor who could feel a patient's abdomen for subcutaneous swelling; at times the Dallas-born engineer could literally feel trembling or temperature changes in a vehicle or building. If it didn't seem right, no one went in. Sometimes Bryan could swear the thirty-year-old was actually channeling the spirit of a thing. It was eerie.

The pellet-shaped door was just under six feet high. Kowalski pulled the latch toward the right. The hatch opened after he put a strong shoulder to it.

"The doorframe is warped," he said into his microphone.

"Woody, was it okay before?" Bryan asked.

"Yes, sir," she said.

It wasn't rust, then. The frame of the vessel was twisting due to the weight of the water collecting on one side of the vessel.

"Gabe, hang back and give it a quick weld," the major ordered. "The rest of you, in."

Captain Gabriel dropped from the lineup. While he fired up the torch, the other team members quickly followed Bryan into the stairwell. The major wanted to make certain that if the hatch slammed shut as the boat settled, and the frame shifted farther, they weren't stuck on the other side. This meant Gabriel would not be following them. Once Major Bryan broke an individual out of the team, he stayed out, barring orders to the contrary. Bryan did not want to have to go looking for his own people in the event someone got lost. In this instance, Bryan felt they could afford to be one man down when they went below.

Two of the team members lit high-powered xenon flashlights. The units were thin and encased in rubber with a thin layer of air and water-resistant O-rings. If the lights were dropped, they would float. The team's lights each punched a pure white hole in the darkness, about four feet in diameter. The personnel with the lights stayed to the rear of the line, one man shining to the left, the other to the right, as the others descended.

The rubber-soled shoes kept them secure on the sloped metal stairs. The team moved rapidly, following a course they did not know well. They had reviewed the blueprints during a single briefing, which might be all the advantage they would have in a real disaster.

The two levels of steps were each two-tiered. Each tier ran fore, then aft. When the team reached the bottom, they ran along a straight but narrow corridor that followed the starboard side of the ship. Bryan gripped the cable coiled around his shoulder. The line would be hooked to the horseshoe grips inside the door so they could move in the flooded, angled interior. Each L.A.S.E.R. member carried something, whether it was a rolled ladder, mallets and crowbars, a pouch of signal flares, a fire extinguisher, or a stretcher for the wounded.

Bryan tasted the salt water in the air, mixed with the grease of the drowning engine. He could not read the Russian labels on the doors but he knew where the engine room was. Another fifty meters or so, then a sharp left. He could hear the dull thunder of the rushing water. It bothered Bryan to see Cyrillic letters on the door. Yeah, it had been a Russian ship for a while but—

The destroyer lurched forward, throwing the team the way they'd come. Their shoes held them where they were, though they reached out to brace themselves against the walls to keep from falling on each other. A moment later the tail end seemed to cough. Then it dipped dramatically, spilling them aft. Once again they managed to stay on their feet. The destroyer stabilized but a loud squealing came from the port side.

"Major, are you all right?"

"Yeah, Gabe," Bryan replied. "Can you see what happened?"

"Negative."

"Puckett?"

"Sir, your tail went down about twenty-five degrees," the chopper pilot told Bryan. "I didn't see an explosion."

The rush of water was louder. Obviously, something had popped in the engine room, but he didn't smell smoke, which meant there wasn't a fire. And the escape route was still clear. Figuring out what and why was not why they were here. L.A.S.E.R. had one job to do.

"Let's get those marines," Bryan said.

He started ahead and the team followed. Suddenly, there were two more coughs and the ship rolled to the starboard pitching them against a wall. Then it nosed up, causing them to skid down the corridor toward the engine room. They had to extend one leg like a brake and crouch in the opposite direction, toward the forward section of the destroyer, to stop themselves from being dashed against the dead-end corridor.

"Sir, I'm seeing clean hull plates!" Puckett shouted. "They popped up from the stern."

"Abort!" Bryan shouted.

The team turned to go as the vessel rolled completely onto its starboard side. They were slammed against the outside hull wall as, simultaneously, the engine-room door crumpled toward them, folding outward along the hinges, and the Gulf poured in and upward. Major Bryan turned but did not move as the men with the flashlights took point. In a rapid-retreat situation, those two were the team leaders. Their only job was to find and secure the exit.

The group was scuttling along the hull as the water rose. It pulled the ship down, angling it higher and making the new floor steeper by the second.

"Abandon gear!" Bryan yelled.

Everyone lay aside whatever they were carrying, making certain it didn't strike whoever was behind them. Now they were able to crawl ahead, making egress quicker on the sloping surface. Bryan continued to hold the cable.

"Gabe, what's your situation?"

"I secured the door and tossed the torch," the big man said. "I'm ready to do some pulling."

"Received."

The team was about twenty-five meters from the stairwell. The water was now a steady roar, amplified by the helmet but strong nonetheless. Bryan did not have to look to see that it was gaining on them. But he did, so that General Scott could see it. If anything happened to them, the video image would help the general do a postmortem on the operation. The water was tossing angrily in the dark, slopping against the sides of the up-ended corridor. Bryan turned around again. As he crawled, he slid the 1/0 gauge cable from his shoulder. He hooked one end of the 8.2 millimeter steel line to the plastic loop of his equipment belt. He grabbed the other end and passed it back.

"Woody, take the end and feed it ahead!" he said into the microphone.

The officer reached back and took the other end. She slid it under her belt, then handed it to the next team member. Bryan's thinking was not to save himself. The water was already wrapping itself around his shoes and making its way up his legs. What he wanted was to get the other end to Gabe. If the big marine could secure the line and pull them out—

The ship lurched again toward the stern, angling farther, and the team slid back. Bryan dug his toes into the floor and put his hands against the wall. If nothing else, he wanted to be able to brace anyone who fell back. No one did. They were good people, alert and strong.

"Gabe?" Bryan said.

"I'm still here. I see your lights."

The team was unable to see straight up while crawling. That Captain Gabriel could see them appeared to give the members an extra kick. They pressed ahead more rapidly even as the destroyer began to roll again, this time toward the port side. Bryan's booties enabled him to crab-walk with the ship as it turned, even as water washed up along his ankles and shins. He glanced up and saw the flashlights swaying wildly as the point men tried to keep their balance using just one hand each. The team prepared for a lot of contingencies, but he really should have thought about top- or side-mounted lights for their helmets on this mission. Those lanterns didn't have the flexibility and pinpoint focus of handhelds, but the guys would have had both hands free right now. Maybe the team needed both.

It never occurred to Bryan that they would not get out of there. Not until the ship continued to roll and then, in a sickening moment of abandon, decided to slide under the surface. He felt the wall he was on, the light he was beginning to see from the forward hatch, the slack in the line—everything went away at the same time. He dropped into the water, butt first, Woodstock falling back on him. The major instinctively grabbed her as he tumbled aft. He was effectively lying on his back with just his head, neck, and forearms above the water. A moment later the water rose around Bryan's cheeks and poured into his helmet. He tried to keep his earphones above water and at the same time attempted to push Woodstock up and off, to keep her afloat. His legs were churning wildly, uncoordinated, as he looked for a place to put his feet and brace himself. He was pissed that this had gotten so badly out of control, and that he was probably going to drown on a goddamn drill.

Just before his face went under the surprisingly warm water, Bryan felt a hard, gut-bruising tug at his waist. His neck snapped down.

"I've got the cable!" Gabe shouted.

Bryan heard nothing after that, save for the bellowing of the

Gulf spilling in around his ears. The distant light of the open hatch wiggled and faded to brown as the water level rose. But the tightness around his waist remained. Major Bryan shut his eyes since they weren't doing any good. He grabbed a breath and held it as he simultaneously found a place to put his left foot. It was a nook of some kind and something came free—a fire extinguisher, it felt like. A moment later Woodstock was above him but no longer on top of him. The major reached out on both sides, feeling for anything to hold on to. A door handle was on the left and he grasped it hard. With foot and hand steady, he turned sideways to try to climb up what was now the left side of the corridor. He reached up, found nothing to grab, and continued to feel around as his lungs began to tell him he hadn't breathed quite deeply enough.

He swore in his head. *A training mission. A fucking training mission.*

Perishing here would have been like getting red dye blown up his ass. Yeah, the guy was wearing his country's uniform, but—*a training mission?* Not even test-pilot stuff, but boot camp for heroes crap.

As his head began to pound all around whatever the skull case seam was called, and his thought process crashed, Bryan felt himself rise. Quickly. His arms and legs flailed as he ascended, looking for another foot- or handhold. The first thought in his oxygen-starved mind was that the ship was being spit up again before going down, which was rare but not unknown if it had burped out an air pocket. His second thought, as he broke the surface and sucked down air, was the right one. Gabe and one of the point men were hauling him up while the other point man pulled Woodstock through the now inverted hatch.

The breath revived Bryan sufficiently so that he was able to grab the sides of the hatch as he reached it. Gabe grabbed the front of Bryan's wet suit, along with a devilishly painful fistful of the flesh and hair beneath it, and pulled him up. Bryan hacked out seawater, which he had apparently swallowed without realizing it. His mouth tasted metallic. Gabe threw a big arm around the major while he unhooked the cable with his free hand. Winking away the Gulf water, Bryan saw the chopper hovering overhead. The prop backwash was muscle-chilling cold. Woody climbed the aluminum ladder with the help of the copilot, who had descended halfway to help extricate the team.

Now that he had a second to get his bearings, Bryan noticed that the sea was rising around them—or rather, that the vessel was sinking fast. The chopper was moving to keep on top of them. The major's mind tapped him on the shoulder, wanted to ask what the hell had gone wrong, but his mouth stayed shut as Gabe hoisted him toward the lowest rung of the ladder. Feeling that he had to overachieve just so he didn't feel like a pussy, Bryan grabbed the second-to-lowest rung.

That'll show 'em, he thought with anemic pride.

He began to climb and motioned the copilot back into the chopper. Bryan knew that Gabriel would be following him and didn't want to have a logjam near the hatch. His own arms were tired, and he could imagine how weary Gabe's would feel after hauling them all out.

As he neared the top of the ladder, Major Bryan turned back to make sure that Gabe didn't need help—and to record, for the camera, the last surface-side moments of the USS *Bundy Meadowood Cherkassov Titanic.*

Looking down at the sea, Bryan saw one of the most disturbing things he had seen since he had joined L.A.S.E.R.

THREE

Corpus Christi, Texas

General Scott was sullen as he stood watching the video play-back of the four "dead" marines rotating swiftly, face-up, on the surface of the Gulf. Major Bryan shifted uncomfortably in his swivel chair. Corporal Vandenburgh was between them, in a swivel chair.

The men were alone in the communications shack. Following the exercise, the entire L.A.S.E.R. team had gone directly to the infirmary, where everyone was found to be shaken but healthy. Afterward the other L.A.S.E.R. members went to their quarters, located in cabins on the northeast end of the base. Woody was miserable. She did not understand how she could have miscalculated the blast.

"This is what I do for a living," she said to Bryan as she left the medical building. "How did I screw this up?"

"We don't know what happened there," the major had told her. "Let's wait and see what the frogmen find."

"The plates that came off," she went on. "Puckett said they weren't damaged. I don't understand how that could happen."

"We will understand it," Bryan assured her.

A four-man navy team had been sent out immediately to go to the engine room, examine and document the site, and pick up any debris that might help to reconstruct the accident.

Lieutenant Black left, unhappy and unsatisfied. Bryan knew

she wouldn't sleep. She'd probably study her own computer blueprints and notes. Meanwhile, Major Bryan and General Scott watched the major's videos, looking for clues. Corporal Vandenburgh had cranked up the audio. They were listening for additional explosions they might have missed when they were on-site.

There was nothing.

The playback ended a third time. Major Bryan turned from the monitor. The cabin's small air conditioner hummed. In the distance, they heard the occasional crack of an aircraft as it broke the sound barrier over the Gulf.

"You know what I was doing while we choppered over to the destroyer?" Bryan said.

"What, Major?"

"I was making up families for those guys."

"For the dummies."

"Yes, sir. I never even told Dr. Headshrink that. It's how I psych myself up for rescues. Guys who are in the service, they know and accept the risks. But families are the ones who sit around worrying."

"Who count on you to fix things, like a surgeon or a plumber."

"Yes, sir."

"And you think you screwed up."

"I don't *think* it. I know it," Bryan replied. "We should have gone in after those four bodies."

"Four dummies." The general was not a feelie-healie kind of man. He kicked people in the pants to get them to stand up straight. Since this was L.A.S.E.R.'s first mishap, he would give the major a little "poor me" time. But not too much. If the team got a call to go into the field in ten minutes, Bryan had to be ready.

"To me they were *bodies*, especially when I saw them floating in the Gulf," Bryan insisted. "They were indistinguishable from dead people."

"You're overreacting."

"I don't think so, sir."

"I do. I'll tell you what you're upset about," Scott told him.

End of self-pity time. Scott turned to Vandenburgh. "Corporal, shut that and excuse us."

"Yes, sir."

Vandenburgh turned off the video and left the shack. Scott took his seat beside the major.

"This is the first time you lost control of a situation and had to make a choice," the general told Bryan. "The instant things went wrong, your concern was for the team and not the people you went in to save."

"Is that a polite way of saying you think I panicked?"

"No," Scott said. "What I mean is, you redefined the mission. You prioritized."

Bryan made a face. "Thank you, sir. But we weren't sent to that destroyer to get *us* out. We were sent to pull those men free."

"Mannequins," Scott repeated. "And you got your team out safely. Two questions. How would you feel if this conversation were about how two or three of your people drowned trying to rescue dummies?"

"Worse. But that doesn't justify—"

"I said two questions, Major."

"Sorry, sir."

"Just as important, do you think you would have done the same thing in a real crisis? If there were guys in that room calling out to you?"

Bryan hesitated for several seconds. "I don't know."

"I do. I think you would have turned the team around and gone in yourself," Scott said.

"Then why didn't I do that?"

"Because it was a drill," Scott reminded him again. He tried to put as much weight on each word as possible.

"Sir, in boot camp when we go belly-crawling through the mud, live ammo zips over our heads. Why? So recruits know what it's like to keep their damn heads down. It's gotta be real. We were going down that corridor and we had people to save. In here." Bryan jabbed a finger at his head. "It was real in here. It still is."

Scott sat still for a moment, then rose. He paced the shack.

"Major, if I thought you screwed the pooch, I'd be the first to say so. I don't. Things came apart and you looked after your team instead of dummies. So here's what we're going to do. We're not going to talk about this anymore. And you're not going to beat yourself up—"

"General, may I ask *you* something?"

"Go ahead."

"Are you going to tell me that you've never done something you wish you could do over?"

The silence that filled the small room was thicker than before. Scott swore he could hear the sun hitting the roof. "I think everyone has that wish, Major," the general replied.

An unpleasant silence followed. Scott sat back down. The general had never been comfortable discussing what he called the "transfer incident." He was much too private and he was still too angry about it. But perhaps that was a reason *to* get into it with the major.

"Major, maybe I'm telling you to give yourself a break because I don't want you doing what I did. What I *still* do, which is replay the damn thing in my head as a form of—hell, I don't even know what it is. Punishment? Motivation? Both, I guess. I assume you know a short version of what happened back in D.C."

"I know the gossip."

"Well here's the frontline recon," Scott said. "I wanted to knock a French officer's nose into his fucking brainpan because he was determined to keep me from going over to NATO. But I didn't. He said I roughed him up. I didn't. I swore at him, I got in his face, but I never touched him."

"I see. NATO. That would have been something."

"'Something' isn't the word for it. They wanted me to head the intelligence operation of the NATO-Russia PJC, the Permanent Joint Council. I would have been the liaison between alliance intelligence operations and Russian intelligence operations. I heard a rumor that the French didn't trust us to have that much power. I went to talk to one of the guys on the intelligence committee, General Augustine Dupre. He confirmed the rumor *and* said that because my wife was military and had been married before, they were going to have to background-check her. He suggested that she may have married me to get access to secret information to give to her former husband, an editor at the *Washington Post.*"

"He couldn't have been serious."

"He was. He was determined not to have me as DIO and tried to provoke me into roughing him up. I didn't. But he said I did anyway, and that was that."

"Who got the job?" Bryan asked.

"Some Belgian. A *Général de Brigade* Charles Leopold. The supreme command couldn't pick a Frenchman or it would've seemed like a mercy fuck because of what I'd supposedly done. So NATO went with the next best thing." Scott shook his head. "I missed a career opportunity, but that isn't the issue anymore. I'm happy with what I'm doing. But he got away with it, and that galls me. You know how many times I've actually thought of going over to Lyons where he lives, meeting him outside his home, and busting him up. I once even bought a plane ticket."

"What stopped you?"

"The window of opportunity passed," Scott replied. "Beating him up now isn't going to bring the moment back. All it'll do is let me vent, which I can do in more constructive ways. Like succeeding. Showing myself that either I made the right call for the wrong reasons, or the right call for the right reasons. I still get pissed, the thing still gnaws at me, but I use that as fuel to drive me on. Now we have this situation. You made the right call to abort. Period. Use the disappointment, the fear, the confusion, next time you're faced with a tough call. But move on."

Bryan's mouth twisted. "With respect, General, I don't even know how to get off that fucking moment when I said to bail, let alone move on."

"It's still too new, too hot in your belly," Scott said as the phone beeped. "You'll get there."

Bryan shook his head as Scott answered the phone. Lieutenant Black was on the other end. Her voice was surprisingly animated.

"Sir, can you come to the hangar right away?"

"Sure. What have you got?"

"The reason the ship went down the way it did," she told him.

"Let's have it."

"Sabotage."

FOUR

Corpus Christi, Texas

Major Bryan and General Scott rode a stealth golf cart to Hangar 5, which was the staging area for L.A.S.E.R. operations. The near-silent, battery-powered carts had originally been painted black for nighttime transportation around bases in Saudi Arabia, Turkey, and other "matchbook" nations, countries where anti-American sentiment could flash without warning. Officers were desirable targets and the stealth golf carts made them less visible. A new generation of carts was being deployed with armor plating, which was how one of the original carts had ended up at NASCC.

Major Bryan was at the wheel. He was not happy with the "look ahead" solution proposed by General Scott.

You were looking ahead, Bryan thought. *Right at the exit. That's the problem.*

Gabe had been the real hero. He had stood there with the other end of the cable hooked to his belt, yanking people out. If they had fallen, he would have fallen. What the hell must the big marine have thought when he saw those uniforms doing a lazy spin on the smooth blue waters?

Bryan doubted whether anything shy of a time machine would satisfy him now. The damn thing was, intellectually he knew that Scott was right. Psychologically, though, what he'd done felt wrong. The major didn't know how to reconcile those.

The general said it would take time. More than a year after the fact, Scott was still a kettle on high boil. The major didn't want to be kicking his own ass years from now. He wanted to move on.

It was a seven-minute ride to the hangar. Because the satellite dish needed to hit the southwest sky to hook up with the secure uplink, the shed had to be located on the opposite side of the base. The steel-frame building was twenty-five years old, with an eighty-meter span and a twenty-meter clear height. The structure rattled far more than the newer structures whenever storms lumbered in from the Gulf. It also had the noisiest tailgate door. But L.A.S.E.R. was still a relatively new unit, and the new units got the older structures along with the hand-me-down golf carts.

Bryan swung around the long north side, toward the entrance, a single metal door toward the rear of the hangar. Office compounds and newer hangars were located on all four sides, along with communications towers, radar dishes, and supply depots. Flight crews were moving about the field, mechanics were working on aircraft, and Major Bryan felt that every one of them was looking at him.

They weren't. But he still couldn't look back.

The men entered the hangar and walked to a room that ran along the entire back wall. The northern side was a research facility, the right side was storage space and a dressing area. Bryan opened the door with a swipe of his pass card. Woody was seated on a stool by her worktable. Fluorescent lights hung low over a black-slab surface packed with computers, discs, containers marked DANGEROUS, empty casings for explosives, detonators, high-voltage ionizers, cables, shock tubes, and electronic initiation systems to commence explosions remotely including the handheld unit Woody had used that morning.

Woody was looking at her laptop. She did not turn or salute but motioned excitedly as the officers entered.

"You've got to see this," she said.

"I've never seen anyone so happy to discover that the integrity of her vessel was undermined," General Scott said.

"I'm not happy, I'm relieved. You don't know what I've been going through."

"I have some idea," Bryan replied.

Woody did not appear to have heard him. "To be entirely accurate, sir, this would not fall under the label of sabotage, but under the Defense Intelligence Agency's new category of 'structural terrorism.'"

"The DIA?" Scott said with surprise. "You're going to tell me they had something to do with this?"

"Indirectly, sir. That's where I tracked the problem to. Old War Department files that were passed along to them."

"Really?" Scott said.

The men stepped up behind her. They looked at the monitor.

"What got you there?" Scott asked.

"Sir, I knew I hadn't used enough C-4 to damage the hull plating to that degree. So I checked the destroyer's background and—"

"Damn."

"Sir?"

"The Allied Naval Transfer Program after the war," Scott said.

"Yes, sir—"

"The Russians did this."

"No, sir," Woody replied. "We did."

Scott looked at her.

"We caused the problem. Through the British."

"Explain," Scott said.

"The HMS *Meadowood* was given to the Russians as part of the process of rebuilding its anti-submarine fleet after the war. According to press releases and declassified documents from the War Department, we did that to help an ally rebuild after the war. But according to declassified white papers, we did it to keep them from immediately building new shipyards. The thinking was that we could saddle them with old hardware to satisfy their immediate needs while we went ahead and built the next generation of destroyers that would be faster and more powerful."

"While the Soviets used their resources to jump ahead of us in new technologies like intercontinental ballistic missiles?" General Scott said. "That doesn't make any sense."

"But that's apparently what they hoped," Woody said.

"Moscow made off with a number of German rocket scientists. The Truman administration wanted the Soviets to spend money on technology that we would then appropriate. Apparently, we had a pretty good spy network in place over there."

"So how did the Russians beat us into space?" Scott asked.

Woody smiled. "They used their resources to build rockets *and* expand Stalin's secret police. They dug out our spies and effectively put a stick in our eye."

"Okay. We screwed up," Major Bryan said. "What's that got to do with the hull plating?"

"According to the War Department, Russian mechanics did not regularly service the naval engines. When something busted, the crew repaired it with whatever they had on hand. The most common problem during the war was running the engines until they overheated and blew."

Scott nodded.

"Okay, I'm missing something here," Bryan said.

"You're missing what our government did to the crews of our Cold War adversaries," Scott said. "Go on, Lieutenant."

Woody sucked down a long breath. "The War Department had the hull plates loosened so that if there was an engine room explosion, the destroyer would go down," she said.

Bryan tasted disgust in the back of his throat. "So what you're saying is that when you blew the engine room, the weakened plates came loose."

Woody nodded gravely. "The think tank figured it would be three to five years before each of the nine destroyers we gave them suffered a mishap of that kind."

"Tell me that except for us it didn't work," Bryan said.

"Actually, Major, two destroyers went down. One in 1949 and one in 1951—"

"The War Department got the time frame right," Scott said.

"What about the crews?" Bryan pressed.

"Most of the sailors made it off safely. Losses were estimated at a total of ten to fifteen seamen, and most of those were lost in the initial blasts."

"Targeted war," Scott said. "Take down the hardware and not the personnel. That was actually considered humane."

"That's correct, sir." Woody tapped the monitor with the back of a pencil. "The analysts quoted here said exactly that."

"What about the other destroyers?" Bryan asked.

"The other seven destroyers were never impacted. The *Cherkassov* was one of the vessels that made it through the Cold War without buckling."

"Kicked in the ass by our own Trojan horse," Bryan said.

"Well—that's the price of forward planning," Scott said. "Sometimes you don't look ahead far enough. Sometimes you do."

Bryan frowned. "Sir, would you have approved of this plan?"

"Yes. When you were in Iraq for the first war, would you have cared that a few dozen artillery shells that we gave Baghdad to fight Iran twelve or thirteen years before blew up in the barrel?"

"No, sir."

"This is no different," Scott said. "The Soviets had a big head start on us in the spying and propaganda business. They'd been outreaching since the Revolution. After World War II they were planting moles in our departing forces like crazy. Hell, they even managed to steal the bomb from us. I remember my granddad reading the Wabash *Plain Dealer* and the Churubusco *Truth* in the 1950s and worrying out loud that we were losing a war I didn't even realize we were fighting. The United States had to do whatever we could wherever we could to maintain balance. If these little time bombs were one of those things, I applaud it." The general moved closer to Bryan. "Our nation was proactive in the face of a sudden danger. It was looking after its people. Sometimes that causes collateral damage—regrettably but unavoidably."

Bryan said nothing. He did wonder, though, how he would have felt encountering wounded Iraqis and being ordered to leave them to die. After all, they were enemies.

Scott looked at Woody. "Lieutenant, I want to thank you. That was a real nice chunk of detective work."

"Thank you, sir." Woody looked at Bryan. "Major, I would like to say something."

"All right."

"I know you're upset about the dummies. But knowing that you were behind me in the corridor today made a big difference. I pushed myself on some very tired arms and legs because I knew you were there to catch me. If you had gone after them, I might not be here."

"Did you think I would go after them?"

"Frankly, sir, I wasn't sure. I hoped you wouldn't. It was still just a drill and we needed all our resources to get out."

Bryan smiled. "Thank you, Lieutenant. I appreciate that." He looked at the general. "And thank you, sir. I'll think about what you said."

"Not too much." Scott pointed ahead with a finger. "That way."

"Yes, sir. Now if you two will excuse me, I think I'll get started on my mission report."

Major Bryan saluted the general and left. The keys were still in the SGC. Scott would be able to drive himself back. Bryan felt like walking.

A brisk wind was moving in from the Gulf. But the sun was still high and it warmed the major's hands. He flexed them. It felt sweet.

Okay, Bryan thought. He was alive and dummies were "dead." He could deal with that. He had to. But Maj. Thomas Bryan made a vow as he crossed the concrete airstrip. A vow on which more than his self-respect depended. It was the cornerstone of any future peace of mind.

Whatever the personal cost, he could never again leave a job unfinished.

Never.

PART THREE

THE POLE

ONE

Stanley, Falkland Islands

With a population of two thousand hardy souls, Stanley is the smallest and most remote capital city on the planet. Stone Silver had read that in the briefing book prepared by the DOD.

The rear admiral loved facts like that. He had always loved knowledge and discovery. That was how he'd ended up at the top of the Ant Hill. That was how he'd ended up in the navy.

Growing up in Vermont, not far from Lake Champlain, Silver was raised with stories about the Lake Champlain monster—Champy, the locals called it. His parents owned a small inn, and he would go through the brochures, hang out on the shores at night, even throw bait in the water hoping to see the monster. It never happened. But while he was out, he watched the currents, the fish, the nocturnal predators. They fascinated him. He thought he might one day become a scientist.

Unfortunately, Silver was a straight C student. His parents couldn't afford college and he couldn't get a scholarship. So he joined the navy, hoping to learn engineering or communications or something having to do with science. He was accepted into the navy's Elint Program—created in 1958 under the banner Operation Tattletale—which designed and launched satellites to spy on the Soviet Union. Fewer than two hundred people, which included the men and women working on it, knew the program existed. The first satellite, GRAB—for

Galactic Radiation and Background—was sent aloft in June
1960. That was a month after U2 pilot Francis Gary Powers was
shot down flying atmospheric reconnaissance over Soviet territory. The Elint Program continued to fire satellites into orbit for
two years, though the navy did not acknowledge its existence
until its fortieth anniversary. In 1962, operations were assumed
by the super-secretive National Reconnaissance Office. But the
navy continued to create and construct the elements that went
into the satellites.

Silver was good with his hands and was put to work machin-
ing and assembling components that were shipped to the NRO.
He was based at the Naval Research Laboratory on the Po-
tomac, where he put in sixteen-hour days and loved every instant of them. Just being in the nation's capital was a thrill and
a privilege. Because Silver showed an aptitude for detail work,
he was moved into circuit-board construction, then design, as
electronics became more and more sophisticated. Because of
his top-security clearance, Silver was involved in other secret
navy projects. He was moved from the Naval Research Lab to
the San Francisco Naval Bay Shipyard in 1968, where he
worked on the new generation of nuclear submarines. He never
left that field, nor did he ever wish to. He always dreamed, in
fact, that one day he would take a midget submarine back to
Vermont and search for Champy.

But at the moment he was in the Falklands, on a short lay-
over before heading to the south pole. Their destination was
pretty amazing in itself, a place he had never expected to find
himself. He had studied the navigation charts and geological reports, but that was sterile and intellectual. He had been too
busy, too preoccupied with tests and deadlines, to take a step
back to look subjectively at the reality of the journey, the place.
The bottom of the world. A place still relatively unchanged
from ages gone by.

Silver stood on the deck of the *Abby* while Angela and her
crew supervised the loading of supplies. He was dressed in
warm civilian clothes. All of the naval personnel were in
civvies. The Falklands were still a British territory, with a significant British military presence still ready to fight off Argen-

tine claims on the 202 islands, as they had done in 1982. Argentine operatives still watched the harbor, and the U.S. navy did not want it getting out that seamen were on board a science vessel bound for Antarctica. By treaty, the south pole was not to serve as a military base for any reason. Since the *D* would not be docking, the letter of the treaty was being upheld. But the navy did not want any embarrassing questions. They also didn't want anyone going down and having a look. That would not only cause security problems, it could endanger the crew of the *Tempest D* as well as any observers in the test area. This was one reason the navy had chosen such a remote spot.

The *Abby* had arrived shortly after sunrise—at 4:30 A.M. Which was fitting, Silver felt, since they had left Kings Bay at sunrise. The morning had been overcast, mist churning low across the sea, but it had cleared by seven and the harbor was now aglow with bright sun. There were white hulls of pleasure boats and the worn hulls of fishing ships, as well as the metal hulls of freighters and tankers. Most were en route to somewhere else, stopping here, like the *Abby*, for supplies. The city itself—which was more like a village than a metropolis—was built on a mountainside where it received daylong and unobstructed sunlight. It was charming and a good way to be reintroduced to civilization after more than a week at sea. Not much noise, no crowds, and everything relatively close by. Silver had just enough time to get a cab, go to the Wool Centre, and buy a sweater of unusually soft Falkland Islands wool. He bought a black one for himself, a white one for his daughter, and a green one for Sally.

The voyage itself had been unexceptional. The weather was generally good, and the hours were filled with checks of systems on board the *D* as well as reviews of the mission plan and emergency procedures. Most of those were the responsibility of the personnel who would be remaining on the *Abby*, who had equipment and gear to rescue the crew in the event of virtually any kind of accident. The team also spent time getting to know the members of the *Abby* crew. Captain Colon and Angela seemed to get along extremely well, but only at the outset. Tension seemed to grow between them as the journey progressed. It didn't affect their work, so the rear admiral didn't ask Colon about it. For all Silver knew, it was simply the pressure of replacing the top scientist at the last moment, or having zero hour so near. After all the years and all the hours that had been stuffed into them, the test was finally, literally, around the corner. People were going to be a little edgy.

So he stood on the deck, in his warm new sweater, and thought about the many ironies that had dovetailed into this moment. Interest in a sea serpent had taken him to space and then back to the sea, where he was about to launch a man-made leviathan. He had spent his career working mostly with men, yet here, in this foreign harbor, the only people on his mind were women—his wife, his daughter, and Charlotte Davies— all of whom would have reacted differently to being here. His wife would have been blissful. She would have loved the openness of everything, the freshness in each breath, the hint of deep Antarctic cold beneath the natural chill of the sea. Elizabeth would have been in professional travel-writer mode. Her microcassette recorder in hand, her eyes running over everything like little machines, she would have been reporting and enjoying the challenge of "understanding the character," as she put it, rather than enjoying the place itself. That's what made her work successful. She sold edge, not puff. And Charlotte— she would have been back in Kings Bay, asking for on-site temperature readings to see how they matched the climatological reports from the navy's Fleet Numerical Meteorology Detachment, Asheville. If they didn't match exactly, she would be riding them to check the data coming in from the Satellite Data Information/Processing Distribution Subsystem to make sure it was accurate. The one advantage the SATIPS system had was it collected data from three different satellites to make sure there was sufficient overlap and no glitches in the data. Mike Carr had sent daily summations from the multisatellite composites, but they lacked the personality of Charlotte's communiqués. There were only facts, not evaluations.

It was strange to be thinking about the three women when both Antarctica and this momentous test loomed. But as food and water were brought aboard on hand trucks—purchased in advance by the Smithsonian Institution—maybe it wasn't all that odd to be looking for humanity. Trying to put beloved faces on something so vast and intimidating. The rear admiral looked toward the south.

It was frightening, frankly, to think of the continent to which they were headed. More so than it ever was contemplating the lake, which seemed too large when he was a boy, or the night sky, which was infinitely greater. Maybe it was the risk, the fact that this was not a tour and they were so far from assistance on the off chance something went wrong. Maybe it was the magnetism of the south pole. This was a planetary pole, he had to remind himself. Not a street lamp or a cell phone tower. This was the big noise. For an officer who had spent most of his time in windowless buildings, not even on a boat, that was awe-inspiring.

Angela and her crew had already been here. The rest of the team from Kings Bay were all extremely focused. The rear admiral would be surprised if they felt what he did, at least now. That was one of the privileges of commanding a crack team: There were moments for reflection. But Silver was willing to bet that things would change when they got under way.

Then there was the project itself. If all went well, history was about to be written. A new form of national defense, but with applications in the civilian world. Charlotte had once written a paper suggesting other uses for supercavitation. Unclogging arteries. Turning aside flows of lava from inhabited areas. Even fishing. "Knock them out and drag them in," she had suggested. What they did here could produce the most far-reaching spin-offs since the Apollo moon program.

And he was the man in charge. It was humbling and chest-swelling at the same time.

The rear admiral wondered if other great advances had filled their creators with the same sense of "event," or if that had come after the fact. Perhaps—no, probably—the Wright brothers, Robert Fulton, and J. Robert Oppenheimer and the scientists of the Manhattan Project were too busy tightening bolts and soldering wires to recognize it. Afterward, they were probably too caught up in the "What hath God wrought?" stuff to savor the achievement.

Right now, Silver was somewhere in between, and liking it. For the next ninety minutes, or so. After they headed back to sea, who knew what he would think and feel?

Which was also part of the adventure.

TWO

The Tasman Sea

So much of life was not just about what we did but how we did it.

When the orders reached the *Destiny* to pick up a passenger on Louisa Reef, Sr. Capt. Chien Gan had expected Captain Biao to do exactly what he did. The younger officer had sent two seamen in the inflatable raft ashore to collect Guoanbu operative Wu Lin Kit and escort him to the *Destiny*. Had Biao not sent two men—an honor guard—he would have been telling Wu that he did not consider him to be an important passenger. For Biao to have gone himself would have been embarrassingly subservient to Wu.

When Wu came onto the bridge, Biao had made the first bow. That was important. If Wu was honorable, he would seek to extend Captain Biao similar courtesies wherever possible, such as informing him of his needs in private and allowing the captain to give orders as if they were his own. That would give Biao face with his crew. If Wu was not honorable, the Guoanbu operative would probably seek to humiliate Biao by expressing his wishes in the presence of the crew.

The senior captain would be insulated from these activities in any case. He would give no orders while the agent was on board. In that way, technically, the vessel was still under naval control. If the senior captain didn't challenge an order that the captain was forced to obey, that signified the superior officer's agreement.

It was all a dance without music, but an important one. Without face a man had no identity. He was what others made him. All it took was a small incident, a lapse in protocol, to rob him of that. An insult unchallenged or a challenge unanswered. It was more complicated in the military because rank did not always permit the correct response. Crews understood this and watched to see how superiors handled difficult situations. If they did not give subordinates face, it was the senior officer who lost respect.

In the days since the *Destiny* had been diverted to Louisa Reef, Wu Lin Kit had been a shadowy dance partner. He had come aboard and thanked the captain in front of the crew. Wu had also asked that his appreciation be extended to the senior captain, though he did not ask to meet him. Asking to see Chien would effectively have been bidding him to come forward. It would have established a hierarchy with Wu on top. Then the newcomer disappeared, save for a brief period every day when he emerged from a small stateroom he had been given— displacing a pair of officers—and talked with his superior in Beijing. Chien knew it was his superior only because the communication destination was registered in the daily radio log of the *Destiny*. It was the office of Chin Liang, director of Remote Field Operations for the Tenth Bureau. After a brief conversation, Wu would take Captain Biao aside and give him new coordinates. The *Destiny* was moving southwest, though Wu did not say to where.

Captain Biao did not want to ask. He might be rebuffed. Or perhaps their guest didn't know. Whichever it was, the senior captain decided it was time to dine with the field operative and ask questions about their mission. He offered through Captain Biao and Wu accepted. Chien asked to meet him in the mess hall instead of in his quarters. The crew would see them and know that Chien had asked for the meeting, since everything Wu did was in secret. They would regard the senior captain's act as one of command. That would give them all a feeling of pride, confidence, and face. Submarine crews rarely knew where they were going. But they knew and trusted the men in command. That was not the case with Wu and it made them uneasy.

The centermost of three stainless steel tables was kept empty. The seven crew members who were dining when the senior captain arrived all rose and saluted. Wu was already there. Chien acknowledged the crew and went directly to Wu. The Guoanbu operative also rose. He bowed politely.

The men had never seen each other, let alone met.

"Thank you for this invitation, Senior Captain Chien," Wu said as they sat.

"I'm honored you accepted."

Wu nodded deeply. "Chien is an uncommon name. Many men would be intimidated by it."

"Because it is 'of the *chi*,' because people expect you to be powerful?" Chien smiled.

Wu smiled back.

"The name is a shortened version of our ancestral town, Chieuan-ga. My great-grandfather used to say that to change it would be to admit it was too much of a challenge. He felt we should try to live up to it."

"Clearly, Senior Captain, you have succeeded."

"The acquisition of confidence is a process," Chien said. *As is the process of finding out who another man really is,* he thought. This was like a children's game where they pat hands. Eventually, the pace increases and the true game emerges. "Tell me, have you been on a submarine before?"

"Never."

"What has surprised you?"

"That's an interesting question," Wu said. "My only points of reference are surface vessels, which are quieter."

"The water amplifies the noise of the engine. It causes sound to carry along the hull. We are never without that, or the drumbeat of every valve, piston, gear, pump, and door. Has it bothered you?"

"No. It is similar to sleeping in a metropolis. You quickly grow accustomed to the horns and the sirens and the people. I was also surprised by the air. There is a metallic taste."

"I have been on submarines for so much of my life that the recirculated air seems normal. Fresh air tastes untamed."

The cook and a server came to ask them what they wanted. Chien ordered sliced soyed goose. Wu requested oyster pancake, which was made of deep-fried egg. Both men asked for Cokes. The senior captain noticed that the other tables had thinned, leaving just a few men, who were quickly finishing their meals.

The colas arrived immediately, having been fetched by the server.

Wu glanced at his glass. "Look at that. There is a steady, subtle vibration on the surface. In the same way that we're all traveling at the same speed, we all shake like that in here. But we also shake when we're afraid." He regarded the senior captain. "May I ask what you fear?"

"Failure," Chien said without hesitation. "Dishonor."

"Intangible things."

"But no less real."

"I agree," Wu said. "Those are my fears in the reverse order. I may fail, but I will learn something in the process."

"Interesting. If you view life as a classroom, you will never fail."

"In the Shaolin temple, my master used to say that life ends in failure for it is our wish that it continue," Wu said. "That is why he took his life. To control the manner and time."

"Did you approve of that?"

"I mean him no dishonor, but it seemed to me a charade, a pretense. He was no less dead for the performance."

"Perhaps he had finished with all he wanted to do," Chien suggested.

"In that case, I would have been disappointed by the master's lack of invention, of imagination. No—I did not see this as a victory. Simply a premature defeat."

Their meals arrived as the remaining sailors were leaving the mess room. Chien told the cook they would call him if they needed anything else. The galley chief took that as a signal to leave the area entirely. He did so. The goose was slightly salty. The senior captain wondered if the cook had used more soy than usual. Or maybe it was something in his mouth. Distaste for the direction of the conversation.

"Do you prefer to eat in silence?" Wu asked.

"Not necessarily."

"We did that at the monastery, never speaking during meals. I didn't like it, though conversation was also impractical."

"Why?"

"We often stood on posts, in the horse stance—that is, with our legs spread wide as we crouched. It's almost like sitting on air. Except that beneath each of us was a sharpened spike. It taught us endurance and concentration." Wu regarded the senior captain. "It was where I learned to watch the master closely. If you made sounds with your food, he struck you in the seat with a bamboo switch. If you didn't read his expression before he struck, if you weren't ready for the blow, it could be bad."

"A useful skill in your work," Chien said. "Reading expressions."

"Indispensable, sir."

"What do you see in me?" It was a leading question, but the senior captain was growing impatient. He wanted to know where his crew was headed and Wu did not seem interested in telling him.

"Right now, Senior Captain Chien, you look like the master when someone sucked soup loudly from a spoon."

Chien grinned.

"What displeases you?" Wu asked.

"I would like to know our mission." It wasn't subtle, but Wu had swung the door wide and Chien had stepped through.

Wu seemed neither surprised nor hesitant. "We are tracking an American ship. I have not wanted to discuss it because I did not know what to tell you. I have more information now. The vessel, the *Abby*, is registered to the Smithsonian Institution in Washington, D.C. She recently made a trip to Antarctica; her course and mission were recorded by GESAMP, the Joint Group of Experts on the Scientific Aspects of Marine Environmental Protection. That's a branch of the United Nations International Maritime Organization. When the *Abby* returned, she went to an American military base and remained hidden for several days. When she set out, she filed the same itinerary with GESAMP. We obtained the file several days later, after it was processed and made public. We flew Chingmy Mok, our expert in maritime activity, to one of its stops. This morning, she reported from Stanley, in the Falkland Islands, that the ship stopped there briefly with three times the crew it had said it was carrying."

"The original journey was a scouting run to a region where they intended to conduct a test of some kind," Chien suggested.

"That is exactly what we believe, sir."

"And have you any idea what the ship's mission is?"

"Our agent took photographs of the ship and sent them to Beijing for analysis," Wu said. "We have built up a considerable database of portraits of U.S. military officers from their Web sites. One of the individuals appears to be Rear Admiral Kenneth Silver. We have further confirmation in that the gentleman went clothes shopping in Stanley. He bought sweaters for himself and two others. One was a very small sweater. The rear admiral has a daughter and a granddaughter."

"What else do you know about him?"

"Very little. He has never been profiled on the U.S. Navy Web site or in their on-line newsletter. He has only appeared in three press photographs, all of those at submarine launchings. His low profile suggests that he is involved in secret operations, possibly involving submarines."

"That is a significant leap to make."

"It is what I do," Wu said. "And there is still the matter of the *Abby* and her secretive stay at the naval base."

"If so little is known about the rear admiral, how do you know about his granddaughter?" Chien asked.

"The rear admiral's wife died recently. The little girl was mentioned in a newspaper obituary."

"Your people are thorough."

"We are, though we thank the *New York Times* for their thoroughness every day." Wu was silent for a moment. "Sir?"

"Yes?"

"There is blood in the corner of your mouth." Wu pointed.

Chien removed the napkin from his lap. He touched the right side of his mouth. There was indeed blood, coming from inside his lower lip. That's why the goose had tasted salty. Obviously, not knowing the mission had been more disturbing than he had realized. Face came at a price.

Chien replaced his napkin, took a drink of cola, then resumed eating. To his surprise, the mood at the table was much more relaxed. Yet it was not talk of the mission that had liberated them, but the senior captain. He had established himself as a leader and removed what was apparently an uncomfortable burden from Wu. Chien had seized an initiative, however symbolic, however inadvertent, which the greatest commanders must be willing to take.

Sr. Capt. Chien Gan had both given, and taken, first blood.

THREE

The Scotia Sea

Thursday was a turning point.

That was the day Captain Colon and Angela Albertson had been standing on the slowly swaying deck of the *Abby*. A stiff wind knifed from the south, but they were comfortable enough in their heavy, fur-lined parkas, gloves, and rubber boots to protect their feet from the icy spray. They were watching a magnificent wandering albatross alternately hover and flap in slow, determined beats across the open sea. Colon related to the big bird.

It was alone.

Colon was beginning to feel that he had been too subtle, too professional, with Angela. In all these days at sea he had never intruded on her bridge watch or monopolized her at mess. Whenever they were standing around below or on deck, he asked about her work, her interests, rarely about her private life. And he was charming. He knew it. That same enchantment had worked on ladies at the Muddy Tracks even when they were sober. Yet he still couldn't get her to say anything like "When I'm finished sending my cover-story e-mails to the Smithsonian about cuttlefish migration, why don't we say hello to some beers in my cabin?"

The captain grew frustrated by her lack of return fire. Angela asked questions about his career, but it was just chat. He wondered why nothing was percolating. Did she only date African-American men? Did she not date men at all? Or did she find him unattractive? That would hurt, but at least he would know. The no-spike zone on the love meter was killing him. Standing beside her on the deserted deck, admiring the desolate scenery, he had resolved to take the next opening and see where it went.

"Did you ever read Coleridge's *Rime of the Ancient Mariner*?" he asked.

"It was required reading in my house," she said.

"Oh?"

"My dad made an animated short subject about it, using the Doré illustrations. It was nominated for an Oscar."

"I didn't know that," Colon said. "Impressive."

"I'll send you a copy of the video when we get back."

"Do you have one here?"

Angela said she did not. Swing and a miss.

They had continued to watch the giant bird with its ten-foot wingspan circle in search of a meal. "I feel like I'm having a celebrity sighting. My dad used to read the poem to me. It was scary, the image of the dead albatross hanging around the mariner's neck."

"According to seafaring legend, an albatross flying alone is the soul of a dead sailor," Angela said.

"Do you believe that?"

"The sailor in me does, but the scientist does not."

"Which is stronger?"

"The part that has rules, that relies on facts. I know that these birds are born on one of the subantarctic islands, then take to sea," she said. "Most of them don't see land for five or ten years before they return to where they were born to mate."

"We have a term for that in the military. From hitch to hitch. Do you have any idea how old this one is?"

"Probably just two or three years," Angela said. "It will be about twenty percent larger in a few years."

"And their life span is what?"

"Fifty years."

"Almost like people."

"Except for one thing," she said.

"Which is?"

"These wonderful birds mate for life."

That sounded bitter, he thought. *Maybe she'll want to talk about it.* "May I ask something personal?"

"All right."

"Were you ever married?"

"Engaged," she said.

"You are?"

"Was. About two years ago, to a fellow ichthyologist from grad school. It didn't work out."

"Why? Because you were at sea?"

"In a way," she said. "I found that I liked being out here better than I liked being with him."

"That's not good."

"No. I figured I'd wait till it was the other way around before I married. Problem is, it's tough to meet guys on the ocean."

Ouch. Colon didn't know if that was directed at him or if it was meant generally. Probably the latter. Still, it stung like a rebuff.

The diving albatross caught a small squid in its sharp, hooked beak. With an audible flapping of its great wings—they could hear it over the wind—the off-white bird with black-tipped wings settled onto the water. It folded itself into a perfect floating device and devoured the wriggling creature in greedy, gulping bites. Then it sat there, riding the sea, resting after its successful hunt.

Colon was about to ask her for a drink after dinner when Angela excused herself to check on their course. She left the captain alone, at sea, like the albatross. He nursed his frustration for another couple of days. Finally, after more than a week at sea, of standoffishness that was driving him crazy, Colon decided to ask Angela what was up with them. Why things not only weren't clicking, why he was getting nothing back either good or bad. They were walking toward their quarters after their evening shift when he asked if he could stop in her cabin for a moment.

"Sure," she said.

"I wanted to ask you something," he said when they were inside. "I don't want this to get in the way of the work we're doing, but—first off, I wanted to say I think you're a terrific woman, beautiful and smart."

"And you want to know why I don't seem to be attracted to you?"

"Yeah."

"I *am* attracted to you."

"You are?"

"Yes."

Now he was completely confused. "So what is it? You don't mix with co-workers or something along those no-crossing-the-lines line?"

"No. I'm just looking for someone very special. Or I should say, specific."

"Can you be more . . . specific?"

"It's one of those 'I'll know it when I see it' things."

"I see. It's gotta hit you like a tsunami."

"Yeah. First instinct, all that. I don't want to have to learn to love and adore someone."

"I'll buy that," Colon said. "In the meantime, doesn't life get lonely?"

"You mean, do I wish I had someone to hold me from time to time? Yeah," she admitted. "And I've got one of those."

Colon felt as if he'd been hit with a sock full of dimes on a side street back home. "You do?"

"Yeah."

"On board? Now?"

She nodded.

"I'll be damned. Who? Dr. Ogden? The rear admiral—?"

Angela didn't answer.

"I mean, if I've got to lose, I'd like it be to brains or rank, not dashing good looks."

"Captain, I'm not going to say anything more except that you didn't lose," Angela said. "The truth is, I like you too much to use you."

Angela gave him a cheek kiss followed by the sweetest, most

genuine smile he had ever seen, with eyes so completely feminine that he felt his insides turn to seawater. In that moment the frustration left him.

After he left, the captain went on deck. He saw the wandering albatross. His "brother" seemed so damned relaxed as he rolled over the high waves.

"Maybe there's something to be said for chastity," Colon thought.

With a grin, Colon turned from the increasingly icy winds and went to his cabin.

FOUR

Weddell Sea

Antarctica was different from any other continent Rear Admiral Silver had ever visited. Not because it was locked in ice and was difficult to reach, but because it announced its presence in a regal fashion, with heralds and fanfare and majesty. He had sensed it in the chill air as far away as Stanley. Now, standing just below the bridge, the feeling was even stronger.

Silver had come on deck shortly after dawn. They were in a region where there were now just two hours of darkness each day. Captain Colon, who was his bunkmate, slept through the end to the brief darkness. Dressed in his sweater and a felt-edged capote that reached nearly to his shins, Silver kept the hood tied tight to protect him from the wind. He had a heavy scarf tied around his mouth and nose and the wind still bit through it, still turned his hot breath to crystals under the scarf. It wasn't helping much, so Silver asked one of the crewmen to bring him a thermos of coffee.

The day before, the *Abby* had traveled west of South Georgia Island. They'd sailed close enough to catch a quick look at the king penguins clustered on the beach. There had to be twenty or thirty thousand of them, shifting about or racing in what appeared to be a mating ritual or early-morning mess call—Silver wasn't sure which. He also noticed a clutch of fur and elephant seals hanging out on or near isolated offshore rocks. There were albatross and seabirds he did not recognize, some fishing in flocks, others traveling alone. Behind all the activity were sentinels as titanic as any he'd ever seen: snow-covered mountains, plum-colored in the rising sun. But only on one side, the north. The other side was still dark. It was like seeing a half-moon, but this was a terrestrial range. Clouds crept by the peaks, but slowly, as though afraid to wake the sleeping giants too suddenly.

Now, just a few hours later, Silver glimpsed the South Orkney Islands, a bump on the far horizon as they entered the Weddell Sea. The science ship was now in the antarctic throne room. At least, that's how it felt to the rear admiral. The winds were less bruising here, the cold less aggressive. Silver dropped the ice-encrusted scarf and lowered the hood. The air felt good on his ears for about three seconds. Then they began to burn; it was still, after all, the south pole. He ignored the pain, a minute or two shy of frostbite. He wanted to hear as well as see.

Silver could hear cries from distant birds and the slosh of the water against the hull. But like the wind they seemed smaller, somehow, than they had the night before. Silver watched the horizon. It was free of morning mist, the water crisp and bright, the skies absolutely clear pale blue. As they sailed south, the continent appeared as a slightly saw-toothed line of gleaming white. It seemed to rise from the sea, growing in breadth and stature as they sailed closer. But the change was in three dimensions. The continent was also coming toward them. And with its approach came something else that was unique in Silver's experience. A sense of age, of time locked in place, of a kingdom indifferent to the events and wishes of the rest of the world. He saw cracks and fissures in the sides of the ice. He realized, as a commander, that these were the soldiers of the realm. Change came with angry protests, a splitting off from shelves and glaciers, a cry to the planet to let it be or it would visit terrible suffering on others.

Silver wasn't a save-the-earth man. He liked to see human fingerprints, human ideas, and human vision on the world. He had never paid much attention to the ozone hole, which seemed very far away from Georgia. But he had to say, it was a lot less far at this moment. He felt slightly ashamed. Not for his inactivity, since naval officers did not have a lot of leeway regarding causes they could champion, but for not having cared at all.

With respect, Silver had to admit that this was a continent with a strong, unique, persuasive personality.

The intercom behind the rear admiral chimed loudly. Silver checked his watch as he touched the button. He was surprised to find that he had been on deck for over an hour.

"Yes?"

"Rear Admiral, we are about two miles from position," Angela said.

"Thank you," Silver replied. "I'll inform Dr. Carr. Has Captain Colon signed in yet?"

The bridge controlled the locks to the door of the hold. All of the crew members had to signal the bridge to go below.

"Not yet. He was up pretty late last night."

"I'm not surprised," Silver said. Even though they shared a cabin, Silver had not heard him come in. That was one benefit of a lifetime spent in the military. Since soldiers never knew when or where they would be needed, they learned to fall asleep fast and deep and wherever they happened to be. This was especially true in R&D work, where Silver often grabbed power naps at his desk while engineers, welders, and cranes did their noisy work around him.

Colon had been going over a checklist of *D* components with Carr's team at the Ant Hill. Though the full-scale *Tempest* would be nuclear-powered, the smaller prototype ran entirely on battery power. Ten batteries were grouped aft, each five-foot-tall panel producing 7,000 amps, 15,400 watts per hour. They could run for forty-five days without being charged, thanks to an innovative oxide-lead positive plate that was laced with calcium. This made for very low charge loss. Colon needed the batteries to run for just two days. Nevertheless, to err on the side of conservation they had put the submarine in hibernation mode on the way down. To keep electronic clocks and gauges from needing to be reset, they were individually powered by small cadmium cells. Last night they woke the *D* and started running their systems checks. Silver had gone to bed when it appeared that everything had come on all right. Obviously, Colon had not.

Silver was about to go below when the intercom beeped again.

"Yes?"

"Rear Admiral, Captain Colon is awake and at his post," Angela said. "He had three and three-quarters hours of sleep and seems a little cranky."

"I'm not surprised," Silver told her. "It's time for him to start dealing with Dr. Carr."

"I heard they were not close."

"No. Though I'm hoping they get past that. I have to say, the captain has seemed pretty content these past few days."

"He has," Angela agreed.

The rear admiral went below. He entered his personal code in the keypad at the door and was buzzed in from the bridge.

And ran right into a shooting war.

FIVE

Weddell Sea

"That is *dumb*," Colon yelled into the phone. "No, I take that back. It is *excruciatingly* dumb."

The captain was standing by the starboard screw of the *D*. He was shouting into the 3324SE unit, holding the briefcaselike console and punching with it as he spoke. Forward, under the bright work lights, two men on aluminum ladders were working on the nose of the *D*. The captain was facing them. One of the men, Ens. Chuck Warren, gestured for Colon to look behind as the rear admiral entered. Colon saluted him with the hand holding the receiver. It didn't matter if he missed some of what was being said on the other end. It was bullshit.

Colon put the phone back to his ear.

". . . no idea what the currents will be like until you're in them," Mike Carr was saying.

"That's why we need mobility," Colon said. "Leaving the towline attached until we're ready to rock and roll won't give us that. It'll also endanger the *Abby* if something happens to us."

"Not according to the sims," Carr replied. "I've got a three-dimensional model on my screen right now that covers the magnitude and distribution of tidal mixing in that region of the Weddell Sea. The team has been going over the latest models all night. We've got semidiurnal barotropic constituents, diurnal barotropic tides, and internal tides. We can compute the interactions of these elements at sea, and they give us tolerable levels of current. But a lot depends on how they hit the offshore slopes, and a lot of *that* force will be determined by what the slopes are like when you get there. We have no idea what kind of erosion has taken place since the *Abby* was there taking soundings. If you get hit in a high vertical eddy—"

"It could spit us out like gristle," Colon said. "I know all about it."

"Maybe so, but you don't seem to be concerned."

"This is a *test* mission," the captain yelled, once again jabbing with the phone. "There are *risks* that come with that. Hell, commercial airlines risk wind shear every time they take off! We can handle some current. If what you describe does happen—which is unlikely but possible—I don't want to be attached to the *Abby*. If the current hits us the wrong way, the towline could actually snap us into the *Abby*!"

"If the *Abby* moves sixty meters to your starboard or port side, there isn't a current in the region strong enough to hurl you into her," Carr said. "We even ran a sim for ice-shelf section NH109 breaking off and sending a tsunami through the region. You won't hit the *Abby*, but the torque of an ice slide could spin you out of the region entirely if you are not anchored. Captain, we're only talking about a half-hour window when you run through your internal checklist. After you've launched, you'll be able to ride the current on your own. That's when we'll release you, and not before."

"A half hour is a year when you're tied to the hitching post," Colon replied.

"But it is, in fact, just thirty minutes."

Colon wanted to strangle the man through the phone, force him to listen. "Don't you get it? If we're tied up, we won't have control of the *D* if something does happen. We'll have virtually no maneuverability."

Silver stopped a few feet from Colon. The rear admiral did not look happy.

"Given all the things that can happen," Carr said, "you will be safer if you can be brought back into the *Abby*."

"That's crap," Colon yelled. "Crap! When the hell did you become a submarine commander?"

"The same day you became an oceanographer," Carr replied.

Colon wanted to kick something. That wasn't an answer. It was "I know you are but what am I?" kindergarten bullshit.

"The bottom line," Carr went on, "is that the computers disagree with you and I agree with the computers. The towline will remain attached to the *D* through the systems check."

"Dr. Carr, you don't know what the fuck you're doing."

"Captain, do we have a dispute here?" Silver asked impatiently.

"Yes, sir," Colon replied. "Dr. Carr wants to keep the umbilical cord attached to baby *D* while we run the checklist. I want to be able to sail her in case something happens."

"The towline will remain attached," Silver said. "Was there anything else?"

That was as firm a slam dunk as Colon had ever experienced. "No, sir," Colon replied.

"Good. Please inform Dr. Carr that we're two miles from position," the rear admiral added.

"Yes, sir," Colon said.

The captain did as he was asked, and Carr thanked him politely—Carr had been annoyingly polite through the entire discussion—then hung up. The captain set the secure phone down and regarded Silver sternly.

"Sir, he's asking me to go into the water with a noose around my pecker."

"I assume Dr. Carr has valid reasons for his decision?"

"They were valid to him, but he's not going to be at the helm of the *D*—"

"That isn't relevant and you know it," Silver said angrily.

"Not *relevant*, sir?"

"You're both acting in the best interests of the mission. But Carr's the one with the brain trust and the sims—"

"And zero experience at sea."

"I hear you, Captain, especially when you interrupt."

"Sorry, sir."

"But I can't, don't, and won't dismiss what he's suggesting,"

Silver went on. "We're launching a complex piece of hardware. We need to be cautious, a little conservative."

"Sir . . ." Colon's voice trailed off in defeat. He just shook his head slowly. "Remember what the Mercury astronauts used to call themselves? 'Spam in a can.' They were just passengers in those friggin' buckets. They were allowed to do one thing: push a button to fire the rockets that took them out of orbit. That was it."

"They all made it back to earth, didn't they?"

"Yes, sir, they did," Colon allowed.

"If I remember correctly, when mission control thought that John Glenn had a loose heat shield, they came up with a possible solution and executed that solution from earth."

"That is true."

"Then it seems we have precedent in addition to protocol."

"Okay. Yes. But we also have a machine that's a lot more complex than the Mercury spacecraft," Colon said. "We need the ability to react if something happens, not wait for Carr to process information."

"Captain, if something happens that quickly, we're probably screwed anyway."

Colon couldn't dispute that. Not because he didn't want to; the rear admiral happened to be right.

"Now, how's our *D* been acting since they woke her up?" Silver asked.

"Fine," Colon said, his voice low and glum.

"Good. Let's go in and have a look."

The two men walked toward the center of the vessel, toward the stubby tower that constituted the bridge. The captain tried to get his brain back to where it had been in Kings Bay, happy just to be a part of this. But now that they were here, about to start the test, Colon couldn't stand the thought of not being in command of his own vessel. Even if the crew didn't know it, he would. And that made him want to scream inside.

Colon stopped suddenly and faced the rear admiral. "Sir, I need to know one thing."

"Go ahead." The rear admiral looked very much the brass hat right now, not the partner he had been for so long.

"If we hadn't made this deal with Carr—"

"It wasn't a 'deal,'" the rear admiral said with open annoyance. "It was a decision."

"Yes, sir. I'm sorry, sir." *That was dumb.* The rear admiral wasn't his enemy. Colon was venting, not thinking. "If Dr. Carr were not in charge, which way would you have wanted this?"

"I would have wanted the *Tempest D* to remain connected to the parent ship until we were comfortable that it was safe to release her. I would rely on my captain and science team leader to tell me when that was. And so you don't have to ask, if there was a disagreement, I would lean toward caution. Captain, we're in waters you've never sailed. Waters different from any you've *ever* sailed. I would not release any potential lifeline until I was sure of what we were doing."

And that was that.

"Are we finished with this now?" Silver asked.

"We are, sir."

Captain Colon and the rear admiral resumed their short walk toward the submarine's midsection. A detachable ladder was attached to the side. The rear admiral started up. Colon followed. Before launching, the seven-step ladder would be removed and the hooks withdrawn to streamline the vessel.

The captain wished that he could vanish just as easily. Press a button and get sucked into a nice alloy shell. He felt stupid and humiliated. He had known he would lose the showdown with Carr. Stone Silver had to support the man in charge. But the rear admiral hadn't even given Colon a winking nudge of support, which had never happened before. Hell, this was the first time the higher-rated officer had ever played the rank card. What really upset Colon now was that Silver believed what he had just said, which shouldn't have surprised him. After all, Rear Admiral Silver was more of an engineer than he was a seaman. Just because the captain and the rear admiral had always gotten along until this last minute, that didn't mean Silver would give him a free hand.

And you're just going to have to get over it, because that's not about to change, Colon told himself.

Once more the captain found himself in a lousy, uncomfortable mood. Angry at the guys in command and having to force himself not to stay that way. He was standing beside one of the technological marvels of the new century. He was going to be in charge of the vessel, if not the mission. And if that wasn't what he wanted, it was far from insignificant.

Remember that, asshole, he told himself as he waited for the rear admiral to climb down the interior ladder, then followed Silver down.

SIX

Weddell Sea

The *Abby* was just sitting there, like a doe waiting for a stag.

The *Destiny* had reached the Weddell Sea several hours ago. They had intentionally approached in the brief period of darkness, since they wanted to be at periscope depth to watch the *Abby*. Wu Lin Kit did not ask to observe the vessel, but when he was offered the captain's viewing post, he accepted. He watched the lights on deck and below, trying to see where the crew was most active.

And why they were active at all at this hour.

There was no way to tell from here what the crew was doing. The radio operator of the *Destiny* detected uplink activity from the science ship, but the communications were encrypted. Clearly, the research they were conducting was not for the Smithsonian Institution. The only thing Wu could ascertain, due to the high waterline on the ship's hull, was that they were carrying extremely heavy cargo. Wu calculated it to be somewhere in the vicinity of thirty tons. This could be a mission to retrieve core samples from beneath the seabed. The vessel could be carrying self-contained laboratories that would be hoisted aloft by gliders or balloons to study the ozone layer. Perhaps the equipment was loaded at the naval base because they had the engineering facilities to do so.

Or it could be a weapon or conveyance the U.S. Navy was testing. They may have ignored the international treaty regarding the region so that no one would see them test it.

Captain Biao was never far from Wu, and the Guoanbu operative kept the officer informed about everything he was seeing. Which wasn't much. Wu did not talk about his thoughts or suspicions; supposition indicated ignorance, and he did not want the crew to perceive him as unknowledgeable.

Wu stayed at the post through the night. The *Destiny* remained in silent mode, with a radio blackout in effect and both human and mechanical onboard movement restricted to avoid extraneous knocks and bangs. At one point the *Destiny* was forced to withdraw when its navigator detected sonar pulses moving through the water. Obviously, the American research vessel did not want to be spied upon. Captain Biao ordered the *Destiny* to retreat at five knots. That was the speed of a feeding blue whale. Because they were running silent, using ballast to carry them down and away, the Americans would hear nothing out of the ordinary. Because it was dark, it would be virtually impossible for the Americans to see them. As long as the "whale" was leaving, they would have no reason to look. Fortunately, the science ship was not using the U.S. Navy's new Low Frequency Active sonar, which might have picked up surface details and been able to make the distinction. That new form of sonar detection was banned from polar waters because the 150 to 160 decibels it produced were sufficient to rupture the delicate membranes in the bodies of marine mammals. The *Destiny* took up a position three-quarters of a kilometer from the vessel, which put it much closer to the coastline of Hope Bay. There, in silent mode, the submarine would be indistinguishable from the large slabs of ice that were floating farther to the north in the dark water.

Sr. Capt. Chien Gan did not come forward the entire night. Wu understood why. It would have put too many commanders in one place, creating a strained and difficult dynamic. But Wu was not thinking much about the two captains. He peered through the rubber eyepiece, doing his job, concentrating on the target and wishing he were closer. He thought back to the Vietnamese fishing boat in the Spratly Islands. He would have loved to float a dinghy over and examine the American vessel with night-vision lenses. But that was too risky. Eventually, the Americans' reasons for coming to Antarctica would be revealed. However, it would have been useful to learn a little more about the science ship's operations, possibly identify some of its crew.

At a few minutes before 5:00 A.M., the sonar operator of the *Destiny* reported something moving in the vicinity of the other vessel. The Chinese were not using their sonar in case the other ship was listening for acoustic surveillance. However, they were using external sensors to listen for sounds from the other vessel.

Wu couldn't see anything. It was extremely frustrating. "Are you certain?" he asked.

"There is no question, sir," the young seaman replied. "It's stopped now. It was a low drone, eighty decibels, and it lasted for exactly twenty-one seconds."

"Is there any other data?" the captain asked.

The crewman looked at two readouts beside the digital clock. "Phase variation was negligible and acoustic intensity was low."

"That would eliminate an engine or anything with a lot of kick," Captain Biao observed.

"Yes, sir."

"Was it definitely in the water, not inside the ship?" Wu asked.

"It was external, sir," the crewman replied. "If it were inside, the hull would have dispersed the sound."

"Might the brevity suggest a test of some kind?" Wu asked. "Perhaps a drill bit or a crane being moved into position?"

"It might," the crewman agreed.

"Could it have been hydraulic action?" the captain asked.

"That is very possible," the crewman replied. "The decibel level would be right for that."

"Suggesting what, Captain?" Wu asked.

"Cargo doors are frequently operated with hydraulic rams," the captain said. "They are lighter weight than gear mechanisms, creating less drag over a long-distance voyage."

"If they open bay doors to lower something into the water, how clear an image will your sonar give us?" Wu asked as he continued to watch the vessel.

"Depending upon the size, of course, we may be able to read significant projections on the surface," the crewman said.

"But that's all?"

"Yes, sir."

Wu stepped from the periscope. "Captain, may I speak with you?"

Biao nodded.

"Crewman, please let us know if the sound recurs." Wu was careful to say "us" to make it a mutual command.

"Yes, sir," the seaman replied.

The two men made their way toward a small extracurricular-vehicular equipment room just aft of the command center. The forward escape trunk was located here. If the submarine went down, this was the hatch to which a rescue ship would attach itself. Wu came here so he could think out loud, which was not something he liked to do in front of subordinates.

"I need to know what the American ship is doing," Wu told the captain. "They have too many crewmen on board for this to be a science mission."

"What do you suspect?" Biao asked.

"I don't know." Wu's voice had an edge even though he was whispering. "The United States navy may be testing a new kind of vessel or underwater mines or missiles or torpedoes. We need to know whether that's the case, and if so, what they are testing. At this distance we can't pick up any detail."

"We can move in closer during one of their sweeps," the captain said. "Once their operation has begun, it will be difficult, perhaps impossible, for them to abort immediately."

"I'd rather not be stationary," Wu said. "We don't want to give them a chance to read us. The upgrades on this vessel are still classified."

"Yes, of course."

"If we sail past the Americans, can your sonar operator compensate for the Doppler shift?"

The Doppler shift is the relative change in the wavelength

and frequency of a wave due to the movement of either the source of the signal or the receiver. If the source and the receiver are moving toward one another, sounds will seem to be higher. If they are moving apart, sounds will appear to be lower. In both instances the sonar image would be distorted.

"Yes," Biao said. "The computer can reprocess the image to compensate for movement."

"Good," Wu said. "If we were to move past the vessel, close to what appears to be an open bay, we would get a better sonar reading of whatever they release. How close can you take us?"

"That would depend on speed and angle," Biao replied. "Let's have a talk with the sonar operator and helmsmen. They're the ones who will have to perform the maneuver and reading."

The captain was excited, and thinking. Wu was glad to see it. That made a good ally an invaluable one.

The men made their way back to the command center. The corridor was extremely narrow and they had to walk sideways. These hallways were kept dark, the shadows used to suggest space that wasn't there.

When the men reached the command center, the sonar operator reported that the underwater bay of the science ship was still open. Clearly, Wu thought, this was not a test of the doors themselves. They had remained open for a reason.

The captain and two of his crewmen talked briefly at their side-by-side stations. Then they began working out calculations on the computer they shared. When they were finished, Captain Biao turned to Wu.

"As long as we remain in motion, we can ride the American sonar in without being detected."

"How?" Wu asked.

Biao deferred to the helmsman, while the sonar operator continued to watch the American ship.

"If you imagine a line through their ship, from stem to stern, that is the horizontal baseline of their sonar," the young seaman said. "Their sweep covers the sea from a starting point forward to a perpendicular position jutting out from the ship, toward our position, and then at a decreasing angle toward the stern. When it reaches the baseline it starts again on the opposite side."

"That's why we read a blind spot on this side," Wu said.

"Yes, sir. It's a big clockwise motion. Given our present location, if we come at the American vessel from twenty-two degrees off their forward baseline, we can reach them and pass beneath them before the sonar completes one sweep. We would effectively be invisible."

"What about feeling our presence?" Wu asked. "You displace a considerable amount of water."

"Roughly forty-five hundred long tons of water, which is over one million pounds," the captain said.

"The Americans will notice a change in their equilibrium," Wu said.

"Yes, but not in time to reel in whatever they've deployed," the captain pointed out.

"So we'll have to move fast," Wu said.

"Correct," Biao said.

"What kind of resolution will we get?"

"We can get close enough to read objects one meter high, sir," the sonar operator told him. "With computer enhancement, that will give us an extremely detailed silhouette."

"And if we maneuver carefully, sir, swing around whatever is deployed, we can try to get a silhouette from multiple angles," the helmsman said.

"From which we can construct a three-dimensional model of the image," Wu interrupted. "Brilliant."

"It's theoretical, but worth trying," Captain Biao pointed out.

"I agree," Wu said.

The captain ordered the helmsman to take on ballast and submerge to a depth of seventy meters. Biao did not notify the crew since they were still running silent. With a barely perceptible jolt, the *Destiny* began to float down.

"We'll watch for the American deployment, get a good sonar picture showing the parameters of the object, and then we'll start our run," the captain went on. "As long as we're moving around a clearly defined perimeter, we'll be able to do this quickly and safely."

"What if the object moves?" Wu asked.

"Any device that is placed in the water will certainly undergo a systems analysis, especially if it is a new device," the captain assured him. "We'll submerge so there is less chance of being heard when we start the engines. Once we start our run, we'll need less than two minutes to reach and pass the object."

The captain and his crew were suddenly energized. Wu was slightly less so, since the idea of literally firing the submarine close to a target held a certain risk. One of the foundations of Wu's martial arts training was that whenever someone threw speed and force at an opponent, it took little effort for that opponent to deflect the strike and turn the momentum against the attacker. All he had to do was move his arm or leg in a circle, intercept the blow or kick, then finish the arc to push it aside. This wasn't exactly the same, since it wasn't an attack. But the use of power in lieu of tact and technique always unsettled him.

Still, Wu wasn't a submariner. He did not know the water or the capabilities of this machine. These men did. That muted his concerns enough to allow him to focus on the job at hand.

It did not make the unease go away.

SEVEN

Weddell Sea

In the small hours of the morning, Rear Admiral Silver joined Angela Albertson on the bridge. Drs. Ogden and Grande were there as well in the somewhat cramped cabin. Aguina Grande, a man of African-American and Cherokee descent, was going to be watching the sonar to make sure no marine animals were in the area. They had selected this region of the sea because it was no longer mating season for any of the animals that habituated the bay. And being away from any of the migration routes, it was unlikely that any whales or seals would simply "happen by." Still, he watched to make sure. With enough notice, once released from its towline, the *Tempest D* could dive or reduce the supercavitation bubble to avoid sending a shock wave against an oncoming animal. Grande was not from the protect-all-aquatic-life-at-any-cost school. His attitude was that anything that got killed at sea got eaten. Nonetheless, Dr. Albertson wanted to do everything possible to maintain the natural ecological balance of the region.

Dr. Ogden was going to steer the *Abby* off to the southwest, toward the shore, as soon as the *D* was in the water. He was waiting for the signal from below, though the actual go-ahead would come from Dr. Carr.

They listened to the checklist items as they were read off. The items were replicated on a computer monitor: Everything on board had to be verified by a hands-on test and by a computer check of the electronics. So far, everything was functioning exactly as it was supposed to. At least, as far as being on-line went. They wouldn't know how it all held together until, as Captain Colon had put it back at the Ant Hill, "We get in the water and turn the ignition key."

Back when it was fun to be around Colon, Silver thought. He didn't blame the captain for being upset, but the rear admiral didn't believe the towline was the reason. It was the metaphor. Colon didn't like being leashed to Carr. But Silver had spoken with Carr several times since leaving Kings Bay. The scientist had worked hard to get up to speed. He was sounding more and more confident. Silver was impressed. He had no problem deferring to the judgment of the scientist and his think tank, especially when he agreed with their findings. Colon would have to adjust.

Happily, Ensigns Warren and LaCosta had been able to work the final kinks from the towline spool and hook—known, rather oddly, as the nose-eye because of its location and shape, respectively. The hook had been sticking but they'd found the right bearings to grease.

Despite the clash of minds and experience, the rear admiral was optimistic. He had been in situations like this before, though never with seven lives and billions of dollars at risk. He was hyper-alert; it did not feel like one-something in the morning, he thought, as the countdown clock reached the two-minute mark.

Angela shifted restlessly behind him. He reached over and gave her hand a squeeze. It wasn't politically correct but it felt right. She gave him a quick smile and continued to watch and listen.

The computer clicked past ninety seconds. Lieutenant Michaelson was manning the radio for the launch. Brance Michaelson had actually been the team's first compromise. His father was California Congressman Steven L. Michaelson, senior member of the Congressional Arms Appropriation Subcommittee. The kid had served on submarines but he was untested in a command-backup capacity. That bothered the rear admiral. But Colon was okay with it—Colon liked to teach, and Michaelson seemed quick on the uptake, so Silver signed on.

Michaelson was on the audio speaker. His voice was also being pumped to the command booth at Kings Bay. The lieutenant announced from on board that the *D*'s hull tubing was "one hundred percent." That meant a test gas had been forced through the liquid capillary system and no leaks or buckling had been detected. It would be ready to take on hydrogen from the seawater when they were ready to ascend. They reached the one-minute mark. The hatch was already closed but Colon ordered it sealed. A hollow O-ring seal was inflated with argon, an inert gas. Argon would not change on a molecular level because of heat, cold, or deep pressure. At the forty-five-second mark, the seal light went on. The crew was locked in.

Silver's heart thumped harder and faster. He had a sudden urge to be on the *D*, to be *doing* something other than standing around on a cold floor with his hands in his deep pockets.

He looked at the clock on the control panel. In thirty seconds the *D* would be lowered into the water. The towline connector locked on command, a screw-top attachment that resembled the open-faced cap used to hold a nipple to a baby bottle.

Angela took a sharp breath. Now she sought out Silver's hand.

"You okay?" he asked.

"Nope. But I wouldn't trade it for anything."

He knew what she meant. There were fifteen seconds to go. Dr. Ogden had his hands on the wheel. He was the only one wearing a headset. He did not need to hear anything except Dr. Carr telling him to move the *Abby*. He did not *want* to hear anything except that all-important command.

The last fifty seconds had passed slowly. Silver had imagined each person's activity, just as they'd rehearsed it on the mock-up at the Ant Hill. The pace changed as the counter hit ten seconds. Time seemed to speed up. The *Tempest D* was virtually cleared to go.

There was no sense of history. None at all. He knew then

what the men on the mural back at Kings Bay had experienced when they'd pushed the envelope.

Pride.

Pride that closed his throat and blurred his eyes with tears as men, not legends, put their fragile lives where their vision was.

EIGHT

Weddell Sea

"We have a target!"

Senior Captain Chien was at the desk in his stateroom. The intercom was on and he was listening to the activity in the control room. The voice belonged to the sonar operator. Captain Biao acknowledged but said nothing more.

Senior Captain Chien did not like what the captain and Wu had planned. It was ingenious and daring, but also extremely dangerous. The action would not only push the tested thrust and maneuvering parameters of the Song-class vessel, it ignored the unpredictability factor. They had no way of knowing what the surface ship would do, or what it was deploying.

Chien had to decide what to do about it.

It was extremely difficult to be the ranking representative of the People's Liberation Navy. Chien's primary job was to assess the hardware and procedures, not to actually run the submarine. If he chose to do so—and he could—Chien would undermine the command structure for the duration of the mission. He also risked destroying the captain's career. Biao would be entitled to ask for a "personal tribunal," a hearing before three vice admirals. If they ruled in the majority that the captain had been "hindered without due consideration," it would effectively end the senior captain's career at sea. To avoid any confrontations, captains typically informed the senior captain of a change in mission parameters. It was an oblique way of asking permission before giving an order. If the senior officer objected, there were ways of letting the captain know.

Biao had not presented this option to Chien.

Perhaps Biao believed in what he was doing. He might have gotten caught up in their guest's enthusiasm for the mission. One of the mottos at the naval base was "A good officer assumes the noble commitments of his comrades-in-arms." A successful reconnaissance of the American vessel would also reflect well on Captain Biao. Or perhaps this was something even simpler. Biao may have felt that by dining with Wu, Senior Captain Chien had created an exclusive and exclusionary rapport with him. This might be Biao's way of creating his own bond with the agent, leaving Chien on the outside and making sure the crew knew it.

Chien could take the slight. The question at the moment was not face. It was the security of the submarine.

Chien rose. Though Wu had the right to order the mission forward, the senior captain would express his doubts. To Wu, not to the captain. That would give the captain the opportunity to side with whomever he chose. If he sided with Chien, the officers could be brought before a "mandatory tribunal," a panel of vice admirals who were guided by articles that effectively pursued the charge of treason. Even so, if Biao joined Chien, things would be extremely difficult for the Guoanbu operative. The crew could not take orders from a civilian.

The senior captain left his stateroom and walked quickly to the control room. He maneuvered confidently through the dark, narrow passageways. He knew when to duck where pipes crossed widthwise, or gauges projected significantly from the hull. Chien had walked the corridors often. Away from men, in hidden corners where no one looked or listened.

When Chien arrived, Captain Biao and Wu Lin Kit were shoulder to shoulder behind Sublt. Tsui Yen, the sonar operator.

". . . it appears to be an oblong shape," the young *zhong wei* was saying.

"How long until full deployment?" Biao asked.

"We have another two minutes or so, sir."

"Wu Lin Kit, may I speak with you?" Senior Captain Chien said.

The men had not heard him arrive.

"Senior captain present!" Biao declared, alerting the dozen men who were bent over screens and gauges in the semicircular command center. The crewmen stopped what they were doing and saluted. Chien snapped off a general salute. His eyes remained on Wu.

"Might it wait?" Wu asked.

That told Chien everything he needed to know. Wu intended to proceed whatever the senior captain said.

"It cannot wait," Chien said. "Your plan concerns me."

"It was Captain Biao's plan," Wu pointed out.

"I know. It has his courage."

"Sirs!" Sublieutenant Tsui interrupted. "The deployment appears to be a miniature submarine. I do not recognize the outline configuration."

Wu regarded Chien. The operative seemed unpressured, confident. "We need intelligence about the American mission. The captain's plan appears to be the best way to get it, and this may be the only chance we have."

"It is perhaps the only chance to get information instantly. A more patient approach may get us more."

"Or it may cost us a fleeting moment of opportunity," Wu replied.

The senior captain felt himself being maneuvered less by the needs of the Guoanbu than by thousands of years of Chinese military history. It was the eternal question: What matters more, the mission or the personnel?

"No vessel comes this far to conduct one test," Chien said. "There is no risk to us merely observing the first trial. Indeed, there will be data to be gained from that."

"Senior Captain, I respect your view. But something may go wrong with the test. We may not get a second look. That is a risk we cannot afford."

Chien finally looked at Biao. The captain was in combat simulation mode, alert and engaged. But was that of his own choice? The two senior officers had left the command center to discuss the objective.

"Captain, have you decided which risk is greater?" Chien was careful to ask in a way that would force Biao to commit.

"Senior Captain Chien, we have been ordered to support Wu Lin Kit. He has set us a task and I am obligated to carry it out."

"That was not the question, Captain." An abstention would be a victory for Wu Lin Kit. Biao would still be obligated to convey his orders. "I ask it again, and trust you understand why I do so?"

"Yes, sir. And I believe that the action, as charted, is a fitting and appropriate first encounter for the *Destiny*."

Captain Biao had not answered the question directly, but he had answered it decisively. In a strong voice, with passion in his eyes and determination in his posture. Further, he had done so in military rather than intelligence terms. In a way the crew would understand.

"I wish you success," Chien said.

Nodding formally to both men at once, the senior captain left the command center. Biao announced his departure. Chien did not see the salutes. He did not feel they were merited. Whether or not the captain had intended to do so, he had shamed Chien by presenting the mission as a matter of naval pride.

The senior captain had known that presenting his concerns carried danger for himself. His judgment had been openly questioned, his honor diminished.

Even so, as he returned to his stateroom, Chien hoped that he was wrong.

NINE

Weddell Sea

Taking the *D* for a swim was far different from any of the tests. Captain Colon was reminded of this as they reached count-down zero and did their "Slim Pickens." The unofficial desig-nation was a whistle-past-the-graveyard tribute to the actor who had ridden an atomic bomb from the belly of the B-52 in the movie *Dr. Strangelove*. It signified the beginning of a haz-ardous journey.

A sailor, a pilot, a test driver, or a fill-in-the-blank could run as many simulations as possible. He could try the seat and con-trols, learn the computers and the comm system, work in full-sized bells-and-whistles mock-ups in big saltwater tanks or with computer-generated sonar images. But until it was all put together, until the real thing took flight or hit the road or got wet, it was all just a big dress rehearsal.

Captain Colon began to feel the difference as the two large booms lowered the *D* into the sea. The submarine vibrated sub-tly. Everyone felt it; this baby was snug. The *D* had three com-partments. The control room was forward; the engine room and escape tower were amidships; and the supercavitation drive was aft. A single corridor with a six-foot ceiling ran down the center of the submarine, with a ribbed hard-rubber floor below to pre-vent slipping, and a black, foamlike polymer above and on projecting handles, pipes, and levers to prevent head-banging in case there were "burps." These had occurred infrequently during simulations, but they did occur: minor, fraction-of-a-second fluctuations in the integrity of the air pocket, which caused the submarine to kick to one side or another, up or down, or at an angle, until the computer could strengthen the weakened area and stabilize the ship. The burps were a problem they'd have to solve before a future Tempest-class submarine could carry torpedoes. Dr. Davies had suspected the problem was due to sudden fluctuations in water temperature. They hoped to get a clearer reading on that in water where the variations would be more dramatic: On day two, the *Abby* would be hosing jets of hot water in the path of the *D* to see how she reacted.

The problem of head-bumping was exacerbated by the *D*'s sloping interior walls, reflecting the streamlined design of the exterior. It was impossible to stand upright anywhere except in the narrow central corridor.

The sound and vibration were noticeably muted when the submarine touched the water. That made the water feel closer, heightened the feeling that you were in a narrow bucket in a big, icy sea. The crew did not react but remained focused on their instruments. Each of the six members was strapped in his bucket seat, arrayed in a sharp U-shape around the interior nose of the submarine. Both the interior lights and the readouts were dim by design. Because everyone was sitting hip to hip, one could not afford to be distracted by activity at the other stations. The crew members were watching their monitors, listening to Kings Bay over headsets, answering questions about readings and equipment when asked. The captain was seated inside the U, with nothing in front of him but submarine. He had a pair of wireless headphones that would allow him to sit or walk, whichever he preferred. A wrist-worn remote let him access the conversation at any station or combination of stations.

Colon felt the temperature climb slightly as they went in the water. He didn't need a computer to tell him the climate controls were on-line. It would have been a very short trip if they weren't. According to the moored thermometers the *Abby* had left behind on its previous voyage, the mean temperature in the water was twenty-eight degrees Fahrenheit. That was near the surface, where the sun's rays could give it a good warming during the day. At one hundred meters down, which would be their deepest penetration today, the sea was a lot colder.

When the *D* was fully submerged—though not yet clear of the open doors of the hold—the release process went to a scheduled hold as control shifted from the *Abby* to the *D*. This was the final planned abort window, the last time they could be pulled inside with a minimum of fuss. By the time the three-minute transfer was over, the booms would be withdrawn and the *D* would be functioning on its own—albeit tethered to the *Abby* by the towline.

Colon sat in his vinyl-covered swivel seat, his elbows on the high rests, hands folded chin-high as he listened to the conversation between Dr. Carr and Lieutenant Michaelson, who was in charge of the switchover checklist. For the captain, listening to each of the sixty-six items was like having to swallow an aspirin without water, one every 2.07 seconds.

"Aft starboard stabilizer?" Carr asked.

"Go," Michaelson replied.

"Ballast control?"

"Go."

All it would take to scrub the mission was a single missed "go." But the engineers and electronics experts at Kings Bay had done their jobs well. There were sixty-six go's.

The *D* "hovered" below the *Abby* by distributing ballast through the hull capillaries. Colon removed one of the earphones so he could listen as the booms were withdrawn. It wasn't so much that he wanted to hear the release of the *D*. He was listening for any knocks or pings that didn't sound right. Once they started the engines, both conventional and then supercavitation, that would be all they heard.

When the arms had retreated, a world of audio color moved in. The sea transmitted sound, and every clang on the *Abby*, even the waves slopping up into the hold, could be heard. Inside the control room the gentle squeaks of the chairs, the hard-edged clicks of the few analog dials, and especially the monotone voices of the personnel—all were distinct and amplified.

"Forward sonar array receiving an all-clear," said Lt. (j.g.) Catherine Bain.

"Thank you," Colon replied.

The spherical sonar, housed in the nose, was a ten-foot-diameter orb that had both active and passive capabilities, for echo ranging or listening. The seventy-five thousand watts of radiated power extended twelve feet forward during supercavitation drive, piercing the air bubble and creating the only liquid-drag surface. The sonar gave the crew a great deal of detail about what lay ahead. At the speeds they would be traveling, long-distance imaging was essential.

"Ballast tanks at absolute neutral buoyancy," said Ens. Jonathan Walters, who was in charge of the ballast and trim tanks. The latter were responsible for maintaining the ship's balance.

"Very good, Ensign."

The control room was absolutely quiet for a moment as they waited for the telltale clack that meant the booms were locked in place inside the hold. It came, followed a moment later by confirmation from the bridge of the *Abby*. Colon put the headphones back just in time to hear Dr. Carr acknowledge that the *D* was free-floating at the end of the tether.

"Captain Colon, you are in command of the *D*," Carr added. "Proceed according to the mission plan and parameters."

Hearing Carr pass along the A-OK was a blowtorch on the back of Colon's neck. "We copy, Kings Bay."

What the captain wanted to say was *Up yours, Mike, and the next time I see your sorry pan, I'm gonna club it hard with the ass end of a cue stick and then dump you in an alley where you can wake up with a cat licking your round fucking cheek.*

"Lieutenant Michaelson, what is the payout on our towline?" Colon asked suddenly.

"Twenty-three feet and on hold, five of that in the water."

"*Abby?* Give me thirty-five feet of slack," Colon said. "We'll descend when the deployment is complete."

"Hold, *Abby*," Carr said.

"What's the problem, Ant Hill?" Colon asked.

"Captain, that extension will increase the FSA by more than thirty percent," Carr informed him after a few moments.

"For two minutes, max," Colon said. The freeze-surface area referred to any unprotected material that was exposed to below-freezing temperatures. The submarine was warmed by internal heat. The cable was not. It would become stiffer as the seconds passed. Though the cable was tested for temperatures down to twenty below, the more towline surface that was underwater, the more the cable would be cooled. That would create an effect similar to windchill along the entire length.

"We don't need to take that risk," Carr said. "The cable will deploy at the same pace as the *D* to a depth of fifty feet. There is no reason to change that."

"It feels too tight," Colon said. "We have no room to maneuver if the *D* shows any instability."

"Is there a sign of instability?"

"No—"

"Define 'feels too tight,' " Carr said.

"Dammit, I can't," the captain said. "It just does."

"Captain, please proceed as planned. Acknowledge."

"Acknowledged," Colon replied through his teeth. That one burned him a lot more than *We copy, Kings Bay*. The extra seven feet of towline would only be a problem if the spool jammed: After fifteen minutes the FSA would cause the line to begin to stiffen and possibly to crack. But even if that did happen, the *Abby* could simply release the connector. The *D* would still be floating close enough to the hold for the arms to collect it—just as they'd do if the towline were still attached. The frustrating thing was, Colon knew this restriction was in there. It was one of those things that he didn't typically make room for in his head until he was in the situation, in the water. The kind of fine-tuning that, typically, he would have been free to change. But not while anal-boy was running the play-book.

Colon gave the order to submerge and deploy cable, both on the same schedule. As the captain did so, he wondered how much the extra slack really mattered and how much he had been squirming against Carr's control.

The submarine began to descend. A ballast descent was like sitting inside an inner tube that was slowly filling with cement. The crew could feel the displacement taking place around them, and pressure from the added volume of water pushing down and in on all sides. Colon could even feel the slight tug of the towline. At least, he believed he could.

"Full stop," Colon said.

"What's the problem?" Carr asked.

"I need more towline," Colon said.

"Why?" Carr asked patiently.

Because having you run this mission is pissing me off and that's not going away. "I'm feeling forward drag." That was true, though Colon could live with that if he had to.

"The instruments read normal," Carr replied.

"The instruments don't have my decade-plus in submarines," Colon protested. "Just give me five feet. I can live with that." The captain had "given" two feet off the original seven and he hoped Carr would do likewise. That was all Colon wanted. A little give in the line and some give from Carr.

Throughout the exchange the bridge of the *Abby* had remained silent. It was not the rear admiral's way to interfere. Colon wondered if the Ant Hill would request his input.

They did not.

"Take your full seven feet, Captain," Carr said. "But the sim we're running says you should descend while it plays out. That will generate extra heat."

Colon felt the weight of Mike Carr slip away. "We copy, Kings Bay, and thank you."

"*Abby* control, increase speed of spool to give seven feet more by a depth of twenty-five feet."

The engineers in the hold acknowledged the order. Colon gave the order to resume descent. The submarine began dropping at fifteen meters a minute. Lieutenant Michaelson announced the descent in two-meter increments. Colon smiled. He felt like a king. He wondered if Stone was pleased or pissed by the showdown.

"Ten meters," Michaelson announced.

Probably pissed, Colon decided. Stone had to know the cable wasn't that big a deal and why the captain was making it one.

"Twelve meters."

"Captain!" Lieutenant Junior Grade Bain shouted from the sonar station. "We've got—something."

"Can you be more specific?" Colon asked.

"Abby's moored thermometers are giving us a rapid temperature rise. Switching to thermal . . . something warm coming from—"

That was all she got to say before she was heaved from her seat.

TEN

Weddell Sea

The rear admiral had been getting ready to give Captain Colon the "down, boy" order when Dr. Carr had come back with his capitulation. A valid one, Silver thought, that gave the captain what he wanted without compromising security. What was interesting was that Carr had obviously begun running a sim when Colon had first made his request. Otherwise, he would not have had the information when the captain came back at him. It made Silver proud.

But only for a moment.

A hard shudder shot through the *Abby*, followed by a loud crack and a series of sharp, splintering snaps, like a string of firecrackers. A moment later sound and chaos was everywhere as the floor rushed up at them and the windows on all four sides of the bridge shattered, the glass blown in and the frames crushed from bottom toward the top. Silver was thrown hard to his left side, against the wall, then flung to his right as he was hit with a sideward-moving spray of water. The geyser was so forceful that it pinned him to the wall and sent the *Abby* rolling to port. An instant later water was storming at him from all directions. Silver lost his bearings as the flood knocked him, his bridge mates, and pieces of ship about the cabin. Wood, metal, and even pieces of ice pounded the rear admiral as he wrapped his head in his arms to protect it. Suddenly, the maelstrom

ended with a loud, pouring retreat. Razor-edged cold replaced
the force of the water. A moment later, with a thumping jerk,
the ship settled at an angle. Silver was standing on a surface
formed by a wall meeting the ceiling. One foot was on each, his
back against another surface—the floor, he suspected, since the
base of the helm control was just above his head. He knew that
by feel, not sight, since the cabin was dark. The sounds were no
longer overpowering. There was only creaking and groaning
and the once-more distant sounds of the sea.

When Silver was sure he was secure, he wiped the cold,
dripping water from his face and looked ahead. Through what
used to be the roof of the bridge. His first numb thought was
that the *D* had exploded, but he didn't see any oil fires burning.
Silver tried to call out but only managed to cough up seawater.

"Who's there?" Angela asked from the dark.

"Silver," he said.

"Silver."

"Yes."

"Dr. Ogden?" she called, a desperate quality to her voice.
When he didn't answer, she called his name again, then yelled it.

"Angela, save your energy," Silver said.

"Dr. Ogden? Is that you?"

"No," Silver said.

It sounded as if Angela was below and ahead. Silver lowered
himself slowly to a crouching position. After feeling around
and making sure the floor—the wall, actually—was secure, he
crept ahead. He felt damp clothes and poked at them.

"Angela, is that you?"

"Yes."

"Hold my hand," he said. "I'll see if I can find Dr. Ogden."

She didn't take his hand, didn't move. He suspected she was
suffering from posttraumatic shock. That was bad, but it was
preferable to panic. He walked his fingers down her sleeve to
her hand and clasped it. It was unresponsive. He held on anyway. With the other hand he felt further. He found nothing.

It was bitterly cold as the wind sliced through the window
frames and the hole in the roof. His cheeks stung and the wet
parka he had on was already beginning to stiffen around him.

"He's not here," Silver said after completing his sweep of the area.

"Where is he?"

"I don't know."

"What happened?" Angela asked.

"Something must have hit us," Silver said. "Is there a flashlight in here?"

"The equipment locker."

"Where is that?"

"I don't know."

"Usually," he said.

"Beneath the radio."

"I'm going to try to find it," Silver said. "You stay where you are."

The rear admiral tentatively released Angela's hand. It dropped. She wouldn't be going anywhere.

Silver started moving around again, touching ahead, left, and right with both hands. A stack of debris was in a V-shaped crevasse where the roof met two walls. It was mostly wood and glass. There was a headset as well; this was all that remained of the radio. There was nothing that felt like a chest or flashlight.

"Do you think it was the *D* that hit us?" Angela asked.

"No," Silver said. "To rise that quickly they would have had to blow ballast. We would have felt that and it would have taken them two or three seconds to rise. Besides, Lieutenant Bain said something was coming at them."

"Did she? Maybe it was an ice floe or a whale."

"Maybe," he said, though he doubted that as well. It hadn't shown up on the sonar of the *D* but on the temperature buoys.

The groaning grew louder for a moment and then the *Abby* dropped, like an elevator. Neither of them screamed; they were too scared. The vessel fell several feet and then stopped just as suddenly. When it did, there was a crunching sound, like a boot in wet snow.

"Are we sinking?"

"Not just yet," Silver said. He was shivering from the cold and fear. He relaxed his body to soften the trembling. "I think we're *on* something."

"Why do you say that?"

"Because of the way we just stopped," he said. "We're badly damaged and listing but we're not sinking."

"Why didn't the emergency lights come on?"

"I don't know," Silver replied.

"The battery must be dead."

Or at the bottom of the sea, Silver thought. Along with who knew how much of the rest of the *Abby.*

Silver felt something to his left and stopped. A small, ragged section of shelf was swinging from a shattered section of wall. Held there by a twisted bracket, the shelf was knocking against something below it. Silver followed the jagged wood down to what felt like a tool chest. He popped the side latches. He felt inside and found the flashlight. That anything should make him smile right now was improbable. But that did. He removed it from the C-clasp that held it and pressed the switch.

Angela cried out as the big white orb hit her in the eyes.

"I'm sorry," Silver said.

Angela raised her forearm to shield her eyes. The statuesque scientist was bent nearly in two at the waist, folded into what used to be the junction of the ceiling and forward wall. He didn't see any blood.

"Can you move your arms and legs?" he asked.

Still blocking the light, she wriggled them all at once.

"Good." Silver turned the light on himself. "Do you see any wounds on me, any blood?"

She lowered her arm. And screamed.

"What's wrong?" Silver yelled.

"Behind you!"

Silver swung the light around. The bridge had been knocked almost entirely loose from the deck of the ship. And just outside the remains of the cabin was the deck of the *Abby.* It had a huge hole, as if it had been blown out. But no smoke was coming from it, not even a wisp, reinforcing the idea of an impact rather than a blast. Silver moved toward that open side of the bridge. The wind was coming from behind so it wasn't as cold facing this way. He was doing a crustacean-style walk to give himself the traction of his soles. Crouched and waddling from leg to leg, he moved along the angled surface. Fortunately, he only needed to cover three or four meters. Gripping the flashlight tightly, he shined it into the hole in the deck.

"What do you see?" Angela asked. "What happened?"

He didn't have the heart to tell her. For a long moment he also didn't have the voice.

"What *is* it?" she pressed.

"Just a moment." Silver wasn't sure she had heard over the howling wind. The words had trouble clearing his clogged throat.

The first thing the rear admiral saw, directly to his left, was Dr. Ogden. The scientist was suspended from the bridge-level deck. He was quite dead. His hand was impaled backward on a sharp horizontal section of flooring. He was swinging slowly over the opening in the deck. His chest was red and flattened. When the bridge was upended, Ogden must have fallen out but not onto the deck and onto what had come *through* the deck. Onto what had pushed him back upward, against the snapped flooring, simultaneously crushing his chest.

Onto the other thing Silver saw.

The charcoal-black nose of a submarine was visible through the open cargo doors of the *Abby*. It was either a Russian or a Chinese boat, he couldn't tell which. But it had their distinctive delta-shaped forward diving planes. He felt sick as he looked down. Apparently the towline from the *Abby* was draped across the submarine. Part of the cable ran along the side of the submarine and back through the hole in the lower deck.

One thing Silver could tell, however, was that most of the sounds of destruction he heard were coming from inside the hole, from the shattered lower hull of the *Abby*. From the point where the submarine had broken through. A submarine that was slowly sinking.

When it did, the *Abby* wouldn't stay afloat more than a minute.

ELEVEN

Weddell Sea

The *Destiny* had accelerated more quickly than Wu Lin Kit had expected.

It stopped the same way.

The submarine had started slowly, like a bus pulling from a stop, even growling slightly as it began its sharply angled ascent. But the *Destiny* had quickly gained speed as it raced toward its target. Wu held on to a pair of the vertical handles at the sides of various consoles to keep from slipping backward. He watched the sonar image as the vessel climbed, studying the constantly changing silhouette that appeared on the screen.

The digitally recorded images could very well get Wu the information he had come for. He was hopeful, then excited, as the submarine began to gain speed. The rubber floor helped him stand as he leaned into the climb. Captain Biao was standing to Wu's left, his hands folded against the small of his back. His balance was impressive. Wu was about to release the handles himself when there was a roar so loud Wu only heard the first moment of it. His ears went blank as he was simultaneously lifted parallel to the floor, as though he were flying. He held the handles for an instant before he flew headfirst toward the command console. Wu struck a crewman, who was the last thing Wu saw as the lights went out. The intelligence operative dropped back on the floor as the *Destiny* swerved wildly and climbed, sending him tumbling back against a chair support. Someone landed on him, then someone hit them both. Wu felt each hard, dull hit. Fortunately, he had been able to tighten his muscles from shoulders to thighs, the way he did in martial arts, mitigating the blows. Finally, the submarine stopped moving. Wu was lying on his stomach, lengthwise, bent around a curved metal surface. The stuffiness in his ears passed quickly as the volume rose on loud ringing. He thought, at first, it was inside his head. Then he realized it was an external alarm. Wu squinted and began to notice spots of white light here and there. Emergency lights, no doubt. He realized then that he was looking toward the stern; looking *down* toward the stern. The submarine had stopped at a steep angle, roughly forty-five degrees.

The Guoanbu operative put his hand underneath him. The metal was highly polished. It could be the periscope base. Wu brought his other arm around and tentatively flexed his fingers. He was lucky. Neither hand nor arm was broken. He turned over slowly so his back was on the metal.

Along the base of the console were lights. These were little more than glowing rectangles, and he realized that they weren't electric at all. They were phosphorescent strips. They showed where things were but did not provide any useful illumination.

"We hit something."

The voice was ahead and to his left. It was soft, buried in the alarm. Wu crawled toward him. He bumped up against him, felt for his face, and found his ear. He leaned close.

"What did we hit?" Wu said directly into his ear.

"Who is there?"

"It's Wu, sir."

"Where is the captain?"

"I don't know." Wu recognized the voice now. It belonged to Sublt. Tsui Yen. The sonar operator was panting hard and fast. Wu wondered if he was hurt. Not that he could do anything about it. "Do you have any idea what we hit?"

"No," the young man said. "We were clear of the target."

"What about that alarm?" Wu asked. "What does it mean?"

Suddenly, the ringing stopped.

"Fire," the man said. "Someone must have extinguished it."

The fire must have been far to the stern, since Wu didn't smell smoke. The extinguishing told Wu that at least someone was active deeper in the *Destiny*. And that whatever had happened, there was no flooding.

"Are you all right?" the young sublieutenant asked.

"Yes. You?"

"I can't feel my left arm," the young man said.

Wu reached over and lifted it gingerly. The man screamed.

"I'll try to help you," Wu said. "First tell me: If the lights are off, does that mean air circulation has ceased?"

"Put your hand against the vent."

"Where is it?"

"Above my station. Look for the triangular lights."

Wu patted the man on his right arm, then looked around for the triangles. He saw them and crept ahead. Now that the alarm had stopped, he heard groans from all around, mostly toward the stern. Crewmen must have been flung in that direction.

It was difficult crawling up the floor. Wu finally turned and did it backward, scooting along on his seat and pushing off with his heels. The back of Yen's chair was angled upward. When it was within reach, Wu turned and used it to pull himself toward the console. Hugging the chair back with his left arm he felt ahead with his right. His fingers found the air vent. The two silk ribbons that showed air was circulating hung limp in the darkness. He pressed his palm to the slats of the vent. It was like exhaling into his hand. There was nothing but the whisper of still, hot air. It was wafting out rather than being blown.

"Nothing," Wu said.

"We may be able to do something about that," the young man said. "The compressors are located in the stern. Whatever we hit was forward. The collision may have damaged the electronics up here."

"Then we should go back there." Wu glanced in that direction. Strips of phosphorescent material were on the floor. "I assume the markers will lead us there?"

"Yes," Yen said.

"Then let's go."

Wu returned to the young man's side. The operative put his left arm around Yen's chest, under his arm, then hung the crewman's good arm around his neck. Rising, Wu bent backward at the waist for balance as the men made their way through the command center.

"What could have happened?" Wu asked. "What was there that we didn't see?"

"I don't know, sir," Yen answered. "We should probably conserve breath."

The seaman was right. The air was quickly growing stuffy. Wu wondered about that. He also wondered whether they had struck the underwater object or the carrier vessel.

Just then, the submarine began to slide—this time, without the reassuring growl of the engines. Wu lost Yen and finally his balance as the *Destiny* slipped toward its stern, simultaneously rotating about its horizontal axis with a high, disturbing scream.

TWELVE

Weddell Sea

Senior Captain Chien had not quite reached his stateroom when the world turned over.

He heard, then felt, the change in attitude when the *Destiny* set off on its mission. He heard the screws turn hard, the ship vibrate and move forward, and the floor begin to slope. He continued walking aft along the downward-sloping corridor. He had been walking almost on his toes when, unexpectedly, he felt the submarine turn hard to port and tilt nearly ninety degrees. Chien was hurled against a wall, hurting his upper arm and spraining his neck from a rough snap. Because the corridor was extremely narrow he did not fall. He reached behind him, grabbed a bracket that held a fire extinguisher, and waited. The submarine did not have that kind of turning capability. He had not felt a collision and there wasn't a current on earth that could simply divert them that way. Not without also crushing them. Even an underwater earthquake would not have produced that kind of shock wave.

The submarine was still moving upward. An instant later it struck something more solid. That rocked Chien back but he managed to hold on, even as the all the lights went out and a fire alarm sounded.

The emergency lights have failed, the senior captain thought as he sniffed the air, searching for the fire. For that kind of catastrophic failure to occur, the main engine as well as the two dedicated battery compartments had to have been disabled. A forward impact would have accomplished all of that.

Chien heard coughing from farther aft. That was probably where the fire was—though he could not be certain there was only one. He faced forward for a moment. As far as he could tell, no smoke was coming from the command section. He would continue aft. Chien removed the fire extinguisher and started down the steeply sloping corridor. The fire extinguisher had a flashlight built into the hose anchor. He switched it on. The walls felt cool, which was good. The fire could not be too severe or the metal would already be heating up.

Chien made his way toward the engineering section. He hoped that at least the emergency signal was working. The "gray radio" as it was called—nicknamed for the heavy metal-alloy box in which it was sealed—was located just above the forward trim tank. In a full-shutdown situation such as this, the gray box was ejected on a small torpedo-like jet. After several seconds flotation balloons would inflate. The device sent out two "condition red" satellite signals. One, a directed beacon, was relayed by satellite to the Chinese navy receiving station in Ningbo, south of Shanghai. The other, a scatter signal, went out across a broad range of frequencies. When a submarine went dead at sea, help from any quarter was welcomed. Not that there was much anyone could do, even if they were in the vicinity. If the air pumps on board the *Destiny* could not be restarted, the crew would suffocate within six or seven hours.

And we will lose our reason before that, he suspected.

The smoke and the silent, airless dark made the submarine seem as if it were alive and malevolent. The ship's systems were dead, yet the vessel still acted like a ghost, clawing at his eyes and throat while its passageways constricted him like a serpent. In all his years at sea Chien had never experienced anything so unwholesome, so frightening. For a sailor to die at sea was an honor. But to die in the belly of a fish—that was bad seamanship.

The senior captain reached the nuclear reactor compartment. The door did not operate with a wheel but opened and closed pneumatically, by pressing a panel to the right. If there was a reactor fire, the panel would not function. It opened. That was another good sign. Chien entered the dark chamber. He smelled the smoke now, tart but thin. The aft escape hatch was next, followed by the electrical switchboard compartment and the engine room. He knew the vessel by heart and felt his way through the reactor chamber. Chien encountered two men who must have been knocked unconscious in the collision. That was not surprising; there were a lot of low pipes and hard, exposed lead shielding on the walls. The senior captain stepped over the men.

As Chien exited the reactor room, he heard the distinctive puff of fire extinguishers. The switchboards were arranged in five rows perpendicular to the ship's hull. The sounds were coming from a forward grouping of switchboards, the ones that controlled the submarine's single propeller. The screw must have overheated trying, and failing, to drive the vessel forward immediately after impact.

"This is Senior Captain Chien. Are there any injuries?" he called out.

"Nothing serious, sir. Are you all right?"

"Yes."

Though the crew had put the fire out, smoke remained suspended low in the air. That was because the ventilators were not working.

Someone found another flashlight and turned it on. It was Lieutenant Mui, the officer in charge of propulsion systems.

"Sir, do you know what happened?" Mui asked.

"I do not," Chien replied. "Lieutenant, repairing the air circulation system is the top priority. How many engineers have you?"

"Three, sir. They were with me, doing maintenance on the clutch. The others are in their bunks or in the rec room."

In a full lights-out emergency, crewmen were supposed to remain wherever they were. That way, officers would be able to consult the duty roster to find whoever was needed.

"Get to work," Chien said. "I'm going forward. If I learn anything, I will send a runner with the information."

"Thank you, sir," Mui said.

Chien thanked the crew for their timely effort with the fire, then turned to go. He didn't take more than a few steps before the submarine tilted backward, throwing him against the others as it began sliding deeper into the sea.

After the initial jolt toward the stern, the *Destiny* dropped straight down. It was not moving at top speed, since ballast was in the tanks. But she was otherwise powerless and unable to stay afloat.

When Chien fell to the deck, he curled himself tight as possible and covered his head with his arms. In a free fall, anything might come loose, and the submarine might turn in any direction. The important thing was to be as healthy as possible when it stopped.

The *Destiny* wobbled from side to side and prow to stern as it descended. Chien was shifted around the narrow corridor, though the rubber flooring prevented him from being tossed hard. He heard sounds like a cello string being played, probably the structure of the submarine being tested by the descent. He heard that and the shouts of crewmen as they were tossed around the sinking ship.

Suddenly, there was a violent thump and Chien was literally lifted from the deck and dropped back down. The submarine had stopped. But it had not gone silent. A low groan came from the stern, followed by an abnormal submarine noise.

The sound of surging water.

THIRTEEN

Weddell Sea

Ernie Colon's first thought—his only thought as he was violently hurled against his harness—was that the supercavitation drive of the *D* had prematurely engaged. That would have accounted for the sudden surge. But the submarine hadn't gone forward or backward, it had spun off to the side. Even a one-jet firing would not produce that kind of effect.

The captain gripped the armrests as the *D* turned quickly in a clockwise direction. Then the submarine stopped suddenly, accompanied by a sound like that of a large branch snapping in a high wind. Everyone was pitched hard to port when the vessel stopped.

The disturbance took three or four seconds, after which the *D* settled back on a relatively even keel. The lights were on and all of the crew were still harnessed in their seats. They were probably shaken and some of them bloodied where foreheads, chins, and cheeks had struck the angled wall. But they were upright and moving. Colon's headset had been flipped from his head. He found it hanging alongside his chair. It was still plugged into the armrest.

"Status report," Colon said.

Lieutenant Michaelson ignored a bloody right palm. He had probably torn it on a console projection.

"All systems are on-line," he said.

Colon slipped the headset back on. "Ant Hill, are you there?"

"We are," Dr. Carr said.

"Abby?" Colon said.

There was no response.

"Repeat, *Abby.* Dr. Albertson, come in. Rear Admiral, come in."

Still nothing.

"What happened?" Carr asked. "Our instruments are showing the *D* has made a nearly complete horizontal turn along with a five-meter rise."

"Ant Hill, have you got the *Abby*?" Colon asked.

"No. Captain, what happened?"

The scientist's voice was even, unexcited. Colon was glad to hear that. It was too early for the captain to know how he himself felt.

"We have no idea," Colon said. "We saw something approaching, but we didn't feel an impact and the engines didn't light. All we know is that we were kicked around for about four seconds."

"Sir, sonar is picking up a large mass to starboard," said Lieutenant Junior Grade Bain.

"Specifics?" Colon snapped.

"Working on that."

"Rockford, ramjet report."

Lt. (j.g.) Wayne Rockford was the man with his foot on the pedal of the supercavitation drive. He was sitting on the port side, to Colon's left. The black-haired young man was looking at his controls, not at the captain, waiting for a command.

"The jets didn't do this. They're silent," Rockford said.

"Bain?"

"Still working, sir," she said.

Colon knew she was. He just wanted to make sure she worked faster. During combat or any kind of in-field trauma, it was important to keep the survivors from slipping into a "woe is us" mind-set.

"Sir, the computer's running a database search of the visible dimensions," Bain said. "It looks like a submarine out there."

"Wouldn't you have seen them?"

"We should have."

"Not if they were running at a minimum of fifteen knots and came at you between sweeps, from below," Carr said. "We just ran a sim."

"Can you narrow the ID for me?" Colon asked. "Who's out there?"

"Checking," Bain said. "It looks like—"

Bain fell silent as something screeched outside the hull, on the starboard side of the nose. It sounded as though someone were running a fork across a clean plate, perhaps the other submarine scraping his hull. Colon suddenly had no interest in finding out what was there. He swiveled his chair to port to where helmsman Lt. (j.g.) Jim Withers was seated.

"Mr. Withers, ready standard drive," Colon said.

"Yes, sir."

"What are you going to do?" Carr asked.

"Get away from whatever is ahead of us," Colon reported.

Withers tapped the series of small, flat panels that brought the two turboelectric screws on-line.

"Sir, the object is moving!" Bain reported. "And there's another object coming into view."

"Toward us?"

"Yes, sir. But . . . from above!" she said, her voice sounding pale.

The scraping sound continued. Colon listened as the propeller shafts began to turn. In a larger submarine the noise would not be as noticeable as it was in the *Tempest D*. There were no clanks or dings. The captain was relieved. That meant they hadn't been dented in the apparent collision or subsequent spin.

Just then the *D* lurched backward. It stopped suddenly, then angled toward the stern.

"Mr. Walters?" Colon said.

"Sir, ballast tanks registering normal," said the ensign. "That wasn't us. We're being *pulled* down."

"Flooding?"

"Negative," Lieutenant Michaelson said. He was glancing at

the small monitor that tracked electric pulses running through the hull. A break in the circuits would suggest a leak. "Our weight is unchanged, hull is intact."

"Speed, Mr. Withers?" Colon asked.

"Screws nearly at full, sir."

"Lieutenant Michaelson, jettison towline," Colon ordered.

The lieutenant turned his chair to the button that released the cable. He pushed it. Captain Colon listened for the ping that would tell him the disengage function had been completed.

It never came.

"What happened?" Colon demanded.

"Sir, automatic tow release inoperative." Michaelson undid his harness and dropped to the deck. "Going manual."

Michaelson opened a small panel under his station. He took a foot-long socket wrench from a hook inside the door and reached into the compartment. It was an awkward reach but he managed to get the socket on the nut that held the towline plate to the nose. He gave it a hard turn. Nothing moved. He tried again, grunting through it. The nut still refused to give.

"It's jammed, Captain!" Michaelson shouted from the compartment. "It may have been dented. I can fix it, but that will take time."

That wasn't good. They couldn't remove the tow-plate itself without letting in the sea.

"Start on that, Lieutenant. Are we sure the cable is still attached?" Colon asked.

Bain glanced over at Michaelson's station. "The connector light is red," the lieutenant junior grade told the captain.

That wasn't good either. It meant they were still getting current from the battery pack in the spool control on board *Abby*. As with the hull, current flow was the means for determining for certain that the cable had been released.

The *D* continued its slow slide backward.

"Sir, we're down seven meters from post-incident position," Ensign Walters informed him.

"Captain, the submarine image is exiting sonar range from the bottom and the second object is growing larger from the top," Bain said.

"Identify," Colon said.

"It's still too far to determine."

Something knocked the top of the hull. It was followed by a second and then a third strike.

"Sonar shows material dropping *from* the second object. Sir—"

"Yes?" Colon pressed.

"That could be the *Abby*. The hold was open. Debris may be falling through."

"Mr. Walters, drop forward ballast to level us off," Colon said.

"Aye, sir."

The nose of the *D* began to drop. But only for a moment. Something stopped them with a jerk.

"Hold ballast," Colon said.

"The cable," Michaelson said suddenly.

"What, Lieutenant?" Colon asked.

Michaelson slid from the compartment. "Sir, I felt it in here. The towline just pulled on us. The whole attachment was jolted pretty hard."

There were several additional bangs on the hull.

"Sir, second object is dropping more debris," Lieutenant Junior Grade Bain said. "Some of it several meters large—"

Another jolting tug interrupted her, this one harder than the others. The *D* began to dive slowly.

"First object back on sonar," Bain said.

"We're descending at one point two meters a second," Withers said.

"That's the same rate as the object," Bain said. "Sir, it's pulling us down."

That thought had just occurred to Colon.

"Second object no longer visible," Bain continued. "Debris field descending, one very large object also dropping."

"Lieutenant Michaelson, are we still getting a red light down there?" Colon asked.

"Yes, sir."

"Mr. Withers, drop ballast to match the speed of descent. I don't want extra strain on that forward plate."

"Aye, sir."

"The big one is the spool," Colon muttered. *The fucking spool* was implied by the captain's tone.

"What do you mean?" Carr pressed.

"The large object that just entered the water," Colon told him. "I'm betting that something did strike the *Abby*, probably a submarine, and tore the towline spool loose. It's going to pull us down."

"Can't you eject it?" Carr asked.

"The join nozzle is jammed," Colon said. "Something must have twisted the cable and bent the connecting bolts." He thought for a moment. As he did, he felt sick. "I'll bet that's it."

"What?" Carr said.

"Sir, we're at twenty-five meters and picking up speed!" Withers told him.

"What's our speed?"

"Three knots and climbing."

"Bearing?"

"Northwest," Withers replied.

"Dr. Carr, what's the depth in that direction?"

"We're working it," Carr said. "You're heading toward the coast—we make the bottom at about seventy meters."

"Mr. Withers, give me minimum reverse," Colon said. "Let's see if we can slow ourselves down."

"Yes, sir."

"Lieutenant, watch that towline plate."

Michaelson acknowledged. Colon listened as the screws powered up slightly. He could feel at once that there was no change.

"Descending at four knots and rising," Withers reported.

"Captain, a moment ago you said you had an insight into what happened," Carr said.

"Yeah. The harpoon effect. The reason reverse engines didn't do squat for us."

"I'm not familiar with that term."

"When a whaler threw a harpoon without realizing there was something snagged on the line, usually another man's leg, the whale would submerge and pull that 'something' down," Colon told him.

"You're saying this other object is dragging you."

"It would explain why we can't bootstrap ourselves."

There was a short silence.

"Captain, the DOD satellite monitor just picked up an emergency beacon from your position," Carr said. "A Chinese signature."

"What kind of beacon?"

"SOS. It's an automated signal."

"Meaning they probably took it on the chin, worse than we did, and their systems are dead," Colon said.

"Sir, the sonar profile fits the Russian Romeo-class submarine," Bain said.

"Bingo," Colon said. "The Chinese have been buying Romeos and refitting them with their own upgrades."

The captain now knew exactly how much dead weight was pulling them down: 31,750 kilos. He also had a good idea what was keeping the two vessels together. The fucking towline. That would explain the pressure on the nose plate. There was just one thing he didn't know.

What they were going to do about it.

FOURTEEN

Weddell Sea

Rear Admiral Silver backed from the shattered bridge onto the deck.

The wind was mercifully calm as he hopped from what was left of the cabin onto the slightly buckled, sloping foredeck. He held the flashlight in his left hand as he extended his right arm for balance. He walked on the balls of his cold feet as he ascended the slanting vessel. It was ironic. The DOD had selected this spot because no scientific stations were nearby, no one who might hear their radio communications or register the punch of the supercavitation drive. That could also doom anyone from the ships who did manage to get to shore. A rescue party couldn't just get in a sled and shoot out to rescue them.

The officer tried not to think about that, or about the submarine and her crew. Perhaps Colon and his people were all right. Perhaps the *D* had managed to cut loose from the science ship and withdraw. The submarine might even come to their rescue. Hope was essential.

Silver tried not to focus on anything except the things he had to do next. Right now he was searching for the motorized dinghy. He tried not to let the light fall on the nose of the submarine that had rammed them. It was a sad and dispiriting image he wanted to forget, not reinforce.

One nine-person dinghy was forward and another aft. Each

contained an emergency kit, stocked for antarctic survival; though Silver wasn't sure they could reach the coast or how long they could survive in soaking clothes, he couldn't worry about that now. He had to get himself and Angela off the *Abby*. He had to try to find anyone who might have been thrown into the water. Fifteen minutes was the maximum anyone could survive in the polar waters. And that was only if he or she was conscious enough to stay afloat.

The dinghy was still attached to the boom that held it above deck. Suspended from two thick ropes, it was hanging back over the deck, not over the water. That would make the hard-rubber lifeboat difficult to release. Somehow, though, it had to be done.

Except for the soft wind and the creaking of the eye hooks that held the dinghy, the sea was disturbingly quiet. He had hoped to hear splashing or the shouts of crew members. There was nothing.

Then, suddenly, there was a sound from belowdecks. A sound that Rear Admiral Silver knew well. The moaning girders, the distinctive whoosh, the heavy gulp of the sea taking in the new vessel. It was the sound of a submarine being launched. Only this wasn't a new submarine being sent to the depths, but the submarine that had hit them, slipping away. The science ship had been designed to float with an open hold. But the impact of the submarine had torn that away, along with a significant portion of the hull. When the vessel was gone, it would leave a significant hole in the hold of the *Abby*. The ship could not remain afloat. There was no time to get the dinghy and try to bring it around.

Silver turned the flashlight toward the bridge. The powerful six-volt krypton light probed the blackness. Angela was still tucked in the corner. He couldn't see her from here.

"Angela, come out here!" he cried.

Either the woman did not hear or else her mind was elsewhere. Dropping butt-first on the icy deck, Silver slid toward the bridge even as the *Abby* began to go under. He could hear the massive *glub* of water that filled the area formerly occupied by the submarine. He heard it pouring into the hold.

"Angela!"

"Stone?"

"I'm here, Angela! Go forward, Angela. Come out."

"What's happening?"

"Don't worry about that. Just come to my voice!"

Silver was nearly at the bridge. The deck settled slightly toward level as water sloshed into the forward section, weighing it down.

"Come on!" Silver said.

Angela didn't move. The rear admiral reached the destroyed bridge and leaned chest-down through the open roof. He stretched his arm inside and took the woman by the forearm. Without panic, she climbed out as the water burbled through the open hole in the upper deck, behind Silver.

The ship was going to go straight down, more or less. That could help them release the dinghy, assuming they could get to it in time. Once the foredeck went under, it would pull the dinghy down to the surface.

It was impossible to move back up the slightly inclined deck holding the flashlight and pulling Angela.

"I'm going to release you!" the rear admiral said.

"No, don't—"

Silver had no choice and no time to discuss it. He let her arm go and she screamed as she scrabbled to keep from sliding back. She managed to get her footing, and guided by Silver's flashlight—which he kept away from Dr. Ogden's body—she moved to the starboard side, toward the railing. She hung on while Silver continued aft, toward the winch. Reaching the dinghy, he wrapped one hand around the railing and probed the base of the boom with the light. He found the release lever and pulled it toward him, then swung back out of the way. The dinghy slid down the deck, past him, and hit the water, which was just climbing above the bridge.

"Angela, get to the boat!" Silver shouted. He turned the flashlight toward the boat so she could see it.

The woman was about ten feet behind him. She was hugging the rail tightly. The water was just a few feet below her. The boat was bobbing rapidly, moving slowly toward the port side. She was looking at Silver with a frightened expression.

"Angela, you have to let go!"

"No—"

"You must get in the boat. We'll be *safe* there!"

"Safe?" she said.

That seemed to register. The young scientist unwrapped her arms cautiously and scurried across the sinking deck. She reached the boat just as the sea reached her. She clambered in. Then Silver released his own hold on the rail and skid feetfirst, on his belly, down two yards of deck that separated them. The rocking motion of the ship sent him the wrong way, forcing him to have to reach for the dinghy to keep from missing it. He grabbed one of the handles, then heaved the flashlight in. He held the hard-rubber grip with both hands and pulled himself over the side as the sea washed around his knees. His feet were still sticking out and he used them to push off the deck. That gave them a nice start toward the starboard side of the sinking ship. He pulled in his feet as the railing passed behind him. The ship vanished with a sound like large breakers hitting the shore. Huge air bubbles popped under and around them, rocking the dinghy hard. Silver picked up the flashlight and slid it under his armpit. He held it and steadied himself between two of the three benches as he waited for the motion to subside.

In just a few seconds the sea was still. The rear admiral turned the flashlight on Angela. She was sitting between the two far benches. Her back was against the side of the dinghy, her arms slung around her knees.

"Are you all right?" Silver asked.

"Yes." Her voice was as flat as her expression.

Silver raised the light and turned it across the sea. He moved the beam slowly, looking for anyone who might have escaped. It was terribly still and silent. Then, after a moment, he thought he heard something behind him. It sounded like coughing. He turned the flashlight around and saw a young man in a life jacket. The crewman was about fifty feet away and doing a rapid dog paddle.

"Thank you, God," Silver murmured.

The oars were attached to the dinghy. Silver released the

Velcro straps, put the paddles in the water, and handed the flashlight to Angela.

"I need you to shine this ahead," he said.

"Okay."

The woman shined the flashlight toward the sea. The beam bobbed here and there as Silver rowed. Angela didn't seem to understand that anyone was out there. That didn't matter. The powerful, directed beam was enough to keep Silver turned in the right direction.

The dinghy headed toward the seaman as fast as the commander could pull the oars. It took just over a minute, though each stroke seemed long and ponderous. They were made more so by the partly soaked, partly frozen sleeves of his coat. It felt good to row, though. The heat generated by the activity warmed him.

They reached the man, who was well enough to climb from the sea on his own. It was Ens. Chuck Warren, a mechanical engineer. He pulled himself up over the side. The wonderful kid, in a glistening leather jacket and wool gloves, saluted as he came aboard.

Silver smiled broadly and saluted back; he damn near wept. He told the ensign to have a look in the large locker behind the last seat, near Angela. He said there should be blankets inside.

"Thank you, sir," the lanky young seaman said, shivering.

Angela was still shining the flashlight across the water. Warren stopped and looked at her.

"I'll take that, ma'am," the ensign said softly.

"All right," she replied pleasantly.

Warren gently removed it from her hand, opened the locker, and reached inside for the blankets. He put one around her and offered one to the rear admiral before taking one himself. Silver declined. He was warm enough for now.

The ensign shut the locker, then settled onto a bench beside Angela. He turned the light on the sea. There were ruptured planks, plastic equipment housing, and papers. Anything that could float. Warren made two slow turns of the perimeter, one near the dinghy and one farther out. There was no one else. He made a third quick pass before shutting off the light to conserve the battery. Then Silver picked up the oars. Warren offered to row but Silver declined. He wanted to keep active.

The dark was absolute, save for the sky, which was rich with stars. It suddenly seemed awe-inspiring to Silver that men, in darkness like this, used no more than those to navigate. He felt both uplifted and humbled as he turned the dinghy toward the southwest, toward the coast.

"Do we know the condition of the *D*, sir?" Warren asked.

"No," Silver replied. "Communications were cut off instantly. Did you see anything below?"

"Just the nose of that baby punching us a new hold. Most of the guys were at the towline spool. That was where the thing hit, amidships. I was forward that, wiping spray off the cable engine. I got knocked on my seat but I found the stairs in the dark. I hung there. I wanted to call out, but there was a lot of really hot steam coming up the well. I was afraid I'd burn my throat."

"Where was the steam coming from?"

"The spool, I think," Warren said. "It smelled greasy. I'm guessing the cable got pulled real fast and superheated the lubricant."

"Isn't lubricant supposed to prevent that kind of mishap?" Angela asked.

Silver was only partly surprised to hear her. It was not unknown for shock patients to become lucid with the proper trigger.

"Well, ma'am, it's designed not to burn, and it didn't," Warren told her. "But if it gets hot enough, the liquid content will smolder."

"I see."

"I turned away and pulled my lapel across my mouth to protect my lungs, and just listened. I didn't hear anyone, though I would have been surprised if I did. That sub knocked us pretty hard. Kicked the towline spool right off its base, popped those six-inch bolts like they were champagne corks."

"What happened to the towline spool?" Silver asked.

"It went down, sir, through an opening in the deck."

The three were silent after that. Now that they had traded
certain death for an uncertain future, Silver had a moment to
reflect on the magnitude of what had happened as well as the
predicament they were in. He tried—tried hard—to look at the
positives. They had the dinghy, they had the emergency gear,
and they were only about two miles from the coast. If they
could make it, they could probably buy themselves a day or
two. For what, Silver was not sure. But as with getting off the
Abby, he wasn't going to worry about that now. He was going to
deal with this one crisis at a time.

FIFTEEN

Weddell Sea

The *D* was sinking. Colon knew that. But the sea wasn't very deep here and they would survive the drop. What the captain had to do was make sure they survived the impact.

The small size of the *D* made it relatively easy to adjust ballast quickly. Captain Colon was pleased with that. If they could blow ballast completely just before reaching bottom, they might make a relatively soft landing. That would give them a chance to try to free the cable and pull away from the other vessel.

Colon was also pleased with the sharp response of his crew. They had drilled for many things, but an underwater collision and subsequent entanglement with another vessel was not one of them. Yet they were handling the emergency with calm, poised professionalism.

It is always that way, he thought. The only reason they trained was to learn the equipment, not the scenarios. The crew had to be able to work everything blindfolded since, in fact, they never knew when the lights might go out.

"Eighty meters," Withers reported. "Angle holding at five degrees negative tilt to the stern."

"Very good. What's the rate of descent?"

Before Withers could answer, the Ant Hill came on.

"Captain, I want you to activate supercavitation drive, full forward," Mike Carr said.

"What?"

"Did you not hear or are you questioning the order?"

"I heard," Colon replied. "Ant Hill, there's another submarine out there."

"Correct. And you need to get clear of the other vessel *and* the towline spool now. They may both come down on top of you."

"I still say 'What?' Ramjet activation may pull the cable loose and pop the nose plate. Hell, a strong sneeze might do that."

"We calculate the outgoing bubble will tear it loose on the other end," Carr said. "If the spool has come free, the *Abby* may be crippled and sinking as well. You have to get clear. *Activate at once.*"

Mike Carr had the computers and scientists telling him what was best. Carr also had the authority to make that call. Colon still believed this was the absolute wrong maneuver, just as he had believed that being lashed to the *Abby* by a tether was the wrong thing to do. Unfortunately, there was no time to wrestle with options. There was really only one issue: whether or not to obey an order.

"Lieutenant Rockford, activate ramjet," Colon said.

"Ramjet on," Rockford replied.

"Go to full forward when ready."

"Full forward when ready," Rockford repeated.

The quiet determination that had filled the tight cabin was replaced, palpably and instantly, by uncertainty. Not just about whether the maneuver would work, but whether the ramjets themselves would work. The temperature seemed to rise as the distinctive whirr of the aft fans filled the hull, the air around them, the seats they were on. It rolled from the stern, growing rapidly in volume.

"Seven hundred and fifty revs per second on the way to one thousand," Rockford said.

"Positions," Colon said.

All checked their harnesses and locked their swivel chairs. The time from activate to full power took fifteen seconds.

"Ninety meters," Withers announced. "Stern dipping, now seven degrees off level."

The sound intensified and the descent of the submarine slowed slightly. That was not the result of the bubble forming around it, pushing the water back; the pressure from the Egg would be equal on all sides and would not affect them. The rise was due to the jets coming on.

"Ninety-five meters," Withers said.

"Sonar says all-clear ahead," Bain reported.

"Full ramjet power in five . . . four—" Rockford said.

"All personnel in position," Lieutenant Michaelson said, after checking the small monitor that reported on belts and seats.

"—three . . . two . . . one."

The sudden forward momentum sent electric sparks along the captain's back, a giddy sense of speed unlike any he had ever before experienced. The "zero-to-sixty" factor of the supercavitation engines was just under five seconds, which meant the crew took nearly three g's dead-on as the *D* moved ahead. Though the submarine was angled upward, the ride felt smooth and swift, like a luge taking momentum into an ascending slope. It was more exhilarating than Colon had ever imagined.

The thrill did not last.

"Skewing slightly to port!" Rockford shouted.

"Aft horizontal stabilizer nonfunctional on starboard," helmsman Withers reported.

The tail fin must have been hit by debris. The acceleration may have weakened it further. They couldn't afford to lose that.

"Cut ramjet!" Colon yelled.

"Belay order, Rockford!" Carr shouted.

Rockford obeyed the command from Ant Hill.

"Carr, we have to shut—" Colon began. He didn't get to finish.

A loud snap at the nose of the *D* was followed by a sudden, lurching tug at the stern.

"Shit," Colon snarled. "Cut the fucking ramjet *now*!"

Before Rockford could kill the drive, the submarine snapped hard toward port. The *D* flipped over a half-turn, nosed down, and went into a power dive, propelled by the twin ramjets. Even as they plummeted toward the bottom, Colon identified at least one calculation Carr had overlooked: whether the towline was free or whether it was wrapped around some other part of the ship.

Like the starboard horizontal stabilizer.

SIXTEEN

Kings Bay, Georgia

"Cut ramjet!" Carr ordered.

Lieutenant Junior Grade Rockford carried out the command. Carr watched as the speed of the *D* dropped. The submarine had a deceleration rate of two knots a second. It had been traveling at seventy-seven knots when it turned. That had knocked fifteen knots off the speed. But they were still heading toward the bottom rapidly, with the ramjet shutting down gradually. If they killed it immediately, the sea would rush in where the Egg had been and slam the submarine. It would be the equivalent of wind shear to a small plane, but across every meter of the hull—top, bottom, and sides.

"Mike, they've got to change course," Dr. Patrick Drake said urgently. Drake was the Ant Hill geologist.

"Give them the new coordinates." Carr did not ask the geologist why. There wasn't time.

"*D* helm, alter five degrees southwest at once," Drake said.

"Port mobility negative!" Rockford replied.

"Vent all starboard ballast into bubble," Colon commanded. "Draw psi at three per second."

That was smart, Carr thought. Putting water into the air pocket would create drag on that side. Adding water at the rate of three pounds per square inch every second would keep the hull from being crushed.

"Increase ramjet deceleration to three knots a second," Colon said. "Adjust working stabilizer to compensate for skew."

The faster deceleration would be pushing hull tolerance, but not outside the theoretical safety zone. The variable in all that was the addition of pressure from the emptying ballast. The team's structural engineer, Dr. Otis Fargo, was already working those computations. He flashed Carr a thumbs-up—then suddenly frowned and raised his other fingers in a "stop" sign.

"That maneuver won't allow the bubble to be depleted in time," Dr. Fargo said gravely.

"In time for what?" Carr asked. The scientist did not mute the speaker. He wanted the captain to hear the conversation.

"The ramjet pocket is going to hit the ice shelf at roughly thirty-one percent full capacity," Dr. Drake went on. "That could provide a shock wave sufficient to bring the shelf down."

"That isn't entirely bad news," Dr. Fargo remarked.

"Why?" Carr asked.

"Having the air pocket in place, partially intact, will ease the blow to whatever section of the *D* impacts the ice shelf," Fargo said.

"If there's an avalanche, what part of it will we catch?" Colon asked.

"There's no way of knowing," Drake said. "We aren't certain how fragile the subsurface sea ice is in that area."

"Is there a better spot to impact a degree or two in any direction?" Colon pressed. "Less rock, more silt, shallower ice—?"

"We don't know," Fargo said.

"Wouldn't a deeper contact-point be marginally better?" asked Dr. Adler Davenport, the oceanographer. "If ice does fall on the *D* and drives it down, the underside would take less stress if there was a cushion of water."

"Wouldn't a lower impact also dislodge less ice?" Carr asked.

"Yes on the first question, no on the second," Fargo replied. "Having the air pocket hit the slope even lower could be disastrous. If the bottom section were to give way, that might weaken the ice wall immediately above it, but not bring that down until after the *D* has come to rest."

"Burying it," Davenport said.

"Or worse, crushing it," Dr. Drake noted.

"Gentlemen, thanks for the input but I'm riding this puppy down with the Egg as is," Colon said. "I want the cushion."

"You're go on that," Carr said.

As the scientists waited, Drake pointed to a map on his monitor. It showed sonar readings from the *Abby*'s previous voyage. "The ice shelf slopes dramatically toward the shore above them. That section of the offshore region may not be affected by a concussion below. The captain is correct. It's better to allow the ramjet to blast the lower ice loose, create a kind of nest, before they hit."

It was slightly absurd to Carr that they were discussing options that would lead to a result that would probably not matter. Whether the submarine crashed or was buried, the *D* would probably be crippled. And even if it came to rest relatively intact, what would they do next?

It was also strange that no one had said anything about the *Abby*. The feeling, Carr guessed, was that no one was "as" concerned because the rear admiral and his team were above water. They assumed that was a safer place to be. But even a surface wreck, in the antarctic, was as much a potential death sentence as the underwater drama they were witnessing.

Everyone in the room was very still. There was nothing to do, no simulations to run, no numbers to process, no more options to consider. Carr didn't even second-guess what any of them had done, from insisting that the towline be attached to the present. All of that would come later. Right now, they were waiting to find out just one thing.

Whether they still had a submarine and a crew.

SEVENTEEN

Weddell Sea

Hoping that additional hull-surface against the sea would slow them somewhat, Captain Colon ordered Rockford to raise the nose as they descended. A "belly flop" landing was risky since it could snap them in two. But a nose or stern impact wouldn't do them a lot of good either.

Carr didn't object. The bastard was finally quiet.

Now that his stupid fucking towline security precaution has sunk us, Colon thought bitterly—now that he had a moment to reflect.

"Second incoming!" Lieutenant Junior Grade Bain warned as she watched the sonar screen.

"Nature?" Colon asked.

"Same profile as whatever hit the towline. It's coming in at what looks like a free fall, twenty meters starboard. Third incoming," she added quickly. "Fourth . . . fifth, all smaller. We've also got the seafloor on-screen, impact imminent."

The tow spool was probably among the debris, along with wreckage from the *Abby*. It would be sadly fitting to survive the crash and then be crushed and can-opened by flotsam. More stuff from the *Abby* that Colon didn't want.

Colon put his feet forward to brace himself and held tight to the arms of his command chair. As he watched the green sonar screen, saw what would probably be the last sweep before they hit the ledge, the captain had at least one final gratification. The supercavitation drive had worked just the way it was supposed to. Charlotte Davies would have been happy. Maybe she *was* happy. Colon might find out for certain in a second or two.

The *D* slowed abruptly, as though it had struck a thick sponge. There was a little "give"—what was left of the supercavitation bubble, Colon imagined—then the impact. The *D* took the hit just slightly astern from the command center. When Colon was a kid, he had climbed into a metal trash can and rolled down a hill. It rattled off course and hit a tree stump. This felt the same, and like that trash can, the *D* didn't split. It complained with a loud, dull "cough"—that's exactly what it sounded like—as it ended its descent. The submarine immediately rolled to port about twenty degrees, leaving them sloping to the left; then it slid backward with a jolting series of thumps. Obviously, the surface was not flat and their downward momentum carried them along the slope. There was a series of deafening bangs during which, at some point—God bless him—Lieutenant Junior Grade Rockford dutifully announced that the air pocket had completely dissipated.

While all of this was going on, Colon listened for the distinctive trickling of seawater. Given the concussion they had absorbed, there was no way of knowing which security systems were still on-line.

After seven or eight seconds of backsliding, the submarine finally stopped, slanting only slightly to port. The lights were still on and air was circulating.

"Everyone stay put!" Colon shouted during the tomb quiet that followed.

While they awaited the impact of the debris shower, the captain asked for an all-systems report. The crew had an order of response, starting with the helmsman. But before Withers could give his status update, the silence was swallowed by a deafening thud to starboard.

"That was a very big signature, probably the submarine," Bain said.

"Location?"

"Twenty-seven meters to starboard—"

There was a second, louder crash, this one on top of them. The crew waited tensely to see if the hull held.

It did.

"One end of the submarine is apparently across our back," Bain said.

"Point of impact?"

Bain studied her screen for a moment. "We're getting a shadow in front of the submarine. It appears to be our bridge. I can't be sure because there are other projections on the hull, probably dislodged pieces of the sea shelf."

"I only heard the one hit," Colon said.

"Yes, sir. These probably piled up behind and around us when we slid down," she said.

"Thank you," Colon replied, trying to project a sense of normalcy.

Rockford and Withers made their reports amid continuous knocks and clangs of falling debris. The sounds lasted for nearly two minutes. Fortunately, either the piled ice or the water slowed them so there were no hull breaches. After they stopped, however, there was another sound, an ominous drumbeat from above. The sound grew into a steady rumble, like a jet approaching the tarmac, becoming sharper and louder until it was all around them.

"We're getting a really big blip," Bain said.

"Location?" Colon asked.

"Everywhere," she said.

This was the avalanche that the Ant Hill had feared. Colon did not have to tell the crew to hang on. The captain's heart was thumping harder than before. Something about just sitting and waiting was worse than riding a maelstrom. He refused to believe that the crew had survived the ride down only to be crushed. But damn, that was loud. Colon knew that the water was amplifying the sound. Still—

The first chunks of ice struck with terrifying force. Everything jumped and rattled, everywhere at once.

"We're blind!" Bain announced as ice covered the nose.

There were a few more heavy hits. Then, within moments, the sound of the landslide grew dull and distant. That was both good news and bad news. The good news was most of the falling ice wouldn't touch them. The bad news was the reason.

The *Tempest D* was buried.

EIGHTEEN

Weddell Sea

"What was that?" Angela shouted.

Rear Admiral Silver wasn't certain. The water was suddenly shaking all around them. They could feel it in the dinghy as it rolled beneath them. The ripples were radiating toward them from along the coast. He continued rowing; whatever it was, they had nowhere to go but toward the shore. His body heat continued to keep him warm enough, in spite of the wet clothes, but his arms were getting tired.

"It feels like an explosion," Ensign Warren said. He shined the flashlight toward the coast. He moved it slowly across the wavelets.

"Do you see any large bubbles?" Silver asked.

"No. Nor debris."

The rear admiral took heart in that. If one of the submarines had exploded due to a fire or imploded because of the pressure, bubbles and wreckage would have reached to the surface.

"An explosion? Are we going to be okay?" Angela asked. It had taken a few moments for Warren's words to register.

"Just stay calm," Silver said. "Whatever it is, we can ride it out."

"Sorry, sir," Warren said. "I should have thought before I—"

The ensign didn't finish. He froze the flashlight beam on a spot between the dinghy and the still-distant shore.

"Hold on, sir. I see something."

Silver looked in the direction he was pointing. He saw it as well, about two hundred meters away.

"It's the other dinghy!" Warren said excitedly.

"Are you sure?" Silver couldn't make it out. Frost on his eyebrows was blurring his vision.

"I am, sir. Only it's upside down."

"Is there anyone around it, holding on?"

"I don't see anyone."

The rear admiral began rowing in that direction and it took nearly ten minutes to reach the dinghy. It was difficult, at first, because they were heading straight toward the epicenter of the ripples. But those died after a few minutes, leaving only the wind, which was blowing away from shore. Fortunately, the current was moving in their direction.

When they arrived, the dinghy was closest to Warren. He handed the rear admiral the flashlight and borrowed one of his oars. The ensign extended the oar to try to hook the guy rope along the side. He slid the paddle up and behind the rope and pulled the dinghy toward them. He grabbed the line with his left hand, put the oar back in the boat, then got his right hand around the rope. He tugged hard, lifting one side of the dinghy onto their own. The rear admiral angled the flashlight low across the water so they could see inside.

The emergency kit was there but nothing else.

"We'd better get that," Silver said.

"Yes, sir."

Silver moved the flashlight even lower so the ensign could see. As he did, the rear admiral squinted at the mooring hooks, fore and aft. They were torn. The dinghy had not been lowered into the water. It had been ripped free, either by the impact of the submarine or by the tidal force generated when the *Abby* had gone under. As Warren worked on the plastic screws that held the kit in place, Silver moved the beam slightly. He looked at the side of the dinghy that was still in the water.

Two bodies were floating facedown. Their hands were hooked around the guyline. Crystalized blood was on their clothing and more frozen in the water, delicate and clinging to their boots. They must have seen the dinghy and swum toward it, but were probably too weak and too waterlogged to turn it over. They died frozen to the rope, probably trying to right the dinghy.

Warren was focused on removing the emergency kit and did not see the bodies. Neither did Angela, who was shivering now. She had slid into the bottom of the dinghy and was hugging herself.

"Got it!" Warren said as he pulled the kit in. He put it on one of the benches. "Do we want the dinghy for any reason? Shelter?"

"No," Silver said. "We'll be all right. Let it go."

"Yes, sir."

Warren pushed the other dinghy off. The boat drifted several meters, riding the currents of the now-calmed seas.

Silver picked up the oar and handed the flashlight back to Warren. He hesitated before putting the oars back in the water. The two dead men were sailors. Burial at sea was honorable and appropriate. But if the rear admiral let the dinghy go, their families would probably be deprived closure.

Assuming that we ourselves are ever found, Silver thought.

"Is there a problem, sir?" Warren asked.

Silver was staring out into the dark, in the direction they had sent the dinghy. It wouldn't be difficult to tow it. But there was something else to consider, something more important than mourning.

Living. Silver did not want to make camp in a morgue.

"Sir?" Warren pressed.

"Yes, Ensign?" Silver said.

"I asked if there was anything wrong."

"No, nothing," Silver assured him as he put the oars in the frigid sea. He rowed purposefully from the dinghy, from the accident site, from whatever mistakes had put them here.

He rowed toward life.

For more than an hour, Silver pulled the oars toward a distant point on the compass, to a section of the Antarctica coast called Graham Land. Covered with ice, Graham Land borders the Weddell Sea from the Hilton Inlet to James Ross Island on one side and mountains on the other. Battered by a confluence of fierce winds from both directions, it is one of those places where an individual does not want to be stranded for long.

But the three-person crew was bound there and they would have to find a way to survive. When they reached the shore, Silver had to travel eastward for nearly a quarter mile to find a spot where the ice passed under the water. Everywhere else the coast rose straight up, like a miniature white cliffs of Dover.

The rear admiral and Ensign Warren got out of the dinghy. It seemed strange to be on a solid surface. Silver had gotten used to the bobbing of the dinghy. Warren held the flashlight with one hand while he tugged on the forward handle with the other. Silver pushed from the water side of the little boat. He was perspiring and did not care to imagine how he would feel in an hour or so. Even with warmers from the emergency kit it was going to be damn cold.

One thing at a time, the officer reminded himself.

The men decided they would secure the dinghy a hundred yards or so from the water, rig some kind of shelter using it, then have a look inside the emergency kits. Silver also wanted food and drink after the long row.

"Limnognathia maerski," Angela said through clattering teeth as Ensign Warren helped her from the dinghy.

"What was that?" Silver asked her.

"Limnognathia maerski," the ichthyologist repeated. "I was trying to remember the name of the animal the Danes found down a cold well in Greenland."

"Tell me about them," Silver said as they started tugging the surprisingly heavy little boat up this steeply sloped surface with its small, rough, rocky projections. He wanted to encourage Angela to stay focused, awake.

"I read about them in *Polarfronten*," she said.

"What's that? A magazine?" Ensign Warren asked, picking up on what the rear admiral was doing.

"Yes. They have an English-language version on-line."

"What did the article say?" Warren asked.

"That scientists have discovered these freshwater organisms, *Limnognathia maerski*, which are only point one millimeter long and don't fit into any known animal grouping."

"You mean, a mutation?" Warren asked.

"No," she said. "A new kind of animal. Like the platypus was when it was discovered."

"I see," Warren said. "Point one millimeter. The little fellow wouldn't make much of a meal."

"Not for us, unless we ate them the way whales eat krill," Angela said with a laugh. "Boy, it's cold. Where are we?"

She's definitely still in a haze, Silver thought. "We're ashore on Graham Land. We'll have you warmed up soon."

"Thank you. I'd like that. Will Howard be joining us?"

It took Silver a moment to figure out whom she was talking about. "I don't think Dr. Ogden can make it."

"That's too bad," she said. "I really like him."

"So do I," Silver told her.

They reached a relatively level spot behind a slightly lop-sided ten-foot pyramid of ice and put the dinghy there. Silver took one of the emergency kits and gave the other to Warren.

"Ensign, would you take care of the heat?" Silver asked. "I'll work on the beacons."

"Yes, sir."

Warren removed the adhesive body warmers from their water-resistant sack. A dozen were in each kit. About the size of a washcloth, each air-activated warmer had a tape perimeter that allowed it to be placed securely on the body. Made of iron, water, carbon particles, and salt, each would last twelve hours and generate temperatures of 110 degrees.

Warren opened his coat and shirt and placed one on his chest. He did the same to Angela. She resisted at first, but relented when Warren let her feel how warm the one on his chest was. He placed it without actually removing any of her garments. Then he handed one to Silver, who waited to apply it. He was still warm enough. They would use the others, as needed, if the blankets failed to keep their extremities and faces warm. These were environmentally responsible, since small space heaters could cause melting of the polar ice.

God knows that's a responsibility I don't want, Silver thought. *Rear admiral loses two ships and melts the south pole.*

Gallows humor. That was a first for him. He didn't know if that was a good thing or not, but there it was. He also wondered if the individuals who had designed the patches had used them to stay warm in Antarctica or if they'd gone to a ski lodge for a weekend. He assumed they were adequate, no more. Right now he would sell his soul for a good-sized kerosene heater.

The rear admiral removed an Emergency Position Indicating Radio Beacon from its rubber case. The case prevented both water leakage as well as electrostatic shocks. Roughly the size and shape of a police radio, the beacon was a self-contained transmitter that, when activated, sent internationally recognized distress signals on both 121.5 and 243 MHz, which were reserved for just such beacons. After removing it, all Silver had to do was open the small, squat tripod base, extend the whip antenna—flexible in extreme weather conditions, compared to static telescopic designs that tended to become damaged in high winds—and turn it on. It would run continuously for forty-eight hours. They had two EPIRBs, which was all they would need. Silver didn't imagine they could survive out here more than four days. He didn't know how those turn-of-the-century explorers had done it. When Shackleton's antarctic expedition had gone awry in 1915, the only emergency supplies they had had was a cat, Mrs. Chippy.

Though the EPIRB beeped every thirty seconds to signal the user that it was working, Silver didn't hear it. The wind was extremely loud, carrying with it a high-pitched and undulating whistle that seemed to come from a movie sound library. His hood was also tied tight against his ears and his teeth were starting to chatter. The sweat was chilling faster than he had expected. Taking one of the warmers from Warren, he put it on his chest. The heat sent waves of well-being that reached his back, upper arms, and waist. His butt was numb but he could deal with that for now. The cold there wasn't affecting any major organs.

Using a pocketknife to hack the beginnings of a pair of holes, then using a chunk of ice as a hammer, the men drove the oars paddle-first into the shelf. The wind was blowing in from the sea, so they turned the bottom of the dinghy toward it. They cut the rubber casing of the EPIRB into strips and used them to tie the handles of the dinghy to the heels of the oars. That created an effective wind barrier. Then, using the knife to unscrew the hinges of the emergency chests, they used the covers as combination ice picks and shovels to excavate a small depression behind the dinghy. That would keep them bunched close together and warm when they slept. When all of that was done, they finally broke out the rations. There were small bottles of fresh water, beef jerky, dried fruit, powdered milk, Melba toast, and vitamins. Each emergency chest contained sufficient rations for three people for two days. At least they wouldn't have to ration. Four days of food was more than they would need.

Dinner—or was it breakfast?—took just a few minutes. When it was done, the three *Abby* survivors snuggled into their pit, Angela in the middle, their feet facing the dinghy. If the boat blew over, they didn't want it hitting anyone in the head. The first aid kit was as elaborate as the meal packets.

Silver and Warren pulled the blankets entirely over the pit. They tucked the edges under their feet and shoulders. It was satisfactorily warm, especially with the adhesive patches on. The situation was far from ideal, but not as bad as it could be. And Silver liked their position better than that of the submariners of both vessels. This thought didn't make him happy. But it ensured one thing.

That he took none of his cold, raspy breaths for granted.

NINETEEN

Kings Bay, Georgia

When he was a kid, Mike Carr had seen an episode of *The Twilight Zone* where a jetliner had gone back in time, all the way to prehistory. He remembered vividly the pilot's remark about how unsettling it was to be receiving nothing over the radio, not even static. Carr couldn't quite grasp what that was like.

Until now.

It was eerie. That was the only word to describe it. No sound was coming from any of the audio monitors. There were no telemetric signals of any kind. There were nothing but baleful flatlines on several LED systems, and empty electronic columns that should have been busy with data but were showing only backslashes, and dead radios with buffers that filtered out static and thus provided them with no sound at all. Just like the television show.

Only real.

All means of communication between the Ant Hill, the *Abby*, and the *Tempest D* were left open. None of the scientists made any adjustments to their equipment. Emergency protocol was for settings to remain where they were for two hours. In the event of a technical mishap on board one of the vessels, the crew had that much time to effect repairs. Most of the damage the engineers had imagined could be fixed in that time. Circuits were modular and easily replaced. Systems that failed had backups that came on-line automatically. Backup failures had troubleshooting checklists that could be completed in under an hour.

The second hour was padding. It was primarily a transition period for the science team, a chance to shift from operation to recovery. That, too, would be an upsetting "twilight zone."

After two hours the Ant Hill would presume a catastrophic systems failure of some kind, which could include external damage that had caused antenna misalignment. At that point they would begin running a Satellite Realignment Program, which would search the region for a signal. The problem with the SRP was that it would temporarily cut communication with the last known location of the vessel. That could cause them to miss each other. Rear Admiral Silver once described it as playing pin the tail on the donkey with the donkey moving. Still, the effort would have to be made. For now, all the Ant Hill could do was notify a list of research bases along the Weddell Sea and inland to listen for standard or emergency radio signals from the research vessel *Abby* or from a Chinese submarine that might have struck it. Most of those bases would not be equipped to lend assistance. But they might be able to relay messages, perhaps give the Ant Hill some hint as to where the vessels might be, maybe a seismic blip from the collision or a subsequent impact, something to help them narrow their search.

Beyond that, the Ant Hill was virtually helpless. Whatever the next step might be would have to come from Admiral Grantham at NORDSS.

If, in fact, there *was* a next step to take.

TWENTY

Corpus Christi, Texas

It had been a week of hard-won ups and easy-to-come-by downs for Major Tom Bryan.

Bryan had spent the first two days after the training fiasco feeling down. Way in the crapper down. He went through the postmortem in a bright, fluorescent-lit training room that looked like an elementary-school class. Some DOD psychologist had probably decided that yellowish walls would be subliminal sunshine for the soul and that big green blackboards would take them to a time of innocence when they were eager to learn and listen. Even the tile floors were cheerful, eggshell-colored with what looked like finely dribbled green and red paint, like Christmas run through a shredder. The desks were pale wood. There were thirty of them, since the room was usually used for squadron flight-crew briefings. Instead of cheering him, the room pissed Major Bryan off. He didn't like being manipulated. He didn't like it any more than he liked fucking up, which he was convinced he had done.

Everything Bryan heard over those two days was a big fat I-beam to everything General Scott had told him from the time they had got back to shore. Supported it strong and sure: L.A.S.E.R. had done exactly what it should have done under the circumstances and Bryan had acted "appropriately."

That was a neutral word and Bryan detested it. It described

the kind of clothes you wore when you went to a reception, or skiing. He'd rather have a red stain. At least that was the blemish of a soldier.

By the third day Bryan had started an uncertain climb from depression. Scott had him work with pilots on survival training, which wasn't something you could do if you were distracted. The major took veteran Captains Puckett, Reno, Highland, and four newer recruits on a three-day field trip to Mexico. The military didn't like to acknowledge this was done, but it was difficult to simulate behind-enemy-lines fear unless you went behind someone's lines. In this case, Bryan and a team of seven recruits parachuted into Mexico, illegally, just south of Brownsville, Texas, outside of Valle Hermoso. They had no provisions or arms. Their objective was to live off the land and make their way back to the United States on foot. Though they suspected they would not be shot if discovered by *federales*, the Mexican federal police officers, it would be an embarrassment to Washington and to NAS. No one wanted that, least of all Bryan.

He rode the team hard as they slept in ditches they dug themselves, soothed calluses with plant sap, and boiled pond water to drink, with worms and grasshoppers added for protein.

Getting away from the base, even for a short while, and having to wet-nurse guys who grew up in places that had a McDonald's and Starbucks on every corner, allowed Bryan to stop obsessing on his screwup. Being out in the field forced him to reprioritize. Perspective was a good thing. They made it back to Brownsville, where a navy chopper came to collect them. Bryan was in a pretty good mood after that, the crew having performed with enthusiasm, professionalism, and contagious camaraderie. Having two guys go through nicotine withdrawal, another through caffeine withdrawal, tends to bond a team. Especially when they're on a three-thousand-foot-high mountaintop where it's thirty degrees and they're sitting in a tight circle for warmth since a campfire might be spotted by "the enemy" and the only hot beverage or smoke consisted of roots they found.

In their absence, General Scott had been working on a new

training exercise. An exercise is generally less ambitious than a
mission since it is conducted on the base and typically does not
involve fire or water. In this case, they were preparing for a
search-and-rescue in the basement of a collapsed building. The
"building" was actually a fifteen-by-twenty-two-foot pit, thirty
feet deep, into which concrete—from a repaired section of
runway—pipes, insulation, wood, and other debris had been
dropped. Their goal was to find and recover a half dozen mannequins that had been left in the bottom. No one knew the condition of the dummies. If they were perceived to be injured
rather than dead, extra care had to be taken in their removal.

Major Bryan was looking forward to the exercise. It wasn't
that he thought he owed something to the dummies of America.
And this was not about ability, but ability under fire. He wanted
to prove to himself and to his team that he could do something
right under pressure.

The day before the test was spent in a "jam session," with the
ten participating L.A.S.E.R. members familiarizing themselves
with the gear they would be using. Some of the team members
had worked with some of the equipment on other rescues. They
would not be doing so this time. General Scott liked to rotate
assignments in case team members were injured and others had
to fill in. They all practiced on each other, using gear from the
rope rescue pack, including a seat harness, static rope, webbing,
anchor slings, rescue winches and pulleys, a spinal immobiliza-
tion and extraction unit, and con-space kits. The latter were
large backpack-carried communications and rescue systems designed for extremely confined areas. The kits included a search
camera, cable splitters, breathing equipment, and jacklike
stress supports to keep local areas from collapsing. It was not
necessary for team members to be expert with the gear, only familiar with it. They would be in constant communication with a
member of the team serving as surface liaison. If they had a
problem, the liaison would have a laptop with instructions for
the operation of each device.

The jam sessions were held in Hangar 24. Major Bryan tried
to keep things relaxed. For one thing, stress levels always rose
the day before a rescue simulation. For another, since team

members were constantly being mixed and matched in smaller groups, it was just as important for them to integrate with one another as it was for them to learn to use their tools.

The night before the search-and-rescue Major Bryan lay in bed anticipating success and dreading failure. As he was reviewing the tactics, General Scott called.

"Major, I just received a call from DOD. You've got a forty-five-and-out," Scott said.

There were no preliminaries, no "Are you awake, Major?" Something was up. Bryan had three-quarters of an hour to select a team, field them, and have their gear on the airfield.

"Mission, sir?" Bryan asked. He got out of bed, the cordless phone tucked under his ear while he went to the closet. The major would have to dress and get his personal gear while he called the barracks leaders to wake the team members he selected. He would also have to call the group's quartermaster to assemble the equipment they might need.

"Cold weather, water, possible deep submergence," Scott told him. "The Hercules is being prepped and the chopper is being loaded. I'm still waiting for details. I'll meet you there."

"Yes, sir."

Bryan hung up and phoned Captain Gabriel. Gabe was the barracks leader for the men; he would contact Lieutenant Black, who was the drumbeater for the women. Bryan had already been putting together a mental list while he was talking to General Scott. He would take thirteen team members with him, those who had experience in water operations—the ones he had worked with on the destroyer—as well as a few who had done survival training in the arctic circle.

The lingering shadow of depression fled. So did doubt. So did every thought but one. A thought that would stay with him until the job was completed, wherever it was and however long it took.

This mission was real.

TWENTY-ONE

Corpus Christi, Texas

Dressed in a battered leather flight jacket and a long red scarf that his wife had given to him twenty-two years before, General Scott waited on the dark airstrip for the team to arrive. The morning was cool, still, and fresh. A slim folder was under his arm and a vinyl map in his hand. The map was like a Twister game surface: large, flexible, and water-resistant. It was a two-year-old map of Antarctica that Scott had pulled from the files.

Major Bryan had been talking these past few days about perspective. Scott knew the major was about to get a lesson in perspective that would test him in a way few men had ever been tested.

The general was standing just outside the large hydraulically operated rear ramp of the C-130K Hercules transport. The Hercules was affectionately referred to as "the pelican of airplanes"—big, ungainly, but able to carry a lot in its craw. With 132-foot wingspan and four powerful turboprops, the aircraft had a range of nearly twenty-five hundred miles and a top speed of 385 miles an hour. The C-130K was the aerial refueling configuration; the aircraft would have to be topped off three times on its way to the Falklands. Ideally, Scott would have liked to get a longer-range C-130H variant, the HC-130H, to make the trip, but there hadn't been time. Apparently, time was extremely short as it was. Minutes, let alone an extra hour or two, could matter. Reaching the Falklands, the crew would land at the RAF Mount Pleasant base, which was opened in 1984 to establish a fighter and transport presence in the islands after the Falklands War. Among the aircraft the British kept there were a Hercules C1, as well as No. 78 Squadron with Chinook and Sea King helicopters. While the C-130K was in transit, General Scott would be in touch with his old RAF pal Air Marshal Moss Holiday to get one of the Chinooks the team could use to fly south. Holiday had been one of Scott's strongest supporters during the NATO showdown. He'd be happy to help. Captain Puckett was rated to fly the Chinook.

Scott heard the team before he saw them. He felt a flood of pride as he listened to their footsteps on the tarmac, double time. A moment later he saw them in the taillights of the plane, running forward in two columns, Major Bryan at the head. Scott had always referred to L.A.S.E.R. as "his" team, but it was Bryan's now. The major had met them at the barracks and run them over in full gear. No slouched shoulders, no casually carried bags. Everything was trim, efficient, formal. Elite military units were always gung ho; they had pride in their heritage and a sense of duty and honor that transcended life itself. These soldiers didn't have a past and were eager to establish a high-bar precedent. Scott had seen it in their efforts since they'd been together, which was probably why the major had taken the destroyer situation so hard.

General Scott knew that Bryan would put foot to ass on this mission, whatever the cost. He was confident that L.A.S.E.R. would do themselves proud. The general foresaw only one problem, which was the nightmare Admiral Grantham had tacked to the back end.

Major Bryan turned the loading over to Lieutenant Black, then walked to where the general was standing. Bryan threw off a sharp salute and General Scott returned it. Even in the dark, Scott could see the light in Bryan's eyes. He was eager to go. Scott handed the major both the file and the map.

"There are some dossiers on the people, a little about the mission that was under way—all my handwritten notes, which I hope you can read—and a map that covers more area than you need and doesn't give you enough on the area you do need," Scott told him. "I'm sorry I don't have more for you at this time. When I get it, you'll get it."

"Sir, not a problem."

"No." Scott hesitated. "There's more, though. You're going out on this because I received a call from Admiral Grantham at the Naval Office of Research and Development, Submarine Systems. They were in trials on a new submarine in the Weddell Sea when they lost the test vehicle, apparently in a collision with an overly friendly Chinese sub. We think the PLN vessel was one of their new Song-class ships. It sent out a distress call that was picked up by satellite. The admiral also fears we may have lost the science ship that was accompanying the test sub on its mission."

"Has he heard from either of them?"

"Not a chirp from the surface ship, and they lost all telemetry from the sub when it hit bottom—where, they think, it may have been caught in an ice slide."

"At least it survived the impact," Bryan pointed out. "Is there ordnance on the test sub?"

"No," Scott said. "We don't know about the Chinese vessel, though it's likely. I've got a call in to the military attaché at their embassy in Washington. I'm also trying to find out if the Royal Navy has a submersible in the region, something you can use. Initial reports are not favorable."

"What's the target depth?"

"That's the good news," Scott said. "They appear to be at about one hundred and fifty feet."

"Wet-suit doable."

"Yes. Major, the big problem with this thing, apart from just getting there in time, is the fact that the navy was testing a military vehicle down there."

"With respect, sir, the Chinese were down there with a military sub—"

"Military proliferation is not the problem," Scott interrupted. "A United States submarine was patrolling and collided with a Chinese sub on patrol. Politically, it's a wash. The problem is that we anticipate a Chinese recovery effort, one that will get there before the navy can. DOD doesn't want them to find our sub."

A jeep purred in the distance. The purr became a growl as it neared. Bryan looked over. The jeep had a glow-in-the-dark no-smoking sign on both doors. He glanced back at the general.

"That's from the quartermaster's office," Bryan said. "BUDs."

"That's right."

"For the love of God," Bryan said. He raised the manila folder. "This is not in the written orders, is it?"

"No," Scott said. Despite the scarf and heavy jacket, the general suddenly felt very, very cold.

"You're saying that if we can't raise the submarine, we're supposed to use the basic underwater demolition kit to blow her up," Bryan said.

"Those are the admiral's orders."

"Even if there are crew members inside."

"There are no alternatives to a failed reflotation," Scott informed him. "I'm very sorry."

"Complement of how many?"

"Seven."

Bryan was silent as the Hercules fired up its massive T56-A-15 turboprops. The jeep stopped at the side of the ramp and one of the two passengers ran over. A lieutenant, he saluted the general and asked for permission to bring the BUDs chest on board.

"Major Bryan is in command," Scott said. "Ask him."

The lieutenant turned to the major and saluted. "I'm sorry, sir."

"Permission granted," Bryan said. "See Lieutenant Black about the transfer."

The lieutenant asked for the major's signature on the bill of lading, then ran back to the jeep. Quickly but carefully, the two men brought the crate on board.

Bryan did not watch them. He was looking at Scott. "Do we know for certain that the Chinese have begun moving into the area?"

"No," Scott said. "We believe they'll make an aerial sweep

of the area, which should occur several hours before you arrive. We're going to try to get them to cooperate with whatever recon information they acquire. They won't put a rescue team in by air, however."

"Why not?"

"The admiral believes they'll try and recover the vessel."

"They will but we won't," Bryan said.

"The Song is a new class of submarine for them," Scott said patiently. "Beijing will need to know why their ship hit one of ours. If the crew can't tell them, they'll hope the submarine can. With our vessel it's different. It apparently functioned as planned. Admiral Grantham's big concern is whatever they were testing. He doesn't want the Chinese to get it."

Lieutenant Black called down from the open bay, "We're ready up here, sir!"

"Thank you, Lieutenant!" Bryan yelled back.

"You'd better hit it. Are there any questions?" Scott asked.

"None, sir."

"I'll e-mail undersea charts of the Weddell Sea as soon as I have them, along with any other pertinent information," Scott said.

"Blueprints of the American submarine?"

"Tough one," Scott admitted. "They're highly classified."

Bryan said nothing.

"I'm sorry it has to be this way," Scott said.

"I appreciate the situation, sir. I'm going to concentrate on getting a brave crew out of a bad situation."

Salutes were exchanged and then the general offered his hand. Bryan shook it. But the major's manner was formal. Not special ops formal but cold, disapproving. Not of Scott but of the situation. As he watched Major Bryan head up the ramp, Scott did not doubt that Major Bryan would do whatever was necessary to fulfill his mission. But at what cost?

As the major was surely realizing, compared to this the destroyer incident was nothing.

Perspective. It could be a killer.

PART FOUR

CONVERGENCE

ONE

Ho Chi Minh City, Vietnam

The two crews on board the Boeing 737 did not have to say it to know it, to feel it, to hate it. Yet there was no avoiding it. Sometimes military service posed risks to the flesh, and sometimes the dangers were no less real for being less tangible.

There was no question to any of the men which was worse.

At one in the afternoon, the 737 had left the People's Liberation Army Air Force landing strip in Zhanjiang on the South China Sea, accompanied by a Russian-made Il-76 jet. Less than an hour later, crossing one time zone to the west, the two planes were on the ground nearly one thousand miles away, at Ha Tay Field, which the People's Army of Vietnam, Air Defense Force, maintained outside Ho Chi Minh City. There, both jets were quickly refueled so they could continue their journey. The Il-76 had a range of 2,160 miles. The 737 had a range of 2,600 miles. The 76 would stay with the 737 for another thousand miles, refuel it in midair, then turn back to Vietnam before heading home. The 737 would continue to the southwest. It would make subsequent refueling stops at Jakarta, Java, and then at the French island of Kerguelen. That would give it enough fuel to reach its destination, conduct a brief search, and then return along the same route.

Sold by Boeing to China United Airlines in 2000 and soon thereafter shifted to the PLAAF, the 737 had been equipped as a reconnaissance aircraft. Like the Chinese navy, the Chinese air force—though the largest in the world—was operated primarily with aging craft. Reconnaissance that was not conducted by satellite was done mostly the old-fashioned way: with binoculars, thermal imaging, and cameras—albeit digital, with an assist from onboard computer enhancement.

Two full flight crews were on board for the twenty-two-hour flight, each consisting of a pilot, copilot, navigator, and radio operator. In addition to staying in contact with the air base, the radio operator was listening for any additional signals that might be relayed by satellite from the stricken submarine. He would be monitoring Chinese and Russian satellites, as well as contacting all of the scientific research stations in the region. They might see or hear something that could help tell them exactly where the submarine was or what may have happened, perhaps radio signals or seismic activity. Shortly before take-off, a report from the Ukrainian Antarctic Center at the Ministry of Education and Sciences noted that an "earthquakelike signature" was recorded by their Vernadsky Station on the Argentine Islands, just off the Antarctic Peninsula. The reading was taken minutes after the distress signal was received from the *Destiny*. The *zhong jiang* in charge of naval recovery operations suggested that the explosion of the submarine engine might have produced a reading like the one recorded at Vernadsky. The vice admiral's office had instructed both radio operators to take careful readings for radiation levels, in the event that the submarine's nuclear reactor had suffered a breach. The navy would want that information before they arrived. If the reactor casing had been compromised, the defense minister himself would have to decide whether to inform the research stations in the region, as well as commercial vessels that sailed these waters.

Only one reconnaissance team was on board the 737, since they wouldn't be needed until the jet reached the south pole. They would spend most of their time in the quarters that were located just rear of the electronics section. There were cots arranged bunk-style along the wall of the fuselage, a washroom, and a small galley. The passengers also included two naval submarine engineers and a three-man supply master's crew, who were in charge of cold-weather survival gear, supplies, and their parachute deployment. The jet was not equipped to land or effect a rescue. That would come later, in four days, when the naval vessels arrived from the Beihai naval base on the Gulf of Tonkin. They would attempt to recover the submarine. However, if crewmen from the *Destiny* had managed to escape and deploy lifeboats or reach shore, an airdrop would help keep them alive until then.

The crew of the 737 and the air force command were disconcerted that in an age of instantaneous communication, when data and video images could race about the globe in instants—going first to outer space to be returned, intact—an effort to save lives had to be done one kilometer at a time.

But that wasn't the worst part. The submarine crew were warriors. They understood the dangers that came with the privilege of sailing this vessel and defending the nation. They were also faceless. The airmen had a manifest in the event that communication was established. But Senior Captain Chien and Captain Biao and all the rest were still names, not people. What made this more viscerally disturbing to the Chinese fliers were two unrelated factors.

First, the accident had occurred aboard the flagship of the first generation of homegrown Chinese submarines. The airmen understood that kind of loss. The PLAAF had recently inaugurated flights of its Shenyang J-8, the first Chinese-made fighter jet. Though the J-8 was not as fast or maneuverable as the most advanced Western jets, it was a proud beginning—just as the first Song-class submarine was considered the strong firstborn prince of a twenty-first-century Chinese navy. To lose the fleet flagship was not just a tactical setback, but a stain on national pride. Therein lay the roots of the second factor that quickly took hold of the crew: an awareness of the personal impact this would have on the men, their careers, and their lives. Even if the airmen were able to locate survivors, this mission would always be remembered for the news it brought, not the men it might save. By association, the two crews on board the 737 would always be shrouded in the submarine's failure.

Like the seamen, they had known there were dangers when they joined the military. But they had never bothered to think of the ones that harmed the man but not the body. The ones that could never be repaired, that were never talked about in training. The ones that caused people to fall silent when you passed.

The taint of failure.

TWO

Corpus Christi, Texas

Strapped into thinly cushioned, fold-down seats that lined the sides of the fuselage, the L.A.S.E.R. team relaxed as the eighty-ton aircraft lifted itself off the tarmac. It was a slow climb, the cabin rattling as the four turbos raised her. The great wings of the plane were placed high on the fuselage; that way, the mountings would not require internal supports that would cut into the cargo capacity. In situations like this, where there was little cargo, just the large cabin, the echo of the engines was even greater. All of the team members had donned headphones that were hooked above the seats—and, in fact, had more padding than the seats. This minimized the noise and also allowed them to hear communications from the flight deck. Once the aircraft reached its cruising altitude of thirty thousand feet, and the sound settled a bit, they could remove the headphones. All except the team's radio operator, U.S. Army Corporal Jefferson Emens. He would be the liaison for any communication with Corpus Christi.

Thomas Bryan was not in the mood for communication of any kind. Despite not wanting to think about what the general had said, he couldn't help himself. This was not a problem that would go away with superior concentration. He tried to tell himself not to think about it. The submarine might be unsalvageable and the crew might already be dead.

But they might not be. And then he would have to kill them.

The major was not naive. He had been in combat. He understood the concept of shooting those who would shoot you. He had taken part in preemptive strikes based on reliable intelligence, even accepting the possibility that the intelligence could be wrong and that innocents might die. He even understood friendly fire and how it happened. But this—

It's a matter of national security, he told himself. That takes precedence over everything. That's why men shield presidents with their own bodies. It's why the submarine crew was down there in the first place, helping to create the next generation of ships to safeguard the nation.

It was the reason he might have to blow them up.

Major Bryan understood why. He understood how. He didn't like them but they weren't the problem. What he didn't understand was *when*. He remembered himself on the destroyer a week before. There, the "when" was the point at which his own team was in danger. And that point was clear: The ship started going down faster than anticipated. What point would that be in the south pole? General Scott had made it clear that Bryan had to make the call. And Bryan knew that call would be made if it became clear the submarine could not be salvaged.

If. That was the big word. If we don't hear anything from inside, no radios, no tapping, nothing that could be interpreted as motion, then we can destroy the target without hesitation or conscience. But what if L.A.S.E.R. was hearing sounds inside the sub right before the Chinese recovery unit arrived? Or as it arrived? Or right after it arrived? What was the drop-dead moment? At what point did the major pull the trigger? The submarine crew didn't get a voice and DOD didn't want a voice. Thomas Bryan was the one who had to decide.

The major glanced back at the large crate the quartermaster's men had loaded. It was secured to the back of the fuselage with a pair of heavy canvas straps. Bryan wondered how his own people would react to the mission overview when he finally presented it. He wondered how they would take the command when he gave it. Some would handle it a little better than he had, some a little worse. Some would be more emotional, some more pragmatic.

But we'll all do our duty, won't we? he told himself.

For weeks the team had been talking about coming up with some kind of motto and designing a uniform patch that incorporated the elements of air, land, and sea, something representative of them all. They couldn't think of a phrase that identified what they did, or even an image. Woodstock had suggested the Statue of Liberty, since she was on a small piece of land in the sea and reaching up to the sky. Though other units used Lady Liberty, it seemed to fit. Yet as the aircraft rumbled through the last portion of its ascent, only one statue image was in Bryan's mind. A statue with which, unhappily, he could identify.

Blind justice.

THREE

Weddell Sea

When Senior Captain Chien heard the sound of rushing water, he did not think. He acted.

It was a hull breach, aft. Chien had dropped the fire extinguisher and the light had shattered. He would have to proceed in the dark. He headed toward the stern, feeling his way and keeping his head low so he didn't hit anything.

"Lieutenant Mui!" the senior captain shouted. *"Lieutenant, are you there?"*

There was no answer. That could mean the officer was hurt or he simply couldn't hear over the roar. It was difficult to tell how bad the breach was because sound was amplified by the nearness of the hull on both sides.

Chien passed through the reactor compartment. The water had not reached here. He closed the hatch manually behind him. That made the sound of the water seem even louder. He continued forward toward the electrical bay. A light was ahead. It was high and unmoving.

"Lieutenant?"

"No, sir. This is *Zhong Wei* Hark."

Chien continued to pick his way forward, toward the light. "Sublieutenant, what is your situation?" he asked as he felt his way around the low-hanging pipes.

"I am working on the air system, sir."

"Where is Mui?"

"He and Khan went to try and close the aft hatch."

Two hatches were to the rear of their position: one at the turbine generator and one aft of that, right before the main ballast tanks and propeller shaft. Chien still did not know how far back the breach had occurred. If it had been far aft, past the turbine hatch, one man would have waited there, ready to shut the hatch in case the one beyond it could not be closed.

"Did they have a light?" Chien asked.

"Only matches, sir."

Chien did not want to distract Hark further. Obviously, the men had left him the flashlight. The air system was the sublieutenant's specialty. If it was irreparable, nothing else mattered.

Chien moved past the young electrician and continued into the dark.

"Mui! Khan!"

The sound of the sea was getting exponentially louder. Part of that was because he was nearer, and part of it was because the water was pressing deeper into the submarine. The senior captain found it odd that the vessel itself wasn't moving. Even being on the bottom, the added weight of the water would cause them to shift from side to side. Unless they were being held in place. He had heard what sounded like detritus striking the hull. Perhaps part of all of the submarine had been buried.

As Chien rounded the aft escape trunk, he began to feel dampness along the hull wall. The spray was reaching here.

"Can you hear me?" he shouted.

He thought he heard a response. He moved ahead more quickly, taking a few bangs and bumps in the process.

"Khan? Mui!"

"Here!" someone yelled.

"Again?"

"Here!"

The senior captain rushed toward the voice. He began to feel water climbing around his boots. He waded into it, moving his arms back and forth to give himself some momentum. He touched an arm and stepped closer to it. He heard grunting. The man was pushing on the door. The water was preventing him from closing it. Since most collisions were forward, and water was expected to run from that direction, the doors were designed to shut toward the back end of the submarine.

Chien saw a match struck. He made his way toward it.

"Who is there?" the senior captain cried.

"Khan, sir. Lieutenant Mui went in! He isn't able to close the aft hatch and ordered me to stay here!"

Water was cascading over the lip of the hatchway. It was halfway up the senior captain's shins. Chien stepped over the lip and entered the ballast room.

"Mui, can you hear me?"

There was no response.

"Mui!"

Again, there was nothing. Nor was there time to search. If the water rose much higher, it would begin spilling into the electrical bay.

Chien felt for the wheel, which was located in the center of the door. He found it. He tugged the hatch toward him. His idea was to pull it shut with himself on the outside. It didn't move. He tried harder and felt faint; it was difficult to breathe with the ventilators down. But the warm, stale, unsatisfying air was all they had. Sr. Capt. Chien Gan fought the dizziness his exertion brought on and pulled harder. The heavy metal door still refused to move. Whatever had caused the breach must have distorted the hull and hinges, causing the door to stick.

Chien stepped around the door, on the inside.

"No, sir!" Khan yelled.

The senior captain ignored him. There was no other choice. The water was loud, sound hammering him from all sides. They were running out of time. He pushed on the door. It moved slightly.

"Pull on it from your side!" Chien ordered.

"Sir, no!"

"I order you!"

Khan did as he was told. The hatch began to close, then slowed, then stopped. Chien heard the hinges squeak. That was where the problem was. He stretched his feet well behind him and put all his weight into his shoulder. He pushed on the hatch while Khan pulled. The door still wouldn't close.

Then another set of hands were pushing with him. Chien heard the grunting, felt arms knock against him as their owner struggled.

The door began to move.

"I couldn't . . . get the other . . . hatch," Lieutenant Mui apologized as he struggled.

Chien wanted to order the lieutenant out, to have him pull alongside Khan. But closing the door in any way possible was most important. The delay might cost them the slight momentum they had recovered.

Chien leaned deeper against the door as he pushed. The water reached the middle of his thighs. It struck him that if he succeeded, this would be the last act of his life. Yet it was a worthwhile trade. He would be dead but the submarine might live, and with it Chinese pride. Except for the loss of Lieutenant Mui, Chien could not regret that. Even then, Khan would report what Mui had done, how he had chosen honor over survival. There was no greater sacrifice.

The door was nearly shut. Chien found a pipe on which to rest his back. He put his foot on the hatch and gave a final push. Despite complaints from the hinges, the door shut. He heard the bolt being thrown on the other side, the ten-centimeter-diameter lock that held it in place.

Gasping from the strain, Chien fell against the door. He felt the wheel being turned; he moved to starboard and leaned against the thrust block of the propeller shaft. He heard Mui panting as he twisted the wheel on the inside. Khan would be doing the same on the other side. Though the door was locked, the wheel would push out the insulation, make sure there was no leakage.

The water rose above Chien's waist. It was frigid and it stung his flesh. But he smiled inside. Cold, suffocation, drowning. Look at all it had taken to kill him!

Mui sloshed over. "It is an honor to have served with you, sir," the lieutenant wheezed into his ear.

Chien felt for Mui's hand. Unable to see him in the utter darkness, he wanted to know where he was. Finding Mui's right arm, the senior captain moved down to his hand and grasped it in his own. Still clasping it, he stepped from the door and faced him.

"It is my privilege to be at your side now," the senior captain said. He bowed to the young officer. "I salute you."

Then he pulled Mui toward him in a traditional embrace. It was done with the full body, back straight, proud and strong.

And then the breach split wider somewhere behind them and the water entered like an angry fist and Senior Captain Chien silently wished his crew well as the sea took him, made him a part of it for all time. . . .

FOUR

Weddell Sea

It was the most horrific thing Wu Lin Kit had ever heard: the roar of the sea echoing toward him in the dark confines of the submarine. Just a few days before that same sound had been so comforting to him as he sat at his tent on the reef. Ordinarily, this was one of the yin and yang contrasts that enriched him. But not when it imperiled his mission, and his life.

Thoughts of the sea itself lasted only a moment, as this was a time to seek practical answers, not philosophical ones. And the immediate question was what, if anything, could be done about their current situation. The *Destiny* had stabilized for the present and Wu had regained his footing. The submarine was being flooded and the air was thick with men and carbon dioxide. Those needed to be fixed, and quickly. He stood on what turned out to be the slightly lopsided deck of the submarine and headed toward the stern, calling out as he walked to see if anyone else was there. Perspiration seemed to be wrung from him. It leaked from his forehead, his neck, both sides of his chest. As the Guoanbu operative moved, he kept his arms in motion, in slow, outward-sweeping circles. In combat, this was the ideal defensive maneuver for fighting in the dark. You could not fail to contact incoming blows and redirect them. Here, it prevented him from hitting anything.

Several crewmen in the command center were awake, a few

alert, and a handful were mobile. Captain Biao was among them. Sublt. Tsui Yen was not. Wu assumed he was unconscious in the command center. Because the electricity was down, the intercom would not work and the captain's point-to-point radio had been smashed. The only way to pinpoint the breach and to find out what was happening in the engineering and electrical sections was to go back there.

Calm and very much in command, Biao led a small party in that direction, Wu among them. The captain left men at different stations along the way. Hatches were to be shut on his command, depending upon where the sea was coming in. The electrical section had to be preserved above all. Wu got the sense from the captain's conversation with other crew members that if they couldn't get the air circulation going within a half hour, there would be little chance of survival.

Flashlights were missing from their hooks along the way— taken, presumably, by other crew members—and the men moved in absolute darkness. Fortunately, it was a straight run to the reactor room. There, the corridor became extremely narrow and wound around several large structures. The sailors knew their way through the chamber, but Wu lagged. They were about to exit this section when the sea sound suddenly became muffled, distant.

Everyone stopped moving.

"They closed a hatch," Biao said.

With the silence Wu heard another sound: a low hum in the walls. It was faint, almost like the sound of a distant airplane. No one moved. There was a sense of expectation; Wu could feel it the same way he could feel fear or aggression in an adversary. Apparently, some electronic system was functioning. That's what it sounded like, anyway. And anticipation was probably the only thing that would make the men stop and listen rather than move forward.

Wu was correct. He heard the high whine of a turbine somewhere aft. It was followed by a burst of fresh, if metallic-smelling, air. A moment after that a few lights came on.

"Every third light," Biao said.

Wu didn't know what that meant. He only knew that it was better than being in the dark.

The captain went to the nearest intercom and pressed a button that connected him to the electrical room. We edged around the other seamen so he could listen. Sublieutenant Hark reported that he had managed to turn on the battery systems—hence, every third light was working to conserve power. He also reported that the breach had been stopped for the moment by Lieutenant Mui and Senior Captain Chien.

"Mr. Khan was with them," Hark said. "He reports, most regrettably, that they shut themselves in the turbine room to accomplish this."

Biao received the news without expression.

"Sublieutenant, have Mr. Khan lower the constant temperature to thirty-eight degrees," the captain said.

"Yes, sir," the electrician replied.

Wu asked one of the other seamen why that was being done.

"The seals on the hatch are in ice water, sir," the crewman replied. "Extremes of temperature could cause them to crack."

Of course. Wu should have figured that out himself.

Biao thanked Hark and Khan for their good work, then sent two men back to help him and Khan work on restoring the main system. He had the remaining two men get blankets and gloves from the equipment stores for anyone who needed them. Wu suspected that as a matter of pride, no one would want to be the first to ask for extra garments. Perhaps the captain would break the stalemate by selecting one first.

When Wu and the captain were alone, Biao turned toward the aft section and saluted the empty corridor.

"The senior captain was a man of dignity and integrity," Biao said. "The nation will miss him. And I will miss him."

Wu couldn't tell whether Biao was being sincere or just polite. He did not seem upset. Or perhaps it was something akin to a phrase he had once read in an American-language handbook: *I have not time to bleed.*

"Would you come back to the command center with me, Agent Wu?" the captain asked.

"Of course."

"Their sacrifice bought us time," Biao said as they walked. "Whether it does any good depends on what we do next."

"What are our options?" Wu asked as they made their way forward.

"If power can be restored, the big question will be mobility," Biao said. "It sounded as if we encountered an ice slide."

"That was the pounding?"

"Much of it, I suspect. That much debris could not have come from the surface. Falling blocks probably caused the breach and may also have us pinned."

"Can we leave the ship to have a look?"

"We have emergency suits for quick transfers, but not for extended extravehicular activity," the captain replied. "That is why we have to see if the radio is working. The emergency beacon has its own power source. I'm more concerned about the high gain antenna."

"Where is that located?"

"On the bridge, atop the periscope. We need to try and raise naval command, let them know that we are alive. It will take three or four days for them to get equipment to this region. If there is a nation that already has resources in the area, they must ask for help."

"Will they?"

"I don't know," Biao replied. "Face may be more important to them than our lives."

"Perhaps. But not more important than our reconnaissance."

"That will be a difficult call for them. They may also fear leaving the *Destiny* or its crew in the hands of another nation, even for a day or two. They may prefer to leave us to our fate and get us when they can."

The captain's tone was uncritical. He understood the concept and seemed resigned to accept Beijing's decision. Wu would accept it, too, though he hated the idea of dying with his mission unfinished.

The men reached the command center. While Biao sat at the radio station, Wu checked the crewmen who were lying on the floor.

"Please leave them," Biao said.

"Excuse me?"

"There is nothing they can do for us, and unconscious men use less oxygen."

"Ah," Wu said. He should have realized that, too.

The intelligence agent checked for serious wounds and saw none. Only then did he leave the men. He stepped behind Biao.

"A minute ago you referred to the high gain antenna," Wu said. "That's for global communication and data transmission. Do we have another?"

"We have a mobile multiband antenna for local radio communication with other ships in the region. That one is also located on the bridge but it's smaller and more flexible. If it isn't buried, it may be usable."

"For what?"

"For contacting one of the vessels we intercepted," Biao replied. "You speak some English, do you not?"

"Yes. But what can they do?"

"If they have functioning sonar, it may tell us something of our condition. Or they may have access to a rescue submersible. We are not that far from the Falklands. The only drawback is that to operate the radio I need to turn on the entire console, which will draw considerable battery power."

"What does that mean in practical terms?"

"Barring the restoration of power and unexpected exertion— for example, from battling another breach—we will overwhelm the CO_2 conversion system twice as fast," Biao told Wu.

"And that would be when?"

"In three hours," Biao replied. "Which way do we gamble? Do we spend time to try and communicate?"

"It is imperative I tell my superior what I've learned, what we saw. Perhaps it will mean something to them."

"Then we have our answer."

The captain removed the compact radio module from its compartment and rejacked the wires in back for battery power. Then he replaced the unit, sat down, and switched it on.

FIVE

Weddell Sea

"All electrical systems functioning, power and air at full," Lieutenant Michaelson reported from his post.

"Radio is down," said Rockford, who, in addition to running the ramjet, was serving as the communications officer.

Captain Colon walked back and forth in the small area between his command chair and the control stations. His arms were folded tight around his chest and his eyes were turned up—to the surface where he wanted to be. He needed only one more report.

When it came, he wasn't happy.

"Sir!"

Lieutenant Junior Grade Withers called out as he made his way forward through the tight corridor. He was holding the wallet-sized DRC for the electronic thermometers. The Data Retrieval Cell plugged into jacks along the hull to read the external temperature. The Ant Hill had wanted to know how heated the air became during the entire supercavitation process. They had never expected to use it to read water temperatures.

"We have a temperature range of twenty-seven to thirty degrees from just forward the rear fans to the propeller," Withers said. "From there to here we are a very consistent twenty degrees."

"The temperature of big slabs of antarctic ice, I'll bet," Colon said.

"That would be my reading of the situation." Withers headed back to his seat. Outwardly the naval officer was calm, like the others.

"Thoughts, anyone?" Colon said.

"We don't appear to have a choice," Bain said.

"We have at least two," Colon said.

Bain seemed surprised. "Sir?"

"We can try to get out of this or we can stay put."

"I didn't realize staying put was an option," she said.

"Even if the *Abby* was damaged in the collision, the Ant Hill probably has a good idea that the mission is all screwed up," Colon said. "They'll send help."

"Sir, even though the *D*'s systems are functioning, we have no way of projecting hull integrity," Withers said. "The ice could be compacting, and if there's enough pressure in one spot, it will crush us."

"We aren't even sure how deep we are," Bain said. "Traditional escape procedures may not work."

"All of that is true," Rockford said. "But if the hull is in jeopardy anywhere, vibrations from turning on the ramjet to get out of the ice could also pull us apart."

"Or it could bring more of the slope down on us," Michaelson pointed out. "In both cases, staying put is the best option."

"So what do we do, flip a coin?" asked Withers.

"Actually, I'll be making any decisions," Colon said.

Withers frowned. "Sorry, sir."

"But the point is well-taken," the captain went on. "We don't have a lot of information with which to make an educated guess."

There was a long silence. Rockford broke it. "Excuse me, but does anyone else hear a buzzing?"

Colon stopped pacing. He listened. He did hear something.

"Yeah, it's coming from the hull," Withers said. "I heard it aft when I was taking the readings. I thought it was CO_2 having pressure tremens in the capillaries."

"It could be," Colon said.

The captain made his way back toward the ramjets. There was definitely a faint sound, like a mosquito close to the ear. It seemed to change slightly in pitch every now and then. He touched a bare section of the hull. It felt cool and still. The sound was coming from somewhere else.

He picked up the intercom, a wireless unit that looked like a cordless phone. It automatically connected him to the command center.

"Captain?" Rockford said.

"Put Lieutenant Bain on the line please."

The lieutenant junior grade got on immediately. "Yes, sir?"

"Turn the sonar on."

"Right away."

While Colon waited he listened. The sound was definitely coming from farther aft. He got on his knees between the two rear fanjet superstructures. They looked like large, raised manholes.

"Sonar is active, sir," Bain said. "We're still not getting any blips."

"Shut down all transducers except for the T-7."

"Done," she said.

That particular transducer—essentially a glorified microphone—was a mine-hunter. It was designed to receive broadband high-efficiency transmissions at low frequencies. Unlike the rest of the sonar system, it was passive, able to receive signals from proximity concussion devices. Unlike the other systems, the operator had to put on headphones to hear incoming signals.

"Sir, I don't know how or why, but we're getting a small oscillating reading!" Bain said excitedly.

"Direction?"

"The signal is coming from a two-degree spread along a very narrow acoustic range."

"Are we picking it up through the ice?"

"No. The dome is buried or we'd be getting regular sonar," Bain said.

"What do you think is making it?"

"Sir, it's in the range of a standard radio frequency."

"Can you boost it?" Colon asked.

"I'm doing that now," Bain said. "It's definitely a radiocast making irregular pulses. Hold on—no, not entirely irregular. The broadcast starts to repeat, more or less, at fifteen- to seventeen-second intervals."

"More or less?"

"The patterns are very similar but not identical."

"Could it be someone broadcasting a live SOS instead of a recording of one?" the captain asked.

"Possibly."

"I need better than 'possibly,'" Colon said.

"The signal strength is variable, so I'd say yes. An emergency beacon would be consistent."

"Thank you."

"But we shouldn't be picking up a standard radio signal at all," Bain went on. "Even if the *Abby* or the other submarine were broadcasting, our antenna is buried. The broadcast would get swallowed by the ice or dispersed by the water. This is weak but sharp. I don't understand."

Colon looked aft. He reached his hand toward the sloping wall. "It's not coming through the water."

"Sir?"

"Did you ever make a telephone using tin cans and a string?"

"No, sir."

"I think that's we have here," Colon said.

"I don't follow, sir."

"Two submarines connected by a metal towline," he said. "I think that's a broadcast from the sub that hit us."

SIX

Kings Bay, Georgia

The Ant Hill's radio operator, Sec. Lt. Eddie Kilbourn, was seated at the eastern side of the operations center, facing the wall. In addition to the satellite uplink, he had several systems at his post, including a ham radio and a CB system. One thing the twenty-eight-year-old had learned in his years as a radio devotee was that you never knew where messages would come from. As a young teenager in Milwaukee, he had once intercepted an early cell phone message on his ham radio, two guys plotting to rob a convenience store in Winnipeg, Canada. He had notified local authorities, who were waiting for the would-be thieves.

The hardware that he was listening to now was a thousand-channel receiver that scanned between 100 kHz and 3,000 MHz. Attached to a dedicated antenna that was keyed to signals from the south polar region, it was picking up two emergency signals. The first beacon, which had started coming in nearly ninety minutes before, was a gray box "condition red" scatter signal employed by the Chinese navy. It was the equivalent of an SOS that was designed to alert any ships, planes, or receiving stations that might be in the region. The DOD confirmed that the emergency signal had been received in Ningbo, south of Shanghai. Satellite surveillance and coded radio communications intercepted in Taiwan suggested that a 737 surveillance

craft had been dispatched to the region along with a naval recovery crew. The DOD decided not to ask the Chinese directly
for recon information since that would open a dialogue about
why the Pentagon was asking about a science ship, and why
that science ship had gone to the region twice in one month.
Such an exchange could provide little information. The U.S.
military would have its own team in the region within hours of
the Chinese flyby.

The more recent signal, and of even greater interest to the
Ant Hill, was a beacon that had been activated just a few minutes earlier. It was coming in through the main satellite uplink
on the frequency specifically assigned to the *Abby*. Triangula-
tion from military and weather satellites in the region showed
that the signal was stationary and coming from what appeared
to be several meters inland from the Weddell Sea. That was a
good sign. Someone would have had to hand-activate the emergency beacon for it to broadcast.

Someone was alive out there.

Second Lieutenant Kilbourn informed Dr. Carr, who informed Admiral Grantham. Yet the grim mood in the Ant Hill
did not change appreciably. The science ship's two emergency
beacons were located in the dinghies. Since the signal was coming from the shore, it suggested that one or more individuals
had abandoned the *Abby*. To have done so in Antarctica, in the
middle of the night, meant the situation on board must have
been desperate.

That the Ant Hill was receiving no signals, emergency or
otherwise, from the *D* was also disturbing as well as perplex-
ing. The *D*'s "Citrus" emergency signal was located in the nose
of the ship, with the sonar array. The yellow, grapefruit-sized
device—hence the nickname—was self-contained and designed to activate automatically if the vessel lost main systems.
Like the black box of an airplane, it was designed to survive
cataclysmic events including explosions—it could take a direct
hit from a torpedo—fires, and up to five thousand pounds per
square inch of pressure at two thousand feet underwater. Nothing in this area was that deep. That it was not functioning suggested one of five things. First, that Citrus had malfunctioned.

That was everyone's best guess, except for Kilbourn. He had tested it himself. It had been working when the *D* left port. Second, it could be buried. The signal was designed to broadcast underwater, even under the ice shelf, but there were limits to how much rock and ice it could penetrate. Third, the collision may have triggered a blast more significant than the designers had anticipated, possibly the explosion of several torpedoes on board the Chinese submarine. That shouldn't have made a difference, however, since the magnitude of the blast would not have been intensified, only the radius. Fourth, perhaps there had been a nuclear core breach on the Chinese submarine. Intense radiation released into the sea could theoretically disrupt the signal.

It wouldn't have done the crews of any of the ships much good either, Kilbourn thought.

Of course, there was also a fifth possibility: that the *Tempest D* was fully functioning and for whatever reason the telemetry simply wasn't getting through. The only explanations the Ant Hill brain trust could come up with were that the submarine had been crippled and gone into a deep trench, which were plentiful in the region; or else it had collided with the polar ice shelf and been partly or fully buried as a result.

In either case—in any case—Kilbourn and the others knew just one thing for certain.

None of this was good news for the crew of the *D*.

SEVEN

Weddell Sea

Wu stood by as Captain Biao sent his radio message. There was nothing else to do. Walking would keep him warm, but it would also use more oxygen. Wu forced his muscles to relax to keep from shivering. Though the digital thermometer wasn't functioning, Wu estimated it was forty degrees.

"What are you sending?" Wu asked.

"A progressive pitch signal. If anyone hears it, perhaps they will try to match it."

"How long will you continue?"

"Another few cycles," Biao said. "It could be the other vessels are lost or our antenna is not functioning."

Biao stopped sending to take an intercom call from Sublieutenant Hark. Though that too would draw power, the young officer was still working in the electrical section. Going back and forth would waste time and air.

"Go," the captain said.

"Sir, there is something very odd happening here. We're measuring an electrical current that does not originate on the *Destiny*."

"How is that possible?" Biao asked.

"I don't know, sir," Hark admitted. "I noticed the spike on our galvanometer. The needle is oscillating between one and two watts, as if someone were turning a dial back and forth."

"Your signal coming back at us?" Wu asked Biao.

"I don't think so. Mr. Hark, are you certain it isn't a flaw in the equipment?"

"Impossible, Captain," Hark assured him. "The only conditions my machine knows are functioning and not. Mr. Khan is looking for a possible source while I continue repairs."

"Captain, could we be receiving impulses from one of the other vessels?" Wu asked.

"How?" Biao asked.

"I don't know," Wu admitted.

"Mr. Hark, did you hear that?"

"I did."

"Is it possible?" Biao asked.

"Only if we are in direct contact with them," Hark replied.

Wu and the captain looked at each other.

"Mr. Hark, what is the duration of each impulse?" Wu asked.

"One second at one watt, two seconds at two."

"Is it still coming?"

"Yes, sir."

"Thank you, Mr. Hark," the captain said. "Please return to your duties but keep watching the needle. Let me know instantly if there is any change. I'll leave the intercom open."

"Yes, sir."

"Someone is responding," Biao said. "But with a different signal to make sure our broadcast is not automated."

"Can we send a signal like the one that is coming in?" Wu asked.

"Yes." Biao was already making adjustments to the radio. "We'll match the signal twice, then vary it. See if we get the same thing back."

While Biao prepared to send out electronic pulses rather than a voice message, Wu began to feel dizzy. He lowered himself into a seat by the captain's post. After sending the signal, Biao looked at him.

"I know," the captain said. "The air is getting stale."

"You said we have three hours."

"To live," Biao replied quietly. "The quality of the air, however, will continue to deteriorate."

That was another thing Wu should have realized. He was tired and his mind was not alert. He felt ashamed showing ignorance once again.

"Captain, the signal has changed!" Hark said.

"One, two, one, two, one, three, one, three?" Biao asked.

"Yes, sir! How did you know?"

"It's what I sent. Thank you. How are repairs coming?"

"Not well, sir," Hark reported. "The seawater short-circuited several key boards. I am not sure we can rig substitutes."

"Keep at it," Biao replied. "Let me know if there are further impulses." He looked at Wu. "We are in communication with one of the other vessels. We need to find out which one, where they are, and whether they are in contact with—"

"Sir, another set of impulses," Hark said. "One watt, five, three. Then it repeated. Response, sir?"

"Not yet," Biao said. "One, five, three."

"It could be a time reference, or map coordinates," Wu noted.

"It could also be—"

Biao reached into a folder at the side of the helmsman's chair. He withdrew a loose-leaf book that was filled with black-and-white maps. He found the one he was looking for.

"If we headed in a southwesterly direction when we slid into the sea, that would have brought us to this region," he said, indicating a section off the coast of Graham Land.

"What makes you think we went that way?"

"Because we were struck from above, probably by a landslide. That means we are close to the shelf. Any deeper, or farther, that wouldn't have happened. You see?" Biao pointed to other charts. "Four hundred and eleven meters to the north, only two hundred and forty to the east."

"You're saying it is probably the American submarine and they are at a depth of 153 meters—or feet, perhaps?"

"Yes," Biao said. "But if we are receiving an electrical spike from the submarine, it means that they have power. Battery power would not be sufficient to register on the galvanometer."

"Then how did they read us?"

"I don't know," Biao admitted. "But it also means that the vessels *are* touching. Otherwise the signal would have been garbled by water or ice."

"The question is, are they buried? Can they pull us up?"

"You speak some English," Biao said. "Can you read it?"

"Well enough."

"How many characters are there in English writing?"

"Twenty-six," Wu replied.

Biao looked at him. "Is that all?"

"Yes." The Chinese alphabet had thousands of symbols.

"Hark?"

"Sir?"

"Send the following wattage back: one, twenty-six. Send it three times then wait for a response."

"Yes, sir."

Biao shut the radio, then rose slowly. He held the chair back to steady himself for a moment. "Let's go back there and see if they understood."

EIGHT

Weddell Sea

"Twenty-six," Bain said.

"Letters of the alphabet?" Michaelson suggested.

"That'd be my guess," Colon said. He was back in his command chair, watching the signal exchange. "Sounds like they're telling us someone on board speaks English, not Morse. So we'll have to do this the long way."

"Can we start by telling them, 'Fuck you for doing this'?" Bain asked.

Everyone looked at her.

"Sorry. Needed to get that out of my spleen."

"You speak for all of us," Colon said. He thought for a moment. "Just to be clear, we're doing one watt for 'A,' two for 'B,' and so on. Correct?"

"Yes, sir," Bain replied.

"Okay. Start with, 'Do you have radio to surface'?"

Bain sent the pulses and then waited. Everyone was at his or her station, monitoring systems. At each unfamiliar squeak or groan, everyone sat very still. There was only one flood door, in the center of the submarine, and no one wanted to have to use it.

After nearly a minute the radio chirped a return message. Bain wrote down the letters as the pulses came through.

"They say, 'Yes. Else systems down,'" Bain said. "They probably mean 'other systems.'"

"So they're running on batteries. Ask, 'How much air?' "

A minute later the answer came back: "Less three hours."

"Jeez," Withers said. "Dead on the bottom."

"Ask them, 'Rescue coming?' " Colon said.

The reply was quick: "Uncertain."

A stilted but informative conversation continued. Captain Colon informed them his ship was American and asked for their nationality. They told him. Colon said that he had power but was stuck, apparently, from nose to midship in ice. The other crew told him they had an aft breach and believed they were also partially entombed. Colon asked the other crew to provide their submarine type. They did not reply. He asked again. They did not answer again but asked the same question he did. Colon also did not reply.

"So they're down here in a new hotshot submarine just like we are," Michaelson muttered.

"And we're both still playing games," Withers commented.

"Yeah, well, we're also wearing different jerseys," Colon said. "There are larger issues than all of us getting out of here." He fixed his eyes on Bain. "All right. This is the big one. Tell them we may have a way out but it could destroy them."

"We do?" Rockford said.

"I'm working on it," Colon replied.

Bain sent the message. The reply was less than a minute in coming: "We die anyway."

Colon wanted to know how many men were on the submarine. Sixty-nine, he was told. He did not answer when the Chinese asked the same question.

"Sir, this back and forth is costing us all time," Michaelson said.

"Do you know a shortcut?" Colon asked.

"I didn't mean that, sir," Michaelson said. "I meant that our situation may be nearly as dicey as theirs."

"And?" Colon's gaze was fixed on the officer.

"As you just said, there are larger issues here. One of them is the *D*. We need to protect her."

"What have I overlooked, Lieutenant?" Colon's voice, like his eyes, were hard.

"Getting out," Michaelson said. "Using the aft jets at half to see if we can at least dislodge some ice."

"Not yet," Colon said.

"Sir, with respect—we are in this situation because of those people." He pointed vaguely toward the stern. "They were probably spying on us."

"Does that mean we should kill them?" Colon asked.

"No, sir. But there is no indication that we would damage them by trying to get free. And we may save ourselves."

"We may also kill ourselves," Rockford said. "We could pull our nose section off because of the cable that's apparently still tied to the Chinese submarine."

"That's a risk," Michaelson admitted. He was becoming agitated. "But so is sitting here, especially if their submarine is on top of us. Our hull won't support that weight forever."

Frowning as though he'd just thought of something— something not good—Withers turned to the computer. He typed in a file name. Rockford was also typing, though he wasn't frowning.

"Lieutenant, it's a crapshoot either way," Colon agreed. "So our priority has to be to try and get more information. The Chinese may be able to give us intel about their position relative to us. If we decide to use the ramjet, that may give us an idea which fan to use. Maybe they've had a look through the periscope, seen what the ice looks like. But we won't get any of that data if they're dead. Now—are there any suggestions about how to help these people?"

"Well, there's one thing we can rule out," Rockford said. "I just checked our database. There are no DSRVs out here."

DSRVs were Deep Submergence Rescue Vehicles. They were self-propelled mini-subs that were lowered from a surface vessel, attached to the escape hatch, and used to ferry trapped submariners to freedom.

"Not even in the Falklands?" Colon asked.

"Nope. Royal Navy submarine activity in the region was cut back in '92. They have most of their fleet in the Atlantic and in the Persian Gulf region."

"That makes sense," Colon said.

"Also, we can't get them any significant electrical power," Bain said. "These pit-a-pat signals we're sending are only pushing enough juice through the cable to light a small bulb. They're tickles."

"Nobody outside is going to hear those," Rockford said. "Even if they had a functioning antenna, the broadcast radius is about twenty miles."

"Meaning they're *screwed*, because there are no research bases within range. That's why we picked this area!" Michaelson said. "Sir, I understand we could use more information. But suppose they're bullshitting us. Suppose they saw our vessel and want to keep us here till one of their rescue ships arrives?"

"Lieutenant, enough," Colon said.

"That avalanche was real enough," Bain reminded him.

"Yes, that was," Michaelson agreed. "But how do we know they didn't hit us just to keep us here, take the *D* as a prize? They may have had a rescue ship en route even before the collision."

"I don't think they'd sacrifice their ship and a full crew for that," Rockford said.

"How do you know?" Michaelson asked. "And I have another question for you. Suppose this isn't a deception. Suppose they're hurt but they manage to get their engines back on-line. They've got to be working on it. Do you think they'll hesitate to try and pull out, regardless of what it does to us?"

"I've thought about that, and I don't know," Colon admitted. "But I don't have to answer for their command decisions, only for ours."

"Actually, there may be a more immediate problem," Withers said. He was still looking at his computer monitor.

"For us or them?" Colon asked.

"Both. There aren't very many Chinese submarines capable of maintaining a crew that size *and* reaching these waters from any PLN naval base in the region. I've had a look at our database." He faced the captain. "Sir, their aft section is filled with water. In any of these larger submarines, just the rearmost area filled with water represents approximately twelve hundred cubic meters. That's almost three hundred thousand gallons. If they're not resting on a perfectly flat surface—for example, if they're across our back—that's going to cause pressure that will distort their own hull—"

"Meaning the seam of their aft hatch door won't hold," Bain said.

"Exactly. And if they flood, that could cause them to roll or drop or do something that could damage us—"

"Because we're still attached by that fucking towline," Colon said. "Where they go, we go."

"That's right, sir. I know you didn't ask, but while I'm all in favor of finding some way to help these people, the first thing we have to do is get disattached. Which means the ramjet."

"But if we do that," Rockford said, "if we fire the engines before getting ourselves disentangled, the *D* thrust could be neutralized by the weight of the Chinese submarine. We would burn the fans out just trying to get away."

"If it's a question of being proactive or just sitting and waiting, I'm for lighting a fire," Michaelson said. He regarded Colon. "Captain?"

"We may have another choice," Colon said. "I want to think it through. In the meantime, we don't try and move until we know to where, from what, and what the risks are. At the moment we're all right. If that changes—"

There was a loud rumble from the front of the *D*.

"That's not a happy sound," Bain remarked nervously.

"Sounds like a new landslide," Withers suggested.

"Either that, or the ice chunks are settling," Bain said.

"Orders, sir?" Michaelson asked.

"Yeah. We ride it out."

Michaelson did not seem pleased. Colon didn't blame him. Allowing your ship to be hammered by ice is not a choice any commander wants to make. But that seemed the least bad of a short menu of bad options.

Suddenly, in addition to the rumbling, a loud, unhealthy-sounding squeal ripped through the *Tempest D*. The sound was coming from the nose section. A moment later the *D* began to nose down toward the starboard side.

"Shit. The ice," Withers said.

"What about it?" Rockford asked.

"It must be pulling the towline as it falls."

Shit was right, Colon thought. The nose attachment didn't like being pulled. And if that popped, they were dead. The few bad options had just been narrowed to none.

"Ready aft ramjet top, but do *not* engage propulsion," Colon said.

"Yes, sir," Rockford said.

The captain's mind was absolutely clear but his heart was slamming for the first time since the accident. He rose and walked to the command array. He grabbed an overhead handle and stood with his legs wide apart for balance. "Lieutenant Michaelson, prepare to release towline."

"Right away, sir."

The submarine began to hum again as the rear fans were powered up. Michaelson moved his hand to the release lever. Colon scanned the deck for signs of water. The access conduit to the nose was directly beneath Michaelson's post. If there was a leak, it would come through there.

"Jets at full," Rockford said.

"Release the cable!" Colon ordered.

Michaelson pulled the small lever toward him. They heard the distinctive snap of the eye-lock releasing the towline. The light below the lever came on, the "all-clear" indicator. Yet they were still angling in the same direction as the rumbling ice, and the nose section continued to complain.

"Sir, I don't understand," Michaelson said. "We've got separation."

"Maybe not," Rockford said. "The cable may be jammed in place by the ice."

"Not jammed, frozen," Bain said. "Our heat may have melted the ice and it refroze around the cable-eye."

"So the latch may have opened but wasn't released from the hook," Withers said.

"Right," Rockford replied.

The *D* continued to nose down to the starboard. They had to stop this descent. It could do the hull more damage and it could drag the Chinese down as well.

"Ramjet engage, one-sixth," Colon ordered, holding tight to the overhead handle to keep from slipping.

"One-sixth, engaging," Rockford said.

There was a slight downward kick from the stern. They heard kettledrum-like pounding from both sides, presumably as the Egg displaced pieces of ice. The submarine immediately steadied and, within moments, had reclaimed some of the level stability it had lost.

Ice continued to slide around them. They still felt the pull at the nose. But they were able to hold their position, which was all Colon wanted. When the landslide finally stopped, the silence seemed thicker, the air closer than before.

"Everyone okay?" Colon asked.

The crew answered in the affirmative.

The electrical surge to the ramjet generated a slight buzz. Colon listened. Below it was a new sound, a soft creaking like a rusty clasp on a mainmast, high and far away.

Some part of the submarine was being stressed, but Colon couldn't place it. "Can anyone tell where that's coming from?"

"Sir, I don't think it's us," Bain said.

There was a hard bump in the aft section. From below. Bain was right. At least part of the Chinese submarine was sliding beneath them. The landslide must have caused their positions to shift. The crew of the *D* was silent, waiting. There were no further scrapes or sounds.

"Captain, the Chinese are signaling us," Bain said.

"That answers the question about the towline," Rockford said. "We're still attached to them."

" 'Cold stop battery,' " Bain said, reading the message as it came through. " 'Air failing.' "

"That new pile-on must have dropped the temperature even further for them," Withers said.

"At least it didn't wreck that aft hatch," Rockford said.

"Maybe, but I'm sure the slip-slide didn't do the seal any good," Withers pointed out.

"Agreed. Which is why we've got to help them," Colon said. "Now."

The others looked at him.

"I was working out a plan before we were distracted," Colon said. "Lieutenant Bain, find out how much electrical cable they can pull from their systems. Make sure they can waterproof it."

"Yes, sir."

"What are we going to do?" Withers asked.

"We're obviously in this together, handcuffed by a towline," Colon said. "We may have to get out of this together."

"How?" Rockford asked.

"We need to jump-start their aft pumps so they can drain off some of that water, put their systems back on-line—"

"*How*, sir?" Rockford repeated.

"We've got to try and power them up," Colon replied.

NINE

Weddell Sea

Wu sat stiffly at the control panel, his backbone straight, chest extended. He was thinking. Not about the mission now but about Senior Captain Chien. Perhaps he had been the wisest of them all.

The Guoanbu operative was doing nothing but trying to breathe, and that poorly. Each breath was shallow and barely sufficient. Despite his best efforts his teeth were clattering. The last series of concussions had lowered the submarine and the temperature, and caused fluids in the battery casing to finally freeze. Ironically, as Biao had explained, the distilled water was in there to keep the battery from overheating. Hark was attempting to drain it, but the batteries were difficult to reach. Intentionally, as irony would have that as well, so it would not be compromised if the compartment flooded.

The captain was beside Wu, writing a log entry by flashlight; the lights had been turned off to conserve the fading battery power though the radio was left on, in case the Americans would—or even could—respond. Watching Biao make what might be his final entry, Wu thought about his own imminent death and about Chien's sacrifice. The senior captain had saved the submarine—for what he probably suspected would be just a short while—and in the process had died with dignity. That small, quiet man now seemed so large and overpowering, while

Wu felt entirely the opposite. Yet it was not just failure that weighed on him now. It was seeing his own force used against him. Wu Lin Kit had decisively dismissed the senior captain. The officer had used that power to assert his superiority. Shame was everywhere his mind went, and Wu did not know how to help himself.

The radio suddenly became active again. Biao stopped writing to take the message. He did not seem excited. Perhaps he didn't have the energy. He jotted down the wattage number by number. It was a longer message than usual. He handed his log to Wu, who wrote in the English-language characters. He was surprised by what he read. It must have registered in his expression.

"What do they want?" Biao pressed.

"Do we have waterproof electrical wire?"

"We do. Why?"

"They want to know how much."

"Maybe ten or fifteen feet in each torpedo tube to open the outside scuttle," Biao replied.

"Voltage capacity and temperature," Wu said. "They want to know that." Each word came with some effort.

"The wires have three-hundred-volt capacity and I expect they are asking for temperature tolerance," Biao replied. "Tell them the wire has been tested to minus ten degrees."

Wu nodded. "There are two more words. 'Out periscope.'"

Biao thought for a moment. Then, suddenly excited, the captain went on the intercom. "Hark?"

"Sir?"

"Stop repairs and have everyone report forward. Bring all the tool kits you can find."

"At once, sir."

Biao rose slowly. He spoke in breathy exhales. "I think . . . I understand. If we can snake . . . the cable out without letting water in . . . the Americans may have a way of retrieving it."

"But they . . . are trapped as well."

"Perhaps help . . . is coming for them," Biao said. "A submersible could also evacuate . . . my crew."

Wu heard clattering, grunts, and stumbling. The exhausted, oxygen-starved crew moved forward with the two remaining flashlights. Their spirit was inspiring. But it was not enough. The Guoanbu operative didn't think he could feel lower than he had just a few moments ago. He was wrong. There was no greater loss of face than to be beholden to your enemy. Wu did not have the right to prevent the others from being rescued. But for himself he saw nothing but the honor of the solution Senior Captain Chien had selected.

Yet perhaps taking your life is not the best answer, he thought. There was still the mission. And as Chien had demonstrated, what better way of completing it than by using your opponent's own actions against them.

TEN

Weddell Sea

"The Chinese say yes," Bain reported.

"Excellent," Colon replied. "Lieutenant Bain, let them know we'll contact them in a few minutes. Lieutenant Rockford, you come aft with me. The rest of you stay here. When we're through, shut the flood door."

"That doesn't sound promising," Withers remarked.

"Just a precaution," Colon assured him.

The captain and Lieutenant Rockford made their way through the narrow passage. When they crossed the middle of the vessel, Withers shut the watertight door. It was comprised of accordion-style panels that rose along tracks from the bottom to top. The idea of the unconventional door was to save interior space and also to contain a slow leak without blocking access to the entire aft or forward section. Colon was glad to see that it closed smoothly. That meant the ice had not yet crushed or twisted the hull. If there had been any change in alignment, the tracks would be slightly off and the door would not have shut.

"A precaution against what, sir?" Rockford asked when they were alone.

"The ramjet caps can be removed so the fan mechanism can be repaired, or the blades can be cleaned or replaced."

"Yes—"

"I'm thinking that if we run the blade in reverse, we will blow into the *D* instead of away from it."

"Also true."

"If the Chinese can feed the electrical wire out, we may be able to capture it. Like a vacuum cleaner."

"And that's the plan, sir?"

"Yes."

Rockford stopped. "Sir—forgive me, but there are three fatal problems with what you're proposing."

Colon stopped. "I'm listening."

"First, passing the wire through the fans would be like sticking a noodle in a blender. It'll be lacerated."

"It's tough wire. We'll run the jets on superlow."

"Respectfully, sir, they'll still be lacerated."

"Not necessarily. What's the second problem?"

"Second, sir, you'll suck up anything else that's floating in the vicinity."

"I'm counting on that."

"You are?"

"Yes. Hopefully, we'll pull in small chunks of ice. That will slow the blades down, maybe enough to keep them from slicing the wire apart."

"That will also destroy the ramjet."

"We can function with three, or with standard drive. Third problem?"

"If you open the cap and turn on the jet, you'll suction the ocean into this compartment."

"That's why I had them close the door."

Rockford glared at him. "Sir, forgive me, but you can't be serious."

"I am. We can afford to take on some water. Our pumps are working. They're designed to keep us from flooding. Let's see if they do."

"Captain—"

"Lieutenant, this mission has stopped being a test drive. This is about survival. We can't get out of here with that towline still attached. We can't get out to remove it. What choice do we have but to try and raise the other thing it's attached to? Namely, the Chinese submarine."

Rockford did not respond.

"If we can get them mobile and coordinate an ascent, the towline may not be relevant. It's a chance, isn't it?"

"Real slim, sir. Even assuming you can snare the cable, how will we waterproof the compartment once it's here? When we close the cap, we'll cut the wire."

"We've got cement designed for leaks, just as I'm sure the Chinese do. We'll close the cap most of the way, slap it on, and keep an eye on it."

Rockford shook his head. "Another big if. I don't see how this can possibly work—"

"Look," Colon snapped, "I know this is a long shot." The captain was tired and exasperated and tired of having his decisions questioned. "But if we don't try *something*—"

"I was going to say, I'll tell you what might," the engineer added.

Colon smiled. "Thank you."

"Sir?"

"I was praying you'd have a better idea. What is it?"

"The center bolt of the ramjet fan is hollow," Rockford said as they continued walking. "I'm thinking that we remove the fan entirely and fish the wire through *there*. That way we don't have to open the outer fan door more than just a few centimeters. The pumps can handle that."

"The ramjet hub is about a fifty-millimeter opening," Colon said. "How do we grab the cable?"

"I can rig a wire noose. That's not the problem. The challenge will be for the Chinese to place it close enough for me to grab."

"How will they do that?" Colon asked.

Rockford replied, "They're the one with the periscope."

Colon went to the intercom and gave Bain a new message for the Chinese submarine.

ELEVEN

Weddell Sea

Captain Biao had not attempted to use the periscope since they had been down here. He hadn't wanted to drain battery power for little return nor divert human resources to hand-crank the unit.

Now he had no choice.

Wu helped the captain and two other men attempt to raise the periscope manually, which required putting steel bars into a pair of slots and turning horizontally, clockwise. They were unable to budge it. The problem was more than the darkness and rapidly thinning air. Apparently, ice had piled on top of the submarine. They could only raise the tower a half meter and they could not rotate it at all. To make things worse, it was facing the ice, not the American submarine.

While the other crewmen continued to remove wiring from the forward torpedo tubes, Wu relayed the periscope information to the American submarine. Wu worked quickly, since he didn't know when the radio might shut down. As it was, he was already losing the higher wattage and the upper end of the alphabet.

The Americans asked if a man could leave the submarine for a brief period.

"Forward . . . escape . . . trunk. Emergency suit," Biao told Wu while continuing to struggle with the periscope.

Wu passed that along. The Americans replied by asking them to send a man out with the cable.

"Bring wire toward light," the Americans replied.

Wu informed the captain. Biao thought for a moment, then summoned Lieutenant Junior Grade Hark. The young electrician was standing in one of the port torpedo tubes. The vertical launch tubes were clustered four starboard and four port. Four or five men were working in each of them, back to back, unscrewing plates and removing the cables within. Hark handed his battery-powered screwdriver to another crewman and came over.

"Sir?" Hark saluted.

"Put on an emergency suit," Biao ordered. "Take one end of the cable . . . through the hatch. The Americans will direct you by light. The oxygen tank will keep you alive to finish here when you return."

"Sir!" The man saluted again.

Hark took the captain's flashlight and moved quickly toward the forward stores compartment, where the emergency suit was stored.

The hot, unsatisfying air was thick with the musky smell of the crew. Plates clanged on the rubber deck as they were removed. Breath was heavy and strained, eerily audible since the rest of the submarine was so silent.

Hark returned with the suit and was also holding what looked like an aerosol spray can with a long hose. Wu thought that it must be the sealant. Hark would have to create an airtight conduit through which the cable could pass. That would mean closing the outer hatch most of the way, then using the fast-hardening, foamlike substance to create a new water barrier once he was back inside.

Another crewman helped Hark put the suit on. The emergency suit looked like a padded gray wet suit. A vest, bloated with a solution of some kind, protected the chest from the pressure, and the gumdrop-shaped helmet had two thickly protected eye holes. At the back, a pair of small air tanks were attached to the helmet. They rested along the shoulder blades of the wearer.

There were no external tubes or pipes that could rupture or freeze.

Hark called to an engineer, who came over with one end of cable. The short, young seaman was huffing and perspiring, the edges of his long sleeves literally dripping onto the deck: He held a coil of what looked like twenty to thirty feet of surprisingly thin silver cable.

Their lifeline was only a little thicker than speaker wire. But then, lifelines throughout the body were thinner than that, Wu reminded himself. Strength was not a virtue of size.

"I'll need more wire when I get back, all that you can give me," Hark said before fastening the floppy helmet. He pointed to Wu's radio. "Bundle the cable here. I will come for it."

The other man nodded.

The captain rose. "You can't stay out for long," he warned Hark. "The suit is not designed . . . for hypothermic dives."

"Yes, sir."

"Good luck."

Hark saluted again and made his way to the escape trunk. The crewman who had assisted him went along carrying the sealant. He would pass it up to Hark once he had entered the air lock.

Captain Biao left to help the engineers remove more cable. Wu had nothing to contribute there and remained seated by the radio. The only light he saw was whatever happened to bounce his way when a flashlight was moved ahead or inside the torpedo tubes.

He could not even help at the level of the lowest seaman.

Wu was unaccustomed to being helpless and ashamed. But the way through that was to accept the defeat and never forget the feeling. It wasn't defeat that destroyed a man. Only giving up could do that.

TWELVE

Weddell Sea

Bain relayed the communiqués from the Chinese ship. Colon was looking forward to a moment of "face time" with one of the sailors—even if it was through an emergency-suit visor. What he was about to attempt went against his military training. It went against Tempest protocols: He was inviting a Chinese sailor to see the *D* up close. But he was willing to risk that, especially when most of the submarine was apparently covered with ice. Indeed, as Colon worked, his thoughts, his imagination, went all over the moral map. Would he take Chinese crewmen onto the *D* if there was no other option?

No. The submarine couldn't hold that many people.

Would he accept however many he could accommodate?

Yes.

Would he allow the Chinese commander to make that decision alone?

He'd have to.

If that decision was made, was there even a way to get the sailors over here?

He had no idea. Colon didn't know how many emergency suits the Chinese had. Probably three or four at most, since they were used mostly for external repairs and not evacuation. Even so, how would they get the seamen inside? The pumps probably couldn't handle that.

While the captain quickly removed the dozen bolts that held the ramjet cap in place, Lieutenant Rockford pulled a fiber-optic line from one of the control panels. He would use it to run a light outside for the Chinese sailor to see.

As the men actually got down to it, the idea of removing the blade to allow someone to enter seemed desperate and implausible. And dangerous. The *D*'s "dredge pump" was a remarkably compact unit, the size of a small vacuum cleaner, designed by Mike Carr. It could siphon twenty-five hundred gallons a day back into the sea. It was designed to compensate for any hairline cracks that might be caused by concussive force from the ramjet that might echo against the hull due to close proximity to the seafloor, running into an extreme temperature variation that corrupted the bubble, or, ironically, passing too close to another vessel.

"The interior air will be squeezed by the incoming water," Rockford explained as they worked. "That could kill us, rupture the capillaries, and crack the hull, and also short out the pump."

So it wasn't a good idea. Colon appreciated Rockford's having been respectful of the idea and Colon's own subsequent dismissal of it.

Rockford finished shortly before Colon did, then helped him remove the rest of the bolts. The fiber-optic line required a quick splice with a five-foot section to reach. Colon hoped they could do without their depth-indicator readout until the light could be replaced.

Using an Allen wrench, Rockford began removing the center screw from the fan. Once the ten-inch bolt was out, the five-foot-diameter fan would still be resting on the central hub.

"Sir, when I start fishing the line through, you'll have to work the door *and* the pump," Rockford said. "They'll have to be started simultaneously."

Colon nodded. That would be easy enough: The two buttons were side by side on the control panel. A pump mouth was located in the base of each ramjet housing. They had been placed there to guard against backwash when the fans started up. If the pump was started first, it would suck up air instead of water. Air intake would "burp" into the mechanism itself. A vent would expel that air, but using it would cause a short delay in the bailing. A great deal of water could pour through in that time.

"I'll only need an opening of about three centimeters," Rockford said. "I'll let you know when it's there."

The doors opened in the center. If the button was not held down, the two panels wouldn't function. Only a one- or two-second tap on the activation button was required to give Rockford his three centimeters. Colon put one index finger on that button and another on the button that started the port, aft ramjet pump.

"Ready, sir," Rockford said.

Colon felt a rush of satisfaction as he hit the buttons. The crew had been sent here to test a machine that was designed to make war on guys like these. Instead, they were using it to help them. That was incongruous but also very American. He could not imagine the Chinese or the Russians or any damn body else doing this.

If they never got out of this, that would be an okay last thing to think about.

Very okay.

THIRTEEN

Weddell Sea

Wu Lin Kit opened his eyes. He felt as though he were back on the beach.

Cool air was blowing hard, with mist in his nostrils, a lazy sense of well-being in the white sunshine. But Wu realized that he was not on the beach. No sand was beneath him, just rubber. He was lying chest-down on the floor of the submarine. The air was circulating and the lights were on. The mist was his own fast-cooling perspiration.

Wu's right cheek was on the floor. He looked at the other sailors, who had also passed out. A few of them were beginning to move. It took the Guoanbu operative a few seconds longer to realize what had happened.

Sublieutenant Hark had succeeded. Power had been restored to the *Destiny*.

Wu heard a voice behind him. He glanced around. Hark was still in his emergency suit, though he had removed his helmet. He was helping the captain get to his seat. Biao was awake but disoriented. Hark obviously wanted the others to find their commander in his chair when they woke. Wu himself was lying just outside the forward escape hatch. Other crew members were spread out fore and aft, some on their bellies, some on their backs, some seated and slumping forward.

Wu took slow, level breaths. It did not take long for him to become alert. He rose to his knees.

"Wait, sir," Hark said. "I'll help you!" He had to shout to be heard through the cowl of the suit.

"I can manage, thank you."

Wu struggled to stay on his knees. His head was still light. The captain had to be helped up; Wu wanted to do this himself. Hark hovered for a moment before moving on to look after the others.

"What did you see of the submarine?" Wu asked.

"Very little, sir," Hark replied. "The light was very dim." He turned to check some of the other men.

"But you saw something," Wu pressed.

"A small section of the hull."

"What color?"

"Dark gray. And there was a fan of some kind. I could just make it out on the far side of the hatch."

"Describe it."

"It was about five or six feet across, like a ceiling fan."

Biao swung his chair around. He looked toward the compartment. "Well done, Sublieutenant."

"Thank you, sir. The Americans made it easy. They lowered a filament into the water. I simply made my way to it."

"How secure is the cable?" Biao asked.

"The water current is very slow here," Hark said. "As long as the terrain does not shift again, it shouldn't slip."

"How close is the other submarine?" the captain asked.

"We are touching, sir," Hark reported. "It is lying across us at an angle, just aft of the con. The ice slide ends where we cross."

"You didn't recognize the submarine type?" Wu asked.

"No, sir."

"What about the size?"

"I would judge it to be smaller than our own vessel. But it is very difficult to say, for I only saw a small section."

Biao rose and walked over. He squatted among the slowly reviving crew. "Mr. Hark, I want you to take a short break.

Have something to eat, and then go back to your post. We need to see if we can get our own power on-line."

"Sir, I'd like to go there directly, as soon as I wake the men I need," Hark said respectfully.

Biao smiled proudly. "Permission granted. Sublieutenant, I will be logging everything you did today in the electrical room, in the sea, and here. You have performed heroically."

"Thank you, sir," Hark said, bowing.

"No. The PLN thanks you."

Hark began rousing the groggy technical staff who had been working in the torpedo tubes when they passed out there. They seemed surprised to be alive. Though they were still at the bottom of the sea in a virtually dead ship, the control room filled with an uncommon sense of euphoria. Wu understood. As his master used to say, *Hope is the best herb.*

When his own senior officers were awake, Captain Biao told them they would still be running the *Destiny* on minimal power. The interior temperature was to be maintained at levels barely above freezing to keep the rear seal as secure as possible. Most of the lights were to remain off. Biao was using the rest of the power to charge the batteries, which had been seriously depleted running the air system. A full recharge took twelve hours.

Wu was not needed and excused himself. He wanted to go to his stateroom and write down what he had experienced, what Sublieutenant Hark had reported. If for some reason the power cable failed, and they perished, the submarine would be recovered. He wanted to leave a record for the Tenth Bureau. It was not yet everything they had wanted, but the situation was still in motion. The Americans had just begun to help. If he managed this properly, there would be more to learn.

Perhaps everything.

FOURTEEN

Graham Land, Antarctica

Stone Silver was surprised to see morning. At least, he assumed it was morning. This time of year, Antarctica had twenty-one hours of daylight every day. Still, he checked his watch and found that it was in fact early in the day. And that was a surprise. It felt as though only minutes had passed since he had shut his wickedly tired eyes. He hadn't expected to fall asleep. He remembered, as a new recruit, riding an overnight bus from Ft. Ritchie in Maryland to Ft. Monmouth in New Jersey. The heat wasn't working and it was impossible to sleep. But he had slept here. Soundly.

Despite the dusting of ice crystals on his parka, Silver was surprisingly warm. The low sun was shining directly on him, from the feet up. It was a hot sun, and there was no wind in their little pit.

Their pit. He wondered how the others had fared. He tried to turn toward Angela but wasn't able to do so. Their combined body heat had melted the ice they were lying on, and it had refrozen. His back and arms were stuck to the floor of the pit. It would have been comical if it weren't so dangerous; he couldn't move at all. The rubber bottom of the dinghy fluttered softly behind his head. The three of them should have slept in that, not used it for a windscreen.

Silver moved from side to side trying to wrench his sleeves free. The ice wouldn't release them. He couldn't even reach the buttons to remove his parka since his forearms were also stuck. His struggles woke Ensign Warren, who found himself in the same predicament. However, the mechanical engineer was able to pull up his right leg, put his heel on the floor of the pit, and slowly pry his leg from the ice. He could then raise his left leg, bend both, and arch his back until he was free. Warren went behind Silver and literally pried him up from the shoulders. The men did not disturb Angela, who was still asleep. Silver did make certain she was still breathing, however.

"Thanks, Ensign," Silver said. "How do you feel?"

"Surprisingly all right, sir," Warren said, shaking powdered ice from his arms. "You, sir?"

"The same. Why don't you get some rations from one of the emergency kits? I'm going to check the beacon."

While Warren went over to the metal chest, Silver walked toward shore, brushing and plucking off the small blocks of ice that had formed on his parka. The emergency beacon was still pulsing. Silver shielded his eyes and looked out at the water. There was nothing to see along the horizon, no boats and no sign of either submarine. He looked closer toward the shore. Some of the wreckage of the *Abby* had reached the foot of the slope, along with several bodies and parts of bodies. He had half-expected to find something like that. The detritus was rolling up and down with the modest waves of the incoming tide. He walked toward the shore to recover the remains. They were bloated and sickly white. But at least they were the bodies of crewmen from the *Abby*, not from the *D*. There was still a chance the submarine had survived—though if the *D* were mobile, it would probably have surfaced.

The two complete bodies were waterlogged and at least twice their normal weight. Silver found it extremely difficult to bring the first ashore. Warren noticed what he was doing and helped. Together, they half-carried, half-dragged the second one from the surf. They covered them with planks from the wrecked vessel. The limbs they found they also gathered. Silver didn't know why he felt compelled to do this. The night before he had cast a body into the sea. Maybe it was the idea of watching them languish like so much seaweed that bothered him. Or maybe it was the mocking simulation of life, the bobbing up and down. In any case, the rear admiral refused to leave the men there.

When they were finished, Silver said a prayer over the makeshift graves, then forced himself to eat a PowerBar from the ration kit. He didn't feel like it, but he could not afford to let his strength flag. When he was finished, he stepped into the pit and checked on Angela again. She was still asleep and she seemed warm enough. He let her be.

Warren stepped up to the rim of the pit. He was crunching particles of freeze-dried coffee. He offered some to Silver.

"No thanks."

"Are you sure, sir? It's tart but it'll wake you."

"I'm a tea man."

Warren regarded him with suspicion. "Seriously?"

"Seriously," Silver said as he stepped from the pit.

"Sir, if I may say, that does seem a curious distinction to make under the circumstances."

"Ensign, you're standing on the bottom of the world chewing granules of freeze-dried coffee. That's curious, too."

Warren thought for a moment. "Touché, sir. Hypothetically, then, would the rear admiral chew on tea leaves if we had them?"

"I might." Silver was studying the mountains to the north. "We need a plan, and now that I can see where we are, it looks as if one's been decided for us."

"What do you mean, sir?"

"The nearest base is thirty miles, over those mountains," Silver said.

"Yes, a Russian weather station."

"In all likelihood the peaks are blocking our emergency beacon."

"I was thinking that myself," Warren said. "I was wondering what my chances might be of making it over."

"Not good, I'd imagine," Silver said.

"Do you have another plan?"

"Yes. Our improvised dinghy screen held against the wind last night and the pit was warm enough. We may be able to construct some kind of shelter with the flotsam and jetsam washing in. And there are probably fish we can hook for food. At some point, the DOD will send someone to search for us. We need to be alive when they get here."

"Yes, sir," Warren said. "But one thing I know from the reading I did is that we may have lucked out with the weather last night. Storms have a habit of moving in and out of here with some regularity."

"I know. Which is why we'd better get started on that shelter. You gather the materials. While the sun's still on it, I'll work on making the pit a little deeper."

Warren walked toward the shore and began hauling in sections of the wrecked *Abby* that seemed useful. Silver watched him for a moment. Warren was young enough to be his son. The rear admiral felt a flash of satisfaction knowing that his daughter was safe. He couldn't imagine what he might be feeling if she were here. "Despair" didn't even come close. He was grateful, at least, that for all the remorse, there wasn't a feeling of guilt, a sense that the Ant Hill should have anticipated a scenario like this. The military always planned for everything but the eventualities that actually happened. Even with sonar, GPS, telemetry uplinks, and a state-of-the-art periscope, a sophisticated submarine like the USS *Greeneville* still had a blind spot, still knocked boots with the fishing vessel *Ehime Maru* in the seas off Pearl Harbor.

The rear admiral removed a small screwdriver from the emergency kit and used it to remove the lid. He went back in the pit, got on his knees by one of the side walls, and started to dig with the edge of the lid. His idea was to create a channel of some kind so that melted ice would run away from them.

As Silver was hacking with the metal corner, he heard Warren whoop loudly. The rear admiral looked over the lip of the pit.

"What is it?" Silver asked.

"Listen, sir!" Warren shouted.

Silver stood and listened. He heard nothing. The wind in the dinghy was too loud. He climbed from the pit, held the dinghy bottom between his open hands to stop it from fluttering, and listened again.

This time he heard a distant drone. And there was no mistaking what it was.

An approaching aircraft.

FIFTEEN

Graham Land, Antarctica

The 737 had picked up the emergency blip while they were still two hundred miles from shore. It was not a signal from the *Destiny*. Air Command ordered them to investigate the signal directly before searching the sea for traces of the submarine. It could be from the vessel they were investigating. It might tell them something about Senior Captain Chien's quarry. AC also felt that if the submarine had managed to surface, any survivors might be with the Americans.

The aircraft dropped to five thousand feet and started to turn southeast when they neared the coast. The pilot did not want to be headed toward the mountains at that height. The crew's reconnaissance officer was using a Remote Observation Binocular System to search for survivors and wreckage. The left eyepiece received input from both thermal-imaging data, to detect personnel, as well as a scanner that used fluorescence to detect iron. Heat showed up in red, iron in green. The right eyepiece was a natural-light magnifier. By looking into both, the observer was able to conduct three kinds of reconnaissance simultaneously.

The recon officer was sitting at right angles to the pilot, directly beside the navigator. He picked up a series of thermal signatures before anything else. There were three, he told the pilot, plus several faint clicks from along the shore. They were

in a small section of the coastline less than one square mile. The
plane descended to four thousand feet. In less than a minute the
recon officer had them in visible light. He boosted the right-side
magnification to twenty, shutting the left eyepiece, which was
set at ten-times magnification. He locked onto the coordinates
and shifted to computer control. The binoculars, whose optics
ran through the bottom of the fuselage, would now track the
sector automatically as the aircraft moved by.

The three individuals were not Chinese. They were dressed
in civilian parkas. The *Destiny* manifest listed nothing like that.
The two who were waving at the aircraft were men. The sex of
a third, lying in a ditch, could not be determined. It was warm,
however, and alive.

Everything the binoculars saw was recorded digitally for
further analysis. The remains of the vessel would be of particular interest to the Chinese Ministry of State Security, to whom
the reconnaissance officer was reporting directly. However,
they could do nothing for the people themselves. They could
only report their position and hope that either someone would
come for them or they could hold out until the Chinese vessels
arrived.

The 737 went out to sea to search for traces of the submarine. They found none. There were no fluid leaks, no dis-
cernible wreckage, no bodies. There was also no hint of a heat
signature. But that was not surprising. If the submarine was below forty meters, any radiant heat would be so diffuse in the
cold sea as to be undetectable.

After circling the sea for nearly two hours, the 737 made another pass along the shore. The changing position of the sun
would alter the shadows, possibly bringing out other details for
the binoculars, specifics about the wreckage that forensic analysts might find useful. The submarine had apparently struck
the vessel these men had been on. How and why might help
them locate the submarine and prevent such incidents in the future.

The stranded men waved again, even more vigorously than
before. They had to know they had been seen: The plane only
crossed the section of shore where they had made their camp.

Perhaps the men were attempting to thank the aircraft. In times like these, hope was as valuable as supplies.

After the low, slow pass, the 737 turned from the polar coastline and climbed back toward its cruising altitude. Fuel considerations made it impossible for the aircraft to stay any longer. The navigator contacted the Il-76 air tanker to arrange coordinates for refueling.

It had been a long trip for relatively little data. But "little" was not "nothing." The crew knew that reconnaissance was not a job for the greedy or impatient, qualities that apparently have been lacking in whoever had commanded the operation in these treacherous waters.

SIXTEEN

Graham Land, Antarctica

"They had to have seen us," Ensign Warren said after running up the icy slope. He had been pulling the last of the debris ashore when the aircraft made its second pass.

"It would seem so," Stone Silver replied as the hum of the aircraft was swallowed by the wind. The air currents were becoming increasingly belligerent as the sun-heated ocean air battled the cold air sweeping from the mountains. Apparently, this spot would be the battleground.

Warren was understandably excited, but Silver suggested that they get back to work since they didn't know how bad the winds would get, or when. Warren agreed and went back to the water to haul the wood up.

Silver had emptied the plastic first aid kit and placed ice inside. It probably wasn't seawater but snow from who-knew-what era. For all he knew it may have washed the back of a brontosaurus when Antarctica was part of some larger supercontinent. If they were here for an extended time, he needed to know if it was drinkable; the emergency kits only contained two one-liter bottles in each. The sun had melted some of the ice and he had a taste before going back to work. He winced from the "seaweedy" taste, which was probably algae that had washed ashore—again, he had no idea when. But at least it was fresh water in case they needed it.

Silver finished working on the ditch. It was now wider and properly irrigated. Angela was awake but just lying there, trying to stay warm. The rear admiral wasn't sure she even understood where she was or why. She responded when he talked directly to her, but was otherwise silent.

For himself, Silver was glad he had something to do. He was having a difficult time processing the events of the night before. They seemed unreal on every level. The loss of the *Abby*, the disappearance of the *D*, the sounds and the flooding and the chaos, the escape, the landing.

The death.

Silver couldn't even focus on an individual to mourn. When his wife had died, the grief had had a place to nest. He could walk around that place and come to terms with it. Here, whenever a memory of one of the crewmen or scientists would flash by and the rear admiral would try to accept that loss, a part of his brain would say, *Why him? What about Dr. Ogden or Ensign Lewis or some other sailor or the crew of the D?* Then a strange coping mechanism would engage. It would shut him down emotionally so that he couldn't mourn at all. He would brood with no way out except to feel guilty for not having been pulled under with the ship and its hands. The only relief was to concentrate on what he was doing. Besides, Silver still had two other people for whom he felt responsible. And for their well-being he had to be in command. The tiny group had no idea what kind of weather the late afternoon would bring, or whether this night would be like the last night, or how their bodies would react to the exertion, to the heat of their sweat followed by the extreme chill of inactivity.

Hopefully, they wouldn't have to find out. Hopefully, that aircraft would report their position and help would come.

But hope was tempered by the knowledge that while there might come a time when they could leave here, what had happened would never leave them . . .

SEVENTEEN

Kings Bay, Georgia

"Admiral, you can't mean that," Mike Carr said.

The scientist had gone to his cubicle to take the call from Admiral Grantham at NORDSS. Carr needed to get out of the command center, to see something other than the glowing monitors in the dark, still room. When he emerged, he felt as though the world had turned radioactive. Everything had a superimposed luminescence, an aftereffect of the screens.

Fifteen minutes before, they had heard from Grantham's aide that the Chinese had spotted three Americans ashore. They were dressed in parkas that matched the description of those that had been part of the gear stored on board the *Abby*. The posttraumatic numbness that had settled on the Ant Hill was lifted slightly. If they could get an RAF rescue chopper down from the Falklands, they could pick up the survivors and have a report from them in just a few hours.

But NORDSS didn't want that. Admiral Grantham said that the rescue team dispatched from Corpus Christi would be briefed. They would carry out any rescue. They would be there within six hours.

"Admiral, we don't know the condition of the survivors," Carr said. "Six hours could put us there too late. The Chinese report said one of them was just lying in a ditch. That individual may need medical attention."

"The crew have all had survival training," the admiral replied. "They'll have to hold on."

"Isn't that a little cold?" Carr asked.

"Doctor?"

"What you just said," Carr replied. "These survivors don't 'have to' hold on. That's something we're forcing them to do. They can be—"

"Dr. Carr, this is really not something you need to be concerned with."

"Not concerned with? Admiral, I'm the mission director!"

"The mission is over."

"Is that an official notification from NORDSS?"

"Doctor, I'm sorry. There are security issues that I'm not prepared to discuss," Grantham said.

"Is the mission officially terminated?"

"Not yet."

"Then I am still in charge."

"Yes, you are. Of the mission. Not of the rescue or its handling. You have your LOAC playbook. Continue to run all options."

"We are," Carr said. "We're not getting anything."

"Keep trying," Grantham said unhelpfully.

LOAC was "loss of all contact." Attempts to restore contact included the all-frequency search for telemetry as well as running simulations that extrapolated events from the last known activities and positions.

"We will update you when we have new information," Grantham went on, "and you will contact me directly with any data you may receive or sim results that may be helpful."

"I still can't believe you're not going after these survivors."

"We are. The way it needs to be done."

The admiral hung up. Carr sat there balanced somewhere between sad and angry. As a scientist, he was patient. He had to be. Results didn't always go the way you wanted them to, or perform on your personal timetable. But here they *had* a result. A good one. And it was being ignored, pointedly, for reasons he couldn't begin to understand. Carr wondered if Grantham was like that all the time with all but his NORDSS partners, if "high-brass cover-your-ass," as Silver called it, demanded that kind of detachment. It made Carr long for the paternal eye of Rear Admiral Silver and even the uneven temperament and acerbic mouth of Captain Colon.

Carr stopped for coffee, then walked slowly back to the command center. He tried to delay his return as long as possible. He wanted to be surprised, to find something new happening there. A signal received, a new search tactic devised, anything. But when he input his code on the keypad and opened the door, the room was exactly as he had left it.

He briefed the other team members and then sat down. The simulations were running for a collision with a Chinese submarine. Because of the presence of the towline that was attached to two vessels and apparently tangled with a third, the permutations and combinations were nearly incalculable.

Nonetheless, they pursued those variations in the hope that something would present itself. Something that merited further analysis.

That did not happen. The hours passed and the simulations gave little hope for the survival of the *D*, and the radios of Second Lieutenant Kilbourn remained adamantly silent.

EIGHTEEN

Weddell Sea

According to Wu's watch—which was still running, unlike the clocks on board—he had managed to get four hours of uninterrupted sleep after writing his report. He had written it on a legal pad, then put the pages in a waterproof plastic container he obtained from the ship's galley. Then he placed it in the small personal locker located at the foot of his cot and lay down. He was still weak from oxygen-deprivation and fear. They were both equally unfamiliar to him, and equally unwelcome.

For a moment upon waking, he had thought he was lying on the deck again, the cold breath of disaster on the back of his neck. It was real cold, but he was on a hard mattress, not rubber flooring. Though a feeling of well-being did not overtake him, he took some comfort in that time had passed. The air was still circulating; Wu could hear the now-familiar hum of the backup generator being powered by the American submarine. Sublieutenant Hark might even have made progress on the *Destiny*'s own wiring.

Wu slipped from the small bed and left his cabin. The corridor was empty. More than that, apart from the engine vibration, it was silent. It could be that everyone was resting to conserve shipwide and personal resources. But what surprised him was the silence from the aft section. He expected to hear the sounds of Hark and his skeleton team at work. Wu started forward, an unexpected urgency in his step. That the ship was still running made him think they might get out of this, that he would be able to obtain the information he was sent to collect.

As Wu rounded the compartment containing the forward escape trunk, he saw that the hatch to the command center was shut. An intercom button was to the right. He pushed it. No one answered. He tried the wheel in the center. The door was not locked. He opened it and entered.

What he saw stopped him in the open hatch.

The small command center of the *Destiny* was crowded with personnel and activity. In the nose of the submarine was a hairline fracture, a semicircle that stretched from the diving officer's station flush on the port side to the helmsman's station starboard. Three crewmen were working with gas-powered torches to try to seal the cracks. The captain was supervising five other sailors, who were wiping the water that was creeping through the fracture in drips. Four other sailors were wringing out the rags they were using. They were using bailing buckets, all of which were nearly full. This activity had obviously been going on for quite some time.

Captain Biao was standing behind the men, overseeing their work. He looked back as Wu entered.

"I was about to summon you," Biao said. A hint of tension was in his voice and in his normally relaxed eyes. "Please let the Americans know that we may lose the forward section."

Wu Lin Kit went directly to the radio. One of the crewmen was blocking it. The young seaman was standing on a metal tool kit, welding a section of hull above the radio. He shifted to the left to admit Wu, then continued to seal the tail end of the hairline fracture.

The radio had been covered with a plastic sheet to prevent water damage. Slipping his hands under the coverlet, Wu prepared to send a communiqué. As he switched on the radio, he was pleased to see that at least he had the upper end letters back.

"Tell them the ice has continued to shift and caused a fine crack nearly a meter long," Biao told Wu. "They may not hear from us. We may have to abandon the command center."

Wu began transmitting. He had managed to send most of the message when Wu heard sounds like an inflated balloon being rubbed. Men began shouting as the cracks started to widen, pushing through the sections that had been welded, tearing them apart in a series of disheartening pops. Water began to enter in fine sheets, sliding from the rupture and from beneath gauges and faceplates.

Biao ordered the command center evacuated. The seamen obeyed as the sheets of water became torrents and the rest of the nose section began to crack lengthwise.

Captain Biao was the last one out and Wu left right before he did. Three men were poised behind the hatch to push it shut the moment the commander passed through. The water was already up to the hatchway lip and beginning to spill over. The men pushed against the rising flood but managed to close the door without much difficulty. Hark had gone over to the cable that was bringing them power from the American ship. The wire was knee-high, secured to the escape hatch and the hull behind it with electrical tape. He had been prepared to peel away the tape and raise the wire to keep it from being jostled and possibly dislodged in the flood.

That wasn't necessary.

Biao ordered the men back into the electrical room. He told Hark and his crew to get back to work on the circuits.

"If we shift because of the ice, we may lose this," the captain said, pointing to the cable.

The captain, Wu, and the others listened to the low roar of the sea as it poured into the forward section. Biao looked up, at the hull. If the escape section was crushed, there would be no way out of the submarine even if they did manage to survive. Wu listened for the sound of metal. He didn't hear it. But he did hear something else, something nearly as bad.

The sound of tumbling ice.

NINETEEN

Weddell Sea

Captain Colon had been waiting beside Bain while she took the message. The only crew member who was not in the command center was Lieutenant Rockford. He had remained in the ramjet section. Though the fan hatch had been sealed around the cable, Rockford was watching for any sign of leakage. The pump was still running. With the fan removed, water would rise in the well. Colon wanted to keep the sea as far from the seal as possible.

Suddenly, the world began to shake. Above, below, and to all four sides came a rocking and buffeting violent enough to knock Captain Colon back against his command station. He grabbed the seat so he didn't hit the deck. Still, he was barely aware of the process itself. He was listening ahead of it, waiting for a sign that the battle was over and they were about to be crushed. When that didn't immediately happen, the captain got the sense that the only thing keeping the *D* safe was the presence of the Chinese submarine beneath them. The chunks of ice hit the *Tempest D*, rolled off the sides, and landed on the seafloor around the Chinese submarine. If ice was piling up around the *D*, they were being spared most of the pressure because of the wider footprint of the submarine beneath them.

Lieutenant Bain turned from the radio. "They suffered a major hull breach forward, and that was before the big stuff started to fall." She continued to write down letters coming from the Chinese submarine.

"That could be what caused the larger landslide," Withers suggested. "Imbalance at the bottom of the pyramid."

"They've had to seal off the forward compartment and won't be able to communicate with us again," Bain added.

The intercom of the *D* came on.

"We're losing them!" Rockford said.

"Explain!" Colon said.

"The cable is being pulled and eating up the slack. We've got about ten or eleven inches left in the coil before it's at maximum extension."

Suddenly, the *D* started to move. It was rolling slightly onto its port side. The Chinese submarine must have shifted beneath them.

"Sir, gauges show the water level is rising in the fan well!" Rockford said. "The pumps are not keeping up."

"Stay on it. Let's see if we settle back."

The sound seemed more powerful on the starboard side, which suggested to the captain that the landslide was pushing the Chinese submarine one way and the *Tempest D* another.

Their slow, agonizing movement made Colon think incongruously of football, which was called a game of inches. If a ball moved a few inches, someone lost a game. If the submarine moved a few more inches, people would lose their lives. It seemed, at that moment, ludicrous that something so relatively trivial should share the same measurement as something so significant.

"She's at maximum extension," Rockford reported.

"Don't do anything yet," Colon said. He did not want to close the door on the only lifeline the Chinese crew had. Not while there was still a chance the motion could stop—

"She's gone!" Rockford yelled.

"Close external fan door," Colon ordered.

The captain heard the distant whir of the motor beneath the continued drum of the falling ice. The irislike door was being shut. They could do nothing for their fellow seamen.

Captain Colon sat in his command chair. He waited with the others as the seconds inched by. Finally, the avalanche stopped.

Colon looked hopefully at Bain. "Anything?"

She shook her head.

The quiet was bittersweet. The *D* had survived and it was unlikely they would hear anything else from the Chinese vessel. The question now before him was what to do: wait or try to use the ramjet fans. Nothing had changed from before, except that the probability of helping the Chinese was even more remote. There was only the *D* to worry about.

Colon removed his harness and got up from his seat. Michaelson had finished repairing the towline release and was resting at his post.

"Lieutenant Michaelson?"

"Sir?"

"Please go aft and help Mr. Rockford replace the ramjet fan."

"Yes, sir." Lieutenant Michaelson unbuckled himself, ducked low to avoid hitting the slanted wall, and hustled back.

Colon leaned toward the intercom. "Did you get that back there?"

"I did, sir. I'm sorry, sir. There was nothing I could do."

"I know there wasn't. We all did our best."

Colon resumed pacing. He had to consider his next move. They had one less consideration than before: helping the Chinese seamen. And they had one more thing to worry about: If another compartment on the Chinese submarine flooded, that could bring down more ice. They'd been lucky twice. He didn't want to press that. He also had to accept the greatest responsibility a commander had to take. The one they hired him for.

His instinct.

In the absence of data, of certainty, that was what any leader used to make a decision. A decision that could decide the fate of an individual, an army, a nation, even the destiny of civilization itself.

Colon was actually relieved he didn't have to make a decision of that magnitude. He didn't know how generals and presidents did it.

You just say the words and deal with the results, he told himself.

He would.

And, barring new developments, he knew what they would be.

TWENTY

Graham Land, Antarctica

Shortly after noon, the day had turned bitterly cold. Part of that was the changing winds and part was the blowing ice. The brisk sea air tore grain-sized particles from the ice shelf and shot them toward the mountains. The mountain air blew them back. The result was a two-faced assault, stinging and cold.

And getting colder.

Stone Silver and Chuck Warren had spent that time erecting a more-than-passable shelter around the pit. They had dug narrow trenches along the exterior perimeter, used a flare to melt the ice on the bottom, then set debris from the *Abby* inside. The men held the planks in place until the ice refroze. They rigged a roof from the dinghy, using the oars to secure it. They ran the paddles through loops of rope, like old-fashioned door bolts. A blanket served as the door. It kept out the wind and the ice. It could not keep out the cold, which, along with food, was going to be their biggest problem.

Angela sat up shortly after 1:00 P.M. She was extremely calm and apparently oblivious to the cold. She wanted to know where they were and when the *Abby* was coming to get them. Silver told her "soon." She seemed to accept that. She also accepted some of the emergency rations.

When the ice storm hit, the three of them sat in the hut, facing each other as if they were gathered around a nonexistent campfire.

"I wonder if it'll look like an igloo when we go back out," Warren said. He was practically yelling so the others could hear him over the bellowing winds and rapidly fluttering blanket and dinghy bottom. "Sleet will probably pile up on the bottom and start to climb."

"I would imagine so," the rear admiral replied.

The rear admiral was sipping a cup of coffee he had patiently warmed in the sun, after deciding that coffee had to taste better than seaweed-flavored water. The coffee wasn't very warm but it wasn't bad. Angela was sitting to his right, Warren to his left. The scientist had her arms around her knees and a blanket around her shoulders. Her innocence, sad though it was, reminded Silver of his granddaughter.

"Is it snowing?" Angela asked.

"It's sort of snowing," Warren replied.

"This is nice." She smiled. "It's cozy."

"Can I get you anything?" Warren asked.

"I'd like to use the phone."

"It's not working," he told her.

"Darn. I really wanted to call my dad. He worries about me."

"Maybe later," Silver said.

"Someone's using it?"

"Yes," he told her.

"Okay."

Warren looked at the rear admiral. Silver looked down and picked at a little ice patch that had formed on the blanket beneath him. He didn't know what to do or say. After a moment Angela rested her head on his shoulder.

"Why am I so tired?" she asked.

"We've had a long trip," Silver replied.

Warren said something else. Silver didn't hear it. A dull thump came from somewhere underground. A moment later the ice undulated beneath them. It felt as if someone were shaking out a towel. The three of them fell roughly toward the door blanket. Silver braced himself against the edge of the shallow pit and got to his knees. But he didn't stay there. A moment later there was a sound like the endless cannon fire at the Memorial Day ceremony. Silver was thrown roughly toward the back of the hut, then down. The wooden walls they had put up flopped outward, the seaward wall of the pit literally crumbled, and Stone Silver looked out at a shore that was dropping into the water in massive chunks.

The rear admiral had no idea whether the lone drumbeat that had started this had been an explosion, perhaps on board one of the submarines. All he knew was that in just a few seconds their perch would be falling into the sea.

Warren was already hauling a screaming Angela toward the landward side of the pit. But he was having trouble getting his footing as the ground cracked and dropped, creating an uneven surface. Silver dug his boots into a newly formed crack and stretched toward Angela to help. As he did so, the crack became a chasm and the ground just below his feet rose up in a door-sized slab, like the opening upper jaw of a whale. Silver slid backward, the windblown ice pricking his cheeks and forehead as the sea swept up and over his legs as he scrambled for a handhold. He wasn't able to get one as the shelf in front of him cracked and fell apart, dumping Warren and Angela on top of him. Silver managed to squirm out from under them, just in time to see the dinghy take flight on the winds from the east, sailing away from them. At the same time the wood they'd salvaged from the *Abby* was snapped and crushed by what was clearly, now, the complete collapse of the ice shelf. Too late, he thought to reach for the emergency beacon. It had already been lost in the explosion of ice and sea.

Silver tried to claw forward only to be tossed backward again, losing his bearings entirely. He heard Angela crying for help but he could not see her, or Warren. He screamed in frustration as he scratched for a grip on what was left of their small section of ice. That wasn't possible as the ocean took it, and them, and a moment later he was flailing desperately to stay afloat. The rear admiral knew that his parka would quickly become saturated and drag him down, so he had to get that off, and his boots. But first, his gloves. He reached for one with his teeth, grunting as he tried to pull it off. He swallowed water and hacked it out, swinging his arms in desperate circles to stay afloat. He could feel his clothes expanding like a sponge, growing heavy.

Then he became aware of something else.

There was a beating sound, very low, coming toward them from over the water. He could feel the deep vibration in the hollow of his chest. It was the last thing he heard before his soaked clothing pulled him under and the only sound was the hollow gurgling of the sea as it covered his ears.

TWENTY-ONE

Weddell Sea

Major Bryan and the rest of L.A.S.E.R. were seated in the belly of a twin-rotor RAF Chinook when he received the update from General Scott. Scott wasn't sure whether a Chinese sighting of three "persons" on the ice was good news, bad news, a deception to scope out rescue efforts, or irrelevant. They could be the only survivors of the disaster; they could be research personnel who just happened to be in the region where the vessels had collided; they could be lookouts, with the rest of the Chinese or American crew in a cave or windbreak inland; they could be tourists who were penguin-watching; they could be Chinese planted there to spread disinformation through an American rescue team. Whoever they were, they may have seen something.

Scott wanted to know.

The HC MkII Chinook was still an hour away from Graham Land when they received the intel. With Capt. Tyler Puckett at the controls, the Chinook was pushing the outer envelope of its speed rating as it raced across the sea. By the time they were just a half mile out, the situation had changed. Radically. Recon specialist Lt. Renny Kodak, who was on forward point in the flight deck with a pair of binoculars, had detected turbulence offshore while they were still five miles out at sea. When they arrived, the turbulence had become what looked like a full-scale shelf-collapse. Even at ten-times magnification—which was enough to pick out a floating baseball cap and read the logo—Kodak could not see anyone in the water. That didn't mean the three individuals weren't there. Acres of bobbing slabs of ice and wind-stirred foam were in the way.

"We hook-and-ladder on my go!" Major Bryan said into the built-in radio. The L.A.S.E.R. leader was standing in the open door of the Chinook, his amber visor turned toward the Antarctica coast, his left hand on the strap above the door, his right held in salute position, shielding his face from the knifing wind. The door was little more than a hatch located just aft of the cockpit. This Chinook was a transport, not a rescue helicopter, but it was all the Royal Air Force had that satisfied the mission parameters the major had worked out en route.

The RAF helicopter was the equivalent of the U.S. air force CH47-D, which the Tennessee-born Puckett boasted he knew "better than the alphabet." Since Major Bryan had never actually seen the laid-back twenty-four-year-old with a book, he did not take comfort from that in itself. But the kid could fly, there was no doubt about that. He never showed any concern, doubt, fear, joy—nothing. He was like a bass player in a jazz band, just hunkering into his job and letting it flow.

Lieutenant Black was busy securing the rolled "rubberungs" ladder to latches at the base of the door. This was a thirty-foot aluminum ladder with rubber rungs for a secure grip. The added weight also kept the ladder relatively steady in high winds and prop wash. Behind her, Captain Gabriel and MCPO Gunther Wingate, USCG, were getting into their long-sleeve wet suits. These were custom-made Rubatex G-231N nitrogen blown neoprene suits. They had backbone cushioning for air cylinders and canister lights. Although it did not apply to their use at the moment, they were extremely warmth-retentive. That would matter when they went after the submarine. In any case, they were the only suits the team had brought. The wet suits also had a thermal lining. This was effectively a dry suit layer beneath the wet suit. The dry suit trapped air between the body and the lining; this kept the diver warm. The wet suit had a thin pocket of heated water between the two suit layers for added warmth. The L.A.S.E.R. team members used coils to heat a half gallon of seawater each, which they poured into the suit lining after it was on. The twin layers made the suit bulky, but the added warmth would give the team time to reach the seabed, execute the mission, then return.

The ladder was rated for eight hundred pounds. One of the men would go into the water, the other would remain halfway up the ladder. According to the communication relayed from NORDSS, a Chinese spy plane had spotted three individuals. Bryan could only make out two of them in the chaos of ice and water. There would be added water weight, which meant they had to get at least one individual into the Chinook before they could rescue the third. That was why Bryan had referred to it as a hook-and-ladder operation. They couldn't simply get the individuals onto the ladder and fly them to ground. They had to get them inside, the way fire departments pulled people from burning buildings.

The Chinook was less than a quarter mile away. Lieutenant Black indicated that the ladder was secure. Gabriel and Wingate finished suiting up. Captain Puckett dropped to within fifty feet of the sea. He would position himself over the target, then do a straight vertical descent to put them in reach of the ladder. That would minimize the horizontal rotor backwash, which would otherwise dislocate and blow the sea into the faces of those in the water.

Gabriel and Wingate stood behind the major. The helicopter door slid open like the door of a van. There was a bar that ran across the top of the hatch and the two officers held that. They ran a sound-check of the earphones and microphone built into the sides of their hoods. The microphones could be fitted into the regulators for dives; at the moment, they were poking from the hood along the right side of the mouth. Though they were wearing masks to protect their eyes from airborne ice and wind, they were not wearing tanks. Lieutenant Black remained crouched behind the ladder, ready to unfurl it at the major's command. Behind them the rest of the L.A.S.E.R. team was equipping themselves for their primary mission.

The helicopter moved into position above the target zone. Guided by Major Bryan's radioed commands, Captain Puckett dropped the Chinook to within thirty feet of the sea. Lieutenant Black watched the major as he watched the sea. He held his right index finger out, parallel to the water, studied the target a moment longer, then turned his finger down. The lieutenant pushed the ladder out.

The silver-and-black rubberung dropped to the sea just a few feet from one of the individuals. Major Bryan could still see just the two, though it looked as though one of them, the one they were above, was reaching into the water. Perhaps he was trying to help the third.

Gabriel was the first man out.

"Gabe, it looks as though your guy is fishing," Bryan said.

"I see that," the captain said as he went down the ladder. "I'll hook him, then go in."

Bryan had not intended for any of his people to go into the water. The major turned and gave a thumbs-up signal to Sgt. Maj. Tony Cowan, USA. Cowan, who was also wearing his wet suit, moved forward. The Ranger was one of the divers Bryan had assigned to the submarine rescue group. Cowan was also a backup for this operation. If anything happened to Gabriel or Wingate, he would step in.

When Gabe was halfway down, Wingate went out. The individual in the water seemed to be pointing to his side. Gabe didn't bother climbing the rest of the way down. He jumped the last ten feet into the water.

"Go!" Bryan said to Cowan.

The young Ranger started down after Wingate. Bryan's eyes remained on Gabriel. A few strokes put the big man beside the individual in the water. Ice chunks of all sizes were bobbing around them. Bryan could see the captain nod. Gabriel then grabbed the back of the parka and literally heaved the individual toward the ladder. Then the officer sucked down a breath and descended.

Bryan wished that he himself werc the one in the water. He watched as Wingate helped the other man up the ladder. The individual slowed. He seemed to be struggling. Cowan went down a few rungs and pulled off the parka, which was obviously weighing the man down. He was a young man in jeans. With

Wingate giving him a push from below, he slowly ascended the rubberung. The major looked out toward the other individual. He was about fifteen feet away and trying to hold on to a slab of ice to stay afloat.

"Puckett—target two!" Bryan ordered.

He didn't want to abandon the spot where Gabe had gone down, but the other individual was in jeopardy. He needed to be extracted.

The man on the ladder passed Cowan and was within reach of the cabin. Lieutenant Black had donned a leather belt that was attached to an eye-hook low in the doorway. Thus secured, she reached out and offered her hands to the man. He stretched his left hand up and she took it within hers. She pulled as he climbed. His teeth chattering, his eyes wide, he crawled up into the cabin.

The company medic, Lt. Moses Houston, USMC, spread him out on the floor. He threw a blanket over him.

"I . . . I couldn't hold her," the man stuttered.

"What's your name?" Bryan asked, leaning into the helicopter.

"Ensign Warren, s-sir."

"Vessel?"

"Cl-classified, sir."

"Sir, let him be for now," Houston said as he rolled over a blue unit the size of a loaf of bread. A tube and an oxygen mask were attached to it. The medic held up the mask. "Ensign Warren, I'm going to put this over your face to get you some warm, humidified air. Then we'll get an IV into you. Get some heat and vitamins into your blood."

"She wasn't . . . swimming," Warren went on. "Just . . . screaming."

"You quiet down," Houston said softly but firmly. "Captain Gabriel is trying to help her."

Bryan turned back to the open hatch. He was impressed with the young man. Knew to keep his mouth shut, even among what seemed like friends. Solid training and good instincts. He looked too tall to be a submariner, though. Bryan guessed he was from the surface ship.

The major watched as the ladder edged slowly toward the other individual in the water. Wingate was on the bottom rung. When they arrived, he leaned over, grabbed the person's upraised hand, and pulled it toward the ladder. Puckett was watching, too. He lowered the Chinook slightly to help the man get his second hand up. They descended just inches to put the bottom rung in the water so, assisted by Wingate, the individual could get a foothold. Wingate swung to the flip side of the ladder so he could help the person climb. He moved up slowly but steadily, dropping the parka on his own as he ascended. Bryan waited until Cowan had a hand on him. The ladder was going to blow out a little when they moved.

"Take us back!" Bryan said into the mouthpiece. "Do you see him?"

"Negative, sir," Captain Puckett said as he nosed around and moved the Chinook to where Gabriel had gone under.

The man on the ladder struggled the last few rungs and had to be dragged in by Lieutenant Black and the major. He fell on his right side, panting. Houston handed Lieutenant Black a blanket. As Major Bryan looked over, she wrapped it around the newcomer, a silver-haired man who looked to be in his early sixties. He took the blanket, then tried to return to the hatch.

The lieutenant grabbed his shoulder. "Please lie down," she said.

"Dr. Albertson—"

"We're searching," Black told him.

The man seemed to accept that. He sat back against the fuselage, beside the door.

"Who are you?" the woman asked.

"Rear Admiral Kenneth Silver."

"Sir," she said, saluting him.

He returned the salute with a trembling hand.

"Are there any other survivors, besides Dr. Albertson?" Black asked.

"No . . . not that we know of."

Bryan turned back to the sea. According to the thin file Scott had given them, Silver was the commander of the mission. He had been on board the surface vessel, the *Abby*. Dr. Albertson was the science officer. She was their cover for the mission. Now they knew which group of survivors they had. And which crew was still down there.

Gabriel's microphone wouldn't work underwater unless it was part of the subvocal system in the air regulator. It had been a little over three minutes since he'd gone in. Bryan sure as hell hoped he had come up for air. They had lost sight of the region when they'd turned. The ice shelf had stopped collapsing, but ice was everywhere, rocking to and fro. Wingate was still at the bottom of the ladder.

"Sir, I'd like to go in," the master chief petty officer said through the comm system. He was watching the water intently, his blue-and-black suit glistening in the icy daylight.

"Negative," Bryan replied. He needed his team. The major felt a sick, sick stirring in his gut. It was far worse than losing the dummies back in the Gulf. *Come on, you big bastard,* he thought.

"Major, drop the ladder—" Wingate yelled suddenly.

"Lower us!" Bryan said to Puckett.

The Chinook began to descend. The bottom of the rubberung was still in the water.

It went deeper into the sea. Wingate stayed dropped to the lowest rung as it started to submerge.

"Stop!" Wingate cried when he was chest deep. He plunged his right arm into the water and held it there. His body was at a forty-five-degree angle as he held tightly with his left hand.

Cowan climbed down so he could grab Wingate if he started to slip. The Chinook was hovering at just under twenty-five feet. Puckett was holding it remarkably steady in the strong wind.

Bryan watched, his heart matching the fast beat of the rotors. After a moment, Wingate yelled for them to take the Chinook up. The helicopter began to rise; two sets of hands were on the ladder. Wingate was holding one set, which belonged to a third person in a parka. Gabriel was holding on by himself—using one hand to hang on and the other to support the individual they had rescued. The person did not appear to be conscious.

Bryan's chest expanded and lightened. He smiled as the

three men worked to get the last person up the ladder and into the cabin. It was a woman. She was unconscious and not breathing. Having just finished with Ensign Warren's IV, Houston turned to her immediately. He got behind the seated woman and executed the Heimlich maneuver. She vomited water, clearing the airway. He did it again and she spit up nearly half as much water. Then he laid her down and performed CPR. While he was doing that, Lieutenant Black helped the other men up. She patted Gabriel on the shoulder before she pulled in the ladder. Bryan told Puckett to head to shore, then saluted Gabriel.

"We didn't see you come up for breath, Captain," Bryan said.

"I didn't," he admitted, still gasping. "There was an air pocket under the ice. I hit it by dumb luck. Otherwise I'd be playing solo trumpet."

The rear admiral looked up. "Captain, God bless you."

"Sir, thank you."

Rear Admiral Silver continued watching the medic work. Bryan crouched beside him.

"Sir, I'm Major Thomas Bryan. We're emergency rescue out of Corpus Christi, Texas."

"Major, I'm pleased to know you." He was shivering violently and pulled the blanket around himself. "What are your orders?"

"All we were told is that a surface vessel, an experimental sub, and a Chinese sub were involved in some kind of collision, sir," Bryan replied. "Your people at NORDSS snagged a message from the Chinese air force, said they saw you."

"The other vessels? Has anyone heard from them?"

"Not a peep, as far as I know."

Silver seemed to deflate. "They're the ones that did this," he said angrily. "They came up through the bottom of our surface ship."

"At any time did you hear any explosions, see any kind of subsurface activity?" Bryan asked.

"Not until this shelf collapse or earthquake or whatever it was," Silver said. His eyes narrowed. "Wait, that's not true. There was a very distinct pop before the shelf came down."

"A pop, sir? Like a muffled explosion or a balloon . . . ?"

"Neither, major. I've heard underwater demolition and this didn't sound like that. It was less of a bang than a groan."

A moment later Angela Albertson wheezed down air. She inhaled so hard that she seemed to be filling her toes. Her eyes snapped open, her fingers stretched, and she immediately exhaled. She began to wriggle and cry but Houston steadied her. Lieutenant Black put her hands on her shoulders and gently held her down while the medic prepared to give her Ensign Warren's oxygen.

Silver smiled. In the direct light of the overhead bulb, Bryan saw the officer's eyes grow damp with more than seawater.

With a gentle bump, the helicopter touched down well inland, away from where the shelf had collapsed. Puckett cut the engines. Bryan nodded to the crew to get ready. The major's own gear was stowed in the back. He would have to get suited up in a moment.

"One more question, sir," Major Bryan said. "This groan—did it come from directly under the shelf?"

"It seemed to. Why? What are you thinking?"

"The Chinese obviously received a distress call or picked up an emergency beacon from this region. We didn't. I'm told their beacons are attached by a tether and float to the surface. They're designed to withstand explosions and implosions."

"That's correct."

"Well, about the only thing that would mute the signal would be a pile-on that prevented the signal from escaping."

"A landslide," Silver said.

"Yes, sir. If something happened underwater, the tether might have been pulled down, and the beacon dragged in with it."

Major Bryan stood as Cowan came forward with his gear. The major put the bag down and began removing his leather flight jacket. "We were going to drag a sonar tow-fish through the sea to try and pinpoint the location before going down, but I'm beginning to think that won't be necessary."

"You believe they went down on the shelf?"

The major nodded as he took off his shirt. "The Chinese flight path took them close enough to your position to pick up your own emergency beacon and have a look. They were here for a reason."

"Following their sub's signal."

"Yes, sir. That sound you heard *could* have been one of the subs decompressing. A hull breach might have sent up a bubble that shocked the ice along preexisting faults. The charts show a lot of unstable ice in the area. The good news is that we didn't see any debris. That could mean the subs are buried, it could mean they're not in this area, or it could mean they weren't impacted catastrophically. Perhaps just a compartment or two of one of them."

"I understand. But, Major, even if they are down there, what do you plan to do? Do you have extraction craft at your disposal? Emergency suits?"

"No, sir. Our team and our overnight bags are it."

Silver did not seem happy to hear that. The naval officer would be much less happy to learn what Admiral Grantham had instructed L.A.S.E.R. to do if the submarine was unsalvageable.

"Our commanding officer and the brass at NORDSS felt it was more important that we get down here as quickly as possible and reconnoiter," Bryan said. "They did not want to risk having the Chinese recovery units get here first."

"I understand," Silver replied.

"Rear Admiral Silver, my pilot is going to take a run along the coast to see if anyone else from your vessel made it ashore. If there are remains and they can be recovered, he and the aircrew will do so."

"Thank you, Major," Silver replied. "What are you and the rest of your team going to do?"

Major Bryan began slipping into his wet suit. "The seabed is 170 feet below us. We're going to go down and have a look around."

"They're a good crew," the rear admiral said, his eyes misting.

The major smiled. "I'll do everything I can to help you tell them in person, sir."

When Bryan finished suiting up, Puckett lifted off and flew them back toward the new section of coastline along the Weddell Sea. As the chopper rose from what was left of the shelf,

Bryan asked Silver one more question. He wanted to know something, anything, about the submarine they were going down to try to assist. The rear admiral was—perhaps predictably—unhelpful.

"I can't tell you about it," Silver replied flatly.

"I don't understand, sir," Bryan said. "Seven of us are about to go down there, hopefully to locate the vessel, and we don't know anything about what we're looking *for*."

"I know, Major. I'm sorry."

"Sir, if we find it, we'll see it."

"That changes nothing. I am not permitted to *tell* you about the submarine."

"So we just look for the one that doesn't have Chinese markings." That didn't come out as sarcastically as Bryan had thought it would, probably because the major cut the edge as he spoke it. The rear admiral was still a senior officer.

"That's right, Major."

He did not seem to take offense at Bryan's remark. Silver added that if the group found nothing, the security of the original mission would not have been compromised.

Silver was moved to one of the benches on the side of the Chinook. Warren and Dr. Albertson were moved to semirigid hammocks slung along the opposite side.

Bryan and his crew moved to the hatch. Ignorant or not, it was time to go. And the major was not sure it would make a difference. A week before they had thought they'd known everything about the destroyer they were boarding. Turned out they didn't, or they would have been more cautious.

Perhaps knowing you're ignorant is better than thinking you know something, Bryan thought.

He would soon find out.

TWENTY-TWO

Weddell Sea

It is not easy being an unprotected man in a polar sea. It was arguably less easy being a cold-water fish on land. Few creatures get to experience both; the L.A.S.E.R. divers were among the chosen ones.

Thomas Bryan and the six other divers were in full gear. In addition to the wet suits, compressed-air cylinders, weight belts, and buoyancy compensators, they carried packets of thermal explosives, spear guns, and climbing gear. The pitons and lines were necessary because they didn't know what kind of tangle they might find below. They might be required to hang on to rock or ice projections against the current or at odd angles. All of that, plus the flippers, made movement in the helicopter cabin and on the rubberung extremely difficult.

Lieutenant Black, Ensign Galvez, and Major Bryan carried one thing more. They had waterproof packs loaded with C-4 and detonators. These could be used on ice or rock; they would be used on the submarine if it could not be salvaged.

It was quite a group, Bryan thought. Armed with explosives, determination, state-of-the-art gear, and virtually no knowledge of their target.

The team descended as the last one had, in shifts. One person went into the sea while the next person waited in the middle of the ladder. Bryan would be the last one in the water. If there had been any last-second instructions from Corpus Christi, or a change of heart from the rear admiral, the major wanted to be there to receive it. As deep as they were going, into waters as cold as these, communications could become iffy.

There were no sickbed confessionals from the rear admiral. Bryan turned his back to the sea and went down the ladder. He felt this particular officer would understand if they were forced to blow up the submarine. That wouldn't make it any easier, but at least there would be someone to share the pain.

The plan was to dive as far as they could as quickly as they could to leave as much time as possible for a rescue. They would be descending close to the ice that had slid from the shelf, hoping it would lead them to one or both of the submarines.

Lieutenant Black was in the lead. Each diver had a small, powerful halogen headlamp on top of his hood. Visibility was only about twenty-five feet in these waters, less than a quarter of what it was in warm-water dives. Particulate matter did not disintegrate as quickly in the icy waters, preventing both sunlight and portable illumination from penetrating very far.

The team descended headfirst in a wide-angle V-formation. Only Black and the two outermost divers, Gabriel and Bryan, had their lights on. The formation allowed them to follow the leader and at the same time look out over as much of the sea as possible. The presence of the ice was at once reassuring and intimidating. Reassuring because it was a road map to the surface. Intimidating because it was big and obviously unstable, composed of surprisingly rectangular slabs and irregular chunks piled in a chaotic heap. Bryan was immediately concerned that using thermal devices anywhere near the base of this could bring the entire mass down. Grains of ice and air bubbles created by the recent collapse and sustained by the gentle currents circulated around the chunks like insects. Each of them kicked off a little of the halogen light, creating a strange firefly effect. More people were in the water than fish. Perhaps that was a result of shoreline predators or perhaps the collapse, but their absence added to the unearthliness of the scene. Fish provided color and there was none, save for the magnesium-white glare of the "fireflies" and the ivory-white faces of the ice. Beyond that there was only blackness.

The group descended quickly. Each of the suits was equipped with a wireless computer, worn on the wrist and connected to the air tanks and communications systems. It had an audible alarm in case the tanks were compromised; it also had a thermometer, a compass, and a depth gauge. The maximum safe depth for an in-and-out scuba dive was 130 feet. Below that, a decompression stop was necessary before returning to the surface. Underwater pressure causes the nitrogen in a diver's air to separate and enter the body's tissues. A stop allows this nitrogen to gas off through the circulatory system and be exhaled by natural respiration. Failing to do that will cause nitrogen bubbles to form when normal pressure is restored, similar to removing the top from a bottle of soda. These bubbles prevent oxygen from reaching the brain, causing disorienting nitrogen narcosis. They also block airflow to the joints and organs, resulting in "the bends." A diver who ventures below 200 feet risks injury from the pressure itself. Any deeper than that and the diver could be crushed. The twin layers of air and water in the L.A.S.E.R. suits would give them some leeway in terms of depth. Bryan had established a maximum depth of 175 feet. If the submarine was lower than that they would have a problem conducting any kind of recon. It shouldn't be, though. According to sounding charts from a Russian expedition in 1978, the maximum depth this close to shore was 170 feet.

The team had just descended below 125 feet when Lieutenant Black reported, "I've got something."

A moment later Bryan saw it, too. And the mission, however unpleasant one of the alternatives had been, no longer seemed quite so clear-cut.

TWENTY-THREE

Weddell Sea

Rear Admiral Silver was sitting on the bench of the Chinook, looking out at the shoreline some two hundred feet below. They had not spotted any wreckage or remains. If anything had drifted ashore, he suspected the collapse of the ice shelf had dispersed or buried it.

Two hundred feet, Silver thought. That did not seem very far. The *D* or its remains were probably not even that deep. Yet right now it felt so distant.

Captain Puckett turned and shouted into the cabin. Though the cockpit was only ten feet away, and the door was open, the loud beat of the rotors made conversation extremely difficult.

"Rear Admiral, sir, the major would like to speak with you."

Silver walked over, leaving his blanket on the bench. He stepped around Lieutenant Houston, who was still working on Dr. Albertson. Though she was breathing on her own, she was not conscious. Ensign Warren was lying beside her, staring up. He seemed relaxed, or maybe just exhausted. Or both. He'd performed like a hero trying to keep Angela from drowning.

Silver reached the cockpit and Captain Puckett gave him a spare headset. The rear admiral slipped it on and adjusted the microphone.

"Yes, Major?"

"Sir, we've found both submarines."

"How is the smaller one?"

"From what we can see, it appears to be intact, though the forward section is entirely buried."

"Can you free it?"

"We're going to try, sir."

"And if not? What are your orders?"

"Sir, if the submarine cannot be refloated, we're supposed to destroy it," Bryan told him.

Silver had suspected that. He had feared it. Yet when he heard it, his insides liquefied.

"But, sir, there may be a problem with those orders," Bryan went on.

"What kind of problem?" Silver asked, his voice cracking.

"Your submarine is lying directly on top of what's left of the Chinese submarine. The center section of their submarine appears to be intact. The crew could be alive there. If we destroy our ship, the explosion will take the Chinese submarine with it. Their recovery team will know exactly what happened. The United States government will have a great deal to answer for."

That was true, especially since they couldn't blame it on the *D*. The submarine did not carry torpedoes. Nothing on board would leave the scoring marks or blast pattern of an explosion, especially one that had been caused externally rather than internally.

"There's something else, sir," Bryan said. "The forward escape hatch of the Chinese submarine is partially exposed. If we can free the American sub, does it possess a rescue capacity?"

"No."

"Then perhaps you can explain something, sir. We're nearly at your submarine. It's lying at a slight angle and I'm seeing what look like hatches—"

"They aren't," Silver said.

Major Bryan did not immediately respond. The silence was damning. But there was the absolution of orders. When your emotions told you to do one thing, your brain forced you to do another. The brain of Stone Silver, of every commander, was plugged into the Pentagon, into centuries of tradition that regarded national security as more important than life. Silver would not be the one to change that.

"Do the orders stand, sir?" Bryan asked.

If Silver contacted NORDSS, Grantham would take it to the Joint Chiefs of Staff. The chairman of the Joint Chiefs would take it to the president with the recommendation that they destroy the *D* and risk the diplomatic fallout. Silver could hear the arguments now. *"The accident was a result of Chinese aggression."* China would reply, *"The United States had no business conducting a military exercise in the region."* The United States would insist, *"It wasn't a military exercise, it was a Smithsonian research expedition."* China would ask, *"Then why did you blow up the submarine?"* They would be told, *"We were trying to free it."*

The president would not change the order.

"If you exhaust all salvage opportunities, your orders remain as issued," Silver replied. *They must.*

"I will let you know what we find, sir." Bryan's voice was hard and formal.

"Thank you."

"Bryan, out."

Silver took a long, tremulous breath. He returned the headset to the pilot and went back to the bench, though he didn't remember doing any of it. He did not feel pride or honor in doing his job. There was only the image Major Bryan had sketched for him of the living tombs.

Silver had not prayed since his wife was near death, and then it was as much a thanksgiving for having known her. This was different. He did not feel like praying. He felt like beating the walls of the chopper.

What stopped him was hope. The hope that Major Bryan and his team might be able to free the *D*. If not, the guilt and sadness was really academic.

There would be nothing they could do for the crew in any case.

Toward the western end of their circuit, past the section of the coastline that had collapsed, Captain Puckett noticed a few planks and twisted metal slats from the *Abby* knocking against the shore. He asked the rear admiral if he wanted to go down to collect them. Silver said he did not. He wanted the Chinese rescue ships to find the wreckage. He wanted them to know their submarine had struck a science vessel here, not a military ship.

A deception till the end.

It was necessary, Silver reminded himself.

But the question of what else was "necessary" and what was "habit" began to bother him more than a little. Major Bryan was a naval officer, yet Silver didn't know what kind of security clearance he had. The rear admiral had never even heard of this team, L.A.S.E.R. For all he knew this was some wild Russian scam. A team trained to speak English, a bogus RAF Chinook—

No. That is exhaustion talking.

Or was it? Silver didn't know. No one did. Which was why there were rules, however unpleasant they might be. If he didn't like them, if Bryan didn't like them, they should have chosen a career other than the military.

Perhaps, when this miserable business was done, they would.

In the meantime, he asked Captain Puckett to hand him a set of headphones so he could monitor what was happening below.

TWENTY-FOUR

Weddell Sea

Major Bryan pumped his legs angrily for a moment, then stopped himself. That would only cause him to consume air faster. He hadn't really expected the rear admiral to kick this back to his superiors. He hadn't expected a stay of execution for the submariners; the Chinook did not have fuel or weather-proofing for an extended stay. What Bryan had hoped for was another idea. Something no one had considered. Something fueled by inside information about the American submarine.

He wouldn't even give me that, Bryan thought as they neared the American vessel. A submarine that didn't look like any he had ever seen. Whatever was special about this ship, L.A.S.E.R. was not in the need-to-know loop.

The team reached the submarine. Bryan took the lead now. The area was crowded with the massive: the submarines, huge slices of ice, and the awesome darkness beyond their lights. Bryan felt small and exposed. If any of these things decided to move, he or his team could do nothing to stop them. It was humbling.

Bryan directed several team members, behind Lieutenant Black, to inspect the Chinese submarine. The others followed the major to the point where the ice met the hull. The pieces at the bottom of the landslide had been compacted and partly shattered by the weight of the mass above them.

"Ensign Galvez, what do you recommend?" Bryan asked.

Davis Galvez was the twenty-four-year-old naval demolitions mastermind. His father, Cleve Galvez, was one of the world's leading "deconstruction engineers." Davis had been helping the family blow up condemned buildings and mountainsides since he was thirteen. Lieutenant Black was his mentor for destroying objects below and above Galvez's area of training.

"Sir, I would suggest a TRD rainbow array at ten, twelve, two," he said.

That was an arc of thermite reaction devices placed at the ten-, twelve-, and two-o'clock positions of the clock.

"What about refall?" Bryan asked.

"Very likely," Galvez replied as he swam along the jagged wall.

"That's not good."

"No, sir, but the ice is still cracking. You can see the bubbles being released. That air was trapped when the shelf formed thousands of years ago."

Bryan told Galvez to start placing the charges. There was no time to debate the what-ifs. While Galvez went to work with a small unit, and another team turned to cutting the towline, Bryan swam toward the underside of the American submarine. As he did, the major got Silver back on the radio. He briefed the rear admiral.

"Sir, I need to know where the antenna is located," Bryan said.

"In the nose," Silver replied.

"I was afraid of that. It's buried. I can't patch in. We need another way to contact the crew."

"Why?"

"If they are mobile, and they don't pull out when we turn up the heat, they could be blown up or crushed."

The rear admiral was silent. Bryan reached the underside of the submarine. He saw what looked like two hatches with flood doors. There appeared to be a vent at the base of one of them. That had to be a pump of some kind; it had a check valve to prevent backflow. There wouldn't be pumps here unless the doors were designed to be opened underwater. Bryan also saw what looked like a scrap of underwater cable hanging from one of the hatch doors. He swam over to examine a snapped end that was floating in the water.

"Do you think you can save the ship?" Silver asked.

"What we can see of her doesn't look damaged."

"Sir?" said Lieutenant Black.

"Go ahead," Bryan told her.

"Major, the escape hatch of the Chinese submarine took some ice but it can be hand-cleared. But it's odd. There's a cable running from it, sealed along the base with waterproofing."

"What kind of cable?" Bryan asked.

"Low-smoke coaxial," she replied.

"We've got the other end here," Bryan said. "Rear Admiral, it looks like one submarine was powering the other until the line broke. *Someone* got in and out. I need to know how."

"Most likely through what you thought were hatches," Silver informed him. "You were right, Major. They can be opened."

"Thank you," Bryan said as he released the cable and swam over to the hatch.

TWENTY-FIVE

Weddell Sea

Colon was standing with Lieutenant Michaelson and Lieutenant (j.g.) Rockford in the aft section of the *Tempest D* when
they heard what sounded like knocking.

Rockford and Michaelson looked at the captain. Michaelson
was holding a jar with red liquid inside. Rockford had created a
dye using drinking water and the red disinfectant in the small
lavatory. It had occurred to the engineer that because of the icefall, rescue workers might not know where to look for them.
The men had been planning to use the starboard pump and a
hose from the john to drive the dye to the surface through the
fan vent on the port side. They couldn't use the pump there,
since that one would be needed to keep the submarine from
flooding when they opened the hatch. They were about to do so
when the sound started.

It was definitely knocking, and the knocking had a pattern.
One-one, one-two, one-three. Someone was out there—
probably from the Chinese submarine, Michaelson suggested.
What else could it be?

Colon didn't know, but there was just one way to find out. He
told Rockford to turn on the pump. When it was running at capacity, Colon opened the hatch enough so they could see who
was down there.

A bright, white beam was shining up at them, and it took a

few moments before the crewmen could squint past it. The light belonged to a man in a wetsuit. A suit with American army chevrons on the upper arm.

"A major," Colon said, saluting.

Michaelson and Rockford followed his lead.

Whoever the man was, this would be tricky; depending upon how deep the submarine had gone, the officer could not come aboard without suffering some degree of decompression.

To add to the absurdity of it all, after returning the salute, the major made a phone sign with his thumb and pinkie.

"I believe he's asking if we have a phone or radio," Rockford said.

"If this isn't the damnedest thing in a day of damnedest things," Michaelson muttered.

The engineer touched his own throat, just below the Adam's apple. The man in the water nodded. Rockford made a twisting motion with his thumb and index finger. The man nodded again.

"Damn—"

"What am I missing here?" Colon asked. He was crouching beside Rockford, trying to peer into the water, to see an additional patch or insignia on the uniform, but the water was too dark.

"I think he's saying he has a subvocal unit," Rockford replied. "I asked if it has an adjustable frequency. He seems to be saying it has."

"What good does that do us?"

"The intercom," Rockford said. "It's wireless. We may be able to talk with him."

Colon was on his feet and at the intercom before Rockford finished speaking. He punched it on. "Lieutenant Bain, what's the system frequency?"

"It's 413.450," she said.

Colon relayed the message to Rockford. He used a pen to write it on his palm, then stuck his hand in the icy water between the blades.

He kept it there only briefly, however. A moment later an all-too-familiar rumbling shook the vessel.

TWENTY-SIX

Weddell Sea

The warning came only seconds before the ice itself, but that was enough time for Bryan to get away.

The major ordered the team to retreat from shore as the rear admiral warned him of a fresh breakup along the coast. They moved away some fifty meters. The divers could no longer see the target area in their lights. Bryan conducted a verbal head count as they hovered in the dark, cold sea. They were more than halfway through their air. The heat was beginning to dissipate from their wet suits into the sea.

There wasn't much time left.

The major could feel as well as hear ice falling in front of him. The water was stirred by the landslide, causing balloonlike currents that hoisted the divers back and up. Bryan had to swim just to stay in place.

"Lieutenant Black, what's the status of the Chinese sub?" Bryan asked.

"We tapped. They tapped back."

"Where?"

"Just forward the hatch," she said.

"So we've got two live crews," Bryan said.

"Yes, but that was before all this—"

Suddenly there was a new sound in their earphones. "This is Captain Ernie Colon. Does anyone read?"

"We copy!" Bryan replied enthusiastically. His improvised link had worked. "This is Major Bryan of Emergency Rescue. What is your situation?"

"Welcome, Major, and thank you. We have full power and apparent hull integrity, and the drives worked last time we tried them," Colon said. "What is the condition of the *Abby* and the Chinese submarine?"

"There are survivors of both," Bryan replied.

"The rear admiral?"

"Safe," Bryan said.

"What about the science crew, the sailors?"

"Some have been rescued, we're searching for others," Bryan replied. He didn't want to tell the captain the truth. Bad news was not a good motivator, and he needed Colon and the crew in top form.

The thundering landslide stopped. So did the jellylike shock waves. Without hesitation the major swam forward and ordered his people to do the same. Through the fresh storm of ice particles and bubbles, Bryan could see the damage done by the new icefall. It had made little forward progress but had buried the two vessels along the sides. It was as if they were inside a massive pyramid. The vessels themselves were like conjoined twins. If one was removed, the other would be consumed by the material it was holding back.

"Captain, I assume the Chinese submarine is dead," Bryan said as he kicked forward. "You managed to get a cable between you?"

"Yes, we had them powered up for a while—they're on batteries."

"How did you pass the cable?"

"One of their men brought it out."

"So they have e-suits."

"Yes," Colon replied.

"Good. Can you take people through that hatch?"

"It will stress the pumps but I think so."

"Can you communicate with them?"

"Not since their forward compartment flooded. What are you planning to do?"

"I'm not sure." Bryan swam back to the underside. "We're going to use thermite to try and get you out. When you move, the ice on top will come down. That's going to hit them hard."

"Major Bryan, Captain Colon—this is Rear Admiral Silver. No one is going aboard the *D*. Do you copy?"

That was not what Bryan wanted to hear. "Sir, we may be able to get a few of the crew members out."

"I heard."

"If we don't make the effort, we will be murdering them," Bryan said.

"Their own people will have to look after them. They engineered this situation and killed most of my surface crew," Silver replied.

"The *Abby* crew is dead?" Colon said.

"All but three of us," Silver said.

Fuck this, Bryan thought. "The Chinese won't be here in time. You must have heard me. Freeing our sub will destroy theirs."

"Major, you will extricate my crew and my submarine and worry about the Chinese when that is completed," Silver said.

Bryan's gloved hands swept through the water with a knife-edged smoothness. They kept him in place while his mind raced. He looked at the hatch on the American submarine, but what he saw were the drowning marine dummies in the Gulf of Mexico. He saw the faceless eyes of mothers, fathers, wives, children born and unborn. He saw the rest of his life, his career in the military, his self-respect. He had never had thoughts like these before, but he had never been in a situation like this: Everything that was to come in his life and others rested upon the decision he made here. It would have been easier had he found the submarine unsalvageable, if he had to destroy it. There would have been nothing he could do to help the crew of the Chinese submarine.

"Sir, murdering foreign seamen was not part of my mission profile," Bryan said. "Request confirmation from my commander."

"You'll get it," Silver shouted. "Now do your job."

There was a loud creaking ahead. Bryan paddled ahead and

looked at the ice. The chunks on the bottom were starting to crack again.

"Major, we're getting fissures up here," Lieutenant Black reported.

"I hear them. How close are you to setting off the thermite?"

"Another ten minutes or so," she reported. "We won't *have* much more time than that."

Bryan swam back to the hatch. "Rear Admiral, I'm going to need that confirmation now. The pilot will put you through to my commanding officer. Captain Puckett?"

"Sir?"

"Reroute the rear admiral's communications, please. At once."

"Yes, sir."

There was a click. That was the end of the rear admiral's participation in this operation.

"Captain Colon, I have very little time to make a very important decision. I'm supposed to let Chinese seamen die. I want to know why."

"Sir, with respect, that is need-to-know."

"I need to know," Bryan replied. "That's an order."

Colon hesitated, but only for a moment. "Major, please cut out all other personnel."

"Puckett?"

"I'm on it, sir," the captain said. "I'm closing down headsets two through eleven for . . . ?"

"One minute," Bryan said.

"Yes, sir. Puckett, out."

"We're private," Bryan said impatiently.

"That fan you saw was part of a supercavitation drive," Colon told him. "Ramjets that create an air pocket around the submarine."

"An air bubble?"

"Yes. Designed to minimize drag. Basically, we fly like a hovercraft instead of sail."

"How far does this bubble extend?"

"Each fan throws out a ninety-degree arc ten feet deep."

"Captain, can you remove the fan from the port side?"

"It'll take about ten minutes. Why?"

"Can you idle the other fan on bottom?"

"Yes—"

"Go ahead and remove that fan," Bryan ordered. "Then get set to turn on the others."

"Why, sir?"

"Because I have a plan and we're running out of time," Bryan told him as he left the hatch and swam toward Lieutenant Black.

TWENTY-SEVEN

Weddell Sea

There was little light and little movement and the air was available in little more than straw-sized doses. It took concentration and effort to find even that. At least, Wu thought, death would ease in. There would be no sharp teeth or claws, no blood or horror. Wu took some consolation in that. His sensei used to say there were two kinds of death. The death of a man and the death of a warrior. A man died in combat. The great warrior was sufficiently skilled to survive combat and die in bed. To him, death came as night and not as the wolf.

Night was most certainly what they were facing now. Even the tumbling, cracking sounds of the ice were insufficient to dispel that. Those storms were far and muted. And if the ice came, it would come swiftly, like a wind that bore down unexpectedly from the mountains—

The knocking on the hatch seemed to stir the air a little; enough, anyway, for several of the crew members crammed in and around the escape trunk to struggle to their feet, to the ladder. One of the engineers had a wrench and he used that to knock on the metal. Whoever was outside knocked back. Someone was out there. Possibly a diver who had received their emergency call.

The knocking broke off after a minute or so, but it had energized the nearly three dozen men who were clustered in the forward trunk and in the stores section beyond. The remaining crewmen were spread through the reactor compartment. Wu found it frustrating to be close to so much power and be unable to tap it. He felt that was a flaw in himself, somehow. His training had been all about using the power of others to his own advantage.

The men on the ladder banged against the hull for another minute or two, then climbed back down. Hope was in the air but little air to sustain that hope. The air seemed slightly thicker than before, the straw pinched at one end. The men said nothing as they sat on the floor of the hatchway. The only light they had was coming from a flashlight tucked in the bottom of the open hatchway and shining upward.

Time passed, though Wu Lin Kit wasn't sure how much. It could have been a few seconds, it could have been longer. He had shut his eyes and may have slept. He woke only because his lungs ordered him to. He needed to be awake to breathe. It took effort now.

The intelligence agent heard a roar. It sounded like a gas oven being ignited. He thought the end had come, but it hadn't. The sound thinned and there was renewed knocking followed by a squeaking sound, one that wasn't coming from the ice. It was coming from inside. From the hatch above. From the wheel in the middle of the hatch above.

There was also a voice. A voice speaking English.

A voice speaking English outside the *Destiny*.

TWENTY-EIGHT

Weddell Sea

It was not something for which the *Tempest D* had been designed.

The submarine had been created to blast through the sea, to speed to or from an enemy. Not to rescue them. Perhaps putting Dr. Davies's name on the nose had tempered her, replaced aggression with compassion. Whatever it was, Colon had agreed to go along with what Major Bryan had suggested: that they use the ramjet and oxygen drawn from the seawater to create a pocket of breathable air between the *D* and the Chinese submarine. The crew of the American submarine had removed the flood door that separated the forward and aft sections of their vessel and were using that as a plank. They were going to try to save some of these guys.

So Colon sat on the edge of the hatch from which the fan blades had been removed. The other bottom-side ramjets had been turned on and were ramping up slowly, so as to disturb the ice as little as possible. The piled ice seemed to be holding, though that could change at any moment with or without the ramjet. After four minutes they were nearing 100 percent extension of the Egg—or rather, the quarter-Egg. The pocket would only cover 25 percent of the *Tempest D*. Colon would not go until that had been achieved.

Which gave him a little time to sit and think. He knew all the reasons not to help the seamen. He also knew he could blame the major for ordering him to do this. But none of that mattered. What he realized, when agreeing to the plan, was that security had already been breached. The Chinese were down here, watching them, probably waiting for them. The captain would have had a problem letting them die for a secret they didn't know. But letting them die for something that was not a secret, for details that had probably been radioed to Beijing before the collision—that was unconscionable and vindictive. He wouldn't have that on his shoulders for the rest of his life.

Hell, the future of the Tempest project might well depend on having the Chinese crew as our guests for a while, Colon thought.

Perhaps the sailors could be persuaded to explain what they were doing in the Weddell Sea. Had they been following the *Abby* as an exercise in tracking them, breaking in what was clearly a very modern Chinese submarine, one that Colon had never seen before? Was the discovery of the *D* luck or the reason for their visit? Security backwash—learning enemy methods from their penetration of your own systems—was a valuable result of a mishap like this.

Colon finally got the go-ahead from Rockford. The hatch door had been removed from between the forward and aft compartments of the *D*. It had been placed between the open ramjet hatch and the bridge of the Chinese submarine. The captain walked out—he *walked* into the parted sea, like a modern Moses—and went toward the wheel on the hatch of the Chinese submarine. Apart from emergency breathing apparatus, which he had strapped on but was not using, he had no special gear.

Being out here was a strange sensation, like standing in a doorway to get out of a sudden squall. The wind was blowing and he could feel the moisture in the air, but he himself was dry. He was chilly, however, wearing just the sweater and trousers he had on board the *D* and made a point of telling that to Rockford and Michaelson. Any shivering they might notice was cold, not fear.

Maybe they would even believe that.

Colon descended into a world that was entirely surreal. He was inside a wedge of air, the base of which was at a twenty-

odd-degree angle from the Chinese escape hatch. Major Bryan
was hovering in the water a few feet behind him. Ice, bubbles,
and even a few fish were beyond. It was like being in an aquar-
ium where you could walk through the exhibit. Or was he the
exhibit?

Colon grabbed the wheel and gave it a sharp twist; it came
slowly, grudgingly. The fat central column had taken some hits
from falling ice and the alignment was slightly off. But the lop-
sided wheel was turning. He called to the men inside and heard
a weak response; perhaps they were responding to the wheel
and not to his voice. Whichever it was, he yelled down for the
English speaker to come to the hatch.

Above him, Michaelson and Withers waited to help anyone
who might come out. The men were probably weak and the
plank would have to be crossed with care. The walls of the ramjet pocket were not solid. If anyone fell through, they would be
crushed by the pressure, swept away, drowned, and frozen in
the antarctic waters, in that order. As it was, Colon didn't know
how many of the Chinese were alive or how many the *D* could
effectively carry or even how much time there would be to
bring them aboard. Once the thermite was ignited, the *D* would
have to pull away quickly. Withers was working on the weight
computations now. Seven or eight additional people would
mean a half ton of additional weight. And that was just 10 percent of the Chinese crew. But the captain refused to think about
that. He would take on as many seamen as possible. If they
couldn't power themselves to the surface, they would find another way. All they had to do was get to the surface, not circum-
navigate the globe.

Suddenly, Bain called to him through the open fan-bay. "Sir,
there's a message from Major Bryan."

Colon turned. The major was watching him closely, just a
few yards away.

"What is it?" Colon asked.

"His team is running out of air," she said. "They have to arm
the detonator."

"How much time will we have until the explosion?"

"Fifteen minutes," she said. "That's the maximum setting."

"Understood." Colon nodded at Bryan. The major acknowledged with a thumbs-up and swam away. "Mr. Rockford, prep the other ramjets and be ready to put this one back in its well. We have to be ready to shoot out of here five minutes before the detonation."

"That's not going to give you a lot of time out there," Rockford said. "Maybe five minutes."

"I know," Colon replied just as other hands turned the wheel from the inside and the hatch began to open.

TWENTY-NINE

Weddell Sea

Wu Lin Kit was confused by what he was hearing and, in the moments that followed, by what he felt and saw. There was a rush of air, like the wash from an airplane propeller. It was forceful, loud, and invigorating. Then he saw a man in street clothes standing in the open hatch of the escape tower. Had they been brought to the surface somehow? They must have been—

The man was mostly in silhouette, backlit by a white light. Two members of the *Destiny* crew were standing below him, on the inside ladder of the escape tower. They had helped to open the hatch. The man outside was asking for the crewman who had been speaking English on the radio.

"I—" Wu said weakly.

"We need to evacuate your submarine quickly," the other man said. "Do you understand?"

It took Wu a moment to figure out what the man was saying. "We must leave," Wu said.

"That's right."

"All right."

The other crewmen of the *Destiny*, strewn through the adjoining corridors, were beginning to stir. Several were asking what was happening. Biao, who had been lying across from Wu, said they were apparently being rescued. He ordered the men who were awake to rouse those who were not.

Wu put his back and palms to the wall of the escape trunk behind him. He slid himself upright. "Who are you?" he asked the man.

"The captain of the submarine you hit," the man informed him. "Why were you here?"

Wu was disoriented but he was not so dazed that he would answer a question like that. He stood, leaning on the inside of the trunk for support. Captain Biao was busy trying to rally the others.

"You will have to ask the captain when we are aboard," Wu said. As the interpreter, Wu would make sure the answers were incorrect. "How many crewmen can you take?"

"I don't know," the American admitted. "Whatever number it is, we're losing time."

Wu went up the ladder. While Biao organized the others, the Guoanbu operative emerged from the hatch, ostensibly to help the evacuation. Standing outside, on the hull of the *Destiny*, he looked with open amazement at what he saw. There was a fan straight ahead, lit by a white light from inside the American ship. The fan was literally blowing a hole in the water, a pocket with walls that shimmered as it rippled along the outer reaches of the light. The ripples must be caused by changes in pressure from the outside. The external force of the jet was incredible, yet it was not blowing them over. The blades must be directing the force outward—it was *astonishing*. The sonar had revealed several such vents on the vessel. Obviously, they created an envelope of air around the submarine.

"Sir, we've got to shut down!" a woman shouted urgently from the opening.

"What's wrong?" the American captain shouted back.

"The ice! The ramjet is cracking it!"

THIRTY

Weddell Sea

It was a scene no one had wanted to see.

Major Bryan had been convinced that activating the fan was a risk worth taking. The force of the jet drive was directed away from the ice wall; the risk of destabilizing it seemed minimal. But "minimal" was just a guess and not the same as "nonexistent."

Captain Colon had concurred.

The captain had worked as quickly and efficiently as possible. It was odd seeing him in the water; it was like watching someone through a frosted-glass shower stall. When Ensign Galvez radioed Bryan that the ice was starting to refracture, the major left the submarine and had a quick look. The fissures were hairline now but lengthening and widening as he watched. The American vessel was just ten feet below and the major made the decision: They had to get the captain back in his submarine and start the thermite countdown.

Colon was not happy.

"We're getting people out!" he said through Lieutenant Junior Grade Bain, who was working the intercom.

"If we don't shut that engine, the ice will punch through your air pocket," Bryan warned him through Bain. "That'll kill you and the Chinese and probably block the fan doors so you can't move when we detonate the thermite."

Colon did not reply.

"He's still evacuating the submarine," Bain reported. "They've got the plank in place and men are starting across."

"Tell him to close the damn door. That's an order."

"Yes, sir," Bain said.

Bryan watched the ice and he also watched his air supply. They had to be out of here in five minutes. They still had to set the detonator, synchronize the countdown with the submarine, and surface.

"Major," Bain said, "he's still—"

There was a whiplike crack. Bryan could hear it through the water, above the bubbling roar of the fan. A huge, wide fissure slashed horizontally across the ice wall. The jagged edges and protrusions above it remained in place for a moment longer, then collapsed in watery slow motion.

"*L.A.S.E.R. evac!*" Bryan shouted into the mouthpiece.

Everyone moved away except Bryan. He did an arcing backward turn away from the wall and dove down to the submarine. He swam around ice chunks that tumbled end over end down the wall toward the submarine. He swung under the aft end of the American ship just as the ice poured over the side, rolling along the top of the Chinese submarine toward the air pocket. Bryan watched as the water bulged in along the side of the air pocket. One Chinese crewman was on the makeshift plank and Captain Colon was helping another man from the hatch as the bulge grew and the bubble simply collapsed on the forward side; the fan could not fight back the water displaced by the ice. The man on the platform clambered toward the open hatch, but Captain Colon remained where he was, still trying to help the man from the hatch as the water rushed in. The Chinese crewman dropped back into the escape tower as the sea struck Captain Colon on his right side. Major Bryan swam in with the water, grabbed the captain around the waist, and hugged him tight. Someone inside the American submarine shut the fan, allowing the sea to flow back evenly, without pockets of air or crosscurrents. That allowed Bryan, his arms still around the captain, to turn upward and flipper toward the open hatch. He reached it and forced the captain through it, toward the waiting hands of his crew. Then Bryan turned and grabbed the door that had served as the plank. He pushed it back inside. The doors of the fan bay were closed.

As the ice stopped falling, Bryan looked down at the Chinese submarine. What he saw was something he would never forget. Two men were struggling to pull the hatch closed. But a torrent of frigid sea and small pieces of ice were knocking it back to full-open. Bryan swam over to help them as larger chunks dropped on the submarine, slamming the metal where the escape trunk met the hull. An ugly crack appeared along the base of the tower, releasing a kidney-shaped bubble of air. The crack suddenly imploded, as though someone had punched through the hull. Water flooded in and air bubbled out. Men who had been in the escape trunk were flushed through the rupture like dead leaves on a windy street. Then the tower itself was compressed inward, like a crushed soda can. Blood mixed with ice crystals and crumpled shards of metal in the clear white water.

Bryan backpaddled from the maelstrom, from the death. He had done just the opposite of what they'd done in their sea trial the week before. He had acted aggressively, swum into danger instead of away from it, sought to save everyone. And he was still staring into the water and seeing death. Maybe the sea always had the final say.

"Major, Lieutenant Michaelson wants to know what's happening," Bain said.

Bryan told her. "How is the captain?" he asked.

"Battered but alive."

"How many Chinese did we get aboard?"

"Eight."

Couldn't be more than one-tenth the crew, a minimal number, Bryan thought. But again, "minimal" was not "none." Those were eight men who would have died waiting to be rescued.

The major turned his headlamp on the new configuration of ice and submarines. It wasn't good. They had set all their thermite, which was now buried somewhere in the ice, unreachable and unusable. Bryan checked his air gauge. He had just over ten minutes of air. His suit temperature was down to fifty-two degrees. It might be necessary to surface and come back down.

"Major, there seems to be a problem," Bain said.

"Go ahead."

"We overheated the pump trying to keep out that last rush of water. It shorted and took the main circuit board with it."

"Meaning?"

"We're running on batteries, sir. We're dead in the water."

"Any chance of repairing the damage?"

"We could do it in time, sir, but the men we took on are going to help us burn through our air pretty fast," she reported.

That eliminated going to the surface and coming back down. Bryan was going to have to think of something else before his own air ran out.

THIRTY-ONE

Weddell Sea

Ernesto Colon had no idea where he was. All the captain knew was that he was coughing up water that tasted like fish and was on his ass and wanted to get up. First, though, he had to determine "up."

The submarine was dark and his brain felt as if it were whirling. And the captain was hurting. Every time he tried to breathe, stabbing blows to his chest, hips, knees, elbows, and fingers told him to stay where he was.

Someone was talking in the captain's ear but he couldn't hear them. His head was ringing. He couldn't speak; his jaw hurt whenever he tried.

Fortunately, the pain did not last long. He had only been in the water long enough to get a taste of decompression.

A taste was enough.

Unfortunately, when the pain was gone and Colon could open his eyes, the lights did not come back on. And when he could finally hear, he didn't like any of what he heard.

". . . we don't have a backup for the entire system," someone was saying. "Just the components, and we don't have time to replace them."

"Okay," Colon said. That didn't mean he understood. It meant be quiet for a second.

Colon got to his side and then to his hands and knees. The

pain was sharp but manageable. The deck was still tilted slightly to the starboard side, but the main lights were out. Colon's eyes stung from the water. Great quantities of ice are in the Weddell Sea, which sweat their saline content back into the water and make it extremely salty. He dragged a wet sleeve across his eyes. It didn't help. He blinked them open, letting tears wash away the burn. People were speaking softly somewhere in the distance—Michaelson and the Chinese sailors. The last thing Colon remembered was helping them on board. Then the cold water hit.

"What happened?" Colon asked.

"An ugly little chain reaction," Rockford said.

Colon looked in Rockford's direction. He was crouching while someone held a flashlight and he was unscrewing a panel above the starboard ramjet compartment. Three other panels hung open on their hinges to the right of that.

"The pump shorted and the seawater that came in carried that electric arc along the whole string of panels. We never waterproofed the inside. The idea was, if the sea got this high, we were screwed anyway."

"What have we lost?" Colon asked.

"Everything except emergency batteries," Rockford replied. "We've got two hours of air for a crew of five, less than half for what we have now. If we turn on the lights that'll cut into the air power, so we're not."

"Can you do anything?" Colon asked.

"I don't know. We never planned on losing the *Abby* and being stuck like this. These chips are not modular. They were designed to perform specific functions."

"Have we still got the radio?"

"The intercom," Bain said.

"What about the rescue team?"

"Major Bryan is aware of the situation."

"That's nice. Has he got a *plan?*"

"I don't know, sir," Bain said.

"What about the Chinese submarine?"

"Lost," Bain said sadly. "The major said they couldn't close the hatch after the bubble collapsed."

"Shit."

"I'm sorry, sir."

"Did the English-speaking guy get on board?"

"Yes," Bain said. "Lieutenant Michaelson is talking to him. He seems to speak a lot less fluently than he did a half hour ago."

"What a surprise," Colon said bitterly.

The captain rose. He stood in the hatchway that used to have a door in it. The door had made it back inside, pulled in by Withers and Rockford. Colon took off his wet sweater and grabbed a towel from the small locker outside the tiny lavatory. Colon wiped his head and put the towel around his shoulders.

"Any suggestions?" Colon asked.

"How about everyone hold every other breath," Rockford joked. "I need time."

"Sounds like it should work, doesn't it?" Colon remarked.

"Yes, sir, it does."

Colon wished they could do that. Tell the body to slow down, go into that slow-breathing trance yoga masters were supposed to be able to do. The heart would slow, the flow of blood would slow, air would be conserved—

The flow of blood, he thought. *The circulatory system.*

"Rockford, stop what you're doing," Colon said.

"Sir?"

"I've got a new project for you," Colon said. "Lieutenant Bain, get Major Bryan on the intercom, ask what he's thinking in terms of freeing us."

"Right away."

"Tell him I need a timetable," Colon added.

"I'll tell him."

Colon walked over to Rockford and Withers. "I don't suppose we can get any kind of supercavitation push from the batteries."

"If we shut off the air and everything else?" Rockford said. "We'd get a twelve-second ride from one of the ramjets, max."

"Do you think you can rechannel the air flow?"

"Our breathable air?"

"Yes," Colon said.

"To where?" Rockford asked. "We haven't got enough air to create any kind of jet-propulsion."

"That's not what I'm thinking," Colon said impatiently. "Can you run it through the capillaries?"

"Probably. Just shunt the vents and run the air through the hoses. Why, what are you thinking?"

"Come with me," Colon said, and led the way forward, to the pump core.

THIRTY-TWO

Weddell Sea

Major Bryan studied the mountain of ice above the American submarine. He couldn't even see the top, only the sharp-edged shadows thrown upward by his headlamp. When he was finished, he quickly flippered toward the Chinese submarine. As far as Bryan could tell, blasting the ice with the C-4 he carried would bring the massive pyramid down, almost certainly crushing the American vessel. The only option was a long shot. It would require both careful timing and that the American submarine be able to move—something over which he had no control. They'd have to work on that inside and they'd have to work on it soon. Bryan was running out of time.

The major's radio came on. "Sir, this is Bain."

"Go ahead," Bryan said. As he dove back down, he slipped off his backpack.

"The captain wants to know when you might be ready to do—something."

"In about six or seven minutes. Does the captain think he can get power back?"

"He has a plan of some kind."

"We need to discuss it," Bryan said. "I think I can get him out, but he'll have to be ready to move on my count."

"May I tell him what you're planning?"

"Inform the captain that I'm going to place explosives along the hull of the Chinese submarine," Bryan said as he reached the Chinese submarine. "I'm going to set the detonators for ten minutes, which is the max that I can give you. The captain has to be ready to pull out the instant the explosives go off."

"Yes, sir. He'll want to know how this is going to help us."

"You're lying across the Chinese submarine. I'm placing the charges so they'll blow the other submarine out. When the Chinese ship goes, you'll drop. Because of the buoyancy factor it will take a moment for the ice to fall with you. You have to be ready to do a zero-to-sixty reverse when that happens."

"I'll tell him that, sir."

"You can also tell him that we'll need to start the countdown in five minutes. That's all the air I have time for."

"Yes, sir. If it's any consolation, we may have less air than that. What the captain is planning will blow through the rest of our battery power."

It was not a consolation. Any more than it was a consolation to contemplate coming back down here, blowing up the submarine, and being able to radio a "secondary mission accomplished" to Admiral Grantham. That was not the reason L.A.S.E.R. had been organized. That was not what Thomas Bryan had been put on this fucking planet to accomplish.

"Lieutenant, the only thing you'll be out of in an hour's time is that submarine," Bryan said.

"I hope so, Major," the lieutenant replied. "Thank you."

Bryan removed the two bricks of C-4 and six timed detonators from his backpack. He peeled off the protective waxed paper from the explosives. As he worked, he could not help but notice the body hanging half out of the open hatch, facing down, being washed to and fro by the current. The arms were twisted oddly from the water pressure, yet they were still extended, waving slowly as they rode the current, the tortured fingers reaching. It was disturbing; the crew member looked less like a man than the dummies did back on the destroyer.

But the major or his team could do nothing for him or his shipmates. Bryan concentrated on the C-4—and the crew that needed him.

THIRTY-THREE

Weddell Sea

Colon was on his back again. This time, however, he was both alert and not decompressing. The captain was lying alongside Rockford in a small forward compartment beside the command console. He was handing tools to the *Tempest* engineer. Rockford had already rerouted the hydrogen pipe and cut the oxygen line. Once the lieutenant released the clamp he had placed there to hold it together, they would be left with just the air that was already in the submarine. That would get old fast.

Hopefully, they wouldn't need it for long.

Rockford was unhooking the air pump from the electrical conduit so it could be reattached to the battery. He was working quickly, efficiently. If he had doubts about the captain's plan, he did not show them. In theory, Rockford had said, the idea sounded right—certainly better than the last one, about drawing a cable over using ramjet suction.

The hull of the *Tempest D* was lined with over a mile of ballast capillaries. Colon's idea was to separate hydrogen and oxygen in the H_2O, as if they were going to activate the ramjets. But instead of using both gases in the Egg, they would pump the lighter gas into the capillary network and dump the oxygen into the submarine. That would give them a little more air, a cushion if something went wrong. The hydrogen would give them instant buoyancy. How much they did not know, nor was there time to perform more than a few rough calculations. They would flood the system and hope for the best.

No, not "hope," Colon thought. *Pray.*

They were nearly finished when Lieutenant Junior Grade Bain reported on the conversation with Major Bryan.

"Tell the major I will update him in a few minutes," the captain told her. He was not happy.

Rockford was working on the last series of shunts. "Sir—" he said.

"I know," Colon replied. "We're going to need propulsion." The Chinese submarine was below them, the ice on top. The changes they were making would only give them lift. "Any ideas?"

"Actually, I'd been thinking about that as a safety net," the engineer said. "I was going to suggest that when we pump in the hydrogen, we don't have to release the oxygen into the *D.* We can fill the blowholes we use to shuck the ballast. That way—"

"We get a kick when we release it," Colon said.

"Exactly. And it doesn't take extra time because we're already breaking out the oxygen."

"Mr. Rockford, you may have saved our asses again. Can you handle the rest down here?"

"Yes, sir."

"I'm going to tell Withers and Michaelson what we need to do."

Colon slid from the compartment and pulled a penlight flashlight from his pocket. He headed aft. It was hot, muggy, and very, very close in the submarine, making the *D* seem smaller than ever. Colon wished they could tap the power his heart was generating. Having potentially workable ideas was one thing. Getting them to mesh, without room for any missteps, was another.

Maybe we should just get out and push, like we used to do with my dad's '57 T-bird, Colon thought, only partly in jest. Or else they could carbonate the water with bubbles from the capillaries, shake the *D* like a martini, and blast themselves out. That used to work with bottle rockets they made from Tupperware containers and the two volatile sodas, club and baking.

Lieutenant Michaelson had placed the Chinese seamen in the corridor that separated the command center from the super-cavitation chamber. Several of them had been put to work replacing the airtight door. The secret of the ramjet drive was probably blown. If they got out of here, Silver wouldn't be happy about that; Grantham would be even less happy. The captain did not wonder what the DOD would order Major Bryan to do if the submarine could not be refloated. The *D* could not be left here for the Chinese recovery vessel to find.

How did this all go so wrong? Colon wondered as he reached the ramjet section of the submarine. The crew of the *Abby* dead, the *D* incapacitated. Was the goddamn towline the problem or was it a result of the problem, a couple of guys looking to win the big sausage hang? If Colon hadn't insisted on extending the line, would this have happened? Or was this all a fortuitous event because now they knew the Chinese were onto them somehow. In the long run, maybe the Chinese knowing—and the DOD not knowing they knew—would have been worse, like the Russians getting nukes in the early fifties. He couldn't get his brain around it all, though he knew that things would probably never change. If people agreed on things, they wouldn't need submarines like this in the first place.

Colon reached Withers, who was looking for electronic components that still worked. The captain took him off that and put him on the vent controls, helping him to switch them to manual operation. Between the two of them they managed to make the change that Rockford could have executed in seconds.

"I'm going to be back here with you, timing this out," Colon explained. "When we get the go-ahead from Major Bryan, we start the water intake and let the oxygen build. It has to be released the instant the C-4 detonates."

"Sir, the vent pipes may rupture before we get to vent the oxygen," Withers said. "They're only rated for sixteen psi."

"We need that thrust, Lieutenant," Colon replied. "If we don't get it, we'll be crushed."

"I understand, sir. But it will take ten to twelve seconds to fill the hull capillaries. The pressure will build in the outgassing vents at two psi per second. The math doesn't work for us."

"Can you vent for three seconds, then start storing oxygen? That should keep us in the pocket."

"Sir, I'll give it my best, but this whole thing is a rain dance. We're shaking things and making lots of noise and hoping it all comes together."

"I know," Colon admitted. "There's just one difference."

"What's that, sir?"

Colon smiled. "Water is the *last* thing we need more of."

Withers smiled back. Colon took the smile forward to see about the countdown. Lieutenant Junior Grade Bain met him halfway.

"Sir, Major Bryan just radioed," Bain said. "He says he has set the timer."

"It's running?"

"Yes, sir. Five minutes to detonation. He wants to give you the four-minute marker."

"Let's go," he said, jogging forward, around the Chinese sailors. "Mr. Rockford, are you ready?" Colon yelled ahead.

"Just finished, sir!" The engineer came out from the cabinet, flashlight under his left arm, and moved over to the controls. He started the ramjet conversion unit, which drew air from the water. From that moment, they had twelve minutes of battery power.

Colon listened as the capillaries began to fill—hopefully with hydrogen. He reached the forward intercom. Bain handed him the headset.

"Mr. Withers, are you ready?" Colon yelled back. His voice sounded hollow in the still darkness.

"All set, sir!"

"Oxygen building?"

"Digital gauge is down but it sounds like it."

"Good. On my 'go' you vent for three 'Mississippi's!'" Colon yelled.

Withers acknowledged. Colon pressed the headphone to one ear and adjusted the mouthpiece.

"Colon here, Major."

"You've got four minutes in twelve seconds," Bryan said.

Colon looked at his glow-in-the-dark watch. The calm he

displayed was entirely external. Inside he was churning from skull to belly.

"Five seconds."

These were the moments that defined a man: the poise with which he faced life-threatening tribulations.

"Four . . ."

And there was no greater responsibility than making decisions on which life itself depended.

"Three . . ."

The *right* decisions.

"Two . . ."

Not to preserve his own life, but those of a dozen others who were relying on his judgment. Command, like the countdown, always came down to this—

"One."

THIRTY-FOUR

Weddell Sea

After Bryan effectively ordered him to be cut off, Rear Admiral Silver remained in the cockpit. He told the pilot to get Major Bryan back on the radio. Special ops guys were a tough and independent breed. Yet while Silver may have spent his career in R&D and not in the field, they were all still military. He intended to remind this officer of that.

Captain Puckett reported that he could not raise Major Bryan. The Chinook had been locked out.

"You're unable to communicate with your commanding officer?" Silver said incredulously.

"We are not, sir." The pilot pointed to the display on the radio. "Major Bryan has input code 12–2."

"Meaning?"

"This is an unsecure line, sir. 'Twelve' is a communications hold and 'two' indicates the presence of a foreign military force. Shall I raise NORDSS, sir, as the major requested?"

"No," Silver said. "Let me know if you hear from the major."

"Yes, sir."

The rear admiral returned to the bench. Grantham would be up his ass about the security breach and Silver would buck that down to Bryan. A major, however heroic, however moralistic, was not the one to determine the disposition of years of effort and billions of dollars. The Chinese had chosen to be where they were, to do what they did. The rear admiral felt nothing for them. Nothing good.

Master Chief Petty Officer Wingate was crouched by the hatch. The door had been closed to keep out the wind. But he was looking out the window, watching for more than the broken bones of the *Abby*.

Wingate turned and shouted to the cockpit as yellow dye appeared on the water, "Team decompressing!"

L.A.S.E.R. used the dye to indicate they were decompressing and would be ready for retrieval in five minutes.

Captain Puckett acknowledged. He continued along the coast for another quarter mile, then turned back. There were no remains and little debris. Silver looked over at Warren and Angela, both of whom had been given sedatives. He himself had declined medication of any kind. He went back to the cockpit and looked out the window. The first of the rescue workers broke the surface.

"Captain, when will you be able to talk to them?" Silver asked.

"Unless the code changes, we won't be speaking until the team is on board, sir," the pilot informed him.

Silver drew air through his nose; it felt like fire when he breathed it out. Bryan had pushed the radio silence too far. The rear admiral wanted to know the condition of his submarine.

The rear admiral waited impatiently as the Chinook moved in to recover the team. When the helicopter was about ten feet up, Wingate opened the door and rolled out the ladder. Silver watched the divers as they started up. He saw seven, not eight.

Ensign Galvez was the first one back. Wingate helped him in and he flopped onto the starboard bench. The ensign pulled off his mask and leaned his head against the fuselage. He was breathing heavily from the full-gear climb up the ladder. After being in a buoyant environment, the equipment felt heavy.

Silver walked over to him. "What's the situation, Ensign?"

"Sir, I'm not really sure what happened down there."

"What do you mean?"

"We were planting thermite to free the sub when the ice

came down," Galvez told him. "The submarine reported a complete shutdown of electronic systems."

"We're talking about *our* submarine?"

"Yes, sir."

"Batteries, too?"

"No, sir. They had battery power. But the thermite was lost. Major Bryan and your captain were trying to free the submarine some other way. We cut the cable that was wrapped around the American and Chinese subs, then the major ordered the rest of us to come back."

Then it was the towline, Silver thought. The nail that had cost them a kingdom. "Is the major still down there?"

"Yes, sir."

"Do you know what they were going to do?"

"I'm sorry, sir, I do not."

Silver thanked the ensign. The other members of the team were coming aboard. He watched the others as they removed their gear. No one spoke; they looked spent. The divers reminded him of training films he had seen years before, of men returning from combat missions. However the battle had gone, there were no cheers, no locker room camaraderie. They were just beaten down. It was something he had never experienced, never even witnessed.

Ensign Galvez shut the door and Lieutenant Black went over to Captain Puckett. The rear admiral followed her.

"Captain, how much hovering time do we have left?" she asked.

"Fifteen minutes," Puckett replied. "That's assuming we're going to try and get back to Stanley with available fuel."

"We are," she said. "We don't want to be here when the Chinese arrive."

"Why not?" Silver asked.

"We managed to get some of their people out, sir," the woman told him. "Your submarine—it's a prototype with a new kind of drive, isn't it?"

"I can't discuss that."

"I understand. The reason I asked, sir, is that the Chinese apparently knew it would be here."

"Do you have information to that effect?"

"No, sir," Lieutenant Black admitted. "But our guests might. They have an English-speaker on board."

The rear admiral didn't like that nugget of information. He didn't like it at all. Signal intelligence was typically collected above-water. Other than coincidence and spying, there was no reason for an English-speaking sailor to be on board that submarine. The Chinese did not do anything by whim. He began to wonder, unhappily, if perhaps the death of Charlotte Davies had not been an accident either. Silver didn't want to believe that but he couldn't dismiss it.

Moses Houston was examining the divers and overheard what was said.

"It's a good thing we took some of them on board," Houston suggested. "If the major can refloat the submarine, sir, you may want to see that our guests spend a few days in a U.S. hospital. A Valium and Demerol drip to relax them—we'll get that information."

"Thank you, Lieutenant," Silver snapped. Houston was taking the side of his superior officer. That was understandable. Silver just didn't want to hear it.

Silver went to the hatch. Black dragged herself up behind him. They stood beside Wingate, looking out the small window, waiting for something to happen. Another man was waiting there, watching. One of the divers.

Suddenly, the water below them began to ripple excitedly. It rose, ridgelike, along a thick, short line from north to south. The helicopter jerked awake, soaring up and away as a wall of water erupted below them, geysering into the sky. Some of the spray reached the windows of the Chinook before it could bank away.

"Lieutenant, what did that look like to you?" Silver asked Black.

"C-4, sir."

"Are you sure? It couldn't be something that triggered the thermite?"

"No, sir. That was an *ex*plosion rather than a meltdown. It also wasn't *im*plosion or landslide, which could be good news," she replied.

"Why?" Silver asked.

"Because the only thing down there that could blow up that way was the C-4 the major was carrying."

Silver continued to watch the spray as it fell back to the sea, sparkling in the sunlight. He did not say what was on his mind, what was probably on the minds of Black and Wingate as well.

He hoped that the detonation was to free the submarine, not to destroy it.

THIRTY-FIVE

Weddell Sea

Standing aft with Withers, Captain Colon had counted down the final minute. The green-tinged phosphorescent dial of his watch shined confidently in the darkness. Rockford had come aft when he was done to help in case the vent didn't work the way it was supposed to.

Not that he could do much in the seconds they had to react, other than to kick something. Then again, kicking the right thing has been known to help.

Michaelson had gone forward to sit with Bain on the intercom. Rockford and Withers had their flashlights trained on the levers they would have to pull, buttons they would have to press. Everything but the intercom had been shut down.

In addition to the flashlights, Colon had given Rockford and Withers the two emergency oxygen masks the *D* carried. He could not afford to have these men pass out. The masks had been provided in the event that repairs had to be made to the air system. The small tanks each contained thirty minutes of oxygen. Repairs taking longer than that would not help the crew. As it was, it was astonishing how fast fifteen people could turn a submarine full of uncirculated air into a sauna. Michaelson had gotten the Chinese sailors to lie down in the corridor, to consume as little oxygen as possible. But "as little as possible" wasn't "nothing" and their bodies, warm from the exertion of their evacuation, helped warm the vessel.

Sixty seconds had never passed so quickly. The captain had listened as the capillaries filled with what was hopefully pure hydrogen. With everything else so silent, the air flow sounded like a moderate wind moving from stern to prow. There was something primal about it, about fighting water with air. The crew in their submarine were little different from prehistoric men in a cave, waiting to see how the elements resolved their conflict.

Yet despite the countdown, despite the forces both bridled and unbridled around them, Colon was not thinking that these seconds might be his last. He was thinking only about what he could control, about what had to happen on a timetable. In twenty-six seconds they would begin the oxygen purge, followed by the explosion of the Chinese submarine. They would need quick forward thrust while the capillaries finished filling. Then, hopefully, the *D* would rise—all of that before the ice dislodged by the blast and the collapse of the Chinese submarine could crush them.

Thirteen seconds.

Colon started counting down from ten for Withers. At three seconds the engineer would have to start their improvised oxygen-thruster. Colon looked up for just a moment to make sure Withers was ready. The young officer seemed to know what he was thinking and nodded.

At five seconds, Withers reasserted his grip on the lever.

At four seconds, as Withers had feared—though earlier than he had feared it—the oxygen bladder that was to propel them forward blew up.

THIRTY-SIX

Weddell Sea

After setting the detonators, Major Bryan had begun his ascent but continued to look back. He was seventy-odd feet from the Chinese vessel when he saw the American submarine blow out a huge air bubble starboard aft. The blast was followed by a lazy rain of small metal shards.

Something inside the submarine had ruptured. Bryan couldn't go back and have a look; not until the C-4 detonated. He waited an eternal moment as an instant later the Chinese submarine blew up. The American submarine dropped straight down as the hull below it erupted outward. The smaller vessel was rocked from side to side by the blast but was unable to get away before the falling ice pounded its stern.

Bryan punched on the intercom. "You're caught!"

"Our forward thrust maneuver failed," Bain reported. "The oxygen tank on the starboard side ruptured."

Shit, shit, shit, Bryan thought. *This can't be happening. Not this close to freedom.* "Is there another air sac portside?" he asked.

"Yes," Bain said.

"Are the pumps still running?"

Bain said they were.

Bryan started swimming down, through smaller air bubbles that were rising from pockets inside the shattered Chinese submarine. As he neared the American submarine, he saw ice dropping onto its back.

"Is the watertight door back in place?" Bryan asked.

"Yes—"

"Get everyone forward and shut it," Bryan ordered. "Tell the captain to keep oxygen flowing into the portside bladder."

"Yes, sir."

However this went, it wouldn't be good. The submarine was caught in a fox trap. He had to do something about that. Blowing up the ice was not an option: that would only bring down more ice. He had to do what a fox would do.

Gnaw off its leg.

Bryan had used all the C-4 but he still had detonator caps. And a plan. As the major neared the submarine, he had to dodge smaller pieces of ice that were cannonballing down from the fresh collapse. They announced themselves with fists of water that warned him to look back. Visibility was impaired by smaller bits of debris tumbling crazily from the site. He swatted those aside with his breaststroke and reached the struggling submarine. Bryan saw where the starboard cell had exploded; he went to the port side. The ship's hull was trembling. It wanted to rise. He would help it.

The major peeled the backing from two detonator caps and slapped the adhesive base on the side exactly opposite the blown oxygen tank. He set the charge for thirty seconds, turned, and swam up and away. Hopefully, the pure oxygen would run the two small sparks into the end zone, giving the submarine far more bang than the caps themselves would provide.

Bryan did not see or hear the explosion. But he felt it, hard, rolling up behind him like a mugger. Bryan was unable to turn and see whether he had succeeded. Even if he had been able, there wasn't time. The only way he could go was up, and he did that faster than he would have liked.

At thirty-three feet underwater, human lungs compress by a factor of two due to the pressure. At ninety-nine feet, they compress by a factor of four. Bryan was ascending from more than twice that depth.

Ascending faster than his lungs could handle . . .

THIRTY-SEVEN

Weddell Sea

Silver watched the sea following the explosion. He felt sick to his soul when the *Tempest D* failed to surface. The rear admiral was convinced that Major Bryan had destroyed it. Only when the diver standing beside him became anxious did Silver realize that the major hadn't surfaced either.

The drone of the chopper was swallowed by a second explosion, one much different from the first. A perfect dome of a bubble pushed through the surface, straightening the ripples and then collapsing, as if it had been punctured. Several smaller bubbles appeared around the perimeter and popped almost immediately.

"Something just vented air," Black said.

"Could it be one of the submarines?" the rear admiral asked.

"Most likely, sir," she said. "But I don't understand why we're not seeing anything."

One of the other divers had been watching behind them. He jumped over to the storage area, grabbed a spare air tank, and turned toward the cockpit.

"Puck—take me down!" he yelled.

"Gabe, are you sure? We don't know who's spitting up what."

"The major could be hurt and he's got to be near out of air," Gabriel yelled. He yanked open the door. "Puck, don't make me come over and hurt you!"

"Descending!" Puckett said.

The Chinook dropped back to within ten, then five feet of the surface. Gabriel didn't bother with the ladder. Holding the tank to his chest, he leaped in. No sooner did he hit the water than the sea began to bubble and dance some twenty-five meters away, toward the shore.

"Possible target emersion!" Wingate shouted back.

"I see it!" the pilot replied.

Gabriel descended beneath the surface as a dark mass pushed its way from the sea. The helicopter glided over to the object while Wingate kept watch on the spot where Gabriel had gone down. It was definitely the nose of a submarine. Silver's throat locked. He was too hopeful to speak and watched with excitement as he recognized the distinctive shape of the *Tempest D*.

"It's ours," Silver said. "That's our submarine."

"We need rescue!" Lieutenant Black shouted into the cabin.

Silver continued to watch. What he could not tell was whether the submarine was intact. It was clearly not a controlled ascent since the *D* rolled to starboard as it surfaced, almost like a spaceship in zero gravity.

Or a dying sea creature, he thought.

Several other team members had gathered around the open door, suiting up as they did. Wingate was already deploying the ladder. Woodstock took her gloves from the locker and pulled them on. She also grabbed her mask and flippers. Galvez was right behind her. Woodstock gave him the last extra air tank in case they had to go underwater. Warren tried to rise but the medic pressed him back down. Silver ordered him to stay in the hammock.

The rear admiral continued to watch through the open hatch. The Chinook's rotors batted countless little peaks from the water and pushed the thin film of water from the hull of the submarine. The *D* continued its slowly twisting rise and then suddenly fell over as though it had been snapped in two. The submarine landed on its side with a hard smack, revealing a rough and ugly tear: It took Silver a moment to realize that most of its aft section was gone. What remained was scalloped metal, shredded plastic, and swinging knots of wire and tubes.

Guided by Wingate, the pilot maneuvered the helicopter so the ladder was over the submarine.

"Is there any way we can salvage that?" Silver asked Wingate.

"Not with this bird, sir," the officer replied. "We hook that and the weight will pull us down."

That meant it would have to be destroyed somehow, and soon.

Woodstock went down the ladder, followed by Galvez. Woodstock stepped onto the hull and removed the flashlight from her equipment belt while the ensign remained on the ladder's lowest rung. A six-foot canvas lifeline connected the two. The hatch was lying partly in the water. Walking in a surfer's stance, Woodstock made her way to it. She rapped on the circular door using the back of her flashlight. A moment later the hatch opened, slapping the water hard. Because the opening was partly submerged, water flowed in as people climbed or jumped out. Galvez went into the freezing water to help those who ended up there. Wingate went down the ladder to take his place. Silver watched, smiling as he picked out Bain and Rockford, then Withers, along with many men in the uniforms of the People's Liberation Navy. All the while the submarine was shifting its position, rolling onto its back and sinking slowly.

Assisted by the L.A.S.E.R. divers, the crew of the D began to arrive in the Chinook. Bain tried to salute as she entered. Her features were haggard and pale and she had trouble raising her arm. She nearly fell back through the hatch, but Lieutenant Houston, who was standing beside her, put his arms on her shoulders and physically moved her to a spot where he had put down blankets. The medic returned to help the Chinese aboard along with the American seamen. The crew of the D were shivering and wet, but Major Bryan and his unit had saved them. Silver didn't know how he would feel later, but at that moment gratitude pushed the bile back down his throat.

Two people were still missing, though, and Silver watched for them. Finally, Captain Colon appeared in the hatch of the D, emerging as the submarine went under. Lieutenant Black pulled him free, and, assisted by Galvez, they swam him over to

Wingate. The three followed Colon up the ladder as the submarine went down.

Colon looked up as he neared the Chinook. He smiled sadly when he saw the rear admiral. Silver held on to the handle at the side of the door and extended his hand to pull Colon in. The captain's hand was wet. Silver gripped it tightly and leaned back to give himself leverage. Before Colon entered, Wingate climbed behind and tapped him on the back. Colon turned.

"Captain, do you know what happened to Major Bryan?" Wingate asked, yelling to be heard in the rotor backwash.

"Isn't he here?"

"No, sir."

"The last communication we had was when our aft section was pinned. The major asked Lieutenant Bain about an air tank—he must have detonated it to free us."

The master chief petty officer went back down to report to Woodstock. She was hanging on the ladder, watching for Gabriel, who was still underwater. Silver pulled Colon in. The captain crouched in the open door, looking out at the sea. Silver did not release his hand.

"They'll find him," the rear admiral said.

Colon looked at him. "I hope so, sir. I don't have to tell you what he just did."

"No. You don't."

Lieutenant Houston came over to look at Colon. The captain said he would be back in the makeshift medical bay in a minute.

"One minute," Houston said.

Colon was still looking at Silver. The smiles were gone. "It's good to see you, sir."

Silver nodded once. He was fighting tears.

Colon glanced at the other two *Abby* survivors. "Just three."

"Just three. Angela took a big posttraumatic hit," Silver said. "It's going to take a lot of time and care to bring her around."

"Fucking towline," Colon muttered; then added, "Sir."

"We make our decisions and live with them," Silver said. "We all had a hand in that one."

"It should never have been deployed."

"Captain, our best guesses and legitimate chain of command said otherwise. Let it go."

Colon shook his head. "Odd you should put it that way. I tried, sir."

The captain went to a free blanket and fell on it. Lieutenant Houston came over to examine him, the L.A.S.E.R. team members moving around the cabin assisting him. They were administering medication, taking blood pressure, getting crewmen out of soaking clothes and covering them with anything that was dry. That included canvas sacks in which some of the gear had been packed.

Silver turned back to the door. Captain Puckett was maneuvering the helicopter back to where Captain Gabriel had gone under. Right now, the rear admiral did not want to think about the decisions he had made or their Chinese guests or anything other than the safe return of the last two officers. He knew that these issues would trouble him for the rest of his life. But he knew something else as well, something he couldn't let himself forget.

That the lost members of the *Abby* crew would be happy to trade places with him.

THIRTY-EIGHT

Weddell Sea

He went from being knocked around by a big, honking bottle rocket to being a lead weight.

The concussion wave had carried Major Bryan at least thirty feet up, allowing his lungs to expand and forcing his joints to cramp. The pain severely disoriented the officer. He didn't know which direction was up or where he had to go. It was difficult enough just to breathe, since his chest felt as if it were being pushed out and didn't want any more air. But the pressure was decompression and not oxygen. He needed to breathe, despite the razor-cut pain caused by inhaling. He felt as though his ribs were going to crack, along with his elbows, knees, and ankles. He finally knew which way "down" was because he couldn't move his arms or flippers and began to float upward. He made a few clumsy attempts to stop himself, to hold his position, but his joints locked up, swollen to immobility. And then he could barely breathe at all, painful or not. He knew his tank had to be nearly empty.

When strong hands grasped him on the upper arms, the major was barely aware of what was happening. He was being held in place; he knew that because the pain did not increase. After a few moments he became aware of someone fussing with his gear. Breathing became a little easier, if no less painful. Someone had jacked into the external valve and given him more air.

Bryan's limbs began to loosen up slightly. Equally important, the major was able to reclaim his mind. The first thing that hit him was how damn cold he was. The major began moving his arms around, then his legs, to expedite circulation and generate warmth. In the glow of his headlamp he actually saw the individual in front of him, saw the face behind the mask. It was Captain Gabriel. The big man's eyes were locked on the major's face, searching for a hint of recognition. After a few more seconds, as the pain and cold subsided slightly, the major nodded. Gabriel released him and gave him a thumbs-up. They waited for several more minutes as Bryan's body adjusted to the current depth. When Bryan felt better, they ascended another thirty feet. Because there were still lingering bubbles of nitrogen in Bryan's system, the rise was not pain-free. But it was manageable.

The rapid decompression had popped a mercury-based conductor in his com system. Bryan could not communicate with his rescuer until they had surfaced, some fifteen minutes after Gabriel had first reached him. The major pulled out his mouthpiece almost the moment they popped free of the sea. Through the roar of the wind, Bryan heard the helicopter. The major turned to his right and saw it about fifty feet off. But he did not see the submarine. His own pain was forgotten, instantly. It was replaced by a feeling of helpless desperation.

"Captain—where is she?" Bryan gasped.

"You raised her, sir," Gabriel told him.

"Repeat?"

"You refloated the forward section of the submarine and we saved everyone who was on board."

"We did?"

"*You* did," Gabriel said, spitting out sloshing seawater between words.

"Fuck."

"Yeah. Whatever you did down there sent her to the surface. The inside hatch got banged up and took on water, but we got the crew before she went back down."

"Our team is okay?"

"Yes, sir."

"Fuck."

The chopper was coming near. Bryan looked over. Lieutenant Black was on the lower portion of the ladder, waiting to help him from the water. He took her hand when the chopper was overhead and, with Gabe's help, got a grip on the second rung. He climbed slowly, on joints that complained, with lungs that still weren't working fast enough to power his ascent. Both of his team members helped him. When Bryan finally reached the cabin, he lost it: He was on his knees when his thighs started to shake and were unable to sustain him. He pitched face-forward, overcome more with the success of the mission than with his own salvation. When Wingate shut the door behind him, the cabin felt as warm and secure as any place he had ever been.

Lieutenant Houston came over. After removing the canisters he rolled the major onto his back. He was out of oxygen and had to use the tank Gabe had brought. The air chased away the last sparks of decompression. One of the team members put a rubber sack on Bryan's torso. It was surprisingly warm. Meanwhile, the medic rolled back the layers of sleeve on Bryan's left arm and inserted an IV. Houston started a drip of fluids to rehydrate him. Despite the cold, Bryan had perspired a great deal in the suit.

"Is everyone else all right?" Bryan asked the medic.

"They're doing quite well, considering what they've been through," Lieutenant Houston replied. "Now relax, sir."

"I guess I can now."

"Yes, sir."

"I don't feel like I should."

"You should."

"Or that I can."

"Don't make me put you to sleep, sir," Houston warned.

"Okay. I'll relax."

The major tried to empty himself of the mission. All that remained was to destroy what was left of the submarine. That could be done when the Chinook met its escort. Puckett could bring team members back with fresh equipment to finish the job before the Chinese arrived. It would be snug time-wise, but it could be done. They could also do a little photo recon of what was left of the PLN submarine. What he had seen there wasn't like any other Chinese vessel he had ever seen.

Bryan lay there, looking past Lieutenant Houston at the cardboard-gray fuselage. The flutter of light and shadow from the rotor skipped across it. Bryan thought about the mission, not anything specific but in general. He wondered how much the failed exercise the week before had fueled him. Wondered if that had made a crucial difference. Suddenly, a pale face looked down, topped by a flat spray of gray. The major raised his hand to his forehead in as sharp a salute as he could manage.

"Rear Admiral Silver," Bryan said.

"Major Bryan," the rear admiral replied, returning the salute. "How are you feeling?"

"Lucky, sir," Bryan replied. "Did you get through to my CO?"

"I didn't try."

"Oh?"

"I know when I'm being sandbagged."

"Oh."

Bryan didn't say anything more. There could be a court-martial. Besides, it hurt to talk. His lips and the inside of his mouth were sore from holding the mouthpiece longer than usual.

"I don't like what you did to me but I understand why you felt it was necessary," Silver said. "But what's more important is that I like what you and your team did for my crew. That took incredible courage and resolve. I'll log the rest as a communications breakdown and leave it at that."

"Thank you, sir."

Silver smiled. He blew to warm the backs of his hands as he turned away. Everything was relative. Bryan felt remarkably warm right now. He patted the pocket watch that had gone down with him. It was snug in a waterproof vest pocket near his heart. He could feel it ticking. His eyes were tired and he shut them. They *had* done well. He would tell that to the crew once everyone had been released from Lieutenant Houston's field infirmary. Right now the major just wanted to savor the feeling of having pulled off this rescue. Far too many Chinese sailors had died, but there was nothing L.A.S.E.R. could have done differently. They had saved lives, not caused them to be lost. Captain Puckett would already have sent that message to General Scott. A brief communiqué for an unsecure line. A message that said, simply, TARGET DOWN. TEAM PLUS EIGHTEEN ABOARD. That would have told Scott that L.A.S.E.R. was safe on the Chinook with seamen extracted from the lost vessel. Once on board the Hercules, Bryan would send a more detailed report about the action.

But that was for later. Right now it was time to rest. For the first time in a week to rest without guilt or doubt.

Not even Brackettville had been so sweet.

THIRTY-NINE

Weddell Sea

Rear Admiral Silver made his way across the crowded floor of the cabin. He asked Colon to point out the Chinese radio operator who spoke English. He was directed to where the evacuees were lying aft, to one who was sitting on the floor between three other men. They were sharing a single blanket, passing it among them. All had their backs against the starboard equipment locker.

The rear admiral knelt before the radio operator. "What's your name?" Silver asked.

"Chan, sir."

"Chan, what happened down there?"

The man frowned and shook his head.

"Down there," Silver pointed, then clapped his hands together. "Crash. Accident. Why?"

"Saw you." He moved a finger to indicate the sweep of the sonar.

"You saw us on sonar," Silver said.

"Sonar."

"And . . . ?"

"We move away. We hit."

"You were leaving," Silver said. "Going?"

"Yes."

"Do you understand 'bullshit'?" Silver said angrily.

The seaman looked at him blankly.

"Sir, how we get free? What that?"

"I'll ask the questions, Mr. Chan," Silver said. "What were you doing in a demilitarized region?"

"Demilitarized?"

"The south pole. No armies. No naval ships. Peaceful."

"Yes. Peaceful. Us."

"No. You were here with a warship."

"Not war. Science," Chan said.

"Who?" Silver asked, sweeping his hand across the Chinese crew.

"Killed. Flooding."

Silver didn't believe what the man was saying. He didn't believe they were on a scientific mission, any more than the *Abby* had been on a research voyage. The rear admiral moved in close.

"Mr. Chan, your submarine was going fast. Not away from us. *To* us. Why?"

The PLN seaman shrugged and shook his head vigorously.

"Why go fast?"

"Do not know." He pointed to himself. "Radio."

"You were near the captain."

"Yes."

"What were his orders? What did he say?"

"He say go."

"Where?"

"Go. Hit line." The young sailor pinched the index finger to the thumb of each hand, then tugged them in opposite directions as though he were holding a thread between them.

Silver moved back slightly. He remained squatting while he studied the radio operator. That part of the story was probably true. The cable would not have shown up on sonar.

Silver rose. The radio operator tapped the rear admiral's leg.

"Thank you. Save us."

Silver tried to smile, but all he was able to do was roll his lips inward. He still didn't trust what the sailor was telling him, but he could do nothing about that right now. The rear admiral walked forward, thinking about everything that had happened. As he did, Colon called to him. The captain was lying on his back with a torn vinyl bench cushion for a pillow.

"Did you get anything from him, sir?" Colon asked.

"Not really," Silver said, crouching. "He said they saw you on sonar, went to leave, and got tangled in the cable."

"Which part of that do you believe?"

"Everything but the 'went to leave' part. I'm sure they were tracking you, moving in for a closer look. They may have gotten snagged and tried to get away, ended up under the *Abby*."

"Yeah," Colon said.

The captain was snarling, though he probably didn't realize it. Silver regarded him for a moment.

"Captain, I was just thinking about this. If it hadn't been the cable, it could have been the drive itself or a sudden maneuver that caused the collision." Silver cocked his head toward the Chinese crewmen. "We planned for whales and icebergs, but we didn't factor them in."

"Risk is part of this business, sir," Colon said. "I know that. It comes with the uniform and the pension. But so does responsibility for one's command. I wanted it. I earned it. With respect, sir, that wasn't factored in either."

"Captain, when we left home, this wasn't war, it was research. It was as much about brains as courage, science as sailing. I wanted to spread that across a few qualified shoulders. Yours, mine, Carr's, Angela's. I still don't think that was wrong."

"With respect, a board of inquiry will probably agree with you, but I'm not sure I ever will." Colon frowned. "Shit, I didn't mean that the way it sounded, sir. I don't think that's why you're saying it—"

"I know."

Colon's attitude seemed to change then. He'd taken his shot and it obviously hadn't felt right.

"You want to know the damnedest thing about all this, sir?"

"Tell me," Silver said.

"The *D* worked. That beautiful lady did just what she was supposed to, and more."

The captain's eyes were moist. Silver managed a tight smile, patted Colon's arm, then walked away. Not because he had anywhere to go, but because he didn't want a subordinate to see that his eyes were damp as well.

FORTY

Corpus Christi, Texas

General Scott and his wife were having dinner at the China Express on Saint Padre Island Drive. He wanted to be out with her, off the base, doing something other than just waiting.

Scott's pager beeped. Anticipating what he would see, he glanced down. His heart began to gallop.

He didn't recognize the number, but he recognized the authorization code preceding it. The caller was Major Bryan.

Scott excused himself—Wendy understood, of course—and went out to his vehicle, a Ram, to return the call on his secure phone. The night was chilly but clear, the parking lot relatively empty. The general had delayed leaving the base until he had received word from Captain Puckett that the team was safe. That was the big thing. He knew it would be at least two or three hours after that before he heard more, before the chopper linked up with the Royal Navy's Bristol-class guided-missile destroyer. With a range of over fifty-seven hundred miles and a maximum speed of twenty-eight knots, it was one of the few vessels that would have been able to reach a rendezvous point before the Chinook ran dry and could also refuel the helicopter if necessary.

General Scott called the Royal Navy base in Stanley. His call was routed to the British destroyer, where a communications officer forwarded it to Bryan. The major was in a small, comfortable stateroom. He sounded tired as he explained what L.A.S.E.R. had accomplished in the Weddell Sea, and what remained to be done. Bryan said he would supervise the return trip and that Woodstock and Galvez would handle the destruction of the submarine.

Scott was sitting in the passenger's seat of his car, looking at the streetlights, smiling big and proud as all hell. He said so. Bryan thanked him. But the major wasn't into hearing compliments. Not at the moment.

"Sir, do you have any idea what kind of submarine that was?" Bryan asked.

"Not a hint."

Scott realized then that Bryan wasn't just tired. He was doing his postmission analysis. Since he didn't have his own ass to chew on, he was chewing on something else.

"It had four big fans that created air pockets," Bryan went on.

"Breathable air?"

"They were able to vary the mix," Bryan said. "And it was strange. The design of the submarine reminded me of something else."

"What?"

"The sailplane I piloted last week," Bryan said. "Same low, long shape. I wonder if it flies through the water, so to speak."

"They've got torpedoes like that. Why not submarines?"

"Whatever it was, they lost a lot of people and the hardware itself."

"Major, there's never been a test vehicle of any kind that didn't blow up, crap out, misfire, and kill people. At least we get to die with our boots on, which is a privilege few individuals get."

"General, I'm from the any-dying-is-bad school," Bryan said dryly.

"That's a junior college. The world changes when you get your BA, your MBA, your Ph.D. You accept the fact that in our business life is the coin of the realm. We use it to buy turf and experience. But that doesn't change the fact that what you did was exceptional, and how you did it was extraordinary." Scott paused. "And I'm glad you're all alive. I'm also proud. Very proud."

"Thank you, sir."

The general hung up.

"Jesus," he said. "Jesus, Jesus, Jesus, thank you." He was smiling broadly. He couldn't hide it and didn't try to. He had needed this mission to succeed, not just for the future of L.A.S.E.R. but for his own self-esteem. They had hidden him here and he had made something of his exile. Something strong and worthwhile. He was so happy right now he felt like sending flowers to *Général de Brigade* Leopold. He had always hoped to do that for the bastard's funeral. But now—

Damn, he told himself, *let it go. You just won.*

Scott left the car. He savored the walk across the deserted parking lot. Quiet, alone, content. He could just be with his wife, enjoy the first unpressured together-time they had had in—Christ, in more than a year. The next day, the next mission, might hold something entirely different. Right now, though, death had been beaten twice.

Once by L.A.S.E.R.

And once by the general who had risen from it.

FORTY-ONE

Scotia Sea

Royal Navy captain Victor Hilton had already been informed by the Pentagon, through his Ministry of Defence, that an important piece of equipment had to be, in their words, "pulverized," before it could be recovered by the Chinese. The captain of the Bristol-class destroyer—which was also named HMS *Bristol*—understood and cooperated completely. The vessel held its position just north of the Weddell Sea while the Chinook was refueled and returned to the crash site.

In the meantime, Rear Admiral Silver was offered the use of the captain's stateroom. He accepted gratefully. Silver showered and then contacted the Ant Hill. NORDSS reported that it had given Mike Carr at least one update, though Silver had not yet had any contact with Carr directly.

The conversation was not pleasant. Silver gave Carr an update, after which he asked for news from the Ant Hill.

"The tech staff is devastated, top to bottom," Carr said. "None of us slept, and Admiral Grantham has given me until 5:30 P.M. tomorrow to resign."

Silver wasn't surprised, but he was angry. So that was how it was going to play out; fast and take-no-prisoners. Including rear admirals, he was sure. "What about the others?"

"Nothing yet. Everyone was sent home."

That was a security move on the part of Admiral Grantham.

Silver knew how that would play out, too. The senior staff
would be notified by courier that they had been terminated and
then locked out of the Ant Hill. The only reason Carr was being
kept on an extra day was probably to be on hand to take calls
like this and turn over any security codes, passes, and keys that
were in his possession.

"I was expecting some kind of suspension until a hearing
could be convened," Carr went on. "But this—and before the
crews have even reached base."

"It isn't you, Mike. It's the magnitude of what happened,"
Silver said. "Also the reality of a possible security breach."

"They were here cleaning out Dr. Davies's files," Carr said.
"I guess even she's a suspect."

"That's normal."

"It's ridiculous. The whole thing is. Hell, they had the johns
wired—they know we didn't do anything wrong."

"They won't believe that until there's an inquiry, which will
be within a month or two. Hopefully, it will put the blame for
the Chinese presence on external elements. The tech staff will
probably be invited back within a few months and the project
will resume."

"You believe it will?"

"It has to," Silver said. "The technology wasn't at fault
here." *We were,* he thought. *The military, the security people,
the men whose job it was to keep this operation a secret.* The
tech staff would be needed to get things moving again. Whether
Carr came back would depend on how the inquiry judged the
towline issue. They would probably find in his favor. It was a
reasonable precaution.

Silver told Carr they would talk again when Silver was
rested. He hung up and sat at the captain's teak desk.

NORDSS was coming down hard on the Ant Hill. Silver
could just imagine what was in store for him, for the officer
who had been allowed to make all the decisions. He would bear
the bulk of the blame, be the focus of the inquiry. *He should
have delayed the mission. He should have put Captain Colon in
charge. He should have stationed a recon team ashore, watching the sea.* They'd bring up everything he didn't do to attack

what he had done. Silver understood the politics, though that didn't help him deal with being alone.

No, Silver thought suddenly. *Not alone.*

The rear admiral picked up the phone and punched in another number. He placed the call directly without going through the secure uplink in the communications center. He didn't even know what time it was. It didn't matter. His heart was drumming and his mouth was dry as the phone rang on the other end.

Elizabeth answered.

"Hi, sweetheart. I hope I didn't disturb you."

"Hey, Dad, no! I was just watching *Leno*. How are you?"

"Okay." It was the most difficult word he had ever uttered. He hoped he sounded convincing.

"You sound tired," Elizabeth said. "Tough assignment?"

"Yes. You've got an 'old soldier' for a father."

"Baloney. Try running around with Sally for a day or two and you'll know the meaning of the words 'feel old.' "

"Funny you should suggest that. I'll be home in a day or two and was thinking I'd like to come back up."

"Really?"

"Yes. If that's all right with you, I mean."

"Of course!"

"This time for more than just an overnighter."

"That'd be great," Elizabeth said. "I'd love it and so would Sally. Say, are you *sure* you're all right?"

"Yes. Why?"

"Well, this is kind of unexpected. Don't get me wrong, I'm delighted. But it's still surprising. Did something happen to make you feel this way?"

"Something did happen," the rear admiral admitted.

"Was it that call you got while you were here?"

"That was part of it." Silver couldn't get into that and didn't wish to. "What really happened was that I took a look around and realized there's no one taking digital pictures of me, or asking me what mommy was like when she was a little girl or letting me feed them raw fish while they sit on my lap."

"Yeah, and no one to get PO'ed at you," Elizabeth ventured.

"Oh—I've got plenty of people to do that," Silver said. "Listen, hon. I can't stay on now. I'll call when I get back to Georgia to firm up the arrangements. I also want to leave time to go to the cemetery."

"Whenever you're ready."

"Thanks. See you soon, Elizabeth. And give our girl a hug for me."

"I will. Wherever you are, have a safe trip home."

The rear admiral felt better when he hung up, even though nothing had changed. He could still be discharged from the navy, honorably but with prejudice, or there might be a court-martial. A resignation would derail that, but that was not salvation, merely escape.

That isn't true, he thought as he left the desk and lay down on the narrow bed. Stone Silver had taken charge of his future. His family—*that* was where tomorrow could be found. Perhaps that was how it should be. That precious aspect of life didn't have to be borrowed or won, only recognized and embraced.

In just a few moments Silver had entered the half-conscious world between wakefulness and sleep. It was a place where, for a moment, there was clarity.

Things end, he told himself. Life and relationships, work and goals. He had carried the ball for the navy a long time. He hadn't scored this time, but he had shown future project leaders a direction. His portrait might not end up on the cafeteria wall, but one day a Tempest submarine would be painted there. And Silver would be gazing through the periscope, if not in fact then at least in spirit.

Then he slept, long and deep.

FORTY-TWO

Stanley, Falklands

Upon returning to the Falklands, Major Bryan and his team were quartered in a Royal Navy barracks just outside Stanley. Not officially a base, it was a housing complex. The British seamen slept in bedrolls. The Chinese sailors were housed on board the HMS *Bristol*, where they were visited by a British medical team. The crew of the American submarine and the surviving members of the support unit were taken to the King Edward Memorial Hospital for the night.

The following morning, Bryan went for a walk along the Public Jetty, the site of a number of quaint restaurants and shops. He met Captain Colon there. The two men—rested and relatively undamaged—stood in their clean uniforms with their backs to the railing, looking out at the sea, with pastries and coffee they'd bought at a small stand. All of Bryan's senses were stimulated here. The coffee was strong and the doughnuts sweet, the air salty and the breeze crisp. It sustained the feeling of satisfaction he had enjoyed the day before.

"How are you guys holding up?" Bryan asked.

Colon grinned. "I'll let you know when the base shrinks tell me. I can't say enough about what you guys did, though. How long have you been at this?"

"Now."

"You're kidding."

"Nope. This was our first mission," Bryan said. "We were organized nine months ago, multiservice volunteers, and have been training our asses off since. This was the first time we had to save anyone."

"Where are you based?"

"NAS Corpus Christi under General Benjamin Scott."

Colon's early-morning languor seemed to vanish. "General Scott? *The* General Scott?"

"If you mean the officer who was wrongly accused of hitting a foreign officer, yes."

"That's the man. Jeez, I wondered what happened to him. Glad to hear he's still slugging."

"So to speak."

Colon took a bite of pastry and grinned. "Yeah. Hey, Major, put in a good word for me, will you? I may be looking for a job after everyone's finished with their inquiries and committees."

"Will it be that bad?" Bryan asked.

Colon nodded gravely. "I'm not really worried for me. I think the rear admiral will get the worst of it."

"Justifiably?"

"I've been asking myself the same question and there are two ways to answer it—yes and no. Yes, because he took on a responsibility no one else wanted—for the reasons we've all witnessed—and no because keelhauling him will be five percent about fixing what he may have done wrong and ninety-five percent about scapegoating." Colon hugged himself against a sudden wind. "But the rear admiral will be okay. With his experience in R and D, he could make a helluva living as a private-sector consultant. Or a lobbyist, which would be ironic."

"Why?"

"Because his son-in-law is Sander Jackson."

"The left-of-left, antimilitary congressman from New York?"

"Yeah," Colon said. "I think he'd enjoy taking the kid on."

"It'd make for an interesting Thanksgiving," Bryan observed. "So tell me. If the buck stops short of you, what's next?"

"I'll go where I'm sent." Colon smiled. "Hopefully, it'll be someplace warm."

Bryan grinned. It was good to see the captain smile.

Other members of both crews began arriving, and Colon made a point of thanking every member of L.A.S.E.R. Shortly after finishing his second cup of coffee, Bryan was approached by someone who jumped from an open-top staff car. The driver said he had come from the Mount Pleasant Air Base and asked Bryan if he would come with him to the hospital. Bryan went and was escorted to an airy courtyard for recovering patients. Rear Admiral Silver had just arrived and was being introduced to the base commander, Air Commo. Arthur Callahan. Callahan had come to see Rear Admiral Silver and Major Bryan. The men sat in the airy courtyard behind the hospital. Callahan was a starched, young-looking fortysomething. He looked up, down, or sideways as he spoke, rarely at the individual. It was a striking change from Captain Colon, who had been eager to connect. Good commanders used eye contact to reinforce their bond with the crew.

"You are still leaving here in two groups?" Callahan asked.

"Yes," Silver said. "The major's team is taking the C-130K this afternoon. We will be leaving whenever the plane from Washington goes back."

"Because of the Chinese crew."

"That's right," the rear admiral said. "The DOD will bring a translator to help 'reeducate' them, I'm told."

"Meaning?"

"I don't know," Silver admitted.

"I see." Callahan's downcast eyes showed that he did understand. Silver was being kept out of the loop. The commodore began to clean a fingernail with another nail. He seemed anxious. "Rear Admiral, though this is not your concern directly, I must tell you that our minister of Defence is not keen to take responsibility for the Chinese sailors. I hope you will pass that information on."

"I would if I understood it," Silver said.

"There was an unofficial request from your ambassador that

we detain the sailors," the commodore told him. "Medical observation and all that. We were to hold them until the gentleman from Washington had a chance to talk with them about the accident. Unfortunately, the ambassador from the People's Republic has informed us that a Chinese commercial airliner will also be arriving tomorrow to collect their submarine crews. The PLN will be arriving first. You can see our dilemma."

"I also know which of those nations is your ally," Silver said.

"Which, may I remind you, is why we have cooperated to the extent we have," Callahan said. "I've been to see the Chinese crew. They seem fit. We have no reason to detain them."

"We need you to."

"Then I suggest you find a reason before tomorrow and send them out on the Hercules. Otherwise, they will be leaving with their countrymen."

Silver turned to Bryan. "Major, what are your orders regarding the rescue of foreign nationals?"

"Our standing orders are they must surrender to a recognized deputy or agent of their government as soon as possible," Bryan informed him.

"So if you didn't know about that Chinese airliner, if Commodore Callahan neglected to tell you what the ambassador wanted, you would take them back to D.C. on the Hercules and turn them over to their ambassador."

"Yes, sir," Bryan said. "Of course, Lieutenant Houston would have a look at them on the Hercules. He might recommend additional medical care when we touched down. That would put them in Walter Reed for a day or two."

"Now hold a moment," the commodore said. "Why would I fail to pass along the wishes of the Chinese government?"

"Because you had a crisis of some kind," Silver said. "Beijing won't believe you in any case. What does it matter?"

"I suppose we could have unexpected problems of some kind," Callahan admitted.

"There you are," Silver said. "Do it," he ordered Bryan.

"Yes, sir."

Callahan rose. He did not seem more relaxed, but at least he was anxious for a different reason. He looked at Silver for the first time. "Rear Admiral, I'm sorry I wasn't able to find you this morning." He looked at Bryan. "And I'm sorry I could not see you off, Major. I got held up on the *Bristol*, looking after our guests. We must have just missed each other."

"Thank you," Silver said, rising.

"I will go back to the air base," Callahan said. "Major Bryan, you can come and collect your seven passengers when you wish."

"Eight," Silver said.

"I beg your pardon?"

"There are eight Chinese," Silver told him.

"Forgive me, Rear Admiral, but there are seven."

Bryan and the rear admiral exchanged concerned looks. Without a word, the two American officers ran from the courtyard. They didn't wait for the commodore but took his staff car to the *Bristol*. The men went on board and headed directly to the crew's quarters, where the Chinese seamen were billeted. The young British guard allowed them to pass. Silver asked him if any of the Chinese had left. The guard said that he had been there since 2:00 A.M. and that none had.

Seven men were in the general quarters. The rear admiral continued down the hall to the latrine. No one was in there. But a stairwell was just beyond it. Someone could have pretended to use the latrine. The door opened out; it would have blocked the view of the guard. The missing person could have continued along the hall to the stairs. If he had entered just before the changing of the watch, the new sentry might not have known anyone was in there. The previous man might not have thought to mention it. After all, though their movements would have been restricted, the sailors were not prisoners.

The American officers climbed the stairs. They went to the damp railing of the *Bristol* and looked over. It was just a few dozen meters to shore. A man could have gone over the side and climbed onto one of the many private vessels moored along the jetty. He would have waited to make sure he was not missed. Then he could have stolen a car or motorcycle or bicycle or horse and left Stanley.

With information fresh and intact. Information about the

Tempest D. Information that, it would now appear, the Chinese had been sent to collect.

The officers went back to the crew's quarters and circulated among the Chinese sailors. They looked down at the exhausted faces of the men. Major Bryan didn't have to ask who was missing. He knew.

It was the radio operator.

"He snowed us," Silver said as the two men left the room. "He snowed *me*. And he was no novice. This guy was smart enough to figure out what we might do, what we planned to do."

Bryan could add nothing to that. "We can go after him, sir. My team can."

The rear admiral shook his head. "If he left when the guard changed, he's been gone for at least five hours. No. We can't do any of what we were thinking."

"Sir?"

"We're going to have to let the sailors leave with their ship. The DOD will have to cover this another way."

"Any idea how?"

"I don't know," Silver said. "I may never know."

The men walked onto the deck and toward the plank. They returned to shore to say good-bye.

"Sir, I want to wish you good luck," Bryan said. "The next few days and weeks won't be easy."

"No, they won't. But I've got a good support system at home and I've worn my country's uniform for a long time. I'm proud of what I've accomplished."

"I'm glad to hear that, sir. I've a feeling you'll continue to serve wherever you are."

"Wherever?"

"Yes, sir. Military or civilian."

Silver's eyes narrowed. "Have you been talking to Captain Colon?"

"I have, sir."

Silver smiled. "I thought so. Well, we'll see how things unfold. I've got a family I'd like to see more of. D.C. might be a good compromise."

"D.C. and compromise. Words that were made for each other."

"And you keep up your good work, Major. You showed great courage and resourcefulness. I hope you understand why I was rattled down there." The rear admiral dipped his forehead toward the south.

"Sir, I'm the one who was rattled."

"How do you figure?"

"I put lives before country and got you into this mess," Bryan said. "I'm not sure that what I did was right, but it seemed the better error to make at the time. Less permanent."

Silver did not reply, which was itself a reply. He did smile, though it was bittersweet.

The men saluted, shook hands, then went separate ways. Silver to the waiting staff car, Bryan back to the coffee stand on the Public Jetty. Some of his team members were still there. They did not ask questions and he did not offer explanations.

The wind from the sea was warmer now and the air less salty. The morning had changed the way lives changed. Suddenly. As Bryan talked to the others about Stanley and gloriously mundane tourist-things, he found himself hoping that if things ever turned for him, he would handle it with the dignity and poise of Rear Admiral Silver.

If not, there was always General Scott's way, a sock to the jaw, he told himself.

Both tactics had given beaten men a way back. And suddenly he knew that was what he needed translated into Latin. The L.A.S.E.R. motto.

There is always a way back.

FORTY-THREE

Stanley, Falklands

Face.

Which gives it to a man: when he dies that another may live, or survives so a mission might be completed? Wu Lin Kit had never faced a more difficult decision. He decided, finally, that were he to die without making a report, all of this would have been for nothing. The loss of the submarine, the deaths. And Beijing might never know exactly what had happened, or why. They would not know if the reconnaissance had been worth it, or if the trail from the American base had been accurate. All that data had to be carried back. When the American sailor had appeared in the open hatch, Wu had informed Captain Biao, with a look, that he was going aboard the American submarine. The captain appeared to understand. Whether he agreed was something Wu would never know. Biao turned away at once, aggressively helping his crew into the air pocket. Wu would mention that in his final report.

Now, against all odds, Wu was in the Falklands. He had left the British ship when the sentry was replaced. The English sailors were talking, and, watching from behind the open restroom door, Wu had gone up the stairwell instead of back to his bed. He dove into the sea, silently, and hid in a fishing boat until just before dawn. Then he went ashore.

The Guoanbu agent did not know what the Americans or

British would do when they discovered him missing. He assumed they would search. He had a feeling the Chinese crewmen on the British destroyer would not be staying in the Falklands for long. The Americans would want to find out what they knew. That was why Wu had left the vessel.

Wu had neither money nor a knowledge of the area. Rather than make his way into the countryside, he decided to watch and see what happened. He did so from Ross Road, which was busy with tourists from the many cruise ships that harbored at Stanley. The visitors' center was located there, along with shops and stands that allowed Wu to stay close to the water without standing out. He was still dressed in civilian clothes, which helped him to stay anonymous. The early sunrise, at four-thirty, made it more difficult to stay in shadow, so he remained in motion. The sun would not set until 9:00 P.M. It was going to be a long day. But Wu was patient. Whenever he saw members of the American crew or British military, he moved away from Ross to one of the side streets so he would not be noticed. He spent nearly an hour watching, with a large crowd, a pod of killer whales that passed remarkably close to shore. He envied the animals their mobility and wondered why men had never tamed sea creatures the way they had horses, camels, and elephants. What journeys ancient men could have taken. What secrets they could have learned. What wars would have been fought.

It was nearly 7:00 P.M. when Wu heard an aircraft coming in low. He looked over the sea and saw the distinctive red-phoenix tail-fin design of an Air China 747. Wu suspected that this was not a routine flight. Most trips to this region were connecting flights from South America or Europe. He decided not to try to get to the airport, since the RAF base was located there as well, but to wait and see whether the passengers came here. It made sense that Beijing would not send a military craft. The PLAAF transports were thirty and forty years old, and none of them were capable of making the journey without refueling. A commercial jetliner could have stopped at any number of airports along the way.

Not long after the Air China 747 landed, another airplane

came in, this one a small chartered jet. So few aircraft had landed during the day, Wu did not believe this was a coincidence. By now it was twilight and Wu felt comfortable moving about the pier. He remained close to the British destroyer. Less than an hour later several official cars pulled up to the *Bristol*. Wu had been expecting that: A two-man honor guard had taken up position on deck, beside the plank. He watched as a total of ten men emerged. Only one man was in uniform, a commodore of the Royal Navy. The men moved toward the vessel and into the ship's lights.

Wu saw several Chinese faces among the group. He walked over quickly but casually, as though he belonged here. Whether these men had come to examine the seamen or to take them home, the Guoanbu operative would be going with them when they left the *Bristol*.

The Chinese were surprised when Wu showed up. He told them he felt fine despite the ordeal and had decided to take a walk.

"No," he told the commodore through an American interpreter. "No one stopped me." Was there any reason they should have?

Wu felt good. Moreover, he recognized one member of the Chinese delegation as Mui Yu-tang, director of the Guoanbu's Second Bureau, the directorate of foreign intelligence. Nothing would stop him from making his report about the new American submarine with its odd streamlining and extremely curious fans.

To Wu's surprise, the Americans did not appear disturbed by his having left the ship. To the contrary, they seemed delighted.

"The design of our new deep-sea rescue vehicle has been validated," one of the American officials said through the interpreter. "It recovered your seamen, as it was designed to do. Our one regret is that the rescue ship was not large enough to carry more of your brave crew."

The Chinese delegation seemed annoyed by the remarks.

"*Our* regret is that your government did not request approval from the international community before testing a military rescue ship in that region," one of the Chinese officials stated.

"With respect, Mr. Deputy Ambassador Yu, this was not a military undertaking," the American replied. "We selected a crew from among naval officers for their experience, not secrecy. It is our hope that when the vessel is rebuilt and perfected the international community will benefit from its capabilities."

"Gentlemen, why not allow me to bring you to your crew so that you can talk to them, and take them home whenever you wish?" the commodore said.

The two groups went aboard the destroyer. Wu was invited to join them—by one of the Americans, not by his own countrymen. Clearly, the Chinese delegation did not believe, entirely, what they had just been told. But the Americans were not attempting to conceal anything. That was persuasive and also discouraging. The idea that the PLN had lost a state-of-the-art Song-class submarine and so many seamen to investigate what may only have been a civilian rescue ship was not going to be well received in Beijing. Men would have to answer for that, some with their careers and some, perhaps, with their freedom. Ambition was considered treason. Wu had command of the mission. On what evidence did he elect to risk such a valuable asset and its crew? For what conceivable gain? Intelligence or personal? What precautions were taken?

What had the senior captain recommended?

The answers were destined to displease the Guoanbu. Since the disastrous end was already known, the actions had demonstrably been wrong. Wu would be unable to defend himself.

Wu followed the others into the destroyer. As he stepped onto the deck, he saw, in the distance, the American officer who had questioned him on the helicopter. Rear Admiral Silver, his name was. The officer stood like a statue, watching them—no doubt contemplating everything that these past two days had cost him. Not just his work, but possibly his career. The American locked eyes with Wu for a long moment. It was a short, bitterly fought war in which the rear admiral charged Wu with murder and Wu sought to counterattack with the only weapon he had, a look that charged him with deceit. Silver shifted his eyes away, unbloodied and unblinking.

And unbowed.

It was ironic. They had one thing in common now: Both had accomplished nothing at sea. Wu had even mishandled the reprieve he had been given.

No. That's not quite true, he thought.

By sneaking off the British destroyer, Wu had confirmed what the rear admiral must have suspected: that Wu was not a radio operator. Silver would now use Wu's own actions against him, as a good martial artist must do. The United States would find the security lapses that had led the *Destiny* to the Weddell Sea. Those gaps would be closed before the U.S. navy tried again to do whatever it is they were really doing. Beijing would not get the answers it wanted. To make things worse, the American divers had probably had a good look at the *Destiny.* They would be able to describe aspects of its makeup, hull, torpedo tubes, and drive to the Pentagon.

I was taught that when a man steps in the arena, he must expect anything, Wu had told Lieutenant Chen back at the Louisa Reef. *That includes the results, which he must accept without excuse.*

Silver, who had lost so much, still had more than Wu did. Even the dead, who had nothing, had more.

They had face.

FORTY-FOUR

Corpus Christi, Texas

Faces.

They could be as dear as breath.

General Scott was smiling as the Hercules taxied toward him. His smile broadened when the rear cargo bay opened and L.A.S.E.R. emerged behind Major Bryan.

The general's L.A.S.E.R.

His team. The one he had fought to assemble and train and put in the field. The one that had just performed miracles under the antarctic ice, of all the miserable damn places on earth.

The major walked over, his flight jacket and scarf flapping hard in the wind. The field was black, the way it was when they had parted, but the mood was defiantly less dark. The two men saluted sharply as Bryan stepped over, and then they embraced. Spontaneously, out of protocol, warmly. Neither man spoke. There was plenty to say but there would be time to say it. In private, quietly, after a toast, not shouted over the wind and the powerful Hercules turbines.

The other team members came over at Scott's waved invitation. He saluted and then shook the hand of each soldier in turn. He looked into their eyes. It was all there: the courage and pride, the challenges and triumphs, everything they had seen, faced, and defeated.

And there was one thing more. It was the clearest of all, and also the most rewarding. He cherished it as they left the field, as he invited the members in for a drink, and then afterward as he slipped into bed beside his wife.

General Scott saw the future.

His, theirs, and those of the men and women they had saved.

**Read on for an excerpt from
Jeff Rovin's next book**

ROGUE ANGEL

Coming soon from St. Martin's Paperbacks

Waianae, Hawaii

General Scott was more anxious than usual.

With most drills, there was room for things to go wrong. The sixty-three-year-old Scott tried to plan them that way. Water usually gave you a few minutes to get out of a confined space before it dragged you down. You could rest during a climb or abort a dive or a jump. There was even an alarm, of sorts, the time they did an underground rescue scenario in an abandoned mine. Those timbers, which Scott had always thought supported the shaft, did nothing of the kind. They were an early warning alert. If the rock walls shifted, the beams shifted and creaked.

Fire was different, particularly the kind of eruptive, liquid fire the team would be facing. It was not forgiving. But this was an area where they needed to drill. Military units could be caught in forest fires or seismic events. L.A.S.E.R. needed experience working in those environments. A volcano gave them both.

The ten L.A.S.E.R. operatives taking part in the drill were quiet as they rode the short distance to Pearl. That was not unusual. The drills were always held in the morning, when the soldiers were fresh but not yet alert, and rarely chatty. Major Bryan and Captain Gabriel were usually the sharpest of the group. Bryan was an early-morning person, like the general, and Gabriel never shut down. The unofficial slogan was, "Once

a Marine, always a Marine." Implicit in that was a readiness to
fight 24/7.

The men were sitting across from each other on the wooden
benches that lined the back of the truck. Neither man seemed
aware of the bumpy ride on wooden benches that had been
warped by decades of sea air. They had never been to Pearl
Harbor, and Gabriel was becoming visibly agitated as the piers,
vessels, and green grass of the port became visible through the
windshield.

"This is hallowed ground," the forty-year-old captain said as
he sipped a Dr Pepper.

Bryan nodded.

Gabriel looked at the major. "You feel it too?"

"I do. Pretty strong."

"Yeah. And right now I'm wanting to kick the heads of the
sumbitches who made it that."

"Already taken care of," Bryan reminded him.

"Nah," Gabriel said. "We got 'em in big brush strokes. You
know what I'm bettin'? That some of those bastards are still
around, livin' happy in little country cottages with sunny days
on the other side of rice paper walls, sittin' in nice silk robes,
paintin' landscapes and drinkin' tea and enjoyin' the families
that these boys never got to have." He chucked his massive chin
toward the naval station. "It ain't right."

"Possibly," Bryan agreed. "But wiser minds in the field at the
time made the deal they did. I have to lean on their judgment
more than a little."

"They were tired of fighting. They had Russians to think
about. If they had been thinking clearly, I'm sure they would
have hunted every one of those animals down." Gabriel turned
his big, innocent-looking blue eyes to General Scott. "What do
you think, sir?"

Scott was sitting beside Bryan. He looked toward the naval
station. The white of the off-shore USS *Arizona* memorial
shone against the bluing sky, commemorating over a thousand
young fatalities.

"I think that for sixty-four years, longer than I've been alive,
those people in their cottages have had to live with the echoes

of what they did—if not for the hurt they inflicted on us, then for the cowardice of the act and the hell it brought on their nation," Scott said. "The stigma of failure is with them each night when they go to bed, it's waiting for them when their sleep is interrupted by ghosts, and it's there when they get up in the morning. It's living rot, captain. And those kids and grandkids you spoke of? They live with the smell of that. Posterity reeks of it." The general's dark brown eyes stared out to sea, back through the years. "The men out here died heroes, remembered and revered. I think everything is just the way it should be."

Bryan and Gabriel both looked at the general. They were emphatically silent.

"Except for one thing," Scott added. "We should be thinking about the present and the future, not about the past."

"Right, sir," Gabriel said. Because that was all there was left to say.

If the captain was still feeling spiritual about the attack, it did not show when they reached the base. The truck stopped beside one of the older piers along the outside of the cove. Gabriel was efficient, as was the rest of the team, as they double-timed down the wharf to the waiting seaplane. Their gear was onboard and Gabriel and Lieutenant Black went through the three large hazmat bags. These contained the suits and ropes they would need to secure the victims and hike away from the crater. The bags would be dropped ahead of them. Army Sergeant Major Tony Cowan and Coast Guard Master Chief Petty Officer Gunther Wingate—"the Dummy Squad"—checked the five mannequins that would be used in today's exercise. The two men laid the figures on the floor beside the forward hatch. The equipment bags were also there, with self-deploying chutes. The mannequins were dressed in fatigues that had been treated with a calcium zinc molybdate flame-retardant and would be ejected without chutes on the first pass. These figures were different from the usual L.A.S.E.R. props. Unlike the hollow plastic dummies used in water exercises, these figures were made of silicone rubber. They would suffer no more than a few scratches and small gouges when they hit the mountainside. The figures were also all female. L.A.S.E.R. Quartermaster

Mary Land procured them from a Web site that sold "love dolls." There were quite a few jokes about that, including a gag marriage proposal from Army Sergeant Bernie Kowalski, the team's structural analyst and expert in the terrain they would be visiting. At least, General Scott hoped it was a gag. "Leighanne," as the mannequin was nicknamed, was wearing a vending-machine engagement ring. During the SOP extraction exercises—named for "sack of potatoes," which was used to describe the disposition and handling of unconscious, dead-weight extractees—Scott warned the group that no dummy was to be given preferential attention. The general was surprised to note that while no one actually looked at Kowalski, all eyes seemed to drift in his general direction, a peripheral scope-out.

The men finished checking the dummies. When they were done, there were no longer any smirks, no mock-kisses, just sharp efficiency. Kowalski broke out the relief maps of the caldera and unrolled them on the floor. Everyone gathered round. The sergeant was fascinated by how all things were built, the earth included. Although he was not a degreed geologist, he had enough self-taught knowledge to instill the confidence of both Scott and Bryan. Once again, Kowalski reviewed the areas where the crust was thickest, where the lava flow was most active, where the smoking vents could obscure vision. He reminded them about what he called "crunchy rocks," jagged, black, metamorphic rocks that seemed sturdy but were extremely brittle. A wrong step could fracture a "crunchy" and drop a L.A.S.E.R. operative down a cliff or into a hole.

When they were done, Air Force Lieutenant Jen Marinelli, a veteran jumper, reviewed the parachute safety checklist with the team. They opened the chutes on the wide floor of the Seamaster and examined the vent and suspension lines, the bridle, and the canopy. Then they packed it all away and slipped the chutes on. A Pearl Harbor crewman shut the hatch, which was to Scott's left. He stayed behind to serve as jump coordinator. He was dressed in a brown flight jacket and matching leather gloves. It was comfortably cool in the cabin now; when the door was opened, the temperature would plunge to near-freezing. The L.A.S.E.R. Ops strapped themselves into the vinyl-covered, fold-down seats that lined the fuselage, and the Seamaster taxied from the pier, thumping from side-to-side. Four powerful Pratt & Whitney J75 turbojet engines were mounted atop the wing. They howled, causing the fuselage to vibrate as the plane surged forward. Behind them, the frothy white wake was like mighty twin contrails as the ungainly, pelican-like aircraft climbed from the sea. It banked almost immediately to the east.

No one spoke. The roaring engines made that inconvenient. A passenger would have to leave the seat, cross the fuselage, lean close to someone's ear, and shout in order to be heard.

As the plane reached five thousand feet, the JC motioned the L.A.S.E.R. "Dummy Squad" to the hatch. The navigator would give them a countdown to "position," the JC would open the door, and the dummies would be ejected. The plane would make a tight circle and return to position. Then the team would leave the aircraft. As Cowan and Wingate went over, Marinelli popped her harness and rose. She was ten on the jump list, after the Dummy Squad. The rest of the team was seated in jump order from one to six. Bryan was number one.

General Scott looked at the faces of his team. Many of those faces were extremely young. He would even describe a few of the younger ones as innocent. They had gone straight from high school to the military and not seen much of life. Nonetheless, they had a sense of purpose about them. Some of that came with them from the farm or the suburbs, from the city or the rocky coastline. Some of that came from training, from associating with resolute and professional men. He could see it in the eyes, which were strong but compassionate. He saw it in the stern set of the mouth. No one chewed the inside of their cheeks or sucked on their lips, not just because they could bite them if they hit something or if something hit them, but because any anxiety they felt was folded away and secured like a flag at sundown. A number of these people had been on the Antarctic mission when dozens of lives were saved because they were at the top of their game. Young or not, they understood the importance of their work. For many, this would be a career. For some, it was simply a chance to acquire new skills before moving on to something else. For others, it was a time to try to understand what was important and what was not. That was perhaps the greatest gift the military provided its special operatives and combat veterans: inner peace about most things. When you've waltzed with death, either leading or following, a long line at the supermarket or a tailgater on the freeway doesn't seem quite as upsetting. Even illness becomes a setback and a challenge, not a defeat. You realize that the ultimate tragedy, the loss of someone close to you, has to be kneaded into the routine of life.

And you get to do things and see places most people did not, Scott reflected, *like the underbelly of a polar ice shelf or the throat of a volcano.*

A green light came on above the hatch. The JC held up two fingers. That meant the dummies went out in two minutes. The L.A.S.E.R. Ops would follow five minutes later. That's how long it would take to make a tight circle and return to the point. Scott looked at his pocket watch. It had belonged to his grandfather, and he had carried it through Korea and Vietnam. Scott didn't need to know what time it was, but at moments like this he liked to feel connected with Quinn Scott. Growing up in Wabash, Indiana, Benjamin Scott first learned about warfare from his grandfather, who had lost an eye at Château-Thierry in June 1917. The five-year-old had learned it was a terrible thing but necessary. He learned that because some men were willing to risk their lives—"and sometimes their eyesight"—little boys could sleep safe in their beds. After hearing that, Scott never took a night's sleep for granted.

Scott rose. He grabbed the red canvas strap that was hanging above the seat and faced the hatch. The general was not as relaxed as his people. He was a point man, an officer who liked to be the first one in. Leading a unit from behind went against his nature. The major watched as the green light went off and a blue light came on. The JC held up one gloved finger and cocked a thumb toward the cockpit. The signal meant he was about to open the door. The Dummy Squad held the handrail beside the hatch. When the plane had leveled off, the airman tugged back the latch and slid the heavy door aft. Bright sky and warm air rushed in, causing the dummies' uniforms to flutter wildly. Cowan and Wingate released the handrail. Each man picked up a dummy. The JC stepped aside and Cowan stood in the hatchway. Wingate would pass, and Cowan would toss. Both men waited until the red light came on. The dummies went out quickly and efficiently, Leighanne being the last. Kowalski blew her a near-invisible little kiss as she flew out back-first. He wore their engagement ring on a cheap gold chain around his neck. The equipment bags went out after the dummies. The chutes were on timers that would open at one thousand feet. They were supposed to land on a slope five hundred yards from the crater. The team would be able to collect them and put on the hazmat gear before moving in on the dummies.

The JC shut the hatch, and the lights above it went dark. The plane banked sharply to the east to make its turn. The airman faced the jumpers and raised his right index finger, turning it in upright circles and then pointing to the port fuselage. That was the signal for the L.A.S.E.R. Ops to put on their crash helmets and line up. In case of an eruption, each of the white helmets had a small blue strobe light in back so they could be located amidst the smoke. Each jumper also carried a high frequency point-to-point radio so they could communicate with the aircraft or with anyone who might become separated from the group.

Because the Seamaster was not equipped with a jump line, the soldiers held onto the handrail. Cowan and Wingate helped each other into their chutes, then took their place in line. As they did, Scott made his way to the cockpit. The door was shut to keep the wind from buffeting the air crew. The general picked up a black phone hanging beside the door.

"Captain Rockefeller, what's the status of the Chinook?" Scott asked.

"On the pad and ready," the pilot replied. "Would you like me to patch you through to the pilot?"

"No thanks, Captain," Scott replied.

The Chinook was the big twin-rotor helicopter that would recover the team when they reached the rendezvous point. L.A.S.E.R. Operative Captain Tyler Puckett was at the controls. If anything went wrong, Scott wanted one of his own men piloting the rescue craft. Puckett had studied the air currents in the area, as well as graphs showing the way air had moved during previous explosions. The Chinook was capable of operating in volcanic air temperatures which averaged 120 degrees directly above the flows. But heat wasn't the only problem. In addition to "laze," Puckett would have to avoid "vog"—volcanic fog, a blinding, suffocating combination of sulfur dioxide, oxygen, air moisture, and sunlight—and "whiteout," the result of onshore winds mixing these various clouds into a caustic, impenetrable soup.

Hopefully, as Puckett told the general when they spoke at five A.M., none of this would be an issue. The volcano would remain "gentle," and the Chinook wouldn't have to collect the team until they were ready.

The Seamaster leveled and swung back toward the point. Scott made his way back to his seat. The L.A.S.E.R. Ops looked like dancers in some surreal ballet, hands on the barre as they shook out legs and stretched arms and limbered themselves for the jump. Scott wrapped his hand around the strap and faced the team as the green light came on. The JC flashed the two-minute signal. Lieutenant Marinelli went down the line once to make sure everyone was ready. She took her place as the blue light came on. The JC held up one finger, then raised his left hand as a stop sign. Everyone grasped the handrail and moved close to the fuselage as the airman opened the hatch. General Scott took a fist of air in the face. He raised a hand to block it and looked over at Major Bryan. Scott couldn't see the major's eyes through the tinted visor of the helmet, but there was no missing his big smile. The short, muscular officer loved high-risk situations. Yet he was cautious when it came to endangering the lives of others. That was what made Bryan a great field commander.

The general gave Bryan a thumbs-up. The JC was still holding up his hand. When the red light came on, the airman stepped back, swept his hand in a clockwise circle that stopped sharply at nine o'clock—facing the hatch—and Bryan went out. Each of his L.A.S.E.R. teammates followed in turn, without hesitation. When Jen Marinelli had jumped, Scott went to the hatch and looked out. Squinting into the wind, he saw coni-

cal canopies begin to unfurl. He immediately picked out Major
Bryan; because he was on point, Bryan's white canopy had a
red circle in the center. Scott watched the higher chutes being
tugged in different directions, the jumpers spilling air from the
sides to guide them closer to Major Bryan.

The general stepped back as the airman closed the hatch. His
face relaxed as the wind had released it. While the Seamaster
turned and headed back to Pearl, Scott made his way to the
cockpit. Once the L.A.S.E.R. Ops landed, Major Bryan would
give the aircraft's radio operator a head-count and a mission
status report. If there were problems, Scott would call in the
Chinook. Assuming everything had gone as planned, General
Scott would return to Pearl and go directly to Communications
Shack C, a small facility located near the Chinook pad.
L.A.S.E.R.'s radio operator, Army Corporal Jefferson Emens,
would also be in contact with Major Bryan. General Scott
would follow the team's progress from there.

Now that the hatch was closed, the general opened the cockpit door. The pilot and copilot were on a slightly raised platform
with the radio operator/navigator at right angles on the starboard side. Despite the age of the aircraft, all the equipment in
the vertical console was state-of-the-art. He was wearing headphones and looking at the radar screen as he waited to hear
from Bryan.

Suddenly, there was a muffled bang from somewhere behind
him. It was like a paper bag being popped in the distance,
barely audible above the screaming engines. That one big burst
was followed by two more which were even louder. At first
General Scott thought they had come from the aircraft, perhaps
engine trouble. He actually hoped they had.

The radio operator was instantly alert, not because of what
he'd heard but because of what he saw. The radar screen was
full of small blips, as if a flock of birds had suddenly flown into
view.

Straight up.

All had not gone as planned.